SCORCHED EARTH

ALSO BY TOMMY WALLACH

We All Looked Up
Thanks for the Trouble

The Anchor & Sophia
Strange Fire
Slow Burn

TOMMY WALLACH
SCORCHED EARTH

The Anchor & Sophia: Book Three

SIMON & SCHUSTER BFYR

New York London Toronto Sydney New Delhi

SIMON & SCHUSTER BFYR

An imprint of Simon & Schuster Children's Publishing Division
1230 Avenue of the Americas, New York, New York 10020
This book is a work of fiction. Any references to historical events, real people,
or real places are used fictitiously. Other names, characters, places, and events are products
of the author's imagination, and any resemblance to actual events or places or persons,
living or dead, is entirely coincidental.
Text © 2020 by Tommy Wallach
Jacket imagery by vectortatu/iStock
SIMON & SCHUSTER BOOKS FOR YOUNG READERS
and related marks are trademarks of Simon & Schuster, Inc.
For information about special discounts for bulk purchases, please contact Simon & Schuster
Special Sales at 1-866-506-1949 or business@simonandschuster.com.
The Simon & Schuster Speakers Bureau can bring authors to your live event.
For more information or to book an event, contact the Simon & Schuster Speakers Bureau at
1-866-248-3049 or visit our website at www.simonspeakers.com.
Book design by Greg Stadnyk
The text for this book was set in Adobe Jensen Pro.
Manufactured in the United States of America
First Edition
2 4 6 8 10 9 7 5 3 1
Library of Congress Cataloging-in-Publication Data
Names: Wallach, Tommy, author.
Title: Scorched earth / Tommy Wallach.
Description: First edition. | New York : Simon & Schuster Books for Young Readers, [2020] |
Series: The Anchor & Sophia ; book 3 | Audience: Ages 14 up. | Audience: Grades 10–12. |
Summary: On the verge of war, Paz Dedios, Athène, and brothers Clive and Clover Hamill,
finally reunited, must make their last stand, which will determine the future of their civilization.
Identifiers: LCCN 2019028897 (print) | LCCN 2019028898 (eBook) |
ISBN 9781481468459 (hardback) | ISBN 9781481468473 (eBook)
Subjects: CYAC: War—Fiction. | Clergy—Fiction. | Brothers—Fiction. |
Technology—Fiction. | Science fiction.
Classification: LCC PZ7.W158855 Sco 2019 (print) | LCC PZ7.W158855 (eBook) |
DDC [Fic]—dc23
LC record available at https://lccn.loc.gov/2019028897
LC eBook record available at https://lccn.loc.gov/2019028898

For Terry, who helped me build a life raft,
and
for Bobby D., who simply deserves a dedication

SCORCHED EARTH

Prologue

Six Weeks After the Black Wagon Massacre

THE BELL IN THE CLOCK TOWER RANG JUST ONCE, EVEN though it was a good ways past sunrise: the first signal, then. Genny Moses glanced out the kitchen window toward Sophia; the glass was foggy with condensation, and her eyes being what they were, she couldn't see more than a few feet beyond the pane. It hardly mattered. She knew what was out there.

"Foolishness," she said to no one. "Plain old foolishness."

Genny Moses didn't truck in rumors. She had no patience for superstition or mythmaking. Back when she'd lived in Amestown, she'd refused to involve herself in the so-called "spiritual life" of the community—not even to throw a garland of wildflowers around the old totem at Midsummer. The day Mayor Evans sold them all out to the Descendancy for a mill, she'd taken a nice long told-you-so walk right through the middle of town and hawked a big ol' gob of spit right where the new church would be built. People thought she cared about the *religion* of it all, but in her mind, that was beside the point; one set of gods would do just as well as any other, thank you very much. What she took issue with was the fact that they'd voluntarily made themselves subjects. Genny didn't like the thought of someone having power over her. Not a king, not a husband, and certainly not children. Yet here she was living in the old Dedios farmhouse, somehow responsible for the welfare of three helpless little strangers.

A year ago she'd hardly known the Dedios family except by reputation. José was a member of the Sophian town guard, and Genny would occasionally see him at Arthur Edwards's house, delivering some esoteric material for the old codger's tinkerings. Both men were dead now, along with that sweet ginger boy who'd seen after the pumphouse. What was his name? Ralph? Rolph? Hardly mattered. Genny had outlived all three of them. That was what she did: outlive, outlast, outstay. Everyone called her the Widow Moses, as if keeping upright while everyone else keeled over was her defining characteristic.

After José got himself killed trying to track down that minister and his family, the call went out from Sophia: four orphans seeking a guardian. Genny had spent the last five years or so looking after Arthur—fixing his meals, mending his shirts, marveling at his mysterious inventions—and knew that her days would quickly become aimless and dull without anyone to tend to. Less than a week later, she'd moved herself and all her worldly goods to the farmhouse outside Sophia.

She'd assumed she'd at least get a little help in the kitchen from the daughter—that firecracker Paz—but the girl was already off on some ill-fated mission of revenge. So Genny found herself a full-fledged mother again, decades after her own daughter succumbed

TOMMY WALLACH

to the plague and passed it to Mr. Moses in the bargain (both of 'em laid out cozy in the cemetery, side by side, with a third plot waiting). It wasn't a role she'd had much interest in reprising, not just because of all the work—the cooking and cleaning, the shouting and scolding—but because of all the feelings it churned up. Here she was with three fresh vessels eager to be filled with love, when all the world had ever done was take the things she loved and dash them to pieces.

Foolishness. She'd hadn't even been here a year. If the worst came to pass, if the war claimed them all, what would there be to mourn? The ceaseless cavalcade of chores? The all-over ache at the end of each day? The heedless way the boys ran from the table after a meal, their cheeks slathered in jam or gravy, no speck of gratitude to be found in a one of them? And why was just imagining their grubby little faces making her cry?

"What's wrong?" Carlos asked, appearing suddenly at her side. Goodness knew how long he'd been watching her.

Genny coughed a couple of times so she'd have an excuse to surreptitiously wipe her eyes. "I'm just wondering how it is that a boy who never seems to shut his mouth can sneak up on a body so quiet."

"You were crying."

"I was not."

"And you've been staring at that loaf of bread forever."

"It's rude to spy," Genny said, sharply enough to end the interrogation. She pulled the knife from the block and began cutting the loaf of bread into the thin slices Terry preferred. The bell of the clock tower chimed again. "Where's your brother?"

"Getting dressed. The uniform looks stupid. And he can't fit hardly anything into that pack."

"Send him in here. I'll help."

Carlos scampered off, and Genny took the opportunity to compose herself. She'd let him see too much; Terry would see nothing. It wouldn't do to look as if she were predicting tragedy. Things could still turn out all right, though they seldom did.

He came in a moment later, and the sight of him nearly set her to blubbering all over again. The uniform was too big for him, bagging everywhere, making him look more like a vagrant than a soldier. All of fifteen years old, but Sophia would let him fight. They needed every man they could get, especially after what the Protectorate had pulled at the *tooroon*. Genny had never cared much for the Wesah—not enough shame for her taste—but that didn't make it right to slaughter 'em like cattle. The Descendancy had to be stopped, and so the task fell to Sophia. There was no getting around it.

Terry set his bag down at her feet. It was full to bursting; here and there the canvas was stretched over pointy bits destined to become holes.

"What do you have in there?" Genny asked.

"Nothin' I don't need."

"We'll see about that." She hoisted the bag up onto the kitchen table, groaning at the weight; the boy would've dropped dead of exhaustion in the first couple of days. "Nothing you don't need, eh?" She turned the bag over and emptied the contents out onto the kitchen table.

Three books, each one a good three inches thick.

TOMMY WALLACH

"I borrowed those from Mrs. Okimoto," Terry said. "She told me marching's real boring."

"It is. You best make friends."

A small hatchet that used to belong to José.

"What if my gun jams?"

"Then you clear it."

Wrapped in a pair of thick denim trousers, a sack of polished stones.

"Frankie musta snuck his collection in there. He thinks they're lucky."

"Rocks ain't lucky. Just heavy."

Something unfamiliar poked out from between a couple of pairs of woolen socks. Genny slid it out and inspected it: a small fluted block of iron, hinged at the center. "What the hell is this?"

Terry picked it up and gave a sharp flick with his wrist; a blade emerged from the slab as if by magic. "Paz made it for me."

"If anybody gets so close you gotta use that, I don't like your odds."

Terry flicked his wrist again; the blade disappeared. "It's coming," he said firmly.

The clock tower chimed a third time.

"That's it then," Terry said.

"Just hold your horses." Genny wrapped the sliced bread in wax paper and put the parcel and a jar of jam into Terry's bag. The boy would likely wolf it all down at the end of his first day on the march, but at least it meant a little more meat on his bones. She cinched the bag shut and set the clasp.

"Come here," she said.

"Why?"

She tightened his belt a notch and tucked his shirt in—a little less clownish anyway.

"Why are you crying?" Terry said.

There was no use denying it now, with him so close he could probably see his reflection in the rivulets. "I'm just angry is all."

"Angry about what?"

The helplessness of the young. The ease with which they were exploited. The number of good men cut down in the prime of life, or before, or after, always in the name of something or other.

"I don't know. I guess about all the things I can't do nothing about."

Terry's expression hardened, as it sometimes did when he was about to perform the role of "man of the house."

"You're helping me, Ms. Moses. And I'm going out there to do something real important. So that means you're doing something real important too."

Genny smiled wanly. "I'd still rather you stayed."

"I wish I could," Terry said. Then he lifted the bag onto his back and headed for the door, where his brothers were already waiting. He hugged Frankie, who whispered something in his ear that made him laugh. Carlos went next, though he could hardly stop sobbing long enough to say an actual good-bye. Terry was still comforting him when Genny opened the front door and went out onto the porch alone. She looked across the fields, to the main road that wound uphill through Sophia, where every able-bodied man in Sophia proper and the hundred towns loyal to it was congregating. At the bottom of the hill, just across the bridge, a cart carried the gleaming body of Zeno's airplane. Genny had seen it plenty of

TOMMY WALLACH

times by now, circling overhead like some thirsty vulture god. The not-so-secret secret weapon. The ultimate heresy in the eyes of the Descendancy's persnickety god. The sight of it now filled her with pride. They would win this war. Terry would come back safe. The world would be a better place.

The boy, a boy no longer, walked past her and down the steps. Carlos and Frankie came to flank Genny at the edge of the patio. The three of them locked hands.

Terry turned around. "I'll see you all soon," he said.

Genny nodded. "You do that."

They stood there for a good long while, watching Terry traverse the bright fields and enter Sophia, where he disappeared into the undifferentiated mass of men, became just one more soldier heading off to the Anchor, and his fate.

"Lord, don't let me outlive him, too," she whispered. And what Lord was it that she thought she was praying to, that would deign to answer her prayers after all her apostasies and transgressions?

She looked down at the boys she had left. Their eyes were red-rimmed and glistening. They needed cheering up even more than she did.

"Come on," she said, corralling them back into the house. She would show them what hope looked like, though she'd never had much of the stuff to spare. She would pluck off their fears like the burrs they'd amass on their sweaters while playing in the woods. That was her purpose now. That was the *something* she could do. "Which of you wants pancakes?"

Neither of them answered, but that was all right. She didn't need an answer. Everybody loved pancakes.

Part I
VICTIMS

Life is nothing but a competition
to be the criminal rather than the victim.
—*Bertrand Russell*

I. Athène

FOOTSTEPS THUDDING ON WET GRASS. SUSURRUS OF rainfall and the rumble of its thunderous birthplace. The distant crash of the surf. Her heart, jolting wild as a wounded deer. So many distractions, muddling the senses, jumbling the thoughts.

Should she have stayed? Kneeling beside Gemma in those first terrible moments, she'd felt paralyzed. She wanted to remain at her lover's side; though Gemma's spirit had already left her body, there were still prayers to be spoken, valedictions to be made. Yet the woman responsible for creating this tear in the very fabric of Athène's reality was on the brink of escape, already obscured behind a thousand translucent curtains of rain. The opportunity for vengeance might never come again, and the fury was lightning inside Athène's belly, crackling, demanding satisfaction.

"*Miina kawapamitin, moon amoor,*" she said—*Good-bye, my love*—and took off running. Clive called out after her, but she ignored him. The hunt was on.

What did she know of her prey? The girl's name was Paz Dedios. She hailed from Sophia but no longer considered herself a member of any particular nation. That meant she knew no loyalty, no higher calling than self-interest, which made her the most depraved sort of creature, a sister to the jackal and the vulture. The Wesah viewed banishment as the ultimate punishment, yet Paz had chosen to banish *herself*—and not just once! First she'd abandoned her family in Sophia, and now she'd murdered Gemma, betraying those precious few who'd come to trust her. And why? Could it really just have been petty jealousy over that Clive boy? What man's love had *ever* been worth the life of a good woman?

These questions mattered, but only insofar as they informed the central riddle: Where would she run to now, this twice-exiled enigma, this beast without a country?

The pasture was large, full of horses still blissfully unaware that they would never see their masters again. Athène couldn't yet think about that other tragedy, the massacre that had taken place down on the beach. It was too large to comprehend, like the depth of the ocean or the number of the stars. Easier to focus on one death—one immediately avengeable death—than to try to make sense of carnage on such a scale.

She stopped. The silvery footprints she'd been following through the grass had disappeared. Perhaps they'd been disturbed by the horses' desultory grazing, or effaced by the torrential rain. Athène closed her eyes and extended her awareness, imagining it spreading out around her like a cloud. Something eddied at the feathered edge, a wayward stitch in the nap of the night. This anomaly seemed to grow louder and clearer as she focused on it, as if she were shaking the dust from some long-buried artifact.

She realized her foolishness just in time, opening her eyes to find a majestic palomino galloping straight at her, Paz clinging to its neck like a barnacle. Their eyes met. Athène was surprised to find no trace

TOMMY WALLACH

of satisfaction in her enemy's gaze—only rank fear. She side-stepped the horse and lashed out with her nails bared, scoring Paz's bare calf.

"*Baytaa!*" she shouted, chastising herself. If she'd grabbed the girl's ankle instead, she might have pulled her off. The horse was already twenty feet away. Athène took the bow from her back and drew an arrow. Her arms shook with cold; the rain blurred her vision. As she pulled the bowstring taut, she whispered a supplication to Fox, master of the hunt.

The bolt flew true as a hound racing to its master's side; there was a distant shriek. Athène watched for Paz's body to slip off the horse's back, but the girl stayed upright even as her horse jumped the fence surrounding the pasture. A moment later, she was gone from sight. Athène cast about for a horse she might use to give chase, but none was close. It was over.

"No!" she screamed, falling to her knees, sobbing along with the sobbing sky. The possibility of revenge had momentarily anesthe-tized her grief; now feeling returned to the wound. Gemma, her lover, her love, her little dancer—never to dance again. Never to sing or cry or laugh or smile or curse or fight or kiss. And the very same night, Athène's people cut down by the thousands, whole *naasyoon* annihilated in an instant, and the Wesah nation scattered to the four winds.

Gemma and Grandmother had seen all of this in their journeys with the dreamtea. There was no avoiding fate. It had been foolish to try.

Athène could see no reason to go on living. She drew her glass knife and brought the point to her chest. One quick thrust and she and Gemma would be together again. She tensed her muscles and sucked in a breath, praying her ancestors would forgive her this final crime.

Something touched her shoulder.

An impossible hope, momentarily buoyed by the vision that greeted her when she turned around: Gemma, miraculously reanimated by the spirits that had always favored her, returning younger and softer somehow, as if every minute in the land of the dead had returned a year of life to her. Athène blinked the tears from her eyes. Something was wrong. The spirits had erred. They'd made a false copy, a travesty of nature. Or else . . .

"Flora." The name was still foreign on her tongue, though Gemma had spoken it often enough.

The girl didn't respond. Her eyes were lifeless and unfocused.

"She got away," Athène said, answering the unasked question. "I am sorry." Flora's expression didn't change. Did she require more of an apology than that? "She had a horse. I could not follow." Still nothing: just that blank face like a sheer stone wall. "Say something!" Athène shouted.

"Flora? Flora?"

Men's voices, carrying across the field like bats flitting through lightless caverns. Clive and the soldier Burns, calling out for their lost lamb. Athène had no desire to speak to either one of them ever again. Both had trusted Paz, which meant both were responsible for Gemma's death.

"I am leaving," she whispered to Flora. "I must be with my mother, my people. And you must be with yours."

Athène turned and began walking briskly across the dark grass, away from the voices. It was a moment before she realized Flora was keeping pace alongside her.

"What are you doing?"

Flora's answer was the same as ever—no words, only the unforgiving ice of those blue eyes, looking straight through her.

"They are calling for you." Nothing. "They are your family." Nothing. "So you are not wanting to go with them?"

A momentary twinge as she remembered not to say *chee* to signal the question; Gemma had taught her that.

Flora shook her head, so slightly it almost seemed a trick of the moonlight.

"Why not?"

The girl refused to answer, but Athène understood well enough; Flora was only doing what little sisters had done since time immemorial—following in the footsteps of their elder siblings. It was sweet, in its way, but also out of the question. There were weeks of hard travel ahead, and waiting at the end, a tribe of wrathful warriors who'd never had more reason to hate outsiders.

"You cannot come with me. You will not be safe."

"Flora! Where are you?"

The men would give up shouting and simply come after Flora soon; Athène had reached the limit of her patience.

"Do not follow me again," she said sharply, and began running.

And what did she expect? That this girl, blood relation of the woman who'd made herself Wesah by sheer force of will, who'd driven Athène crazy beneath the blankets night after night, who'd hunted like she was born on the plains, would simply obey? Flora loped along beside her, lithe as a cat, silent as a spirit. Athène sped up, faster and faster, until at last Flora could no longer keep up. The girl slipped, sprawling out on the wet grass.

That would teach her to challenge a Wesah warrior.

And that would teach Athène to dash the dreams of a grieving sister. Flora's wail was piercing and pure: a siren's song, drawing Athène back against her will.

"I am sorry," she said, helping the girl to her feet. "Come. I'll bring you to your people."

Flora didn't look happy with that conclusion, but she allowed herself to be led back the way they'd come. Athène almost called out to Clive and Burns to announce her approach, yet the hunter's sense hadn't quite left her, and she stayed silent.

It was all that saved them.

Just in sight of Gemma's body, and had some part of her hoped it would have all been some terrible mistake, and Gemma would be standing there with open arms? Athène dropped to her stomach and wrenched Flora down beside her. A cadre of Protectorate soldiers was milling around the site of the murder. Likely they'd been sent to the pasture to kill any Wesah warrior foolish enough to come looking for her horse. Clive and Burns had been bound at ankle and wrist and were already being marched back downhill toward the beach. There was no hope of helping them, nor of retrieving Gemma's body.

"Come," Athène whispered to Flora. As quickly as they dared, the two of them began crawling away, their movements masked by the unceasing, uncaring rain.

TOMMY WALLACH

The girl rode well enough, and in spite of the long days, never once complained. In fact, she never said anything at all; the closest she came to words were the tears that trickled down her cheeks for hours after they stopped for the night. Athène seldom allowed herself the indulgence of crying; in a way, it was as if Flora were mourning for both of them. Still, she was glad when the fourth day had passed, and the time had come for the ritual.

It was early evening. They'd made camp by a shallow, sandy-bottomed stream. Flora was hunting for mushrooms in the woods nearby, just at the edge of sight. Athène took the opportunity to pre-pare what little she needed: a circle of river stones and some fire-wood, her glass blade, and the bone comb that she and Gemma had shared. The wood, heavy with rainwater, took a long time to catch. The kindling was still smoldering beneath the larger logs when Flora returned to the campsite. She frowned at the unfamiliar setup.

"For your sister," Athène said. "It is our way. Come. Sit."

Flora set her mushrooms down in a row—"Little Stumps," as they were known in Wesah. Poisonous, unfortunately, but the girl would learn.

The two of them sat on opposite sides of the fire, which burned brightly now. Athène closed her eyes against the sting of the wood-smoke and began to sing. It was an old song—some said the first song. It told the story of Sparrow, Fox's wife, who took to the sky during the flame deluge and was struck down by a ball of fire. Fox followed her into the darkness, stole her from the very bed of Crow—who'd fallen in love with her—and began carrying her back up the great stairway to the land of the living. But Sparrow grew heavier with every step, and at the very threshold of escape,

Fox's strength gave out. Sparrow slid back into the darkness, gone forever. At that moment, Crow appeared to Fox and chastised her.

"All must come to me someday, Fox. The morning that Mother Sun refuses to open her eye, you and Wolf will come to me as well, and then the world shall be born anew."

When the song was finished, Athène stood up. She drew her blade and raised it up to the level of her neck.

Flora gasped.

"Do not be afraid," Athène said. "I am no longer wanting to die."

She began sawing through the thick braid that hung halfway down her back: years to grow, seconds to destroy. Like a life. Gemma had been eighteen years old. So little time. Such a loss as could hardly be borne.

At first it seemed as if the sound were coming from the very air, from the trees or the earth, from some place beyond human perception. But it was only Flora, her lips barely moving, her voice scarcely more than a whisper. The first words she'd spoken since they'd been traveling together, since Gemma had been taken from them. A Descendancy song, one that Athène recognized. The last strands of the braid came away. She dropped it into the fire, curl and crackle, a smell like the way she felt inside. But the gods, to say nothing of her grief, demanded more. She brought the blade to her scalp and cut as close to the skin as she could, gripping at the root, tearing where she had to.

When it was done, she knelt to pick up the bone comb. Not much there, only a few silky yellow hairs. She threw them into the fire to burn along with her braid. Flora was still singing, but she stopped when Athène began to speak.

TOMMY WALLACH

"For four days, Gemma is walking beside us. The *otsapah* say that mourning must end here. Our grief ties Gemma to this world. Now she leaves us, to live forever with Crow in the land of the dead. We may keep our sadness, but we will not wish Gemma alive again."

Flora stood up and kicked the burning logs, provoking a cloud of ephemeral fireflies, and then turned away.

"Spirits trapped here become ghosts," Athène said. "They become monsters. Is this what you want for your sister? If you are to travel at my side, you must be a Wesah. You must be a woman. So let go this childishness. Let Gemma rest."

Flora turned back around. There was a new softness in her eyes: ice melted to cool water. She leaned forward and drew Athène's blade from its sheath.

"Hurting me will not help anything," Athène said.

But that wasn't Flora's intention. She went to stand over the fire and flipped her loose, lank hair over her shoulder. The glass knife reflected the dancing flames. The locks fell like sheaves of grain, like leaves in autumn. Flora's tears sizzled on the ashy wood. When it was finished, she lay down in her blanket and fell asleep. Athène watched the gentle ebb and flow of the girl's breath as darkness crept slowly over the forest glade. She closed her eyes for just a moment, and when she opened them again, a revenant was hovering behind the fire, gazing around at the world she'd never touch again. Her whole body was the color her eyes used to be, and her eyes were crimson.

"Where will you go?" the spirit said, in her perfectly imperfect Wesah.

"To my mother."

"Why?"

"To convince her to help me avenge you."

Gemma shook her head, disappointed. "You promised to let me go."

"But what should I live for if not vengeance?"

"You may still live for vengeance. You must. But not for me." The presence floated over the smoldering embers of the fire, like smoke. "Do it for our sisters. Do it for our people."

"I will try."

"I know. And when it is done, you will come to me."

"And nothing will ever part us again."

Gemma glanced upward, and then it was as if something pulled her out of sight and space. Flora turned over and let out a slumberous sigh. Athène lay down next to her and quickly fell asleep. She dreamed an ocean of blood, and it was no nightmare.

2. Clover

THE FLOOD OF RECOGNITION, OF RELIEF. HANDS GRASP-ing in the darkness. A few precious words. Clover felt someone grab the back of his shirt and pull. He held fast to the bars, shouting for a little more time, but more hands had him now, and he couldn't keep his grip. He heard the clank of metal smashing into metal—someone trying to break open the lock on his father's cell—as he was dragged back up through the workshop and into the yard.

The windows of the Mindful safe house had all been shattered; a constellation of glass glittered on the grass between a half-dozen motionless bodies. From inside came the sound of a baby wailing: little Liam, an orphan now. All because Clover had led the Protectorate here.

He shoved the shame down into the depths of his conscience, where it would keep company with the rest of his regrets: killing Lila, unknowingly infecting all those people in Edgewise, helping Sophia weaponize Kittyhawk. The guilt was like a pressure inside him, and he wondered if it would come out all at once someday, release like a coiled spring or a catapult. Or maybe it would only densify and curdle, harden into some black, ineradicable tumor.

Someone had alerted Marshal Ertmann of Clover's return, and

now the stone-faced soldier galumphed across the yard, already asking his first question from ten feet off. "Who the hell is that man down there?"

"He's my father, Honor Daniel Hamill."

"But why would . . ." The marshal frowned. "But isn't he . . ." Finally he gave up on asking a question and settled on a statement. "Daniel Hamill is dead."

"Go ask him how dead he is."

"Don't get smart with me. Even if that is your father, you're still gonna swing for working with the Mindful."

"I'm not working with the Mindful."

"Oh no? Then why did you run straight here?"

Clover had to choose his words carefully; Ertmann wasn't going to like hearing he'd been manipulated. "Someone told me my father was being held here. I couldn't get him out without your help."

"What are you saying? That you tricked us into chasing you?" Clover nodded. "If you wanted our help, why not just ask for it?"

"Because you all think I'm a traitor."

"You *are* a traitor. Everybody knows you defected to Sophia."

Clover couldn't see any reason to hide the truth any longer. "The Epistem and the Archbishop *ordered* me to defect. They wanted someone on the inside."

"How convenient that the only two people who could corroborate your story are dead."

"Actually, it's extremely inconvenient."

"And what about the girl? Is she a spy too?"

"Kita," Clover whispered. One more thing to feel guilty about: he'd completely forgotten about her. But she hadn't come down to

TOMMY WALLACH

the cellar with him, so if Ertmann didn't know where she was, she must've found someplace to hide, or else managed to escape the property somehow. Good for her. "Her name's Kita Delancey. She's no spy, but she risked her life for me and my father."

"What a hero," Ertmann muttered.

Clover turned at the sound of voices. Four soldiers emerged from the bullet-riddled portal of the workshop, carrying between them a gaunt and bedraggled figure Clover could barely recognize. Daniel Hamill was dressed only in a muslin loincloth, and his ribs poked out through the dun and dusty skin of his chest. His head lolled, as if he'd been drugged.

"Please," Clover said to Marshal Ertmann. "Let me talk to him."

"Why? So you can conspire against the Descendancy all over again?"

"I already told you—"

"That you were a spy working for the Epistem. I heard you. It's a nice story. Might even be true."

"It *is* true."

"Maybe. And maybe that's Daniel Hamill back there. But it's not my job to sort it out. Now move." Ertmann grabbed him by the wrist and dragged him back toward the main house. Clover craned his neck to look over his shoulder.

"Da!" he cried out. "Da!"

But the unfamiliar figure on the other side of the yard didn't even look up.

Most people would've dreaded the thought of spending weeks in near-isolation as a suspected enemy of the Descendancy—but

Clover wasn't most people. After a few interrogations in the Bastion, during which he'd described the events of the past few months without mentioning either his wavering loyalty to the Descendancy or his involvement in the Edgewise influenza outbreak, he'd been moved to a holding cell in the Library. These chambers were traditionally reserved for monks who'd overstepped the anathema rules in some way; thus Clover's "cell" was really just a tiny study, complete with a desk and two—but no more than two!—books at a time. Bernstein stopped by a couple of times a week, so Clover had some sense of what was going on outside the Library walls. He knew of the Black Wagon Massacre, of Sophia's official declaration of war, of the Edgewise quarantine and the attempt to establish a new port farther down the coast. What he didn't know was anything that actually mattered—what had become of Clover and Paz, of Gemma and Flora, or of his father.

In order to keep these burning questions at bay, he'd embarked on an odd pet project that now devoured the majority of his days and many of his nights: mastering the Wesah tongue. He wasn't entirely sure why—perhaps out of some sense of culpability over what the Protectorate had done at the *tooroon*, or a head start if he ever wanted to abandon the Descendancy and become a missive. Whatever the impetus, after reading a basic primer on Wesah grammar, he'd found his curiosity piqued. It was a genuinely interesting language; for example, articles could be used to differentiate both by gender and state of being (i.e., animate or inanimate). Thus an egg could be known as *li zaef*, the egg, or as *ôma li zaef*—*ôma* for inanimate, *li* for masculine, and *zaef* for egg. This odd syntactic duality had led most scholars to conclude

TOMMY WALLACH

that the language must have been synthesized from two distinct dialects.

Because a language could only be truly mastered by speaking it, Clover had taken to making conversation with himself, a pastime he was deeply absorbed in when company arrived that afternoon.

"*Taanishi, dishinikawshon Clover.* Hello, my name is Clover. *Taanshi kiya?* How are you? *Nimiyo-ayaan. Kiya maaka?* I'm fine. How about you? *Nimiyo-ayaan, marsi.* I'm fine, thank you."

"*Mafwe!*" Clover jumped, upsetting the notebook on his lap. Bernstein stood in the doorway, chuckling at Clover's reaction. "That's all I know how to say. I don't even know what it means."

"It means 'Oh my goodness,' more or less. You really should learn more of the language. Then I wouldn't have to talk to myself like a crazy person."

"I'm an old dog. No new tricks for me. Besides, it's optimistic to think there will be anyone left to speak Wesah to a year from now. Chang's aim seems to be total eradication."

"All the more reason to learn it. It would be a shame if an entire language were forgotten."

"Thousands of languages have been forgotten. Everything is forgotten eventually. I thought I taught you that."

Clover sighed. "Yes. Everything will be forgotten and nothing will be redressed. We're all going to die someday. The sun is destined to burn out. It's a wonder I didn't hang myself from the rafters studying under you."

"Well, here's a surprise, then. I've actually come today with some good news."

Clover's thoughts ran immediately to his father. "You've found him? He's alive?"

Bernstein nodded. "Better than that. There's a crowd gathered outside the Bastion as we speak. Apparently some young woman has been going around the city telling anyone who'll listen about how the Protectorate is holding the hero Daniel Hamill against his will." Some young woman: that could only be Kita. Who else even knew that Clover's father was alive? "They say Chang will be back in the Anchor any day now. When he arrives, he's going to have to reckon with the public."

"Reckon how?"

"Plenty of people think Chang took things too far at the *tooroon*, and they have their doubts about the official story surrounding the Epistem's and Archbishop's deaths. With the Mindful making trouble all over the city, Chang is running low on political capital. He can't afford to execute an Honor who was held prisoner by Sophia for the last year. My guess is he'll free your father in exchange for a public pledge of loyalty to the new regime."

"And me?"

"You're the hero's son. He'll have to make you the same offer."

Clover sat back in his chair. "*Mafwe*. That's the sunniest prediction I've ever heard you make."

"You're right," Bernstein said, putting on a familiar frown. "I should probably double-check my calculations. I must have missed something."

The halls of the Library were different than Clover remembered. Quieter. Emptier. Bernstein said many of his fellow attendants had

TOMMY WALLACH

left the city after the death of the Epistem, fearing an institutional purge, and those who'd remained had learned to keep their heads down. Clover happened upon an attendant he recognized from his days as an apprentice, but the man scurried away as soon as they made eye contact. It was fear—floating on the air like the millions of dust mites that would one day reclaim all these books, turning them into so much waste. Clover had seen these mites once, under the magnifying scope in the chemistry lab. He'd expected to find them monstrous, but they were actually quite beautiful—opaque and gemlike, sprouting quavering tendrils in every direction.

It was dark outside the windows; though most of the clocks had been allowed to wind down, the few that still functioned showed the time to be a little past eight o'clock. This was the first time Clover had been allowed out of his cell except to answer the call of nature in nearly six weeks, and he'd yet to be told why. The soldier who'd come to get him wasn't exactly chatty; they marched in silence through the desolate stacks and up staircase after staircase, toward an inevitable destination. And what would be waiting there at the top of the Library, where once Clover's whole conception of reality had been turned on its head?

The soldier stopped just outside what used to be Epistem Turin's office. "Go on," he said.

"Alone?"

"You afraid, traitor?"

"I'm not a—" Clover let the words die in his throat. What was the point? People would believe what they wanted to believe. He opened the door and stepped through.

His first thought was that he'd mistaken the geography of the building somehow. Though he'd traveled along the same halls and climbed the same stairs as before, somehow he'd ended up in a completely different place. Here was Turin's office, except everything that had marked it as his was gone. The bookshelves that stretched all the way up to the second floor had been completely emptied of books; in their place were hundreds of useless, ugly knickknacks—taxidermied birds and rodents, small clay pots fired with sneeze-shaped patches of metallic glaze, framed drawings of horses and military parades, various pieces of Protectorate regalia and surplus pageantry, a few geodes (quartz, pyrite, limonite)—anything and everything except words on paper, except knowledge. Apparently, it wasn't enough to murder the man; Chang also had to murder his memory.

"Hello?" Clover called out.

But he could already sense there was no one there. The hint of a breeze caressed his arm. He traced it to the hidden door in the wainscoting, which had been left cracked.

Clover could remember the first time he'd stepped through that portal—naked, terrified, innocent. It felt as if centuries separated him from that day, and from that version of himself. Then, the walkway atop the Anchor wall had seemed no less than the entrance to a new dimension. Now, it was just another parapet; if and when Kittyhawk flew over the Anchor, the pilot would be able to see this pathway laid out beneath him as clearly as a river. Strange how perspective could alter things so completely. The passage began to slope downward. Clover pulled his arms into his sleeves, but he knew there was nothing he could really do to protect himself from what was coming. And though he wasn't

TOMMY WALLACH

looking forward to the pain, he couldn't help but be excited at the prospect of seeing the anathema stacks again. The light turned crepuscular, faded away. Clover stretched out his sleeved hands, wincing in expectation of the first prick of the blackberry bushes. Step after step, deeper into the dark, but still he felt nothing. He must've misremembered the distance; time had been extremely malleable the last time he'd walked this path. Yet now the gloom had begun to take on a distinctly rosy tint. The corridor jogged to the left and the tint became a flame; someone had screwed a sconce into the wall and fitted a torch into the bracket. In the sphere of illumination, Clover could make out where the brambles had been cut away, their bleeding stumps peeping out of the holes in the stone floor. The vegetal detritus had been swept into piles at the edges of the passageway, creating a clear sight line for hundreds of feet. The starkness of it, the violence implied by all those severed vines, affected Clover viscerally. He might've lost his religion somewhere along the way, but his respect for and devotion to the Library itself remained intact. For the path to the anathema stacks to be laid bare like this seemed the most terrible of heresies, and the implication . . .

He began running, as fast as he could manage along the uneven stone bricks, until he nearly fell into the pool that used to offer succor to those who'd survived the brambles. From that raised platform, he gazed out over the great chamber hidden within the Anchor wall.

"Daughter's love," he whispered.

Those materials once deemed too explosive for anyone but the Epistem and Archbishop had practically become public property.

Dozens of men, some Library monks and some wearing the red and gold of the Protectorate, were freely exploring the anathema stacks—idly leafing through ancient texts, tossing them aside like rubbish or else making copies at the desks that now lined the walls to either side of the fatally pitted central bookshelf. So absorbed were they in these desecrations that Clover's appearance was hardly remarked.

"Is Grand Attendant Bernstein here?" he asked the nearest monk.

"In hell, probably," the man answered.

The words themselves implied aspersion, but nothing in the monk's demeanor read as hostile. "Hell?" Clover said.

The monk pointed toward the other end of the chamber. "That way."

Memory had gilded the lily of his last visit to the stacks; where Clover remembered the chamber being enormous, practically a mile from end to end, he now traversed the whole thing at a brisk walk in less than a minute. Guards stood on either side of a doorway that gaped out of the sheer stone.

"I'm here to—" Clover began to say.

"Go on," one of the guards interrupted. "He's waiting for you."

Clover passed through the portal and down a corridor lined with lanterns radiating a suspiciously perfect yellow light. He leaned close to the frosted glass of one and could clearly make out the bulb and its searing filament. Electricity, here in the basement of the Library itself—Chang truly had swept away the old order at a blow.

The corridor opened up onto a chamber about the same size as that which housed the anathema stacks: a workshop, not so different from the one at the academy in Sophia. At least a hundred men and women were hard at work, scurrying between the engines and forges, the generators and the anvils, through air heavy with the smoke that wasn't captured by the fans built to carry it up and out through the roof. Most of them were making guns—some small, some as big as the one Chang was said to have deployed at the Black Wagon Massacre. Clover watched as a monk dipped a tray of bullet castings into a steam bath. He was a strange-looking man, freakish even; though his skin was dark, it seemed somehow etiolated, as if he'd never spent a moment in the sun.

"It's rude to stare," a voice said.

It took Clover a moment to put a name to the face: the illustrious Ruzo Chang, Grand Marshal of the Protectorate, de facto leader of the Descendancy. Here was the man who'd killed Archbishop Carmassi and Epistem Turin, who'd ordered thousands of Wesah slaughtered at the *tooroon*. Clover suppressed the urge to spit in his face.

"Clover Hamill," Chang said. "I'm sorry we haven't been able to meet before now."

"I'm not."

Chang chuckled. "You and your brother are two of a kind, aren't you?" Clover didn't answer; he wouldn't be baited. "Let's go for a little walk, shall we? There's something I want to show you." He gestured toward the eastern wall of the chamber, where another two Protectorate soldiers were standing at attention. At a signal from Chang, they reached into their shirts and produced elaborate brass keys on necklaces. After fitting these keys into nearly invisible chinks in the stonework, the soldiers began to turn them, around and around, as if winding a clock. A loud grinding sound came from the wall—rusty gears activating other rusty gears.

"I learned this trick from one of Turin's notebooks," Chang said.

At first glance, it seemed as if the stonework at their feet had become a kind of whirlpool, a perfect circle of bricks spinning and sinking at once, like a screw slotting into place. It stopped about four feet below the level of the floor, revealing a wrought iron staircase spiraling even farther downward, lit with yet more electric lights.

"Close it up after us," Chang said to the soldiers. "I won't be back today."

They began to descend. After a few dozen steps, Clover heard the grinding of the floor rising back into place above them. Stone dust plinked atop the steps and feathered his hair.

"Where are we going?" he asked.

Chang stopped and looked over his shoulder. "To see some old friends." He smiled, as if in expectation of something sweet to come. "And to make a deal."

3. Paz

T HE TWO OF THEM ROLLED DOWN THE HILL IN A CLINCH, flipping over and over, hands scrabbling for any kind of advantage. Paz felt as if she were trying to get the better of an animal, rather than a person. The slope steepened vertiginously, absurdly, until they were falling through clear air, whirling as they went, still biting and scratching and screaming with the fever of battle. They fell for minutes, for hours maybe, nothing but black sky all around them, stars sprayed like spittle in every direction. The ground arrived as a thunderclap. Paz found her arms pinned beneath the Wesah warrior's knees. The tribeswoman began to intone something with a liturgical gravity, which gave Paz time to wriggle one arm free and draw her knife. She lashed out, but without any leverage, the attack was naturally deflected by her opponent's vest.

The warrior brushed the blade aside like a bothersome fly, but Paz no longer cared. Her attention had been captured by the woman's armor; the cuirass had been hardened in a shape that left room for a bosom. Descendancy women never wore armor, and the Wesah weren't technologically advanced enough to produce this sort of cured leather. That meant this piece had been made specially for *this woman*. And there next to the seam, Paz could just make out the brand of its maker: *RP*, circled twice.

The tribeswoman raised her blade and brought it down with all her strength, piercing Paz's heart and evicting her from the dream.

She woke shivering beneath the thin blanket. The horizon had just donned its first pale corona, inflaming the thin scudding clouds that scarcely seemed to move across the sky. Her belly rumbled; other than a few handfuls of berries and a couple of mealy apples picked off the ground, she hadn't had anything to eat in days.

Her first thought was to wonder where Clive was; then she remembered everything that had happened. Blinking back tears, annoyed at the way they found their way out anyway, she rose and carefully peeled the dressing from her side, so she could wash the wound out in the nearby stream. Athène's arrow had only grazed her, but the last thing she needed now was an infection. Luckily, the horse she'd stolen had been fitted with a saddlebag, inside of which she'd found a few arrowheads, some rope, and the blanket, the edges of which she'd cut away to make bandages.

Had she been wrong to run? Of course she'd wanted to hold her ground, to plead her case before that improvisatory tribunal, but there'd seemed precious little hope of exoneration. Neither Flora nor Athène had any reason to give her the benefit of the doubt, which meant everything would've rested on Clive, who knew her capacity for duplicity all too well. She didn't think he had it in him to hurt her, but if he'd handed her back over to the Protectorate, she'd never have seen the light of day again. She simply hadn't been brave enough to bet her life on the depth of his love.

　　　　　　　　　　　　　　　TOMMY WALLACH

So was it he who hadn't trusted her, or she who hadn't trusted him?

After the adrenaline wore off and Paz found herself alone, riding a stranger's horse toward no particular destination, she realized there was only one way to clear her name: find the woman who'd actually murdered Gemma. The killer had a head start, but probably assumed no one would be pursuing her; only Paz knew what had really happened in the pasture, and would she really seek a second round with the woman who'd clearly only spared her life on a whim?

Paz found an abandoned campsite the very next morning, the embers of the fire pit gray and wet with dew, but in the days since, there'd been nothing. The trail had gone cold . . . until now.

The dream tried to slither out of her grasp, but she grabbed hold of it by the tail and dragged it wriggling back into her consciousness: *RP*, circled twice. It wasn't much to go on; the Wesah woman might very well have acquired the cuirass from someone other than the person who'd made it. But if she'd bought it specifically in preparation for the *tooroon*, there was every chance it came from somewhere close by. Towns were few and far between this deep in the outerlands, and not many would have an armorer of that caliber. RP, whoever he or she was, would be known for many miles around.

Paz had happened upon a road early the previous morning, but for safety's sake had camped a little ways off. She returned to it now and followed it to where it met another, larger road, which wound through the hills to the northwest. Once, she had to hide in a ditch while a large delegation of Protectorate soldiers passed by. They were uncharacteristically quiet, almost solemn. Paz wondered if they'd known what was going to happen at the *tooroon*, or if Chang had suprised them, too. Not that it mattered; they were complicit anyway.

It was another three days before Paz spotted a town, the first she'd seen since leaving the coast. There wasn't much to it aside from a general store—already closed for the night—and a pub called the Alehouse, from whose open windows wafted the homely scents of fresh-baked bread and roasting meat. Paz pulled open the door but froze on the threshold. The place was packed—far busier than a small-town tavern had any right to be. Even in the weak light of the lanterns on every other table, she could see why: Protectorate soldiers took up half the stools in the place. It had to be the same unit that had passed her on the road. The disciplinary tattoos on her face would make her instantly recognizable to anyone who'd seen them before, but there was nothing to be done about that now; a couple of the soldiers had already glanced her way, and it would only make them that much more suspicious if she left without ordering anything. She went to the bar, trying her best to look natural, and took a seat next to a man and woman in their sixties. They were already deep in their cups, and from the easy manner of their arguing, probably married.

"It's on the way," the woman said confidently. "Felt it last night just as the moon was coming out. An early turn."

The man sniffed. "No such thing. Turn's a holiday."

"Turn's a state of mind. When it's cold, it's turned. That's why they call it the cold turn."

"Load of bull. September thirty. Two months off."

"Tell that to the fields o' dead sweet corn when the first frost comes."

"It's fucking July!"

"Excuse me," Paz said. "I'm trying to find someone, a tanner probably, but one who makes armor. He'd have the initials RP."

The man screwed up his shine-shattered features. "RP, eh? RP . . ."

"Roberto!" shouted the woman. "There's your R!"

"Roberto's family name's Lombardo."

"So?"

"And he's a farmer."

"People can do two things. Anyway, he's not much of a farmer. You see how he takes care of that land?"

The couple went on arguing, having seemingly forgotten the initial question, or that Paz was even there.

A fist knocked plangently on the wood of the bar. "You drinking?" asked the tender. He was a young man of twenty or twenty-one, whose striking good looks had yet to be tarnished by the sunless, sleepless life of a barkeep.

"Sure. Whatever's on the tap there."

"Nothing's on the tap. Not for years, anyway. All we got is shine, and it's not good shine either."

"Then you better change your name."

"Juan?"

"Not *your* name, Juan. The Alehouse."

A wisp of a smile below the wisp of mustache. "My da came up with that. He was the brewer in the family. I don't seem to have the knack."

She smiled back at him. "I doubt that. You look like you've got all sorts of knacks."

Juan was momentarily nonplussed—oh, the dependable innocence of country boys. Maybe he'd have the information she needed, but what mattered more right now was that she find a graceful way out of the pub. A couple of the Protectorate soldiers had begun to pay her a little more attention than she liked.

"Nice to meet you, Juan. I'm Irene. You feel like gettin' some air?"

Agate, a barmaid with the complexion of a rotting apple, offered to take over for a bit so Juan and "Irene" could take a turn around the town, which Paz had learned was called Oleanna. She delayed asking after the mysterious RP, allowing herself a moment to enjoy the fantasy that she had no ulterior motive, no mission, no past at all.

"So, Irene, I'm guessing you're not from around here."

"What gave me away?"

"Basically everything about you."

"I'm from the Anchor. Third Quarter, if that means anything to you."

"A city girl. Makes sense. That where you got those tattoos?"

She felt herself blush. "I've had some hard times. I'd rather not talk about them."

"Sure. Sorry. Tending bar, you get used to asking people about their troubles."

They walked in silence for a while. Paz could feel herself relaxing for the first time since she'd come upon Gemma in that clearing.

TOMMY WALLACH

"So what brings you to Oleanna?" Juan said.

"Long story. Call it an adventure."

"A girl like you shouldn't be adventuring. It's not safe."

"Tell me about it."

"And you aren't married or nothing?"

Paz held up her naked ring finger, and remembered the time Clive had wrapped his pinky around it, like a promise. "Nothing doing."

"Good."

He clasped her hand and pulled her to him—gently, but with a winning sort of chivalrous ardor, as if he'd just slain a dragon for her. His breath smelled of shine, and his cheek was rough with stubble, but she didn't imagine it would be so bad to kiss him a little, just to pass the time, just to remember that somebody could want her. And yet . . .

"I'm sorry," she said quietly.

To Juan's credit, he let her go immediately, his playful passion turning to mortification. "No, it's my . . . I just thought you . . ."

"It's fine. You're very sweet. But I can't. There's someone else."

"And he lets you wander the countryside alone? No offense, but he sounds like a damned fool."

"He can be. He has been. But so have I."

They walked on, but things were different now; there was a certain sort of magic that could exist between strangers only until the question of romance was resolved. "You know, I should probably get back to the bar," Juan eventually said. "With all these soldiers in town, we've been pretty swamped."

"Of course." Paz felt the urge to apologize but suppressed it; she had nothing to apologize for. "One thing before you go, though. I'm looking for someone. A tanner who goes by—"

"You think we don't know what those are?"

The voice came from behind them, somewhere in the darkness; two soldiers materialized behind the cindery tips of their cigarillos. Paz recognized them from the Alehouse.

"Can I help you gentlemen?" Juan said.

"No, but we can help you," said the younger of the two soldiers. He had an unhealthy pallor and was probably half a dozen drinks deep.

The other soldier looked like the kind of man who enlisted because he wanted the excuse to hurt people. "Those rings on your girl's face are disciplinary tattoos. Protectorate gives 'em out to Sophian sympathizers."

Paz looked desperately to Juan. She should've kissed him; that might've made all the difference now. Only, something strange was building behind his eyes, an unseemly sort of mirth that finally erupted as boisterous laughter, surprising her and the soldiers in equal measure.

"You think I give a shit?" he said. "This ain't the Descendancy, and it ain't Sophia, either. I couldn't care less which country this girl calls home. Besides, if the rumors are true, you boys just got finished slaughtering a bunch of innocent women and children. So I don't see how you're in a position to judge anybody."

"Innocent?" the older soldier said, teeth bared in an aggressive travesty of amusement. "We'll show you innocent."

The younger soldier took the cue and grabbed hold of Paz's arm. It didn't hurt, but she started screaming bloody murder anyway. As she'd hoped, Juan immediately leaped into action, flooring her assailant with a single punch; unfortunately, the boy pulled her down with him as he fell. The older soldier reached for his sword, but Paz kicked him hard in the shin, which gave Juan time to close the distance between them. The two men grappled; Paz had to roll to the side to avoid being stepped on. Juan's thick boot landed just inches from her nose, and she found herself staring at a mark branded into the leather.

"RP," she whispered, just as Juan deftly flipped the older soldier to the ground and mounted him. The fight devolved into a messy, indecorous affair of half-landed punches, torn clothes, and grunts. It reminded Paz of the way Frankie and Terry used to wrestle.

"What in hell's going on here?"

Another Protectorate soldier arrived from the direction of the tavern, this one sporting an extra couple of ribbons on his breast: an officer, then. Juan and his sparring partner tried to find their feet with some measure of dignity.

"He punched Ollie," the older soldier said. "And she's got disciplinary tattoos."

"So do you," the officer replied.

Paz hadn't noticed the word tattooed around the older soldier's wrist—*inebriate*.

"Not like those, though. They only put those rings on Sophians."

Paz knew it wouldn't do any good to deny it. She rose to her feet, hoping to look as much as possible like a penitent standing chastened before the Dubium. "He's right," she said. "I fell in with a bad crowd in the Anchor for a while. It's why I moved out here. I wanted to start over."

She smiled angelically and watched the officer melt. "Please accept my apologies on behalf of the Protectorate," he said. "It's been a, uh, difficult week."

"Of course. I completely understand."

"Good." He glanced at the older soldier, who was helping a woozy Ollie to his feet. "Let's forget this ever happened, eh? Next round's on me."

The three men headed back to the public house. Paz went to Juan and used the hem of her dress to stanch the blood dripping from his nose.

"I'm sorry about that," she said.

"Don't be."

"I just have one more favor to ask and then I promise I'll leave you alone forever."

"Does it involve any more fighting? Because I'm not sure I have it in me."

"No more fighting, I promise." She wiped away the last bit of blood, then leaned forward and gave Juan a tender kiss on the cheek. "I just need to know where you got your shoes."

Paz rode hard for the next three weeks. She'd wake long before sunrise and go for four or five hours at a stretch, until her every pore was seeping sweat, then find a shady spot to nap away the afternoon. She'd start up again when evening fell and ride until either her body or her horse cried uncle. Though she'd stop briefly in the towns she passed to make sure she was still going in the right direction, she didn't partake in any unnecessary conversation; she'd learned her lesson in Oleanna.

The township of Cody was announced by a sign at the side of

the road advertising a population of 980, amended to 981 in flaking red paint. Paz tied her horse to an acacia outside the town limits and entered on foot. It was midday, and some kind of market was on in a quaint square bordered by flower boxes. At least a hundred people strolled among the stalls, each one tended by a sunburned farmer or thick-armed craftsperson. Crates gaudy with ripe fruits and vegetables competed for the eye's attention with ceramic bowls finished in kaleidoscopic glazes and brightly polished iron tools. Paz palmed a peach while the vendor was haggling with another customer and brought it straight to her mouth. The juices exploded beneath her teeth, overflowing, dripping off her chin, eliciting an involuntary groan of pleasure: She couldn't remember the last time she'd tasted something so delicious. In fact, the experience of eating it was so purely ecstatic that her first thought upon looking up and seeing the face of her quarry across the square was that she must be hallucinating—some sort of peach delirium.

She blinked hard. When that failed to expunge the impossible vision, she closed her eyes and dug her knuckles into her eyelids, rubbing vigorously. But once the phosphenes had dissipated, she was faced with the same view as before: the Wesah warrior who had killed Gemma and beaten Paz to within an inch of her life, done up like a typical Descendant woman going to market of a morning—in a knee-length blue cotton shift, with a shiny black ribbon in her hair and a wicker basket over her arm. Her companion, a slightly pudgy man with a round, good-natured face and a dramatically receding hairline, was easily recognized from Juan's detailed description—the notorious RP. He and the

Wesah woman walked through the square arm in arm, like any other couple in love.

Paz took another bite of the peach, thinking how much Clive would've appreciated this surreal turn of events, and fell into step behind them.

4. Clive

THERE WAS A POINT AT WHICH PAIN COULD NO LONGER reach you. It was as if you'd been knocked unconscious; the world could go on beating you all it wanted, but you wouldn't feel a thing. Clive realized he'd reached that point when he saw the soldiers coming toward him and Burns across the pasture. He'd lost his parents, his little brother, and his faith all in the space of a year. Now the love of his life and his lifelong best friend had been taken from him in a single blow, and Flora was off somewhere in the mist on her own. What was his freedom even worth now? What did he have left to live for?

The journey back to the Anchor seemed to last forever. They were traveling with Chang, his honor guard, and another fifty or so soldiers, and though Clive and Burns had had their ankles shackled, they were somehow expected to keep pace. By the end of the first week, Clive had developed the sores that would remain his most effusive companion for the rest of the journey, that would make sleep so slow to come and the days so slow to pass. He and Burns were kept at opposite ends of the formation during the day and in separate tents at night, ostensibly so they couldn't conspire against the Descendancy any further. Clive did his level best to get himself killed—hurling invective at the soldiers, dragging his feet, pretending to wake up screaming several times a night to interrupt his captors' sleep—but it was no use. After what he'd done in the Bastion—murdering his fellow soldiers in order to free Paz—Clive had become a symbol of the sheer malevolence that threatened the Descendancy; the Grand Marshal needed his execution to be a spectacle.

Clive could remember seeing a lamb just after its shearing, quivering in this unexpected and inexplicable new chill, bleating with confusion. He was that lamb now, defenseless, shorn of anything and everything that had mattered to him. He'd put all his hopes and faith in Paz, and she'd betrayed him. He still found it impossible to understand, so much so that he sometimes began to doubt what he'd seen—Gemma lying cold and bloodless on the grass, and Paz kneeling over her, knife in hand. And yet what other explanation could there be but the obvious one: Paz had killed Gemma.

It didn't bear thinking about. Nothing did anymore. He tried to keep his mind as blank as possible, watching, as if from a great distance, a young man marching silently and inexorably toward death.

It was nearly a month before they reached the Anchor, but the sight of the capital looming on the horizon like some great misshapen toadstool brought no comfort to Clive's heart. He'd long since stopped thinking of it as *home*, and now it promised something far worse than painful memories and a sense of wistful dislocation. The detachment passed beneath the Southern Gate, bursting into the hum of city life, of beggars and pickpockets, artists and artisans, children just finished with their school day and drunkards already a few ales deep—familiar and strange at once. Clive couldn't shake the feeling that something was *off*; a nervous energy seemed to radiate from every face, every storefront, every tree. This was wartime. This was the threat of extinction. Every act and every action took on existential proportions. You were either helping to save the Descendancy or else speeding its destruction; there was no such thing as neutrality anymore.

The soldiers peeled off for the Bastion, leaving Clive and Burns alone with Chang and his black-suited honor guard. People genuflected as the Grand Marshal passed, or shouted brief and ecstatic encomia.

"They missed me," Chang mused.

"They're tellin' you what you want to hear," Burns said.

"No. That's you telling yourself what *you* want to hear. I have this city in the palm of my hand."

Chang marched them straight to Annunciation Square, which was bustling with the morning's commerce. A line of pillories had been set up at the western edge of the plaza, just in front of a jeweler's shop. Only two were in use, and the holes in the unoccupied stations made a perfect row of unsettling, unblinking eyes.

"You're putting us in the stocks?" Burns said.

"We have to show you off a bit," Chang replied. "To build up the anticipation."

Clive didn't resist as two members of the honor guard unlocked his manacles and fitted his neck and wrists into the pillory. When they lowered the top, he half expected it to take his head clean off. They removed the shackles from his legs next; at least now the sores on his ankles would have a chance to heal.

"Look there," Chang said, once Clive and Burns were both firmly secured. He pointed at an empty section of the square, where a couple of men appeared to be measuring something out with string. "Do you know what they're building?"

"A giant statue of you pissing on an annulus?" Burns guessed.

"A gallows. *Your* gallows. When I decide the time is right, everybody in the city is gonna watch you swing from it."

Chang headed off across the cobblestones, stopping every few feet to glad-hand some merchant or another, his honor guard sticking close behind him.

"He's a fool," Burns said.

"He's not the one in the stocks," Clive replied.

"But he didn't kill us. He should've killed us."

"Did you not hear the bit about the gallows?"

"I've been advising him, you know. The whole way back from the *tooroon*. About how to handle the war that's on its way."

Clive craned his neck so he could look Burns in the eye. "Why the hell would Chang want your advice? He hates you."

"We hate each other. But we both want what's best for the Descendancy, and he respects my judgment. As he fucking well should."

The crowd moving through the square had already begun to notice the new prisoners; their glances conveyed a combination of morbid curiosity and distaste. A group of kids ran past, then circled back around a few seconds later. One of them picked up a loose stone and tossed it to himself, considering his options.

"Don't even think about it," Burns growled. The children all scurried off, but Clive didn't take any consolation in the victory.

His neck was already beginning to chafe. The chimes of Notre Fille tolled the hour. Night was coming. When darkness fell, and the shine started flowing, who knew what these so-called civilized people might be capable of?

Five bells, and the sky started to lighten. Clive didn't remember sleeping, only waking with a start over and over again—at a piece of cobblestone ricocheting off his shoulder, or a drunkard urinating on his feet (the warmth of it almost welcome), or a couple of streetwalkers shouting about how much they were looking forward to watching him die. Burns was snoring lightly; according to him, real soldiers learned to take sleep where they could get it.

Seven bells, and the Anchor began to come to life. Street vendors set up their stalls; shopkeepers flipped the signs in their windows. The stray dogs of the city, who'd spent the night skulking around the pillories like vultures, retreated to their kennels and hideaways. Clive could smell the coffee brewing at Grimaldi's Café.

Nine bells, and the square finally looked full; these harried men and women were all on their way to some important job or another, so only had time to fling a cursory gibe or desultory gobbet of spit in the general direction of the pillories. One called out to Clive by name; the two of them had gone to school together but had never much liked each other. Clive pretended not to notice.

Eleven bells, and the gallows construction crew arrived. Four men set to work hammering and sawing, occasionally throwing guilty glances over at the poor souls in the stocks. They seemed to be taking their time; Clive wouldn't have put it past Chang to have directed them to work as slowly as possible, so as to draw out the psychological torment for his prisoners.

One bell, and the lunch hour came to a grudging end. Children were compelled to give up their games of tag and follow their exhausted mistresses back to the schoolhouse. Men scraped their plates into the public waste boxes around the edge of the square or just onto the ground, where the leavings were set upon by the dogs, who'd returned for just this bounty. Satiated and jolly, the citizens of the Anchor put off returning to work by dawdling at the pillories, making all manner of threats. Clive was roused from a daydream of Paz by the sharp snap of a leather belt across his calves; even through the fabric of his trousers, the sting was excruciating.

Three bells, and the sun revealed itself to be the cruelest tormentor of all. Clive could feel the back of his neck and hands burning; they'd begin to peel come nightfall. And though he was starving, the thirst hurt a hundred times worse. Thirst like lust, like ambition, like any want that could be fed and fed and yet never diminish. He imagined standing beneath a waterfall with his mouth wide open, taking in an entire river's worth of water and still wanting more.

Five bells, and the first cool breeze ruffled its way through the ornamental trees and topiaries of Annunciation Square. The men at the gallows called it a day; their half-finished construction lay like a conquered beast at the center of the plaza. A madman stopped by to lecture Clive and Burns for nearly an hour, gesticulating wildly and pacing with the limitless energy of a young preacher, until his gibberings about the end of the world almost began to make sense.

Seven bells, and at last the sun dipped below the skyline. The gas lamps were lit, while candles flared to life in the windows of the

TOMMY WALLACH

tall apartments that surrounded the square. A group of teenagers took turns throwing rotten vegetables at the pillories. Clive licked the tomato pips from his face and was grateful for every one.

Nine bells, and something like peace descended on the square. Couples strolled across the cobblestones arm in arm. A fiddler played a mournful rendition of "What a Weight," glancing forlornly at his violin case whenever people passed. Outside Grimaldi's, diners were finishing up their meals, sipping contentedly from white porcelain teacups.

"Someone's coming," Burns said.

A group of silhouettes clarified as they passed beneath one of the gas lamps. The one in front was tall and broad, his uniform aglitter with medals: Chang. The four strapping figures beside him were members of his honor guard. The other silhouette was short and slim, and moved with a pronounced wariness Clive would've recognized from a mile away.

"Clover?" he said.

"Clive?"

His brother ran to him, as if they might embrace, but of course the stocks made that impossible.

"How are you—how did you—" Clive realized he hadn't expected ever to speak to his brother again. But he remembered the promise he'd made to himself, if he ever did get the chance. "I'm sorry," he said. "Clover, I'm so sorry." The tears spilled down his cheeks; he wasn't physically capable of wiping them away. "Back in Sophia, I wasn't thinking straight. I can't believe I hurt you."

Clover shook his head. His eyes glistened in the moonlight; his voice quavered. "I can't believe I didn't trust you about Irene."

"That wasn't your fault. None of it was."

There was so much to say, too much, but here came Chang, standing between them, speaking over them. "What a lovely reunion," he said. "I'm pleased to see the two of you getting along."

"As if you care," Clive said.

"Oh, but I do. See, if you hated each other, all my leverage would go right out the window." Chang turned to Clover. "I've decided to let you and your father go, but on one condition: both of you work for me now. You will shout your loyalty to me and my government from the rooftops, or I'll hang your brother from that gibbet over there. Do you understand?"

"Yes," Clover said without hesitation, as if he'd been prepared for exactly this proposition—which, of course, he probably had.

Clive was delirious from hunger, thirst, and exposure, so he assumed he must've heard Chang wrong. "Wait, did you just say something about Da?"

"He's alive," Clover said. "I know that sounds crazy, but—"

"That's not possible. We saw his body."

"Sophia faked his death, so the Descendancy wouldn't know he'd been taken. I'll explain everything, but first, what about Gemma and Flora? Are they at Mitchell's place?"

"Flora ran when we were taken prisoner. But Gemma . . ." Clive trailed off.

"Gemma what, Clive? What happened to her?"

Clive couldn't bring himself to tell the whole story. Some part of him still felt the need to protect Paz. "She's gone. I'm sorry."

"I think that's enough catching up," Chang said. "Clive, enjoy your last night in the stocks. Tomorrow morning I'll be moving you to the Bastion."

"Why?"

"Because if I leave you out here, someone's bound to kill you sooner or later."

"What about Burns?"

"Yes. What shall we do with Burns?"

"Just fucking kill me already, would you?" Burns said. "I'm that sick of listening to you talk."

Chang smiled. "You'd like that, wouldn't you? If I put you out of your misery."

"Damn right I would. But I'm sure you've got some idiot reason for boring me with another ten years of—"

It happened too quickly for Clive to track: Chang drawing his sword—a strange weapon, steeply curved, without a cross guard—and chopping downward; Burns shouting out some incomprehensible presentiment of disaster; the blade biting into his left thigh just above the knee and sliding on through flesh and bone and flesh, until it burst free and the bottom half of his leg fell away like a dead tree branch. Blood gushed from the wound, a black cataract making canals of the cracks in the cobblestones. Not twenty feet away, a woman in white petticoats fainted. Burns's eyes rolled back into his head and he went limp in the stocks.

"Take him out and tie the leg off loose," Chang said to his honor guard. "Let him bleed out in the dungeon nice and slow."

Two of the guards took Burns out of the pillory and carried him away. The others marched a dumbstruck Clover off toward the Bastion. And Clive was left alone with the riot of his thoughts. His father was alive. Burns would soon be dead. He and his brother were now firmly trapped under Chang's thumb.

One of the stray dogs who frequented the square, a good-natured mutt who'd managed to get her front paws up onto the pillory once so Clive could pet her jowly face, approached Burns's amputated limb. The dog looked at Clive, something like shame in her eyes, then grabbed the half-leg between her teeth and ran off into the night.

5. Athène

THE VILLENAÎTRE: ATHÈNE'S HEART SEEMED TO WITHER in her chest at the very sight of it. Here, she'd been happier than she'd ever been before, happier than she would ever be again. Here, Gemma had ceased to be a citizen of the Descendancy and become Wesah in mind, body, and spirit. Here, they had pledged their undying love to each other.

Foolish, really, to associate so much irretrievable joy with a place that had been important to her long before she met Gemma. She'd probably been to the Villenaître a dozen times over the course of her life; yet the months she'd spent here in the full flush of love stood out so brightly that all the others became mere shadows—so much wasted time. That contrast cut even deeper now that Gemma was gone. The Villenaître had become the tomb in which Athène's contentment would be permanently interred.

She realized Flora was watching her, judging the upwelling sadness in her eyes. "It is only memories," she said. "Not grief."

Flora blinked—a sort of micro-shrug—and looked away: *sure it is.* Athène liked to think she'd become expert at reading the girl's facial expressions by now; she'd had to, as Flora hadn't spoken a word in weeks. Athène felt attuned to the girl's moods and needs as she'd never been to anyone else's—even Gemma's. Something told her when Flora was hungry or thirsty, when she might need to answer the call of nature, when she was too tired to travel any farther. Was this what it was like to be a mother? Whenever Athène had imagined herself raising a child, suckling some squalling newborn at her raw nipple, the baby had seemed an implacable nuisance at best, and an insatiable parasite at worst, leaching time and energy in equal measure. But in taking care of Flora, she'd begun to understand the strange comfort one could derive from being depended on by something helpless; it was a burden, yes, but more in the manner of a heavy blanket than an overladen basket.

In a few minutes, they would pass beneath the inscribed archway of the Villenaître: MAY ALL YOUR DREAMS BE NIGHTMARES. At the *tooroon*, Andromède had enjoined the Wesah to travel to the Kikiwaak di Noor—their permanent colony in the north—but that was before Chang had unleashed his weapon, before the Wesah nation found itself facing annihilation. There was no doubt in Athène's mind that the tribe would convene here at the Villenaître, where they always came in times of trouble.

"You must stay by my side at all times," she said to Flora. "There has never been much trust for those who are not raised in the tribe. Now, it will be very much worse. Do you understand?" A moment of eye contact was all Athène could expect as acknowledgment.

She steeled herself for what was to come. Andromède undoubtedly blamed herself for what had happened at the *tooroon*, which meant she'd be thinking defensively now, about how best to ensure the survival of the tribe. She had to be convinced this was a mistake. Maybe it was too late to avenge Gemma's murder, but there was still time to avenge the sisters they'd lost to Chang's savagery.

TOMMY WALLACH

However much it hurt to be here, Athène would not leave the Villenaître until her mother agreed to lead what remained of their proud nation to war against the Descendancy.

It was the first time Athène had ever passed through the gates of the Villenaître to find no one waiting on the other side of the archway. The empty plaza pulsated with summer heat; a dust devil lifted a few blades of golden grass and tumbleweed, dropped them silently back to earth. The totems that used to decorate the square had all been ripped out, leaving deep gouges in the red earth.

Athène looked to Flora. The girl's eyes were closed; she was listening to something. And now Athène heard it too—an atonal murmur floating on the air like a scent. They followed it across the dirt square and up the wide, shallow steps of the central longhouse. Athène pushed aside the thick woolen curtain and the murmur immediately became a full-throated moan, so loud as to feel like an assault, especially when paired with the noxious odor of festering wounds—casualties from the massacre at the *tooroon*—and the feeble light that crept in at the edges of the curtained windows. Inside the longhouse, many hundreds of Wesah knelt on rugs or the bare floor, all of them facing toward Grandmother, the tribe's most senior *otsapah*, who stood on a plinth at the far end, leading the lamentation. Athène swallowed a lump of bile and pulled Flora into the miasma.

She'd heard of this ritual—*li Shansoon de Kornay*, the Song of Crow—though as far as she knew, it hadn't been enacted in decades. It was the ultimate funeral service, observing the death and rebirth of the world itself, carried out from sunrise to sunset for one full cycle of the moon. There was no way to know how far it had progressed, but Grandmother had almost certainly waited for Andromède's arrival to begin, which meant there were probably weeks remaining. Athène moved quickly down the rows of mourners, seeking her mother. There would be no pride of place here, no hierarchy. All were the same in the eyes of Crow, the great god of death, who maintained the balance between Fox and Wolf. It was difficult to differentiate faces—there was so little light, and every tribeswoman wore the same tormented expression—but Athène eventually managed to disqualify all of them. Was it possible that Andromède had decided not to come to the Villenaître? Could her shame really run so deep that she couldn't bear to face her people at all?

Grandmother stepped down from the plinth as Athène and Flora approached. The keening continued undiminished while they spoke.

"That girl should not be here," she said, nodding at Flora. "She is an outsider."

Athène bristled at the use of the term *dahor*; she remembered how it had made Gemma feel. "Where is my mother?"

"She does not wish to be disturbed."

"But she is here? In the Villenaître?"

The *otsapah* didn't answer; she was staring intently at Flora, as if trying to read something behind the dead crystals of the girl's eyes. Her expression softened. "Gemma is gone, isn't she? And this is her sister."

"Her name is Flora. She is under my protection."

The *otsapah* nodded, as if something she'd predicted a long time ago had finally come to pass. "Andromède is at Pchimayr, doing penance."

"Thank you, Grandmother."

"I hope when you have finished speaking with her, you will join us here. We owe it to the spirits of those we've lost."

Athène took a page out of Flora's book, and said nothing in response.

"Your sister was coming here every morning. All day, she works. Like a missive." They'd stopped outside the *otsapah*'s hut; some new girl could be seen moving about inside, preparing the place for Grandmother's return from the ritual. "She was so frightened that I think she has no magic inside her, only illness. So one day, she steal a drink of the dreamtea." Athène had to imagine where a normal girl would be asking questions, creating a dialogue with a version of Flora not traumatized by loss. "The dreamtea gives people—how do you say?—like dreams, but awake. Your sister sees very clearly when she drinks. She had much magic in her, I think."

And just what was it Gemma had seen that night, while wandering the sands of Pchimayr, the Little Ocean? She'd said it felt like watching the past and the future intermixing, and discovering that both were brimming with death. Perhaps the gods had been trying to forewarn her about what would happen at the *tooroon*— but what good were signs you couldn't interpret? What use were warnings without solutions? They were merely reminders of your impotence, of the absurd fantasy of free will.

Or maybe the journey engendered by the dreamtea really was just a delusion. Maybe those fits of shaking that had overtaken

Gemma now and again were merely symptoms of a disease. Magic or madness? Divine intervention or cosmic indifference? It didn't matter one way or the other anymore. Maybe it never had.

They walked past the fields where the Wesah raised and kept their horses and up the dunes, stopping to gaze out over the stone jetty that projected across Pchimayr only to coil back on itself like the tip of a fiddlehead fern. Andromède stood at the very center of the spiral, still as a statue.

"Stay by the water," Athène told Flora. "If anyone comes, run to me."

She removed her moccasins and began to walk along the smooth stones. She'd always liked the way it hurt, like someone angrily massaging the soles of her feet. Her mother was kneeling on a blanket, cleaning something in the ruddy water of the lake. Silver and scarlet, the blade glinted in the sunlight. Andromède's bangles lay in a pile among the rocks, and thin lines of blood ran down her arms. There was historical precedent for this sort of self-mutilation—specifically with chieftains who'd suffered losses in the internecine wars that had once been a mainstay of Wesah culture—but like the ritual going on in the longhouse, Athène had never seen it firsthand.

"Did Grandmother tell you to do this?" she said.

Her mother splashed water across her arms to rinse away the blood. "It was my decision. To help with the grief."

"And has it helped?"

"Yes."

Athène knelt down next to her mother and drew her own dagger. She pulled up her skirt and placed the blade against the skin of

TOMMY WALLACH

her inner thigh. Press and release: a thin white line where the blood fled in terror. The pain called to her like a siren, promising a very specific sort of relief.

"That is not yours to do," her mother barked.

"No?"

"I am Andromède. The tribe is my responsibility. You have nothing to pay penance for."

Athène laughed at the absurdity of that statement. "Gemma is dead."

"Many of our sisters are dead."

"But I was responsible for Gemma. I promised I'd keep her safe."

Her mother sniffed, gave a curt nod. "One then. Just one."

Athène pulled the blade a short ways across her thigh; it burned cool, shed ruby drops down her calf and onto the blanket. When she was finished, her mother took the blade and shook it clean in the water.

"I want to know your plan," Athène said.

"Plan?"

"After Grandmother finishes the Song of Crow."

"It will be as I said. The tribe will travel to the Kikiwaak di Noor."

"You want to run."

"This war has only just begun. Countless more will die. I cannot prevent that. It was a mistake to think I could. But I can ensure that no more of the corpses will be Wesah."

Athène stood up, momentarily towering over her mother, rivulets of blood running like bright veins along her leg. "We are a part of this war now."

"No. The war is between Sophia and the Anchor. It had nothing to do with us until they tried to use us."

"Only one side tried to use us. The other tried to exterminate us."

"Even if we were to join with Sophia, we would still be fighting *their* war."

"So don't join with Sophia."

"Are you suggesting we fight for the Anchor?"

"Of course not!"

"Then what? There are only two sides, Athène! What is it you want to convince me of?"

Athène fumbled to make herself understood. Her mother had lost sight of the fact that there was more to existence than just existing. There was honor. There was principle. There was courage. "That you are being a coward!" she finally said.

At any other time, a statement like that might have seen her banished from her mother's presence for a month. But Andromède took the blow with equanimity; when she spoke, there was only sadness in her voice.

"Perhaps I am. Perhaps it is wrong to run. But I would rather be remembered as a coward than for there to be no one left to remember me at all. Now leave me to my grief, and I'll leave you to yours."

Her mother turned away, setting the blade to her arm again, rocking it back and forth to widen the next scar. Athène was too full of anger to risk saying anything else. She strode back along the spiral, splashing through the shallow water as if she might make a point merely by making noise. Flora was waiting at the water's edge, her expression as impassive as always.

"My mother will not see reason," Athène said in English. "She

TOMMY WALLACH

thinks we should do *nothing* about the men who kill thousands of our sisters! She wants a whole nation to flee like a little boy frightened of his mother! Can you believe this?"

But there was no point in talking to Flora, who would give nothing back, who had nothing to give. After a moment of staring wrathfully into the girl's face, Athène stormed back up the dunes and down again toward the square. She felt capable of any act of violence or heresy, and when she caught the first strain of the keening from the longhouse, she followed it like a bloodhound, not knowing if she was going to run screaming into the middle of the ritual, or slap Grandmother across the face, or break down in tears in the doorway.

So it was no conscious decision that saw her fall to her knees next to her sisters and take up their lament as her own. She couldn't have explained why that suddenly seemed the most natural thing to do, except to say that even if she'd begun to come to terms with the loss of Gemma, she had yet to contend with that other, larger tragedy, or with the fact that the Wesah people, to say nothing of her mother, would never be the same again.

After a few minutes, she noticed that Flora was kneeling beside her and had begun to wail along with everyone else. If the Wesah were bothered by the audacity of this yellow-haired *dahor*, they didn't show it. Perhaps grief this profound knew no nation but the purely human. Athène moaned until her voice was raw, until she was nearly dizzy. Then she kept going. She would see this demon out of her; she would reach the shore on the other side of this ocean of sorrow.

And when that was done, she would deal with her mother.

6. Clover

THERE WAS NO LIGHT BEHIND ANY OF THE WINDOWS, and all the curtains were drawn. Clover knocked, but no one answered. He tried the handle.

"Hello?"

The door creaked, far louder than his voice had been. Dust particles danced in the light from the gas lamp outside, swirled where he passed. (And what did the lungs do with all those glittering splinters, once they were inhaled? Did they live on in the body forever?) The house looked derelict. Thick cobwebs hung from the rafters like streamers, and the floorboards were gritty with dried mud and leaves; no one had swept the place in a long time. He went to the kitchen and found the cupboard bare. Clearly Mitchell didn't have the first idea how to keep house without a woman's help.

The plangent sound of sawing floated up from beneath Clover's feet. He took the stairs slowly, not wanting to surprise the old man into cutting off a finger. But when he was only a few steps from the bottom, the sawing abruptly stopped.

"Gemma?" Mitchell said. The desperate hope in his voice nearly broke Clover's heart. "Is that you? Flora?"

"No," Clover said. "It's just me."

He reached the workshop floor. Mitchell stood before a thick chunk of cherrywood held in a vise. His disappointment radiated even as he tried to summon up a smile.

"Clover. Thank God you're safe."

"It's good to see you, Mr. Poplin."

Mitchell was transformed since Clover had seen him last. The ruddy vigor that used to belie his age was gone, transformed into a pallor bordering on translucence, an existential thinness. He'd grown a wild silver beard that sparkled with wood shavings, and his clothes fairly hung off him; if the scene in the kitchen was anything to go by, he probably wasn't eating much. Clover saw the minute hesitation in the old man's eyes—a fear of what he might learn—before he overcame it. "My granddaughters—are they with you?"

"No. Flora's still . . . away."

"But you saw her? She's all right?"

I have no idea. "She's fine. Right as rain."

"And Gemma?"

"Gemma . . ." His father had taught him to be sparing with his lies, that even hard truths carried within them some intrinsic value that counterbalanced the pain they might cause. But faced with a lonely old man who'd survived his entire family, Clover's resolve collapsed. "Gemma's watching after her sister. The two of them had to stay out east, to do some work for the Protectorate."

Mitchell coughed gruffly, as if this might mask the wetness in his eyes. He fitted the saw back into the groove he'd already cut in the wood. "So I imagine you'll be looking for a place to stay."

"If you don't mind. And it's more than just me. My da, too."

"Your da?" Mitchell looked at him as if he might be crazy. "Your da?" he repeated.

"It's a pretty long story. They're still questioning him over at the Bastion, but he'll be free by the end of the week. Chang wants him to give a sermon next Sunday."

"Daughter's love. Daniel Hamill alive." Mitchell made the sign of the annulus on his chest. "If that's not a miracle, I don't know what is."

"My brother's here too. In the Anchor, I mean. But the Protectorate—"

"I don't want to hear one word about that boy," Mitchell interrupted. "Not a single goddamned word."

"Why? Did something happen between you two?"

"Morning after Flora's birthday, I woke up and both of 'em were gone. Haven't seen either one since. She never woulda left the house on her own, not without telling me. Which means your brother convinced her somehow."

"He wouldn't have taken her unless he had a good reason."

Mitchell didn't look convinced. "Anyway, the upstairs bedrooms are all made up. You're welcome to stay in either one. Until the girls get back, of course. Then we'll find somewhere else for ya."

"Thank you, Mr. Poplin."

"My pleasure." The old man considered for a moment, then set his saw down again. "Hey, what do you say we go out to the pub and get some food? All of a sudden, I'm hungry as a goddamned wolf."

Clover paced the hallway between the front door and the kitchen: back and forth, back and forth. There was so much to say, so much

TOMMY WALLACH

ground to cover. He couldn't imagine lying to his father as he'd lied to Mitchell, yet to tell the whole truth—all the people he'd hurt, the crimes he'd committed, the lustful and impious thoughts he'd entertained—seemed just as unimaginable.

Someone knocked on the door.

"That must be your da!" Mitchell shouted from the workshop.

"I know it is!" Clover shouted back, too nervous to be polite.

Standing at the door, he pulled his shirt down and straightened his spine. He tried on a smile and quickly discarded it as false. He was scraping the dirt out from under his fingernails when a second, more emphatic knock made him jump.

"Sorry," he said, undoing the latch and opening the door.

His father stood on the landing, flanked by two soldiers. He looked a lot healthier than he had the night of the raid on the Mindful safe house; Chang had probably held on to him this last week so he could be cleaned and fattened up—otherwise folks might get to thinking the Grand Marshal had tortured a war hero.

"Hello, Son," he said.

"Hey, Da."

Clover gave in to his emotion, practically leaping into his father's arms in full sight of the soldiers. Tears sprang to his eyes as he squeezed for all he was worth, breathing in the familiar smell, feeling the ticklish rasp of beard on his cheek. Finally embarrassment overcame him and he let go; easy enough to do, as his father hadn't ever embraced him back.

"We'll be outside, should you need us," one of the soldiers said.

Clover frowned. "You're staying?"

"The Honor remains a prime target for the Mindful," the other soldier explained. "The Grand Marshal has ordered a full-time escort for the time being, to keep him safe."

"Right," Clover's father said. "To keep me safe." He began to close the door but stopped halfway. "And I'm not an Honor. Not anymore."

"No?" said one of the soldiers. "So what should we call you?"

"How about Daniel Hamill? That's my fucking name." He shut the door the rest of the way.

Daniel Hamill. It had an unpleasant civilian ring to it, a crudeness in keeping with the shocking exchange Clover had just witnessed. Only a few people had ever had leave to refer to Clover's father that way: his wife, Eddie Poplin, a few select Honors and bishops. It was the name of an ordinary man, where Clover had always seen his father as something closer to a god. Now it was *Daniel Hamill* who turned to face his son. *Daniel Hamill* who coughed, the sound of it thick and worrisome. *Daniel Hamill* who sighed ruefully, as if disappointed in something, and walked into the kitchen.

Clover followed, heart in his throat, anxious for reasons he couldn't entirely understand. Mitchell could be heard hammering away downstairs. Clover had asked for some time to talk to his father alone, but he regretted it now; it would've been nice to have a third person there, to help alleviate the tension. His father sat down at the kitchen table and regarded the board of cheese and sausage that Clover had prepared. He picked up a slice of meat with his left hand, and Clover saw where Lila had amputated the index finger at the distal phalangeal joint. Suddenly he felt a little less guilty for what he'd done to her.

"I want you to tell me everything that's happened since the last time I saw you," Daniel said, his tone flat and even. "Don't leave out a single detail. I'll know if you do."

Clover had hoped there would be more small talk before they reached this point, but no part of this reunion was going how he expected, so he began to relate the events of the past year. It was uncomfortable talking about himself like a character in a story, particularly as this fictional Clover approached his fatefully immoral decision to walk with Irene in the Maple Garden; he was surprised that his father was able to restrain himself from giving an impromptu lecture on the dangers of lustful thoughts. He went on, describing the scene outside Sophia and how it felt when Clive's bullet ripped through his shoulder. Here, at least, he'd expected some kind of reaction, but his father's expression remained unreadable. He grew more confident, efficiently laying out how he'd spent his days at the academy, how his father's Filia had led him to Lila's study, and the truth of what had transpired there. He paused after that, waiting for judgment.

"Go on," was all his father said.

He rounded out the tale quickly—the unwitting poisoning at Edgewise, his return to the Anchor, and finally, his unlikely plan to free his father by leading the Protectorate to the Mindful enclave.

"I think you already know the rest," he said quietly.

"Yes. I think I do."

They were quiet for a few moments. Clover picked up a cube of cheese that crumbled into tasteless paste in his mouth. He felt exhausted, exposed. There could be no recovering from so much truth telling; now Daniel Hamill had proof of what he'd always suspected—that his youngest son had no moral center, no faith, no hope of redemption in the eyes of God and his Daughter.

"I'm proud of you," his father said gruffly.

"Proud?" Clover was surprised to find himself less than over-joyed at this unexpected vindication. "I killed innocent people. I betrayed my own blood."

"You survived. In spite of everything."

"You used to say life was about more than just living."

"I didn't know anything back then. I was a child." His father's tone was bitter and self-deprecating. "And what of Clive? I know where he is, but not how he got there."

"I haven't been able to piece it all together, but it seems like he and Flora got in some kind of trouble with the Mindful. They ended up on the run with Paz."

"Is there something going on between her and your brother?"

"You'd have to ask him."

"What about Flora and Gemma?"

"Clive lost track of Flora at the *tooroon*. And Gemma—she's dead."

Daniel looked to the stairs that led down to the basement. "Does Mitchell know?"

"I couldn't bring myself to tell him."

Daniel nodded. "Clover, I have one more question to ask you, and it's an important one. I need you to answer honestly."

"Okay."

"Do you still believe?"

"Believe?"

"In the religion you were raised with. In the Descendancy."

"Of course," Clover replied immediately. "I mean, I had some doubts when I first got to Sophia, but they went away as soon as I found out what Lila did to you."

Daniel's eyes betrayed his disappointment. Perhaps Clover hadn't been emphatic enough. He tried to formulate a better response, some more enthusiastic proof of his faith and loyalty, but his father didn't give him the opportunity. "I'm tired," Daniel said, standing up from the table. "We should both get some sleep."

Clover felt a sting behind his eyes but refused to let it show; he'd hoped they would stay up all night talking. "Sure."

"I'll say good night to Mitchell. You and I can speak more in the morning."

His father lumbered down the hallway like an invalid, like a stranger. Clover let a few tears fall, wiped them away with his sleeve. He went upstairs and undressed, washed his face in the basin. He'd just slipped under the covers when he heard it, a cry of anguish splitting the silence, penetrating wood and plaster and stone as if they were paper. A pain that shouldn't have been inflicted; a truth that needn't have been told.

On the walk from Mitchell's house to the Delancey workshop, Clover could tell who was on their way to Notre Fille purely by the quality of their Sunday finery: a veritable rainbow of velveteens and crinolines, an exhaustive display of the milliner's art, and a couple hundred white suits and frilly dresses containing an equivalent number of unhappy, uncomfortable children. The best and brightest of the Anchor were all turned out for Honor Daniel Hamill—heroic survivor of more than a year in Sophian custody—and his grand return to the ambo.

Clover and his father had scarcely spoken since that first night, and when they did, the conversation was inevitably cursory and curt, as between two acquaintances with little in common: a reunion in name only. Daniel had spent most of his time locked in his room, preparing today's sermon. He'd come downstairs to eat a couple of times a day, but always radiated an aura of aloofness that would brook no disturbance.

So instead of reconnecting with his father, Clover had whiled away the past week with Kita, at least whenever she wasn't putting in her hours at the family workshop. He knew he owed his and his father's freedom to her, but it wasn't gratitude that brought him to her doorstep each afternoon; he genuinely liked her. Their daily strolls around the Anchor even had the whiff of the romantic to them—or would have anyway, if not for the Protectorate soldier always keeping pace ten steps behind them to ensure they weren't up to anything nefarious.

Thankfully he'd been able to evade his escort this morning, and so he arrived at the Delancey workshop unaccompanied. One of Kita's siblings told him he'd have to wait outside, as she was still getting ready. It was nearly fifteen minutes before he heard her voice on the other side of the door.

"You better not laugh," she said.

"Why would I laugh?"

"Just promise."

"Okay. I promise."

Kita pushed the door open a crack and slipped through. She'd been right to warn him; his first instinct *was* to laugh. It wasn't that there was anything funny about a girl getting all dressed up; he'd just never seen *her* dressed up. She wore a black shift that was prettily frayed along the hem, and her hair had been combed into a braid of Gordian complexity, swooping in and out and back around again. Her bone-white shoes had little violet ribbons at the toes.

"I see you smiling," she said accusingly.

Clover swallowed his amusement. "I'm just surprised is all. You look . . . I mean, it's nice."

"I know it is. The lace alone cost two arms and half a leg."

He thought about offering his elbow to her but chickened out at the last second. Though he was ninety-nine percent certain that she liked him, that one percent of doubt kept him paralyzed. It was his first experience with someone maybe having a crush on him, rather than the other way around. Oddly, he found it just as disconcerting, if in an entirely different way. Poor Gemma, who'd endured his amorous attention all those years; he'd thought he was being so subtle, but in retrospect, she must have known all along.

"Whatcha thinking about?" Kita said.

"Nothing."

"Bull. I bet you're thinking about what your dad's gonna say at the service. Did he give you a preview?"

"In a way."

Clover had woken that morning to find his father standing over his bed, wearing an expression stuck somewhere between anxiety and anger. "What is it?" he'd said.

"You will not come to the service this morning," Daniel replied.

Clover sat up against the headboard, still dazed with sleep. "Why? Did I do something wrong?"

"No," his father said, then quickly reconsidered. "Yes. And we'll discuss it when I get back. But you are not to leave the house until then. Do you understand me?"

"Yes, sir."

"Good."

Clover had given his father a good twenty-minute head start before ignoring this injunction completely.

"I mean, does he really think I'm going to miss this?" Clover complained to Kita. "It's ridiculous. I'm not a child anymore."

"You should go easy on him. You know what they did to him at Sophia."

"I guess. I just wish he wasn't acting so strangely. It's like he's become a completely different person."

Annunciation Square was packed with those who'd come to hear Honor Hamill speak. They all jostled to get into the church first and nail down a prime spot, to see and be seen. There was Chang, surrounded by his honor guard and the members of his new Gloria—a sop to those who needed to believe the Church still had any sort of influence in the Anchor. By official decree, there would be no replacement Epistem or Archbishop elected or appointed; the complex checks and balances of tripartite leadership had given way to dull autocracy.

By the time Clover and Kita entered the nave, the pews had already filled up. The spillover congregants were instructed to stand at the very back of the cathedral, just inside the doors.

"I can't even see anything," Kita said. "This is stupid."

"It's a sermon," Clover replied. "There's nothing to see."

"Can I get on your shoulders?"

"No."

"Why not?"

"Because we're in church!"

"So?"

"So no."

The crowd went quiet; something was happening. Clover got up on his tiptoes and craned to see between the two annoyingly tall men in front of him. Bishop Allen was already standing at the ambo. He looked thin and beleaguered. The wattle of loose skin under his chin shimmied as he scanned the audience.

"Who is it?" Kita asked.

"Bishop Allen."

"I thought he got kicked out of the Gloria."

"He did. I guess it didn't take."

Someone nearby shushed them.

"Welcome, citizens of the Descendancy, to this very special Sunday service," Allen said. "It is my great pleasure to welcome back Honor Daniel Hamill, who was taken prisoner by Sophia over a year ago and subjected to all manner of gruesome horrors. He's come here today to speak of his ordeal, and how we all must stand united against the threat of Sophia. Honor?"

A thunderous wave of applause filled Clover's ears as Daniel Hamill climbed the steps up to the ambo, shaking Bishop Allen's hand along the way. He took his place and stood there in silence until the audience quieted down. It was an old trick, one Clover had seen his father employ hundreds of times before, but usually with a sort of beatific patience, as if he could wait forever. Today Daniel looked nervous, frantic even, his eyes darting around the room as if seeking out some enemy lying in wait.

At last the Honor deigned to speak. "The Lord enjoins us not to hate our enemy, but to love them. So when I was first taken, I sought to love the men and women of Sophia, even as they tried to break me. Even as they did this"—he held up his mangled finger to a gasp from the congregation—"and much worse besides. But as the weeks passed, my resolve began to weaken. I believed the Daughter had forsaken me, and a hatred grew in me unlike anything I'd known before. I felt capable of any act of desecration, any act of violence. I was as ready to kill as I was to die. That was when Director Zeno, the leader of Sophia, began to bring me books, books I would never have been permitted to read in the Anchor.

"At first I refused to open them. I tried to convince myself it was out of piety, but the truth is I was afraid of what I would learn. I was afraid those books would make me doubt. Then one night I dreamed I was walking in the garden with Aleph and Eva, and they reminded me that every human being is a descendant of those who ate from the tree of knowledge. I woke up hungry for revelation. I plucked the fruit from the tree, and it turned my conception of the universe upside down. It shook my faith to the very core."

Concerned whispers like rustling papers, a palpable sense of fear. Daniel Hamill looked up to the great stained-glass windows along the eastern wall of the nave. "Sophia is on the march," he said. "As I speak, her armies travel swiftly through the veins of the Descendancy, and they will not stop until they've stilled our very heart, this city we call the Anchor." He went quiet for a moment, then threw his arms up to the sky. "I welcome them!"

Chang shot to his feet, barking something to his honor guard. The entire congregation erupted in shouts of dismay—with Clover probably the loudest among them—but his father would not be silenced. "You are welcome here, Sophia! Deliver us from this benighted age! Deliver us from dogma! Deliver us from evil!"

TOMMY WALLACH

7. Paz

THERE WAS AN ADDITION STUCK TO THE SIDE OF THE house like a barnacle, its unpainted clapboard walls and rusting steel roof contrasting with the sturdy planks and orderly shingles of its host. It could only be RP's workshop. Paz decided to begin her infiltration there, farthest from where her quarry was most likely to be sleeping. The doors were secured with a thick iron chain, but the thin wooden walls were rotten near the ground, so Paz was able to pry the boards off with her bare hands. The nails screamed as they were pulled from their berths, bending as if melting. It was scarcely five minutes' work to make a hole big enough to squeeze through.

She'd kept her eyes on the couple for most of the afternoon. They'd walked the market for nearly an hour before returning home with a basket full of melons, a bunch of carrots, and a rabbit the breeder had clubbed over the head right there at his stall. Crouched in the bushes, Paz had watched through the windows as the Wesah woman prepared lunch. Afterward, the two of them retired to their bedroom. (Paz hadn't been able to make out the details of their exploits through the closed curtains, which was probably for the best.) A while later the couple took another few turns around town and stopped in at the local public house for a drink. Paz got the sense RP liked to show the Wesah woman off; scandalized glances followed them wherever they went. Certainly the people of Cody were responding to the novelty of a Wesah tribeswoman living outside her *naasyoon*—and with a man, no less—but just as shocking was the oddness of this particular coupling. RP was chubby and short, neck-deep in middle age, while the Wesah woman fairly glowed with youthful vigor. Yet these sorts of partnerships were common in civilized society—security and support exchanged for a pretense of devotion and love. It was Paz's mistake to think the Wesah were above such transactions.

The couple returned home again a few minutes past sunset, and Paz took up her position outside. She'd watched from the woods until the last candle was blown out, then waited another half an hour, just to be safe. In spite of these precautions, she could still feel her heart beating hard as she rose to stand inside RP's workshop. Moonlight gleamed through the cracks between the clapboards, making a starscape out of the studs and bolts scattered on the counters. Sickle-shaped tools hanging from the walls enacted a portion of the moon's phases. Paz stepped gingerly toward what she hoped was an internal door connecting the workshop to the house. Something pulled at her shoulder; the rope she'd purchased at the market earlier that day had looped itself around the bottom of a bucket. She shot out a hand and managed to get her fingers around the handle just in time to keep it from falling over.

"Daughter's love," she whispered—a strange habit she'd picked up from Clive. A hollowness bloomed in her heart: Was he still alive? And if so, was there any chance he still loved her? She shook her head, silently chastising herself: this was no time to be clouding her concentration with thoughts like that.

She continued on across the workshop, more carefully now. On the way, she picked up a scrap of light that turned out to be some kind of rasp, serrated along one edge—though her plan was to avoid fighting, only a fool would confront a Wesah warrior completely unarmed. She reached the edge of the chamber and two shallow steps that led up to a door. The hinges were mercifully silent: one of the advantages of sneaking into the house of a craftsperson.

The room beyond had no windows; it was as if someone had applied a fresh coat of black paint to the darkness. She followed the sound of torrential snoring through another doorway, sliding the rope off her shoulder as she went. Though it would've been easy enough to kill the warrior in her sleep, Paz couldn't exactly exonerate herself with a corpse. For this to work, she had to get the tribeswoman out alive.

RP lay on his back at the center of a large bed, his striped socks pointed straight up at the ceiling. The Wesah woman was curled up next to him, entirely submerged in the patterned quilt. Paz had cut the rope into three shorter strands, and now she set aside the rasp she'd found in the workshop and gently laid those strands across the sleeping couple—one at the level of their chests, another at their waists, and the third at their ankles. She looped the ropes around the bottom of the bed, slid under the mattress, and gathered all six ends together on one side. Starting with the middle strand, she crossed the ends over each other and slowly tightened them against the bed frame. RP's snoring attenuated; he muttered something. Here was the dicey part; with a great heave,

Paz pulled as hard as she could and quickly made a knot.

"What the hell?" RP said blearily. He sat up but was forced back down when Paz put her weight into the topmost rope and knotted those ends as well. RP's ankles were still free, and if he'd had the presence of mind, he might've slid out. But already his moment was past; Paz cinched down the final rope, pinning him to the mattress in three places.

She stood up and surveyed her handiwork. RP wriggled beneath his bindings, swearing a blue streak, but the Wesah woman remained a motionless comma beneath the quilt. There was no way she could have slept through all that; this had to be some kind of subterfuge—unless she was simply ashamed to show her face after being caught so easily.

The creak of a closet door. Understanding dawned on Paz just as something hard and heavy smashed into the side of her head. Her legs turned to water beneath her, and though unconsciousness beckoned like a bathtub full of warm water, she managed to keep it at bay.

The Wesah woman had never been in bed at all. Maybe she'd noticed Paz way back in the market, or else heard her fumbling around in the workshop only a few minutes ago. Either way, she'd had time to place pillows or blankets under the sheets to approximate her sleeping form and then hide herself away in the closet. Strange that she hadn't come out sooner, or at least warned RP what was about to happen; Paz easily could've killed him by now, if that had been her intention.

"Noémie, what's going on out there?" he asked. "I can't see a damn thing."

Noémie: it could have been a false name, only it rang a bell—a

TOMMY WALLACH

story Gemma had told during the *tooroon*. This girl had been Athène's lover before Gemma took her place, and then she'd been banished from the tribe for trying and failing to kill her usurper. Suddenly the events of the past few weeks all made sense. Noémie had come to the *tooroon* with one goal in mind: vengeance. To that end, she'd enlisted the help of this foolish old man, whose armor would ensure that when she faced Gemma, she wouldn't come up short a second time. And she hadn't.

"I no know," Noémie replied. In a painful turnabout, the Wesah woman quickly and expertly bound Paz's wrists and ankles with two lengths of twine. A moment later a lantern flared to life. "You," she said, recognizing Paz at last. "Why you are here, *chee*."

"You killed Gemma," Paz whispered.

"Yes."

"But everyone thinks I did it."

"Think you kill," Noémie said, exploring the idea, slowly breaking into a smile. "Think *you* kill." And now she was actually laughing, so hard she could scarcely breathe.

"Girl!" RP shouted. "Cut these goddamn ropes already."

Noémie was still chuckling as she picked up the rasp Paz had left on the floor, running her fingers lightly along the serrated edge. Paz made sure her face didn't betray a hint of fear; she wouldn't give the woman the pleasure. "Do it," she whispered.

But Noémie decided to see to RP first. She went to the bed and began sawing through the rope around his waist. Paz tried to get to her feet, but she was still too dizzy. Blood trickled down her neck. The sawing grew louder.

"Careful there," RP said.

Err-eee. Err-eee. Err-eee. Faster and faster. If Noémie didn't stop soon . . .

RP screamed as the rasp completed its journey through the rope and continued on into his stomach. Paz put her hands over her ears to drown out the ragged scrape of metal on bone. Of course Noémie felt no loyalty to this man; she'd only been using him—for food and lodging, for his skills as an armorer. Probably she'd only come back after the *tooroon* to hide out for a while before trying to wheedle her way back into Athène's good graces, now that Gemma was out of the picture. Paz's arrival had only triggered the plan a little early. Yet another death to weigh on her conscience. Yet another entry in her deep register of sins.

RP's screams died out, gave way to gurgles and grunts, then a final exhalation. Noémie stripped off her nightdress and used it to wipe her hands clean. Then she took a set of traditional Wesah clothes out of the closet—leather skirt and blouse, a fur-lined jacket, moccasins—and quickly dressed.

"We go now," she said.

"We?"

But Noémie had already left through the front door. Paz was lucid enough to stand up, but the bindings around her wrists and ankles forced her to shuffle like an invalid. She tottered outside, where Noémie was just bringing a horse around.

"You no run," the tribeswoman said, then mimed drawing a blade across her throat. She mounted the horse and set a blanket down behind her as a kind of pillion. With her ankles bound, Paz had to ride sidesaddle, which she'd always hated, and hold on to Noémie's skirt for balance.

"Where are we going?" she asked.

"Special place. Place of my people."

"Why are you taking me?"

Noémie cracked her neck, the knobby bone at the base protruding like a creature trying to escape from under the skin. "You my gift," she said, looking over her shoulder so Paz could see the madness in her eyes, the satisfaction in her smile. "You best gift in world."

8. Clive

THERE'S A STORY GOING AROUND ABOUT YOUR PAPA."

"Oh yeah?"

Clive's cellmate, a slim and bespectacled twentysomething named Theo, leaned out from the lower bunk. He spoke low, as if there were any need of discretion in a place like this. "They say he led this big service at Notre Fille yesterday, but instead of giving a sermon or reading from the Filia, he pledged his allegiance to Sophia."

"Sure he did."

"I'm just telling you what I heard."

Theo had been arrested for synthesizing gunpowder in his basement without official authorization, and though he wasn't exactly the sharpest knife in the drawer, he didn't seem the type for idle gossip. Still, something must've gotten mixed up as the story made its way down to the Bastion dungeon. "You heard that my father pledged his allegiance to the people who tortured him for a year? The people who are trying to destroy our entire civilization?"

"Miguel told me. And why would he lie about it?"

Miguel was one of the guards. "To hurt me, or confuse me, or just for the fun of it. Who knows?"

"I imagine a lot of people do, actually." Theo disappeared back behind the lip of the bunk, no doubt returning to the book he'd been reading ever since Clive got here; every time he finished, he'd just start over again from the beginning.

Clive leaned back against his pillow and sighed. Life had truly come full circle. Here he was, a prisoner of the Bastion, when less than a year ago, he'd been looking at Paz from the other side of the bars. He spent a lot of his time thinking about those days; in spite of the circumstances, his visits to the dungeon had been a kind of courtship. The whole time he was meant to have been grilling her for information, he'd been falling in love.

He didn't feel any less in love now, in spite of what Paz had done. That is, what she *might* have done. In the weeks since the *tooroon*, Clive had pictured the scene a thousand times. And though the hard facts hadn't changed—Paz crouched over Gemma's body, covered in blood and holding a knife, then fleeing the scene as if her guilt were a foregone conclusion—he simply couldn't accept that she was the killer. There had to be some other explanation, some larger story he couldn't see. Otherwise, the world was darker and more terrible than he could fathom—and God knew it was already dark and terrible enough at the moment. Though Paz had described the bleakness of the dungeon in agonizing detail, it was one thing to hear about it, quite another to live it. This was boredom on an epic scale, boredom that bent the very nature of reality, that slowed the river of time to a treacly trickle. You clung to anything that helped mark the passage of the hours: the bowls of cold leftovers from the Bastion mess that Clive knew from experience hadn't been that good in the first place; the arrival of new prisoners, always greeted with cheers of welcome from those already imprisoned—the seemingly fraternal welcome masking a bitter schadenfreude; the twice-a-day spot checks, during which a guard would turn over the mattresses and look for any cracks or holes in the walls, pinching his nose with his off-hand the whole time. (Clive could no longer smell the revolting bouquet of the dungeon—one small blessing anyway.)

Things got a little better after his first week, when the prisoners were gifted a distraction in the form of mandatory labor. One morning they were chained together and marched upstairs into a large, light-filled chamber that Clive recognized as one of the Bastion dormitories, only repurposed now as a workshop. Two tables ran the length of the room, both large enough to fit fifty men to a side. The tools the prisoners would need for their work were already laid out like place settings at a dining table.

An attendant waited until they were all seated to explain how they would henceforth be spending their days. Bullet casings cast in the foundry beneath the Library—publicly acknowledged but still informally referred to as "Hell"—would arrive in two parts, which the prisoners would glue together with resin. When that was done, they would cut grooves into each casing by rotating it against a metal wheel, and finally seal the whole thing with wax. A few prisoners—unapologetic members of the Mindful or else die-hard religious zealots who still clung to the Filial dictum of nonviolence—refused to aid the Descendancy war effort, and they were sent back down to the dungeon with a promise of half rations going forward, but everyone else welcomed the change of pace: the food upstairs was fresher, the days passed more quickly, and you could even get some sunlight on your skin if you got a seat near the windows.

TOMMY WALLACH

It was almost enough to make Clive forget that Chang might summon him for a public hanging in Annunciation Square at any moment.

That morning began like any other, with the slow shuffle upstairs and along the wide halls of the Bastion, the uncoupling of the manacles as the prisoners took their seats in the workshop, the leisurely introduction of conversation. But after about an hour, Clive glanced up from his work to find everyone looking toward the workshop doors, where a group of Protectorate soldiers were crowded around something. "What's going on?" he said.

Theo, seated just to Clive's left, tapped his temple knowingly. "Just me being right again. Like always."

As Clive watched, the soldiers separated to reveal the impossible: a new prisoner who looked exactly like his father, or a malnourished and haunted version of his father, anyway.

"That can't be him," Clive said, though he knew how uncertain he sounded. "Why would he be here?"

"I already told you. He's a Sophian sympathizer. They've probably been questioning him ever since that service at Notre Fille."

"Da!" Clive called out, but was quickly shushed by one of the guards. There was nothing for it but to wait until lunchtime came around, when the prisoners were given fifteen minutes to fill their bellies and massage the ache from their fingers. As soon as the food arrived—one pockmarked apple, one scoop of peppered potatoes, one disconcerting assemblage of wilted greens—Clive made a beeline for the window, where a pale revenant in the shape of the late Honor Daniel Hamill stood gazing out over the Bastion training fields.

"Da?" he said. "Is that really you?"

His father turned to him, smiling weakly. "Yes and no."

But there could be no question now that Clive had heard that voice—deep and limpid, somehow more convincing than the average voice. The very sound of it made his heart hurt with a longing for something irrecoverable—a time when their family was whole, and war was just a word you heard in fairy tales and old songs. He wanted so badly to embrace his father, or at least to feel as if his father wanted to embrace him. But neither of them moved.

"Clover told me you were alive," Clive said. "But I don't think I believed him until right now."

"I don't blame you."

"You didn't really turn on the Descendancy, did you?"

"I'm here because I told the *truth*." He gestured with the puckered stub of his left index finger. It had been amputated at the last joint. "This is how the world has always treated prophets. We're ignored until we can't be ignored. Then we're silenced."

Clive's stomach dropped as he realized the full implications of his father's imprisonment; Chang had no reason to keep either of them alive anymore. He wasn't sure which was worse: the fact that his death was now practically assured, or that his father had made that grand public disavowal of the Descendancy knowing full well what it would mean for his son.

"Da, what happened to you in Sophia?"

"What happened to me?" His father paused to eat a spoonful of potato; his hand shook so badly it seemed unlikely it would ever reach its destination. "I thought I was handling the torture well. But when you realize that what you've experienced so far is

TOMMY WALLACH

only the barest fraction of the pain that will soon be brought to bear, you lose hope very quickly. I think I would've gone mad if she hadn't brought me those books to read." Another long and precarious journey of spoon from tray to mouth; Clive would've offered to feed his father, but he knew it would only embarrass them both. "Of course I knew it was all part of a strategy to turn me against the Descendancy: first cruelty, then kindness. But as I read those books, I found all my old pieties and certainties falling away. Ariel opened my eyes."

"Ariel?"

"Director Zeno."

Was it something in Daniel's voice, that subtle softening as he spoke her name, or else in his eyes, momentarily disappearing into reminiscence? Clive felt betrayed on behalf of his mother, but he knew that was rank hypocrisy, given everything he'd done for Paz.

"Did you . . . care about her?" Clive asked.

His father nodded, still half-immersed in memory.

"And did she—"

"I don't know. Maybe I was just another piece on her chessboard. But it doesn't matter. By that time, I was fully converted to her cause. When she was convinced of that, she sent me to work with the Mindful here in the Anchor. I haven't heard from her since."

"Clover said the Mindful had you locked up in a basement."

"That was my idea. I figured if I could fool Chang into thinking I was a prisoner, I might still be of some service to the cause."

"Which is why you gave that speech."

"Now everyone knows the truth about the Descendancy. It's

only a matter of time before the whole putrid edifice comes crashing down."

Daniel smiled at the thought of this apocalyptic outcome, while Clive tried to get his head around everything he'd just learned. Not only had his father fallen in love with the leader of Sophia, the woman responsible for the death of his wife, but he'd also been turned against his religion, his country. The foundation of Clive's identity had just collapsed under his feet; he was falling through space.

"You're upset," Daniel said.

"I think that's fair to say."

"But why? You and I are the same. We've both ended up here, enemies of the state, men without a nation." True, yet it felt false, or at least incomplete. The paths by which they'd reached this destination were so different that they changed the very nature of the destination itself. Clive had never taken a side; the vagaries of love and duty had led him here. But his father had *chosen* this outcome. "I owe you an apology, Clive. Your whole childhood, I was trying to sculpt you into a copy of me. If you dared to question anything, I came down on you like the Daughter herself."

"Clover had it worse."

"Because he *always* doubted. Your mother liked to joke that his first word was 'why.' I tried to keep both of you from that sort of curiosity, from thinking for yourselves. Now I see how wrong that was. When people are governed by fear—whether of divine punishment, or savages coming for their children, or just the idea of change—they're too easily manipulated. All it takes is one man willing to exploit those fears."

"Or one woman." They were silent for a moment. Then Clive whispered, "So you really want Sophia to win this war?"

"I do."

"But what about all the good the Church has done?"

"That doesn't disappear just because now it's time for something better."

"And you're that sure Sophia *is* better?"

Before his father could answer, a guard called an end to lunch, and they were ordered back to their stations.

Back in his cell that night, Clive replayed everything Daniel had said, holding the arguments up to the light to see where they were thinnest, trying them on to see if they fit. He realized with some chagrin that up until now, all of his choices had been based on personal, rather than political, considerations. He'd agreed to interrogate Paz as a kind of penance for what he'd done to his brother. He'd helped her escape in order to save Flora. He'd kept running because he'd fallen in love. Through it all, he'd seldom given much thought to the big picture. But now, facing down what were almost certainly his last few days on Earth, he had to ask himself the fundamental question: Who did he want to win the war—the Anchor or Sophia?

Another week passed. Clive's hands grew knobby with calluses and blotchy from epoxy residue, and he'd developed a cough from the invisible fragments of lead that flew up from the grinder. He hadn't been able to speak to his father again; the guards must have been ordered to keep them apart.

One morning he was ordered to stay in his cell when the other prisoners were taken up to the workshop. A few minutes later, two members of Chang's honor guard came and escorted him to a nondescript office upstairs, leaving him alone with a fat man in a gleaming white apron.

"What'll it be, Hamill?" the man said, tenting his fingers and turning them inside out with a thunderous crack.

Clive had never heard of a torturer asking for suggestions. "What'll it be?"

"To eat. I'm Chef Fernandez. I'll be preparing your last meal. Anything you want. Opportunity of a lifetime." He frowned at Clive's silence. "You know they're hanging you, right?"

It took Clive a moment to recover his senses. "Yeah. I just didn't know it was happening today."

"Today, tomorrow. What's the difference?"

"A lot can happen in twenty-four hours," Clive said. Now that the moment was at hand, he realized he'd been foolishly hoping Paz would pull off yet another last-minute rescue.

"Keep dreaming, kid. And while you're at it, tell me what I'm cooking."

"I can really ask for anything?"

"Within reason. I couldn't fry you up a baby, no matter how nice you asked."

Clive considered requesting something punitively complicated, as if he might stave off the inevitable that way. But he couldn't quite see fit to denigrate such a famously symbolic ritual, one that connected him to all the men and women put to death—rightly or wrongly—throughout history. "Back when I would go on tour with my father's ministry, my ma would make this stew," Clive said. "At least a couple of times a month, using whatever she happened to have around. And before we ate it, she would tell the whole story of what went into it. The potatoes were a gift from that farmer in Grandsville. Flora picked the sage from behind the little general store on the road into Two Forks. Clover caught the rabbit in a rope trap. The salt and pepper—"

"I get the drift, kid," Fernandez interrupted.

"Sorry. I know that's not a very specific description, but it's what I want. Just make me a stew with whatever happens to be around. One that's got a story to it."

Chef Fernandez smiled slightly. "I've got a story for you right now, kid."

"What's that?"

"I met with your father just before you, and he asked for the same damn thing."

The stew was still warm in Clive's belly when Chang's honor guard returned. They escorted him out to the hallway, where his father was already waiting.

"How was your dinner?" Daniel asked.

"Not a bad one to go out on. You?"

"Same."

They traveled quickly across the city to Annunciation Square. Though Clive had prepared himself for a crowd, the sight of it still took his breath away. A good ten thousand people had come to witness the executions—packed onto the balconies and the roofs, hanging out of windows and off lampposts, snaking back along the alleys that fed into the plaza. Clover was probably out there somewhere, unless he didn't have the stomach to watch; Clive certainly wouldn't have blamed him for that. The bells of Notre Fille began to sound, and the spaces between the chimes were filled with boos and hisses. The crowd parted for the prisoners, and through the opening Clive could make out the hangman. His pointed black hood looked ridiculous, like a child's Hallows' Eve costume. Clive paused at the foot of the gallows and gazed upward; the nooses circumscribed two ovals of clear black sky, like gateways to another, more peaceful world. Bishop Allen stood beside them.

"Go on," one of the guards said.

Clive looked to his father. "I guess you don't believe in heaven anymore, huh?"

Daniel smiled sadly. "How's that for timing?"

9. Athène

THERE WAS NO LONGER ANY SPACE LEFT IN THE LONG-house proper. Over the last two weeks, the majority of the Wesah who'd survived the Black Wagon Massacre had made their way to the Villenaître, drawn there by what Grandmother would call the spirits, and what Athène would call basic self-preservation. Now the ritual spilled out of the longhouse, bodies filling the plaza from end to end, close to four thousand tribeswomen kneeling on blankets in the dirt, their faces expressing every conceivable variation of grief. The sound of their sorrow could be heard for miles in every direction, streaking across the marshland like a volley of arrows. Athène knew this because she'd abandoned the ritual days ago, choosing instead to pass her time hunting the birds and small game that lived near the Villenaître, whose food stores were running dangerously low. Flora went with her on these sojourns, and turned out to be sur-prisingly adept at laying snares. Now and again they would run into missives who were also out hunting. The men who served the Wesah had shown admirable courage during the massacre, rushing Chang's gun even as many Wesah fled the hailstorm of bullets; only a few dozen of them had made it back to the Ville-naître, where they learned they would not be allowed to join their sisters in the longhouse—insult added to literal injury.

There would have been something noble in refusing to take part in the ritual out of a sense of solidarity with the missives, but Athène could claim no such lofty justification. In truth, she'd abandoned the Song of Crow because she couldn't bear to sit in one place for so long. Every morning for the past week she'd woken up with a pounding headache and a swirl in her belly, symptoms she attributed to her growing anxiety about the future. The ritual would be over in a few days, and then the tribe was to travel north to the Kikiwaak di Noor. There, Andromède would have the Wesah hide like frightened mice while the fate of the world was decided without them. Athène had tried every method she knew to change her mother's mind—flattery, cajoling, bargaining, invective—but Andromède remained certain of her course.

"It makes no sense," Athène said, kicking at a rock that remained stubbornly stuck in the mud. She spoke in English, just in case Flora ever decided to contribute something to the conversation. "My mother thinks what happens at the *tooroon* is her fault. She says we should not have gone. But this is not her mistake. Her mistake is making us go with our teeth hidden." It was an idiom in Wesah, and though Athène knew those seldom translated well into English, she didn't care; she was only talking to pass the time, to momentarily drown out the distant, dolorous drone of the lamentation.

A pair of ducks floated lazily in a shallow pond beyond a stand of reeds: a fine offering, which would earn Athène a place at Andromède's table tonight—and another chance to convince her of the folly of her plan. She took aim and drew back the bowstring. Seconds later, one duck flew off into the sky, bereft but alive.

TOMMY WALLACH

Athène and Flora returned about an hour before sunset. For appearance's sake, they knelt down in the square and joined in the lamentation, but after only a few minutes, Athène was distracted by a movement near the archway leading into the Villenaître—two women entered the settlement, one leading the other on a leash, as Descendant folk were known to do with dogs. There was something familiar about both of them, but it wasn't until Flora leaped to her feet with a gasp that Athène realized who they were. The girl with the rope around her neck was Paz, and holding the leash, impossibly, was Noémie.

Athène could feel her heart thumping in her chest, the goose bumps stippling her skin. She wanted to scream. She wanted to cry. Here was the woman who'd killed Gemma beside the woman who'd tried but failed. Could it be said that either one was better than the other, or more worthy of mercy?

"Stay here," Athène whispered to Flora. She stood up and made eye contact with Noémie, gesturing for her old lover to follow her. Only when she was certain they were far enough from the square that they wouldn't be overheard did she turn and draw her dagger, pressing the blade into Noémie's neck. "Why are you here?" she growled.

Noémie didn't flinch or fight back, only held Athène's gaze with guilty, pleading eyes. "I brought you the girl."

Athène glanced at Paz, who was tightly gagged. "How did you find her?"

"I went to the *tooroon* to look for you. I wanted to make things right. But before I could find you, I saw this one fighting your

Chemma." Noémie had never learned to pronounce Gemma's name correctly, or else refused to. "They were all the way across the pasture. Too far for me to help. I am sorry."

"What is that bitch telling you?" Paz managed to say around the gag. Noémie backhanded her across the cheek, and the girl fell to her knees.

"Then what happened?" Athène said.

"I chased after her, but she rides fast. It took me weeks to catch her."

"And then you brought her here? Why?"

"For you! Everything I do is for you." Noémie's voice softened, and Athène couldn't help but remember the old days, when they'd been in the first flush of love. "You broke my heart, Athène. But that is no excuse for what I tried to do to your Chemma. I know that now. I want to make amends."

Athène finally lowered the blade. "It's not that simple."

"Maybe not. Maybe you will send me away again. Maybe you will kill me. Whatever you decide, take your vengeance on this one first. There will be no better moment."

Athène turned her attention back to Paz. The woman was in a sorry state: hair matted; unshod feet calloused and blistered; ankles, wrists, and neck all chafed from her bindings. And yet somehow she retained that ineffable beauty Athène had found so remarkable the first time they'd met, when her scouts had discovered Paz foolishly loitering at the margins of their camp. It was a dangerous beauty, the kind that left people shattered in its wake—and according to Gemma, Paz had been unsparing in her exploitation of it. Her machinations and seductions had resulted in the deaths

TOMMY WALLACH

of Gemma's father and younger brother, the estrangement of the Hamill brothers, and who knew what other crimes and catastrophes. And as if that weren't enough, she'd murdered Gemma in cold blood. But why? Athène had spent long hours considering the question and could find no satisfactory answer.

She went to where Paz was crouched in the dirt and leaned down, sliding her dagger along the woman's cheek. Then, with a tug, she cut the gag loose.

"What are you doing?" Noémie said. "The girl speaks only lies. You know this."

Athène addressed Paz in English. "Before you die, tell me why you killed Gemma."

Paz stretched out her jaw, which had been forced open by the gag. She tried to speak, but her throat was too dry and all that emerged was a coughing fit. Finally, after swallowing twice, she managed to rasp out two words: "I didn't."

"See?" Noémie scoffed. "She just denies it. You're wasting your time."

"Why are you lying?" Athène demanded. "I saw you holding the dagger. I saw the blood."

"I was trying to help her. I was hoping we might . . ." Paz trailed off. After a moment she began to laugh. "You'll never believe me, will you? So what is it you want to hear? I did it because I was jealous. I did it because I was crazy. I did it for Sophia, or the Anchor, or for God and his fucking Daughter. Who even cares anymore? Let's just get this over with."

Noémie was right. Paz was an inveterate liar. There was nothing to be gained by interrogating her. Athène would simply have to live without closure, without understanding. She placed the point of her dagger at the girl's breast, just over the heart. She could feel its flutter—that most fundamental, animal fear, impossible to conceal.

"Fine," she said. "Then take your secrets to the grave."

One quick thrust and it would be done. Her muscles tensed.

"Stop!"

Athène froze. Flora had just spoken for the first time in nearly six weeks. "What is it?" she said. "This woman killed your sister." A tear ran down Flora's cheek, but she wouldn't speak again. Her exclamation hadn't been an instance of a dam bursting; it was merely the one word she knew couldn't go unsaid.

Athène sheathed the dagger.

"You're making a mistake," Noémie said.

"Maybe. Which is why I need counsel. We will take the killer to my mother."

Six women sat on smooth stones around a blazing fire. The ritual had ended for the day, and the Villenaître was overflowing with Wesah, but this area on the dunes overlooking Pchimayr was reserved for Andromède and her guests alone. The moon gazed down placidly on its breeze-rippled reflection. Five of the women ate succulent scraps of duck off smooth skewers carved from driftwood, drank birch tea, and chewed the wintergreen leaves at the bottom. The sixth sat silent, her hands and ankles bound, waiting.

Andromède picked a sliver of gristle from between her front teeth. "It is a riddle," she said at last. "We can't know what happened. It is possible your Gemma attacked Paz, rather than the other way around."

"I told you what happened," Noémie interjected. "You would believe the word of an outsider over that of one of your own?"

"You are not one of our own," Grandmother said, though there was no rancor in her voice. "You were banished for trying to do what this one succeeded in doing."

"Which is why I nearly died to bring her to you!" Noémie made a visible effort to calm herself. "I have made mistakes, I know. But that one there"—and here she pointed a quivering finger at Paz—"is a monster. She desecrated Chemma's body. So many cuts—a Wesah would never do this. I will not be treated as if I am no better than her!"

"Enough!" Andromède said. "You have been heard, Noémie."

Athène stared into the fire. In the dancing flames, she summoned up the moment she'd come upon Gemma at the pasture's edge: skin so pale, flaxen hair turned umbral with rainwater, eyes open. Paz knelt beside the corpse, weeping with remorse, still holding the bloody knife. The rain had been falling so hard, Athène had seen nothing until she was only a few feet from the body, so close she could almost feel the warmth of . . .

The rain: like a thousand layers of milky glass, obscuring and distorting the world. Watering the seeds of doubt. Athène stood up and began pacing around the fire. "I have one question for each of you," she said, first in Wesah and then again in English. She stopped behind Grandmother. "Have you ever known of a Wesah who returned from banishment?"

The *otsapah* frowned. "Never. But this is a unique situation."

Athène addressed her mother next. "Why didn't you approve of my taking Noémie as a lover?"

"Because I didn't trust her," Andromède said.

Noémie snorted but was smart enough to hold her tongue. Athène passed by Flora, who wasn't much for answering questions, and went to stand behind Paz. "Gemma told me you and Clive were lovers," she said in English. "You trusted him. So why did you run?"

Paz's voice was still hoarse, but she answered without hesitation. "I'd betrayed him before, more than once, really. And even if he had believed me, you wouldn't have. I was too weak to fight, so he would've had to defend me. And you probably would've killed us both."

Athène completed the circle, ending up behind Noémie.

"Where were you standing when you saw my Gemma die?"

Silence. Stillness. Noémie turned around just in time to see Athène draw her blade. "There's nothing I wouldn't have done for you," she whispered.

"I know," Athène replied. With a flourish, she opened a crimson smile across Noémie's throat. Andromède jumped to her feet, as if she might be able to stop what was already done. Gurgling some last apology or indictment, Noémie slumped to the ground. Athène wiped her blade clean on her thigh.

"You are lucky," she said to Paz in English. "I am almost doing this to you."

Andromède finally recovered her wits enough to speak. "Child, are you mad?"

"I will never forget that day," Athène replied in Wesah. "The rain was so heavy you couldn't see more than a few feet in front of you. Noémie said she saw Paz and Gemma fighting from across the pasture, but was too far away to help. Then, just now, she described the wounds on Gemma's body. She could only have seen them if she'd been standing close by."

"Couldn't she have gone to the body afterward?"

"No. She would've had to start chasing Paz right away if she hoped to track her in that storm."

"So she was the one who killed Gemma?" Grandmother said.

"Yes. Because I loved her."

Andromède still looked shocked. "But didn't you love Noémie too?" she asked.

Athène regarded the corpse at her feet. Noémie's eyes glittered lifelessly, like glass, and the pool of blood was blackening to a crust where it encroached on the fire. "I told Gemma I didn't, but now I think that was merely the lie that soothes. I will always love Noémie, for how hard she fought."

"So you have killed what you love."

"Yes. I suppose I have."

Andromède was looking at her as if seeing her for the first time. But was that incredulous glint in her eye admiration, or horror?

Three days later, as the sun sank and the sky narrowed its palette to the shades between pink flesh and red blood, the great ritual of mourning finally came to an end. The *otsapah* clapped three times, and after singing one last hymn to Crow, enjoined the thousands of Wesah present to rise and embrace one another. Standing at the top of the longhouse steps as her mother had requested, Athène was surprised by the sudden buoyancy of the tribe, slightly embarrassed it had taken her this long to realize that rituals such as this one did not come about by accident. The lamentation had never been self-indulgent or superstitious, but eminently practical: the only way to recover from a sadness this deep was to allow oneself to feel it completely, to wallow in it. The tribeswomen had gorged themselves on grief until they no longer craved it.

As the embracing continued, some of it shading into the frankly amorous, Andromède emerged from the longhouse and came to stand between Athène and Grandmother. Andromède had put on her brass crown and a white robe lined with stoat along the collar—as regal a costume as she possessed. Athène hadn't seen much of her mother since the night that Noémie and Paz arrived at the Villenaître, but as far as she knew—and in spite of all her supplications—the plan was still to depart for the north as soon as possible.

"Sisters," Andromède said, repeating that one word until the crowd calmed, "the Song of Crow has been sung. I hope tonight we can celebrate again with something like the joy we used to know." A cheer went up: the Wesah were ready. Athène noticed Paz and Flora standing near the front of the crowd, looking painfully out of place. "And though it is time for the tribe to move beyond this terrible tragedy"—Andromède's composure faltered, her voice cracked—"I fear I cannot move on with you. History shall always know me as the leader who oversaw our greatest defeat, whose eyes were set on such high principles she failed to see the snakes at her feet. Thus I renounce the title of Andromède and will retire here to the Villenaître to live out what life remains to me." This last statement put an abrupt end to the nascent gaiety. Athène couldn't believe what she was hearing: How could her mother abandon them in their time of greatest need?

Andromède went on. "In the past, whenever the tribe's leader has stepped down, there has been a period of conflict. Whole *naas-yoon* have died fighting to see their chieftain become Andromède. But we can no longer afford to sacrifice our sisters so carelessly. This is why Grandmother and I have come to you today in humble supplication. With your approval, we would name my successor, rather than see the tribe torn apart in choosing her."

If her announcement of abdication had been a pebble thrown in a stream, this new revelation was a boulder. It seemed every single tribeswoman was speaking at once, but through the cacophony, one word made itself known above the others: *Who?*

Athène was just as curious as the rest of them. She glanced over and saw that both her mother and the *otsapah* were staring at her. She frowned, understanding and not understanding at once.

"Sisters," Andromède shouted. "You know my daughter, Athène. She has been a chieftain for three years now. Her *naasyoon* has carried out dozens of raids, and all who've traveled with her know her to be a skilled hunter and a fierce warrior. More than this, she knows our enemy better than anyone here."

The clamoring of the tribe grew even louder. "Because she was fucking one of them!" someone cried out over the din.

Grandmother raised her hands. The crowd quieted out of respect. "The woman you speak of was named Gemma," she eventually said. "I journeyed with her, and I saw her heart. Though she may have been born an outsider, she died a Wesah. I believe that the spirits led Athène to Gemma, just as I believe the spirits are leading us to Athène now."

The tenor of the tumult began to shift—outrage giving way to skepticism. Andromède must have sensed it, as she signaled for the tribe's attention again.

"Let me tell you one more story before we make our decision," she said. "A few days ago, a Wesah tribeswoman called Noémie arrived in the Villenaître. Many of you knew her. She was banished from the tribe last year, but she'd come to plead for forgiveness, not with honest contrition, but by spewing lies—lies I was fool enough to believe. But not my daughter. My daughter saw something I could not. She *did* something I could not. Noémie had been her lover once, but when Athène had to choose between love and justice, she chose justice. She took her vengeance—without hesitation or doubt. That is why she must be the one to lead us now. So we can take *our* vengeance. What do you say, my sisters?"

In the silence that followed, Athène heard the wind whistling through the palisade around the Villenaître, playing it like a thousand flutes, before the music was drowned out by the sound of the beleaguered remnant of the Wesah nation all cheering at once.

Athène stepped forward and bowed her head. Her mother placed the brass crown on her brow. Their eyes met, wet with tears. The cheering broke into a chant. Athène turned to face the tribe, raising both her fists in triumph when she realized it was *her* name they were calling out.

"Andromède! Andromède! Andromède!"

10. Clover

THEY WALKED THE SNAKING PATHWAYS OF PORTLAND Park beneath a lowering sky of gray-silver clouds. The trails were nearly deserted, and for just a few minutes more, Clover allowed himself to pretend he didn't know why.

"What's that one?" Kita said.

"A dogwood," Clover replied.

"And that one?"

"A magnolia."

"And what are these thingies here?"

"Daylilies. If you're trying to distract me, it isn't working."

"It wouldn't say much for you if anything could distract you today. I'm just trying to fill the space." She was quiet for a few seconds, but Clover could sense another fusillade of idle talk coming. "Do you think you like plants so much because of your name? 'Cause clover is a plant, and your name's Clover. That's a pretty funny coincidence, don't you think?"

"Not really. Most people like clover."

Kita groaned. "You're not listening. What I'm trying to say is do you think a person's name could change them somehow? Like, if your name was Killer Hamill, would you be more violent or something?"

At first blush, it seemed like a stupid question. But as Clover turned it over in his mind, checking it for ripeness like a piece of fruit, he sensed there might be some merit to it. "That reminds me of something I read about once, back when I worked for Bernstein. Subconscious suggestion."

"What's that?"

"It's like if I mentioned water a bunch of times while we were talking, you'd be more likely to want some. Or the way just seeing the annulus makes me worry about whether I'm having sinful thoughts."

"I do that too! Stupid annulus."

"When I was a baby, I must have heard people talking about 'clover' a hundred times a day. That had to affect me somehow."

"So I'm right?" Kita grinned. "I knew it."

"Maybe you are. But honestly, I hope not."

"Why?"

"If you believe what's written in the Filia, none of us really have free will, because God knows everything we're gonna do before we do it. I thought science was an antidote to that. Like, if I could understand how the world worked, it would mean I had some control over it. But maybe it's the opposite. Maybe understanding the mind would mean understanding how every choice we make is built into us from the beginning. Maybe I didn't have any choice but to be interested in plants. Maybe every road leads to God."

Clover could see Kita trying to make sense of his maundering. She was clever in her way, but not particularly given to deep thoughts.

"Well," she finally said, "I guess it means we have to be really

TOMMY WALLACH

careful what we name our children, huh?" She giggled, her cheeks reddening. "I mean, you know, our children *separately.*"

"Right. Got any good ideas?"

Kita considered for a moment. "Triumph?"

Clover grimaced. "Sounds like a soldier."

"Is that bad?"

"You wouldn't want to limit his opportunities. What about Wisdom?"

"He'd be lucky to survive primary school with that one. How about Serenity?"

"Serenity's for the stupid. Maybe Chastity?"

Here it was Kita's turn to scowl. "I wouldn't wish that on my worst enemy."

They didn't say anything for a moment. The mention of children and chastity had injected a sort of fizz into the conversation; Clover immediately felt guilty for thinking about romance when his father and brother were going to be executed in a matter of hours.

The path emerged from under the cover of trees and joined up with the one that circumscribed Surrey Lake, a man-made pond near the center of the park. Even on an overcast morning like this one, there would usually be a dozen paddleboats out on the water—you could rent one for three bronze shekels from the little hut at the end of the pier—but today the surface of the pond was flat as a mirror, and the boats were all tethered to cleats along the dock, floating beside it like a bunch of upturned leaves. The door of the hut was closed.

"You ever taken one of those out before?" Kita asked.

"A couple times when I was young, with my parents. What about you?"

"Not until today."

She skipped away from the path and down the pier. Clover caught up with her just as she'd succeeded in freeing the rope knotted around the farthest cleat.

"You're just gonna steal it?" he said.

"We'll bring it back when we're done."

"What if the boatman comes?"

"Then we'll pay him. Or pull a runner." She jumped down into the boat, nearly losing her balance as it rocked. "Come on."

Reluctantly Clover climbed aboard. Kita pulled the line in and grabbed hold of the oars, and with a few quick strokes, set them gliding briskly toward the center of the pond. A little clutch of ducks had to paddle out of the way, and Clover watched them bobbing gently in the boat's wake. He sat opposite Kita, who was tapping her feet happily against the hull, occasionally tapping at his feet as well. It made him think of the first time he'd come to Portland Park with Paz, and the moment when the back of his hand had brushed against hers as they'd walked the bowered trails of the Maple Garden.

He pulled his legs into his chest and held them there.

"You chilly?" Kita said. "You can have my jacket if you want."

"I'm fine."

The turn was only a couple of weeks away now, and Clover's eighteenth birthday a few weeks after that. He wondered if he would see another summer, or another birthday. Clive wouldn't. Clive had only a few hours left. Would he be cold up there on the

TOMMY WALLACH

gallows, wilting under the gaze of ten thousand people who'd come to watch him die?

"Clover, are you crying?"

"No," he said, then laughed at himself as he blatantly wiped the tears away. "Why would I be crying?"

Kita stopped rowing and set the oarlocks. As the boat kept gliding forward, she crawled across the bottom of the hull and all the way up his body, pushing his knees down so she could lie on top of him and wrap her arms tightly around his back. He knew he was supposed to put his arms around her, too, but he felt paralyzed, numb. After a moment, she pulled back, so her face was only a few inches from his. She brushed the hair out of her eyes, but her hands were wet from the oars, and her bangs stuck to her forehead like sea wrack, like a disciplinary tattoo. "Are you afraid of me or something?" she whispered.

"No."

"Then kiss me."

"It's either I'm afraid of you or I kiss you?"

She smiled. "That's right. It's your decision. Exercise your free will."

But she was wrong. He could do both things. He could kiss her even though he was afraid that she'd betray him like Paz had, even though he was afraid for his father and his brother and Flora, for the Anchor and Sophia and the Wesah nation, for the future.

So he kissed her, and she kissed him back. They lay there for the next hour—holding each other in a rowboat in the middle of an empty pond in the middle of an empty park in the middle of a city on the brink of war—as if there were nothing in the world to be afraid of.

Clover had known the executions would be a spectacle. Scouts had confirmed that Sophian forces were only a few weeks away from the Anchor, and Chang had decided to try to weather the siege rather than meet the enemy on the battlefield. It would be the first war in living memory, and the citizens of the Descendancy were understandably apprehensive. They needed the chance to blow off some steam as much as Chang needed to take his victory lap.

Still, Clover hadn't expected things to be quite this carnivalesque. From blocks away, he could make out the stilt walkers towering over the crowd, each of them wearing the white makeup and bright red wig that the city had come to associate with Zeno. Jugglers and two-bit magicians competed for eyeballs while fortune-tellers and lay preachers made their appeals to the ear. There were dozens of stalls offering everything from singed chicken kebabs to illustrated Filia; a couple of enterprising children sold handmade signs featuring facile, jingoistic slogans: TRAITORS HANG and LONG LIVE THE DESCENDANCY. Someone shot off a firework, which burst prettily against the darkening sky.

The gallows stood empty; the nooses twisted and untwisted in the breeze. Was it foolish of Clover to hope that Chang might show mercy, or else decide to keep his prisoners as bargaining chips for some future negotiation? Or maybe his father and Clive had managed to escape somehow, as they'd both managed to do so many times before.

As if on cue—divine punishment for irrational hope—the bells of Notre Fille started chiming. The desultory hubbub began to focus and intensify.

TOMMY WALLACH

"Something's happening," Clover said.

"You know it's nothing to be ashamed of if you wanna leave," Kita said. "It's not as if you can do anything to help them now."

"I know. But I have to be here."

The crowd cracked open like a coconut, clearing a path through the square. Clover grabbed Kita's hand and led her into the crush of gawkers, weaving his way up to the foot of the gallows. The first person to climb the steps was the hangman, dressed all in black. Bishop Allen came next, wearing robes of red and gold to signal the Church's absorption into the Protectorate. He looked right at Clover but didn't appear to recognize him.

The crowd's enthusiasm reached a fever pitch as the prisoners were escorted up to the gallows by Chang and his honor guard. And there they were, looking the same as ever but for the ragged prison garb and unshaven cheeks: Clive and Daniel Hamill, reunited at last. Clover felt a strange, shameful surge of jealousy that he wasn't up there with them.

Kita squeezed his hand. "You okay?"

Clover didn't answer. Chang was approaching the edge of the gallows platform, as if it were a stage. He motioned for the crowd to quiet.

Of course. The bastard never did pass up an opportunity to give a speech, did he?

11. Paz

THE PERFORMANCE HAD DRAGGED ON FOR NEARLY AN hour now and showed no signs of stopping. It was an old story, brimming with false identities, cross-dressers, ironic misunderstandings, and an unceasing torrent of melodrama. But while the production itself might not have been anything special, the circumstances surrounding it certainly were. Village pantomimes such as this one averaged an audience of a couple hundred people at most; yet today there were thousands watching the earnest town players strut and fret about the stage— or trying to watch, at any rate; the town square wasn't nearly big enough to contain the entirety of the Wesah nation, even in its diminished state.

Paz had assumed the tribeswomen and their missives would quickly grow bored of the show, given that the vast majority of them couldn't understand a word of the dialogue. But as the pratfalls and pretenses piled up, their laughter only grew more uproarious. According to Athène, the closest thing the Wesah had to theater was the *otsapah*'s recitations of the tales of Wolf and Fox. They'd never seen two people embrace onstage, or duel with wooden swords, or be transformed into donkeys by a vindictive fairy queen. Paz couldn't tell what they were enjoying more: the story itself, or the fact that men and women were willing to do such ridiculous things in front of an audience.

"We should go," Athène whispered.

"All right," Paz said. She leaned over to Flora. "Can you look after yourself for a bit?"

The girl nodded. After saving Paz's life with a word, she seemed perfectly content never to speak again.

Paz followed Athène back through the crowd and out of the square. Once again she was struck by the improbability of her new position as right-hand woman to the new leader of the Wesah. Though she liked to think it was because of her intellectual capabilities, or at least the fact that she spoke English better than any of Athène's other advisers, she suspected she owed her station more to the vagaries of sentiment—guilt and grief, nostalgia and longing. Paz had known Gemma, had loved someone who had loved Gemma: a tenuous link, perhaps, but in the weeks since they'd left the Villenaître, it had already begun to blossom into something not unlike friendship.

Paz had always fantasized about life as a Wesah tribeswoman, traveling the byways of the world surrounded by sisters you knew would give their lives for you. She was pleased to discover the reality wasn't so far removed from what she'd imagined, if slightly more violent.

"You really think she came?" Paz said.

"I do."

After Athène assumed the mantle of Andromède, she'd immediately dispatched a rider to the closest town known to be a part of what the Sophians called their "telegraph network." There her emissary was to extend Zeno an invitation to a parley in an outerlands town known to have recently switched its allegiance from the Descendancy to Sophia. The tribe departed the Villenaître the next day, and reached their destination in under two weeks. The mayor himself had arranged this pantomime to celebrate their arrival—impressive, really, given that he'd been informed of it only a couple of days ago—and now it was time to see if they'd get anything more for their troubles than a mediocre drama. Athène's invitation had specified just this hour on just this date at just this specific inn. But the question remained—would Zeno actually show up?

They identified the place by the rank smell that wafted out of it—*alesweat*, Paz's father used to call it—as there was no sign or marker to distinguish it from the houses around it. But as they climbed the wide steps up to the porch, gunshots rang out from inside; stuttering light briefly painted all the fogged ground-floor windows blue-white. A moment later, half a dozen men in various states of inebriation came running out the front door and dispersed into the night. The heavy silence following the fusillade was abruptly broken by the bathetic bounce of a piano, somehow jaunty and foreboding at once. Paz looked to Athène, who could only shrug: *your guess is as good as mine*. They drew their daggers, though such weapons would be useless against a skilled gunman, and went through the open door.

The inn was homey and full of clutter—pots and pans and wicker brooms all hung from the walls as decoration. A large elk head gazed out from over the hearth, its severed neck black from years of smoke damage. A dozen or so tables were patterned with the legacy of who knew how many thousands of mugs of ale, like a drunkard's homage to the annulus. The bar was on their left when they came in, and just beyond it stood a ramshackle old spinet. The figure at the bench sat hunched above the board, her red hair dangling over her hands as they danced across the keys. A huge silver gun with two barrels and two cylinders rested on the top of the piano, leaking twin plumes of smoke. At the bottom of a stairway that climbed the rear wall of the inn, a large bald man with red suspenders lay in a pool of his own blood.

"Don't mind him," Zeno said without looking up from the piano.

Athène sheathed her dagger and motioned for Paz to do the same. "He attacked you?"

"Not exactly. I just happened to meet one of the girls he employs upstairs. She told me she was fourteen, and not very convincingly. I asked the gentleman behind the bar if he would consider allowing her to leave, and he said she still owed him money for room and board. We had a frank exchange of ideas on the subject of unpaid labor and, well, you can see how it turned out."

"Good riddance," Paz said.

Zeno abruptly stopped playing. "I know that voice." She turned toward them as she closed the lid of the piano. Something like a smile made a fleeting appearance on her lips. "Paz Dedios."

"Evening, Director."

"Still alive after all this time. You never cease to surprise."

"I'm just as surprised as you, believe me."

Zeno stood up and walked behind the bar, perusing the bottles on the shelves as if they were books. Occasionally she'd stop to uncork one and sniff before replacing it with a grimace. "I was glad to hear from you, Athène. Or is it Andromède now?"

"Andromède."

"And so young, too. But there are advantages to that. Age calcifies thought. You notice that X and Y always seem to go together, and soon, whenever you see X, you think Y. X and Y become inextricable. So you forget about Z. And it's always Z that's going to kill you." Somehow Paz doubted it was a coincidence that Zeno's name happened to begin with Z. At last the director located a bottle whose smell didn't disgust her. "Looks something like wine, anyway," she said, before pouring them each a glass. She raised hers in a toast. "To collaboration." Her hazel eyes took on a red and sinister tint in the light from the candles on the bar. They all clinked glasses and drank. "An interesting word, collaboration," Zeno continued. "It means both to work together with an ally and to secretly cooperate with an enemy. Tell me, which one are you interested in?"

Paz was impressed at how quickly Athène replied. "The Descendancy slaughtered my people. But I cannot punish them alone."

"So you seek a partner in vengeance?"

"More than vengeance. If the Anchor wins the war, they will come for the rest of my people."

"Do you think they'll win?"

Athène looked to Paz. "She does."

Zeno raised an eyebrow. "Really?"

"I don't know who'll win," Paz said. "I used to think the Descendancy didn't have a chance in hell. But now I'm not so sure. Chang is ruthless. The Protectorate is well-trained and outfitted. The Anchor was built to withstand a siege. Before the Church lifted the ban on anathema, you would've had a clear advantage, but now, who can say?"

Athène frowned. "Anathema? What is this?"

"Guns," Paz explained. "They have guns now."

"Ah. Yes. Big guns."

"We don't know what the future holds for Sophia and the Wesah," Paz said to Zeno, "but we know it's better than the alternative. Join with us, fight by our side, and we will win you this war."

Zeno swirled her wine in its glass. "And what will you do, once you've won me this war?"

"We will survive," Athène said, a boast and a veiled threat at the same time. "That is all we want."

"Is it, now? What a refreshingly humble aim." She offered her glass, but only to Athène this time. "Fine. An alliance."

"An alliance," Athène said, meeting the toast. They drank.

"So when do we strike?" Paz asked.

"Are you in a hurry?" Zeno replied.

"Every day we wait, the Anchor will be getting stronger."

"Which is why I began the assault many weeks ago." Zeno refilled all their glasses, emptying the bottle. "The first blow should arrive any day now."

"Our scouts say your army is still weeks away from the Anchor," Athène said.

"That's true. But I sent a little surprise on ahead. And it's my hope that you and your sisters will help me deliver another one, to Edgewise this time."

There was a creak at the back of the room. In a flash, Zeno drew a second gun from somewhere on her person—this one smaller and more elegant, plated in what looked to be either copper or rose gold. A girl stood halfway up the staircase, staring over the railing.

She wore a tattered white nightgown, and her legs were thin as birch saplings. This had to be the one Zeno had mentioned; she didn't look a day over eleven.

"He dead?" she said, pointing at the body.

"He ought to be," Zeno replied, holstering the gun. "But you never can tell for sure until you've checked the pulse."

The girl came the rest of the way down the steps and approached the corpse. Unafraid, she pressed her fingers into the man's thick neck. Paz could hear whispers coming from the shadowy enclave at the top of the stairwell—some unknown number of other women conferring.

"Goddamn it!" the girl said, advancing on them as if she was thinking about throwing a punch. "What the hell are me and my sisters supposed to do now? Cusick took care of us!"

"He took advantage of you," Paz said.

"And so will whoever comes along next! It's not as if we're gonna get to run this place just 'cause he's gone. This is Amestown, all right? People here ain't civilized unless it serves them to be."

Athène reached out and touched the girl's arm. "What is your name?" she said.

"My name's go to hell."

"Nice to meet you, go to hell. I am Andromède, the leader of the Wesah nation."

"So what?"

Athène smiled. "So tell your friends to come downstairs. I have an offer for you."

The tribe traveled west for most of the month of September, moving swiftly across a landscape exhibiting its last hurrah of beauty—

golden grasses, sunbaked earth, a canopy of reds and oranges threatening to become a carpet at any moment—before the cold turn dragged it unremittingly toward bleak winter. The sweet scent of decay floated on the air, and the weather became unpredictable. They rode through sun and storm, across fields still high with corn and cotton and those where the wheat and barley had been harvested weeks ago. The tribe kept to the Southern Tail, a sort of vanguard for the Sophian force behind them. Though their numbers would've been enough to dissuade any kind of organized opposition, they soon learned that the Anchor had put out a call for all able-bodied men in the Descendancy to come to the defense of the capital, so there was no sign of resistance—not even when they forced their way into homes to empty the larder and raid the coops and pens.

Paz found the power intoxicating. She'd spent her whole life dreaming about bringing down the Descendancy, but even in the most improbable iterations of that dream, she'd never imagined she would find herself traversing the outerlands with the Wesah, aggressively dominating town after town in a relentless drive toward the Anchor. At the same time, Athène was developing a ruthlessness that made Paz nervous; the chieftain still refused to kill a woman—no matter how belligerent or insulting—but any man who stood in her way for more than a moment was unlikely to live to regret it.

Only one town presented the tribe with anything more than the most cursory kind of opposition, a hamlet called Trinity, just east of the mountain range known as the Teeth. Paz had visited the place twice before, once as a spy and again as a prisoner. When the

Wesah first arrived, they thought the town was abandoned. But once they reached the plaza in front of the hyperbolically ornate church, at least a hundred men burst out of the houses all around them, brandishing a pathetic collection of makeshift weapons— pitchforks and hatchets, kitchen knives and a couple of rudimentary bows. They'd been dispatched with only a handful of casualties on the Wesah side, but Athène's anger was as great as if she'd lost a thousand. Standing at the center of a veritable pile of corpses, she'd turned her eye to the august silhouette of the church.

"Come with me," she said to Paz, leaving the rest of the tribe to begin ransacking the town for supplies.

The doors were unlocked but heavy as stone, closing behind them with the finality of the grave. The marble floor drew echoing slaps from their moccasins.

"What are we doing?" Paz said, but Athène didn't answer. The chieftain had that hunter's glint in her eye. Past the ambo, a door opened into a tiny office, where an old man in Honor's robes sat at a desk, scribbling in the margins of a Filia.

"Martin, I told you—" He broke off when he saw them, hand going instinctively to the elaborate golden annulus he wore on a chain around his neck. Athène drew her dagger.

"There's no need for that," Paz said, though she knew it would make no difference. She could still remember this kind of rage; she'd felt it for years after Anton died, blaming the Descendancy for everything that had ever gone wrong in her life, but it burned only dully now. Athène was still new to her pain, drunk on it.

The Honor backed up against the whitewashed wall of his office and drew his Filia to his chest, as if it might protect him somehow.

TOMMY WALLACH

Athène stabbed just below it and ripped the blade outward, disemboweling the man where he stood. He collapsed, curling inward like a pill bug around his precious book. Athène reached down and unclasped his necklace. It was actually made up of a series of annuli arranged around a central pin, like the orbital path of planets around the sun. She held it up and tapped one side; the rings all spun at different rates, in a mesmerizing, interweaving dance.

"Pretty," she said. "Would you like it?"

Paz shook her head. "You shouldn't have done that. He was no danger."

Athène's face clouded; her eyes narrowed. For the first time in weeks, Paz remembered that she was only alive because the girl who had become Andromède saw fit to keep her alive. She backed up a step, instinctually, but Athène closed the distance between them in a heartbeat. Now it was Paz up against the whitewashed wall, just beside a thick streak of vivid red blood.

"That is true," Athène said. "He was no danger. *I* am the danger."

There was an odd playfulness in the chieftain's manner, but it was only at the last moment that Paz realized why. Her fear gave way to curiosity just in time, as Athène stepped into her and their lips met. After some hesitation, Paz let her hands find the curve of Athène's bare stomach, which had an unexpected tightness to it.

The kiss didn't go on for very long. Athène pulled back with a sigh. "So beautiful, but no passion."

"Sorry," Paz said. "I guess I only like kissing men."

Athène laughed. "Maybe one man in particular, yes?"

Paz thought about kissing Clive in the dirt along the old mining road, and on the docks in Settle, and another few thousand times—wherever and whenever they could get a moment alone. It hurt to remember, yet she wouldn't have given up those memories for anything. "I try not to think about him too much. Otherwise, I—hey, you okay?"

Athène's expression had turned sour; she looked as if she might be sick. "Yes," she said, putting a hand to her mouth. "It is nothing. I am only hungry."

But suddenly a dozen little signs and suggestions coalesced into an explanation: Athène had been nauseated the last few mornings, and she'd claimed a couple of meals smelled rotten, even though everyone else agreed they were fine.

"Athène, are you pregnant?"

The chieftain swallowed hard. She looked disappointed in herself, for giving away the game. "You can tell no one. The tribe is still not trusting me. They must see me as strong."

"How long have you known?"

"Only the last week am I sure."

"How did it happen?"

"Just before the *tooroon*, Gemma and I bring a missive into our bed. Rugaru was his name. Dead now. Like her." Athène put her hands on her stomach, as if communing with the child inside. "We would have raised her together. A strong girl. A warrior."

"I'll help, if it ever comes to that." Paz wasn't sure why she said it, or if it was a promise she could fulfill; they just felt like the right words for the moment.

"Thank you, Paz. But I am preferring someone who likes to kiss me. Now come. We have much to do before we sleep."

Athène left the office. Paz followed, but not before looking down once more on the old man. He still had the Filia clutched to his chest, the pages stained red with blood. There was a time when the sight of a dead Honor would have filled her with a sense of righteous satisfaction. But that time was long past now. She reached out and slid his eyelids shut, wondering how many more decent men would have to die before this was over.

12. Clive

LADIES AND GENTLEMEN OF THE DESCENDANCY, I WELcome you to Annunciation Square," Chang bellowed. The crowd cheered enthusiastically, a sparkling sea of bottles and steins raised toward the gallows. Most of them had probably had a couple of drinks already; nobody wanted to watch an execution sober. "I know that many of you aren't native Anchorites, but have heroically answered the call to fight in the holy war that is upon us."

"Heroic?" Clive heard his father say. "They're only here for the twenty gold shekels they were promised after the fighting's done."

Had Chang really promised that much to every soldier? Twenty gold shekels was a veritable fortune; the Descendancy couldn't possibly sustain such a large payoff—unless their fearless leader didn't expect all that many soldiers to be around to collect.

"Sophia's army will be upon us in a matter of weeks," Chang continued. "They plan to lay siege to our city, to try and starve us out. But they will fail. We have set aside stores that will last us for over a year. They'll beat against our walls like waves against the shore, and when the time is right, we will strike like this."

He snapped his fingers and was rewarded with a deafening roar of approval—as if winning a war could ever be so simple. Clive glanced over to his father, hoping they might share in the tragic absurdity of the moment, but Daniel didn't seem to be paying attention; his gaze was firmly directed at the sky, as if he were looking for a sign from the God he had forsaken.

"We're gathered here today to celebrate our city's strength," Chang said once the crowd had quieted again, "by executing two of the Descendancy's most vile enemies. A father and a son. One concealing his malevolence behind a minister's robes, the other behind a Protectorate uniform." The crowd booed and hissed, peppering the gallows with rotten fruit and small stones—though the guards and the hangman probably got the worst of it. "Perhaps you've heard of this sad, cowardly organization that calls itself the Mindful. There are no more than a few of them left, skulking in the shadows, papering our city with their filthy propaganda. We will tear it all down just as we will tear all of *them* down. Our victory begins now."

Chang punched the air—the signal his men had been waiting for. Two members of the honor guard dragged Clive by his bound wrists to stand directly beneath the noose, where the hangman fitted the rope around his neck. He'd been in this same position not so long ago, above the beaches of the *tooroon* with Burns. But Burns was dead now, as was Gemma and probably Flora, too. So many lost. Clive wished he still believed that he would see them all again on the other side, but all he expected to find there now was darkness. The fear reared up in him like a desperate animal—he didn't want to die!

"Da?" His father was still staring up at the sky, completely ignoring the hangman drawing the noose tight about his neck. "Da!" Clive shouted.

Chang turned around to look at the condemned. "Any last words?" he said.

"Plenty," Clive replied.

"Good. Keep them to yourself. I want you to die unsatisfied."

The crowd cawed and shrieked like a flock of ravenous birds. Clive wondered how many of the people out there knew him personally— folks he'd gone to school with, or performed for back in the ministry days, or trained with on the fields of the Bastion. All of them so eager now to watch him hang. A low-pitched drone sounded beneath the cacophony; in his frantic state, Clive imagined it was a sort of auditory distillation of the people's bloodlust.

"Clive! Clive!"

He'd avoided looking at anyone in the first few rows so as not to see their hatred and cruelty so close up. But he would've known that voice anywhere, even through the drone growing louder every second. Clover had one arm on the lip of the gallows, almost as if he might climb up, and the other around the waist of a stout, bright-eyed girl Clive vaguely recognized. He smiled at this unexpected scrap of grace. To know his brother had found someone to give him some comfort and consolation in these dark times—it was better than any last words could've been.

"Da, look," Clive said to his father. "Clover came!" Chang descended the gallows steps as the hangman took up his position beside the lever that would drop the platform. Through it all, even with Clover calling out his name, Daniel Hamill wouldn't stop looking up. "Da!" Clive shouted. "Look at Clover! Look at me! Da!"

As last his father turned his attention away from the sky. His eyes were clear, almost joyful. "She's here," he said to Clive. Then he raised his voice to its full ministerial volume: "She's here!"

Clive looked upward, realizing as he did so that the drone he'd been hearing wasn't coming from the crowd. A shadow appeared behind the clouds, like a fish swimming just beneath the surface of a river. A moment later it dipped into view, a revelation in silver, a demon, a miracle—moving more quickly than should have been possible, as if reality itself had suddenly come unspooled. As Clive watched, it began to shed small gray pellets, almost like bird droppings. The crowd was transfixed; by the time they realized what was happening, it was already too late.

The air filled with screams. Those citizens at the edge of Annunciation Square tried to flee back up the narrow alleyways, as the first bombs began to land, throwing up terrible bouquets of jagged stone and torn flesh. The hangman jumped down from the platform and disappeared into the crowd, while Chang was quickly spirited away by his honor guard. At the same time, a small group of men and women were making their way up to the gallows. They seemed unperturbed by the bombs, efficiently extricating Clive and his father from the ropes around their necks and wrists. The woman helping Clive said something, gesturing toward the eastern edge of the plaza, but her words were drowned out by the cries of the wounded and the drone of the flying fish, which had finished its first salvo and returned to the clouds.

As soon as he was free of his bindings, Clive ran to the edge of the platform and scanned the square for his brother, but the smoke made it difficult to see much of anything. Notre Fille had been hit; the bell tower appeared to have been blown clean off, and the eastern wall had been reduced to rubble. Dozens of bodies were strewn around the cobblestones and at the bottom of the large craters carved out by the bombs.

"Clover!" he cried out. "Clover!"

"Come on," his father said behind him. "We have to leave before Kittyhawk—"

"You do whatever you want," Clive interrupted. "I'm gonna find my brother." He dodged past his father and ran down the steps. There were four bodies underneath the gallows, blown there by one of the explosions. He'd checked only the first two—neither of whom were Clover—when a hand closed around his wrist, holding him in place.

"Daughter's love, Clive," his father said. "There isn't time for this."

"Isn't time? He's your son!"

"I know. But the plane . . ." He trailed off. The "plane" had just dropped below the clouds again. It was returning for a second assault.

"Run!" his father shouted. Clive obeyed this time, charging alongside his father toward the eastern edge of the square. But so many of the cobblestones had been blasted loose by the bombs, leaving pockmarks and ridges and little fires everywhere; it was impossible to move quickly. Clive glanced over his shoulder and saw the bombs exploding along the rooftops. Too late.

He was lifted off his feet, and for a brief fantastical moment, knew what it was to fly. Then the ground was hurtling back toward him again, and the world mercifully disappeared.

A city on fire. Blood running through the streets. That drone like a drill boring into your skull. Clover's little body torn to pieces.

Clive sat up screaming, glanced around like a cornered animal. He was lying in a bed in a wide, low-ceilinged room with wooden beams and gray stone walls. If this was hell, it was nicer than he'd expected; if heaven, a little underwhelming. As his eyes adjusted, he realized he knew this place: the vestry at Ratheman Chapel in the Second Quarter. His father had let him give the homily here once, to an audience of exactly eight people.

Nearby, the woman who'd untied him atop the gallows was bandaging the shoulder of some other man. "Daniel," she shouted, "your kid's up."

The door that led between this makeshift infirmary and the chapel proper opened, revealing a few dozen people milling around the nave; they could only be members of the Mindful. Clive pushed himself back against the thin pillow as his father came to stand at the end of the bed. They observed each other.

"You knew," Clive said, "about that thing in the sky."

"The pilot cut it a lot closer than I would've liked. He was supposed to interrupt Chang's speech."

"You knew it was coming and you didn't warn me. You didn't warn Clover." Clive shook his head. It was one thing to align yourself with Sophia; it was another to put that loyalty above the safety of your own flesh and blood. "I used to look up to you," he whispered.

If the blow landed, Daniel didn't show it. "I hope you will again."

Clive swung his legs over the edge of the bed and stood up. He wobbled, abruptly aware of the many scrapes and bruises he'd sustained in the attack, but managed to stay upright. In the nave, the Mindful members were engaged in some sort of impassioned debate—probably about which innocent people they would murder next. Clive didn't want anything to do with them, or with any part of this war. He was officially done. The large front doors of the chapel were boarded over, but he remembered there was a back entrance behind the ambo. He already had his hand around the doorknob when he was pulled up short by the sound of a gun being cocked.

He turned to find his father holding the weapon. The rest of the Mindful had gone quiet, watching to see what would happen. "Please," Daniel said. "It isn't safe out there."

Clive snorted. "It doesn't look very safe in here, either."

"I mean it, Clive. I can't protect you outside these walls. And you're a risk to all of us, now that you know we're here. I can't just let you leave."

Maybe that was true. Maybe the once honorable Daniel Hamill really had changed so much that he could shoot his own son in the back. But if that was the world they lived in now, Clive would be more than happy to see the end of it. He turned back around and opened the door.

"Do what you have to do," he said, and walked out into the night. He left the door open behind him, waiting for the sound of the shot. But it never came.

TOMMY WALLACH

Interlude

KNIT ONE, PURL ONE. KNIT ONE, PURL ONE. FRANCIE didn't need to think about what she was doing, or even look at her hands. They carried out the familiar motions on their own, while her mind wandered from memory to memory like a cow in a field, chewing a bit of grass here, another bit over there. Shitting it out and starting all over again.

In spite of the must and the dust, Francie could still see this place as it had been the day she and her late husband Drew opened it—as *Debenham House* back then. They'd retained the services of all the best craftsmen in Edgewise to build it: carpenters and blacksmiths, bricklayers and masons, even a down-on-his-luck Anchor-trained artist to paint little Filial scenes in all the rooms. But the murals had all flaked and faded by now, their once-vivid colors turned dull and murky. Francie had painted over most of them with her favorite color—a shade of green she called "sea foam"—but if you looked closely, you could still discern the outlines of the scenes underneath, tenacious remnants of the past lurking beneath the surface of the present.

Why was it that a once-beautiful thing gone to rot left a more bitter flavor than a thing that had never been beautiful to begin with?

Francie had been beautiful once. Boys would stop and stare, happily married men would try to catch her eye when their wives weren't looking, the sailors and stevedores down at the docks would whistle and hoot when she passed. None of them knew her secret, which was exactly how Francie liked it. Sometimes she would tuck a lock of hair behind her ear, and the memory of making that same gesture thirty years ago would momentarily convince her she was a teenager again, and that any man who gazed upon her would inevitably be struck speechless with desire. But that was just wishful thinking: men's eyes slid right off her now, like she was scarcely a person at all.

Knit one, purl one. Start a fresh row. Probably for the best; Daughter knew all that attention hadn't always served her well. They were nights she didn't like to think about now—flirtations turned aggressive, refusals that were ignored.

Let those memories lie, Francie. Move along to a greener patch of grass.

She'd kept the fire burning since the sun went down, and now the lobby of the boardinghouse—called Francie's now—felt claustrophobic with heat and smoke. She put down her knitting and went outside for a breath of cool air. Used to be Edgewise would still be bustling this time of night, but the outbreak last month had changed things. Though there hadn't been any new reported cases of the plague in at least a week, the city was still effectively quarantined. Half the quays sat empty, and the seaside taverns were quiet. Everyone was a little bit poorer, a little bit colder. Business at the boardinghouse was particularly bad; it would've been even worse if people knew that a boarder had died of the plague right on

TOMMY WALLACH

the premises. But Francie had handled it, bundled the corpse up in the dead of night and paid an old dockhand to carry it out to the trench where they'd burned all the other bodies. Even so, most of her rooms were unoccupied at the moment; she'd even stooped to taking in a few working girls to make ends meet—something she'd sworn she would never do.

Across the street, Honor Olmstead sat on the bench outside his church, smoking a cheroot. His teeth were so stained from the tobacco it made Francie a little sick to see him smile; so it was a good thing he seldom did. He waved at her, and she waved back. They hated each other.

She was just about to go back inside when she heard a cry from somewhere up the road.

"Did you hear that?" she said to the Honor.

"Sure did," he replied coolly.

"Sounds like somebody's hurt."

"A cat, maybe."

"That was a person."

"A whore, then. Those girls like to play it up, act like they're enjoying themselves."

Francie knew that sound all too well; she'd endured a few dozen varieties of the ecstatic performance over the past few weeks. The boardinghouse had painfully thin walls. "It ain't that."

Olmstead shrugged. "Whatever you say."

Francie squinted. A match flame appeared at the top of the road leading into town. Then another. And another. "People are coming."

The Honor was curious enough that he stood up and joined

Francie in the middle of the road. He squinted into the darkness. "People come. People go."

"Not these days." Dozens of torches now, and more coming down the road every second. Francie jabbered out of nervousness. "Can you believe what they're saying about that airplane? Flying around like an eagle, dropping things on people. Frightens me to death, I'll tell you. How can a body fight a war against the sky?" The flames floated higher than they should have, like a hundred ruby will-o'-the-wisps—it was a moment before Francie realized it was because the torches were held by Wesah warriors on horseback. And now the quiet of the night was shattered by a different sort of cry. A cry of triumph, of ardor, of incitement.

A cry of war.

Francie didn't personally have a problem with the Wesah. She'd met plenty of tribeswomen over the years, had even lodged a couple, and they'd been about as civil as anybody else. One time a sallow-looking man had shown up with a Wesah girl of maybe fifteen and taken a room upstairs. After thinking on it for a few minutes, Francie had marched up there and told him he'd have to take his custom elsewhere. The look on the girl's face had haunted her ever since—how someone could beg for help without saying a word— but really, what was Francie supposed to have done? If she'd gone to the sheriff, he might've killed the girl just for being Wesah, or else taken her for himself.

Yet it was the shame for not having done more for that girl that kept Francie rooted in place as the Wesah bore down on her, even though she knew there was only one reason they would arrive in such numbers in the middle of the night, particularly after the horror that Grand Marshal Chang had visited on them at that big old get-together of theirs.

"What the hell are they doing here?" Olmstead said.

"Honor, I think you should go inside," she whispered.

But it was already too late for that. The first Wesah were passing by, and Francie lost sight of Olmstead for a moment. The warrior women whooped and hollered, fearless, exhilarating. Candles and lanterns were lit in windows up and down the street, as if magically switched on by the cries of the Wesah. Francie heard something like a slap, something like a gurgle. When the flow of horses had passed, she saw Honor Olmstead lying on the ground with a neat X cut into his chest. Two tribeswomen stood over him. One was tall and broad-shouldered, with blunt, masculine features. The other had a more feminine physique, though Francie had no doubt she was every bit as ferocious in a fight. The larger warrior peeked around the church door while the other looked across the road. Fancie met her gaze; the warrior's eyes were inviting and threatening at once, like deep water, and she still had her blade drawn; a drop of blood fell from the tip.

"You," she said, angling her head like a curious bird, "you man or woman?"

Francie laughed nervously. "A girl could get offended by a question like that."

The tribeswoman didn't appear to understand. She said something to her companion, who looked Francie over and then shrugged, saying something in Wesah that anyone could have translated as *I don't know*.

"I'm a woman," Francie said, as if this were obvious.

"Show," said the first warrior.

"Excuse me?"

"Your parts. Woman parts. Show them."

It had been such a long time since Francie had dealt with anything like this. Not since her school days, boys and girls alike mocking her for the way she spoke and the way she walked, her father taking his anger out on her while her mother hid away in the kitchen, humming to drown out the sound. But Francie had left home, transformed herself as much as a person could, and even met Drew, who'd loved her and whose demons played nicely with her own. And though she knew she ought to be afraid of these women who'd come to Edgewise tonight with killing on their minds, her outrage crowded the fear out completely.

She advanced on the larger warrior, until another step would bring them nose to nose. "Kill me if you're gonna kill me. Otherwise move along."

They stared at each other. Francie thought about how it was almost funny, that her very life could hinge on *this*, the very thing that had nearly killed her as a child, that she'd survived only by the grace of God himself. Drew had always told her her talent for finding the humor in things was one of her best qualities; so when the notion came to her, she decided she might as well indulge it. Angling her chin downward, she looked up at the warrior out of the tops of her eyes and batted her eyelashes: the blameless innocent with a heart as pure as gold.

The reaction was nearly instantaneous. Both of the tribeswomen burst out laughing. Without another word, they turned and went into the church, stepping over Olmstead's body on the way. There seemed a kind of justice in that; a couple of years back, the Honor had worked out what Francie was, and though he'd kept her secret, he'd made no bones about the fact that he saw her as an abomination.

"An abomination who's alive," she said to his cooling body. "Unlike some abominations I know."

Sad to think there'd be no one to give the homily this Sunday. Francie liked watching the churchgoing folk from her window—all prim and proper, primped and polished. But she hadn't actually *gone* to services since her falling-out with Olmstead. Maybe she could start again, whenever the Anchor got around to sending a new minister—if they ever did.

Francie understood what the Wesah had in store for Edgewise now. It was a shame, really: there were some good men in this town. But not many. A scream carried up the hill, the crack of a gunshot. Francie made the sign of the annulus on her chest and went back inside.

Knit one, purl one. Knit one, purl one.

Part II
VAGRANTS

But Paradise is locked and bolted, and the cherubim stands
behind us. We have to go on and make the journey round
the world to see if it is perhaps open somewhere at the back.

—*"On the Marionette Theatre," Heinrich von Kleist*

1. Clive

HE SAT AT A CORNER TABLE, THE COWL OF HIS ROBE UP around his face, nursing his pint of ale and watching the empty stage. The Budding Rose was packed wall-to-wall tonight. At the table next to his, a pair of women sharing a single feather boa were taking turns kissing a handsome young man dressed in a foppish suit. Up at the bar, a group of thickly bearded Protectorate soldiers were working their way through a veritable military parade of shots, slamming the glasses upside down on the table as they finished them, loud as gunfire. A pretty girl in pigtails was making eyes at Clive, but even if he'd come looking for that kind of thing, odds were she'd expect to be paid double her usual rate. He sipped at his ale, which had also cost a fair bit more than he'd expected; imminent apocalypse did strange things to economies.

Finally the gas lights at the front of the stage flared to life. Two girls emerged from the wings. One carried a calliope and wore a crisp white sailor's suit trimmed in blue, cut to look as risqué as possible. The other wore an outfit designed to be removed—a titillating puzzle of stockings and gloves, stays and snaps, buckle and bustier. The girl with the calliope sat down on the edge of the stage and began to play a sinuous melody in a minor key. The other girl

closed her eyes and swayed along with the rhythm. The Protectorate soldiers started hollering as the swaying transformed into a full-
fledged dance, and soon after, even the most pleasantly distracted
of the venue's patrons found their attention drawn to the stage. The
dancing girl pulled at each finger of her right-hand glove in time
with the music, then peeled the whole thing off to a drawn-out glis-
sando that elicited a collective groan of pleasure from the crowd.
Even Clive found himself momentarily hypnotized, though it was
the other girl he'd come here to see.

This was the Anchor on the eve of war—a place of heedlessness,
of abandon. Part of it could be traced to the diminished influence
of the Church since Chang's coup, but in Clive's opinion, the root
cause was simple fear. Kittyhawk's next attack could come at any
time of the day or night, and Sophia's army was said to be only
a couple of days out from the Anchor. People were taking this
opportunity to live the lives they'd always wanted to live, to become
the people they felt they really were underneath all the habit and
decorum. It was a sobering thought, that only in the shadow of
death could a person become his truest self—but Clive's head was
full of little else but sobering thoughts these days.

It had been just over two weeks since the bombing in Annunciation Square, since Clive had left the Mindful hideout at gunpoint. In
that time, he'd been introduced to a whole new side of the Anchor.
He'd always been part of some community before—first the Hamill
ministry, then the Protectorate; now he was just a man adrift, and
to his surprise, the city took him in. He'd gotten drunk with a crew
of masons working to rebuild Notre Fille. He'd played dice with the
beggars who rattled their cups in the alleys of the Second Quarter.

He'd befriended a middle-aged streetwalker whose generous offer to discount her prices he'd turned down as gently as possible.

Of course, his first order of business after leaving Ratheman Chapel had been to transform himself into something unrecognizable to both the Protectorate and the Mindful. He'd snuck into the sacristy of a church, where he'd stolen some old minister's robes and shaved his head clean—the same indignity that had once been inflicted on Paz. Disguised as well as was possible, he'd spent his days wandering the city looking for his brother and his nights sleeping in houses of worship he knew welcomed the indigent (and once, a secluded corner of Portland Park). Mitchell Poplin would've taken him in, of course, but Clive could only assume the Grand Marshal was keeping tabs on the house, which meant neither he nor his brother could risk going anywhere near it.

The dancer had begun to shed her clothing in earnest now, each fallen layer revealing another, prolonging the seduction, earning her another jangling fanfare of copper coins. Clive watched the calliope player, who scarcely seemed to be present. She played by rote memory, her fingers dancing over the keys, her thoughts far away. Talent really did run in the blood.

The music changed just as the dancing girl reached the final threshold, standing tall and proud in nothing but her underclothes. The melody that had guided her through the carefully choreographed striptease gave way to a boisterous waltz—accompaniment to a bawdy song about baking full of painfully obvious double entendres. The calliope player joined in on the choruses, harmonizing with the melody line: *"I can't handle all of your lovin', there's a little too much bread for my oven."*

When the song was done, the audience showered the stage in shekels. A barmaid swept them into a basket while the two musicians took their bows and sashayed offstage. Clive drank down the last of his ale and followed them. In a little alcove next to the kitchen, the two girls were dividing up the spoils from their performance. They looked up as he came in.

"The fuck *you* want?" barked the dancer, revealing her coquettish onstage persona for the pretense it was.

Clive pointed at the calliope player, whose name was Hannah. "Her."

"We're musicians, not whores. And you oughta be ashamed asking for something like that in your robes and all."

Clive had forgotten he was dressed like a minister. He still had his hood up, but was surprised Hannah had yet to recognize him. "I just want to talk."

"Sure you do."

"Hush, Michaela," Hannah said. She looked at Clive. "How much for talking?"

"Five silvers."

"You got yourself a deal." She stood up. "And if I'm not back in ten minutes, Michaela'll send those soldiers at the bar looking for me. You understand?"

"Loud and clear."

"Good."

She took his hand and led him through the kitchen and outside, into an alley empty but for a bin full of food scraps and a thin layer of mist.

"You really have five silvers? Let's see 'em."

Clive reached into his pocket and took out everything he found there. Hannah picked through it with her index finger. "A button, some lint, and two coppers. I knew it."

"I'm sorry. I had to get you out here."

"Even if I *were* that kind of girl, and I'm not saying I am, this would hardly get you more than a tickle." She cocked her head. "You're young, though, aren't you, especially for a minister. The way everyone's acting these days, I'm surprised you have to pay for it. Let me see you better." She pushed back the cowl of his habit, rasp of rough cotton across his shaved scalp. Recognition flooded her face. "Clive?"

"Hello, Hannah."

The girl's cheeks reddened, but the shame was quickly replaced with anger. Clive just missed getting his hands up in time to deflect her slap, which set his head to ringing. "Why didn't you say something sooner, before you made a fool of me?"

"I didn't make a fool of you. I don't care what you get up to. I don't judge anyone for anything anymore."

"Says the man in the Honor's robes." Hannah Delancey sighed her way into a sideways smile. "You Hamill boys are nothing but trouble. Always have been. I told Kita as much, but she didn't listen."

It was because of Kita that Clive was here in the first place; there had been something familiar about the girl Clover had brought to the interrupted executions at Annunciation Square, but it had taken Clive more than a week to realize why: she'd borne an uncanny resemblance to Louise Delancey. He'd gone to their family workshop straightaway, but the place was teeming with Protectorate soldiers—Chang had drafted many of the city's best craftspeople into "the war effort," a euphemism for whatever he wanted, whenever he wanted it. Clive staked the place out for a couple of days until he finally spotted someone he recognized: Louise's sister, Hannah. He'd followed her when she left earlier this evening, unaware he'd end up at an underground burlesque show.

"How's she related to you?" Clive asked. "Kita, I mean."

"Cousin on my da's side. Clover came by last month asking after Louise, I guess, and Kita's been starry over him ever since."

"You know where they are?"

"Why?"

"Because he's my brother. I'm worried about him."

"Are you then? 'Cause I was worried about my sister when she told me she was trying to get at you. And then she ended up dead."

"I wasn't the one who killed her, if that's what you're implying."

A couple of the Protectorate soldiers from the bar lurched through the back door of the Rose and into the alley, belting out the chorus of Michaela's song as they went. Clive kept his eyes firmly latched to the ground.

"I could kill you with a word, couldn't I?" Hannah whispered. She gazed after the soldiers, and Clive wondered if he should start running now. But where would he go, and to what end? The soldiers disappeared into the mist. "You know, Louise used to have such a crush on you. But you were so pious. Couldn't even be bothered to flirt. And there was some girl your parents wanted you to marry, wasn't there? What was her name?"

"Gemma."

"Right. Gemma. Louise always hated her. Called her 'the little angel,' like it was an insult."

"Well, she's dead too, if that's worth anything to you."

"It won't bring Louise back, will it?"

Clive knew Hannah was just trying to rile him, but he didn't have the patience for it. "Listen, if you want to punish me for not loving your sister, or not saving her, that's your right. But I've lost plenty of people myself. I've *been* punished. I don't want to lose my brother, too."

"You mean the brother you shot in the back?"

This was pointless. He was getting nowhere with Hannah, and to add insult to injury, it had just begun to rain; he needed to find shelter for the night. "Never mind," he muttered. "I'll find him without your help."

He'd made it a dozen steps up the road before Hannah called out after him. "My family keeps a warehouse in the Seventh, on the corner of Aurora and the Black Road. My da had a couple apartments built on the second floor. He thought he might rent them out, but he couldn't ever be bothered to find tenants."

Clive turned back around. "Thanks."

"I hope you find him," Hannah said, her voice thick. "But I still think you did my sister wrong."

Clive put his cowl back up. "I'm sure I did," he said.

Passing through Annunciation Square on his way across the city, Clive was once again taken aback at the extent of the damage. Notre Fille had suffered the worst of it; apparently, the bell tower had collapsed and crashed through the ceiling of the nave, where it had reduced half the pews to splinters. Repairs had already begun on the eastern facade—an enormous sheet of canvas flapping against six stories of rickety scaffolding covered what would otherwise have been dozens of exposed rooms and hallways—but there was unlikely to be enough stone on hand to finish the job, and no one would be quarrying anything until the siege was over. In other words, the great cathedral might never be itself again.

The rain began to fall more heavily, beading up in starlit sparks along the arms of Clive's velvet robes. He pushed his hood back and let the drops land on his bare head, remembering how heartbreakingly beautiful Paz had looked after they'd shaved her down to the scalp in the Bastion dungeon. God, but he missed her.

He was soaked to the skin by the time he reached the Seventh Quarter and the intersection of the Black Road and Aurora Lane, but at least he didn't have any trouble finding his destination. The second floor of the warehouse was cantilevered five or six feet out over the street and prominently labeled: DELANCEY FACTORY WAREHOUSE. The latticed windows that made up the whole southern-facing wall were white with moonlight diffused through the clouds. He tossed a few wet pebbles against the panes—shattered glass, Flora glowering down at him from her bedroom, Gemma's gentle but firm rejection of his proposal, the shame still as keen as ever, even after all this time—but nobody appeared. That didn't count for much, however, if Clover and Kita were trying to lie low.

After an optimistic stab at simply opening the warehouse doors, he went around to the back of the building. There were windows along the ground, placed to provide light to the basement, but all of them were latched. Clive glanced around to be sure no one was watching, then pulled the right sleeve of his robe over his fist and

TOMMY WALLACH

punched through one of the panes. Gingerly navigating the treacherous stalagmites of glass, he lifted the latch and swung the window open.

Between the dense garlands of cobwebs and the junk piled up everywhere, the basement might as well have been expressly designed to dissuade trespassers, but he managed to fumble his way across without making too much noise. The rickety stairs shook and shifted as he ascended to the ground floor of the building, which housed nearly a dozen wagons in varying stages of completion—some scarcely more than buckets with wheels, some bonneted like village girls on their way to church, some oversize and double-wheeled, built to military specifications. The Hamill ministry used to have two Delancey wagons; one had been left in the woods behind Amestown, and the other along the mining road north of Wilmington, Eddie Poplin's body still in the back, and little Michael moldering just a few steps away.

Distracted by the memory, Clive didn't hear the footsteps drawing subtle creaks from the floorboards. It wasn't until he felt something loop around his ankles that he realized he wasn't alone; the cord tightened as someone pushed him forward onto his stomach. Knees dug into his back, one on either side of his spine.

"Who are you?" It was a girl's voice, though she was trying to deepen it into a growl. "What do you want?"

"I'm looking for my brother."

"Your brother?" She pulled his hood back and leaned over to get a better look at him. Her voice became unexpectedly amiable. "Clive! It's you! Where'd your hair go?" She slid off him and pulled the cord loose from his ankles. "You're just in time for dinner."

Clive followed her through the darkness to a doorway, beyond which another set of stairs led up toward a flickering golden light. It came from the grill of a large potbelly stove centered against the wall. Clover stood before it, gently shaking a skillet.

"I told you it was just the rats—" he said, but stopped short when he glanced their way.

"Hey," Clive said, and barely had time to open his arms before his brother came crashing into his embrace.

2. Athène

THE JOURNEY FROM EDGEWISE TO THE ANCHOR WAS uncharacteristically slow, as the tribe wasn't accustomed to traveling so heavy. Athène had ordered them to take anything and everything that might be useful, and now the horses' saddlebags bulged with jars of food, coats and scarves, and even some guns they'd taken off the Protectorate soldiers guarding the docks. There had been a larger military presence in Edgewise than Athène had expected, and the fighting had been fierce. In the end, she'd lost nearly eighty warriors.

There were still many who didn't believe she should have been made Andromède, and Athène knew their doubts would only be heightened if they found out she was pregnant—not because chieftains weren't allowed to have children, but because the tribe was about to go to war. Pregnant women were known to make unwise decisions, to be easily flustered; they even had a name for it—*li taanpet di taanfaan*, the storm of child. She needed her people to trust in her strength and single-mindedness, not worry she might flee from battle in order to protect her unborn baby. To that end, she elected to make the trip to the Anchor hidden away in the back of one of the stolen wagons, rather than on horseback. This was something of a heresy with the Wesah, but at least it meant she could rest whenever she needed to, and suffer her morning sickness away from prying eyes. Paz and Flora rode in the back with her—the two Descendant girls both knew she was pregnant, along with a select few elder tribeswomen—while a young missive named Hanson drove the oxen. Their wagon was near the back of the Wesah procession, which stretched for a good mile along the road. The tribe ran into many groups of travelers every day—usually Descendant families fleeing the Anchor, but occasionally Protectorate scouts and even one *naasyoon* that hadn't been at the *tooroon* and so knew nothing of the massacre. Any non-Wesah men were killed, while the women and children were sent on to Edgewise, now the only city in the Descendancy—and probably the world—to be populated *exclusively* by women and children.

Athène reclined on a pile of cushions taken from various Edgewise homes, feeling almost embarrassingly regal. Flora was reading a book, while Paz gazed out on the black ribbon of road unspooling behind the wagon. The two girls had been somewhat aloof since they'd all left the coast. Athène found it hard to believe that after everything they'd seen, they could be bothered by what she and her sisters had done to the men of Edgewise, yet there was no other explanation for their reserve. She didn't like it; in the days to come, Wesah lives might very well depend on the girls' loyalty. There was no room for doubts or divisions.

"We are come to the Anchor soon," she said, hearing the grammatical error but unsure how to fix it. Now that she didn't have Gemma to speak with for hours a day, her English was quickly deteriorating. "Already Zeno should to begin her . . . what is the word? Seep? Seed?"

"Siege," Paz volunteered, just as Athène had hoped; even at her most taciturn, the girl couldn't resist showing off her intelligence.

"Yes. Siege. I think this is not good way to make a war, to sit and wait for the enemy to starve."

Paz's eyes flashed. "It's better to take them by surprise in the middle of the night?"

Athène was glad for the show of anger; wounds needed to be exposed to the air if they were ever to heal. "All fighting is about surprise. You try to surprise me. I try to surprise you. Your strength meets my strength. That is right way to make a war."

Paz snorted. "None of this is right."

"No," Athène conceded. "But it is necessary. The ships that come to Edgewise carry things to help Chang win his war. Without those ships, maybe there are no guns at the *tooroon*. Maybe there are less swords waiting for us at the Anchor. The men we kill in Edgewise seem innocent, but this is trick. This is illusion. No matter how they look, they are . . ." She shook her head, stymied by language. "I do not know how to say in English."

"Complicit," Paz said.

Athène didn't know this word, yet something seemed to loosen in Paz when she said it, as if they'd reached some kind of understanding. It would have to do for now.

Athène didn't speak again that night, or the rest of the following day. She wanted to savor this liminal period, to gather her thoughts and prepare for what was to come. She already had a plan in mind, the sort of plan that Fox was known for, as clever as it was dangerous. The thought of dying didn't frighten her anymore, but to be the chieftain who saw her people wiped off the Earth—such ignominy would surely follow her beyond the grave, beyond the very bounds of time. What if all that awaited them at the Anchor was another massacre? What if she saw herself as Fox but turned out to be Crow?

By the time the tribe reached the Anchor, Zeno's siege was already in place. Massive guns, even larger than the one Chang had brought to the *tooroon*, were set up a few hundred feet from each of the city's four gates. Though Athène could see no sign of the airplane at present, Zeno had already explained how it would be used to inspire the maximum possible fear and uncertainty in the citizenry: striking at random intervals and in random locations. Zeno's hope was that morale would eventually weaken to the point that the people of the Anchor would beg Chang to surrender. In this way, Sophia could win the war without ever fighting a single traditional battle.

Which wasn't to say Zeno was unprepared for traditional battles—many thousands of soldiers, culled from the towns and villages around Sophia, had answered her call, and their canvas tents checkered the hills around the Anchor. Nephra, an older tribeswoman who had once been Athène's mother's most trusted companion, took charge of setting up the Wesah encampment while Athène went to speak to Zeno.

The director's tent was fifty times the size of a normal one, like those used by the circuses and Descendant ministries Athène had seen traveling the Tails. She had to wait while the soldiers standing guard outside announced her. A moment later she pushed her way through a dozen scowling advisers to find Zeno standing over a table on which an impressively detailed model of the Anchor had

TOMMY WALLACH

been constructed. The director wore the same dull gray uniform as always, but her freshly dyed hair was as vibrant as a blown ember.

"Andromède," she said, her voice betraying the pleasure her face so seldom did. "Welcome. I hear the attack on Edgewise went well."

"We lost eighty warriors."

"To cripple the Anchor's supply line and appropriate four wagons full of supplies. This will feed the siege for weeks, to say nothing of what it cost Chang."

"So your strategy is not changed? You sit out here until they give up?"

"There is no reason to risk lives unnecessarily."

Athène bristled, though this was mostly performance; she needed Zeno to feel a little guilty. "Only Wesah lives."

"Our lives too. We lost Kittyhawk a few days ago, along with our best pilot. And don't forget, I didn't force your hand. I suggested that a strike on Edgewise would be strategically valuable, and you agreed to carry it out."

"Yes. And now I am asking you for something in return. I must go into the city. This plan you have, to starve the people—it is slow and cruel. Many innocents will die. But if I kill Chang, maybe this whole war is over. Do you agree?"

"Agreement is irrelevant," Zeno said. "The Wesah are not my servants. You can do whatever you want."

"It is not this simple. I need distraction to get inside the Anchor."

"Distraction?"

"Yes. Sophian lives. Risked. Necessarily."

"Ah." Zeno frowned. "How many?"

"Why not eighty?"

"And what would you have these eighty do?"

"Attack the southern gate, draw the attention of the soldiers. I will go in through the river."

"The river? How?"

It was one of the secrets Athène's mother had passed on to her with the title of Andromède. Many decades ago, there had been a period of relative peace between the Wesah and the Descendancy, and the Andromède of that time had been granted access to the tunnels that ran beneath the Anchor, so she could come and go without fear of being harassed at the public gates. Even as relations had soured between the two peoples, the key that opened the door to these tunnels had been passed down from leader to leader; Athène now wore it on a chain around her neck.

"I have my ways," was all she said.

"When?"

"Tonight. One hour after sundown."

Zeno smiled to herself. "We could've gone by the chimes of Notre Fille, if the bell tower hadn't been destroyed. I think I'll rebuild it to match the one in Sophia, when the city is mine." She disappeared into this reverie for a moment, then seemed to remember Athène. "You'll have your distraction, Andromède. Good luck."

Zeno went back to playing with her model, and Athène returned to her sisters.

The Tiber River entered the city at the northern edge of the Sixth Quarter, made a slow 180-degree turn, and exited at the southern edge of the Seventh. At the outlet point, a semicircle about thirty feet across had been cut into the bottom of the Anchor wall and latticed with thick steel bars that churned the water just before it cascaded down a twenty-foot drop to the natural riverbed. At the bottom, a narrow stone walkway ran alongside the river for a good half a mile. It dead-ended at a flat steel panel gone rusty with spray from the cataract. In the murky twilight, Athène couldn't make out any sort of keyhole.

"How do we get in?" Paz asked. She and Flora had opted to accompany Athène; both were eager to return to whatever passed for normal life in the Anchor these days.

"I do not know," Athène said. "My mother tells me only there is door."

Flora got down on her belly and plunged her hand into the river, as if there might be an answer below the waterline. Athène tried the stone wall on their right, checking between the granite blocks for some kind of hidden mechanism.

Meanwhile, Paz was running her fingertips along the smooth surface of the metal panel. "Could I see the key?" she said.

Athène took off the necklace. Paz frowned as she examined the key.

"It hasn't got any teeth," she said.

"Teeth?"

"That's how keys work. The ridges line up with tumblers in the lock. But without any teeth, this could never open anything. Unless . . ." She touched the key to her belt buckle—*click*. It stuck there, as if with sap.

"What is this?" Athène said.

"A magnet," Paz replied. She started tapping the key against the metal panel, as if searching for something. There was a resonant *ping* when she found it: the key adhering to the metal. Paz turned it and the panel swung inward, revealing a glistening tunnel, gaping like the mouth of some hungry, toothless monster. Flora lit the lantern they'd brought and plunged through the doorway, every bit as fearless as her sister.

The walkway turned to the right and then became a kind of switchback, reversing direction every few hundred feet. Everything was wet, water leaking down from the aqueducts above them. Mushrooms craned out from the cracks in the stonework, and here and there a spangle of sunset light arrived by way of a steep-angled shaft in the ceiling.

"Is there any chance you're going to tell me why you're doing this?" Paz said suddenly.

She'd stopped walking, so Athène did too. Flora, however, kept moving; the sphere of light floated off into the black. "I already tell you. I am here to kill Chang."

"How? You won't get within a hundred feet of him with a weapon."

"So I use my hands."

Paz shook her head. "You're smarter than this. And so am I. What are you hiding?"

"You worry too much," Athène said with a smile. "Now come. We must reach the end of this tunnel before Zeno sends her soldiers to the gate."

They walked on in silence. The tunnel turned back toward the river as they drew up level to it again. Here was another half circle cut into the Anchor wall, another lattice, but the passage was blocked on this end by a door made of iron bars, rather than another panel. A section of one of the bars was rubbed smooth; Athène assumed that was where the key was meant to go. Beyond the lattice, the river wound through what she'd been told the Anchorites called a "park," which apparently was a portion of natural land placed in the middle of a city so people could pretend they weren't in a city. Above and to the right, silhouettes could be seen moving along a low stone wall that ran about eight feet above and parallel to the river. At the top of a set of stairs leading down to the water, something flared red, like a firefly.

In one smooth motion, Athène ripped the lantern out of Flora's grip and threw it into the river behind them. Then she put her hands on Flora's and Paz's chests and shoved them back against the wall. The firefly—which was actually the tip of a cigarette—came hurtling toward them down the steps. Barely breathing, Athène watched as a Protectorate soldier came to stand just on the other side of the iron bars. He peered into the tunnel.

"Hello?" he called out.

There was a skittering sound from somewhere close by. Athène got her hand over Flora's mouth just as the rat ran between their legs and out along the walkway. She felt the girl shudder.

"Fuck!" the soldier said, leaping backward. The cigarette flew through the air and was extinguished in the river.

"What is it?" someone out of sight said.

"Fucking rats. Made me lose my cigarette. Roll me another, would ya?"

The soldier climbed back up the stairs. He and his companion must have been stationed here to guard against anyone coming through the tunnel. There was nothing to do but wait and hope Zeno would be as good as her word. Athène watched the river flowing fast out of the city, like a body purging. A strange gray dot grew larger as the water carried it between the bars of the lattice and past them into the tunnel. Athène wondered if she'd nodded off for a moment, because she'd imagined it was a corpse, even though it hadn't been at all the right shape—one of her fallen sisters floating like a felled tree on its way to the mill, swaddled in dark cloth, arms crossed over her chest. A fan of blond hair around her head, soft as anything . . .

She came to her senses suddenly: even the most distant gunshot had that sort of incantatory power. She waited to see if it was only coincidence and was gratified to hear another few pops soon after. The soldiers at the top of the stairs were whispering, a brief argument that ended in both of them running off toward the gunfire. Athène pressed the key to the polished spot and turned; like magic, the door opened on its cleverly concealed hinges.

They jogged along the river and then up the narrow stairs, at last arriving at a wide cobblestone street.

"*Li boon jheu*," Athène whispered under her breath. Over the years, she'd met a handful of Wesah who'd seen the Descendancy capital—most of them elders in her mother's *naasyoon* who'd visited back before relations between the two peoples had soured. She could remember their attempts to describe the Anchor, and how she'd dismissed their awe as vaguely traitorous, refusing to believe the Descendancy could ever create anything truly beautiful.

"One town is like any other," she would say.

"But it is not a town," they would insist. "It is a city."

"What is a city? Just a big town."

TOMMY WALLACH

But the difference between this place and the average outer-land village wasn't a question of size, but ambition. The buildings Athène could see were all at least three stories tall, running along both sides of the street as far as the eye could see. Gas lamps spaced out every few hundred feet or so burned brightly, their flames sky blue at the base, making perfect little puddles of light on the cobblestones. A horse-drawn carriage clattered by, and through the window Athène saw a man in a black-and-white suit and a woman in a lacy dress laughing uproariously. The driver was also wearing a fancy suit for some reason, and as he passed, he looked down at her like some kind of minor deity.

"You've never been to the Anchor before, have you?" Paz said. Athène shook her head. "It's something else, isn't it?"

Athène didn't recognize the idiom, yet she understood anyway. "Yes. Something else." Was there a first moment of compunction, at her intention to sweep all this history and craftsmanship away like a pile of dead leaves? No—the heart had to be hardened. She touched the brass crown she wore on her brow, as if to draw strength from it. All creation was but a sculpture made of ash, built by the dead and for the dead. In the eyes of the gods, something was not better than nothing—it was just different.

A ways down the road, a young girl appeared beneath one of the gas lamps and disappeared just as quickly; Flora was already on her way home.

"Guess she's in a hurry," Paz said.

"Yes," Athène replied. "You should go with her."

But Paz hesitated a moment longer. "I've got my suspicions—about what you're planning, I mean. But I hope I'm wrong."

"Why?"

"Because I want the Wesah to be better than the rest of us. I want *you* to be better."

More gunshots sounded, cries of pain: eighty men.

"There is no better or worse," Athène said. "We all do what we must."

"There is no must," Paz countered, but she smiled when she said it. Flora appeared and disappeared again, even farther away now.

"Say good-bye for me. Flora is a good girl. Like her sister."

"I will."

Paz lunged forward; Athène flinched. But it was only an embrace, unexpected but welcome all the same. They held each other for a few moments, then Paz pulled away. She suddenly looked very small and fragile among all those big buildings, all the dangers of the city. "Take care of yourself, Athène," she said, and walked briskly up the street, brightening and darkening as she passed beneath the lamps.

"You as well," Athène replied, though Paz was already too far away to hear her.

3. Clover

SOUP BUBBLING MERRILY ON THE STOVE, SENDING FORTH tendril hints of its composition. Rain drumming hypnotically against the windows overlooking the street. The hearth fire, crackling like footfalls on dry leaves. So many cozy, homely sounds: but no words. For the past fifteen minutes, Clive had been perched on a stool by the window, gazing out at the rain. He rocked absently forward and back; the floorboards were uneven, so the legs of the stool didn't lie flush. Clover kept auditioning possible icebreakers in his head before discarding them as too direct, or too indirect, or too trivial. Time was short; Zeno's forces would arrive at the Anchor within the next forty-eight hours. They needed to make a plan. But that would require speaking.

Finally Kita, standing over the stove in the checkered blue-and-white apron she'd found age-stained and moth-eaten in a cabinet, coughed theatrically for Clover's attention.

He looked at her.

She glared back.

He shrugged.

She mimed the concept of talking with her hand.

"What do I say?" he mouthed.

"Anything!" she mouthed back.

They were still engaged in this riveting silent back-and-forth when Clover realized his brother was watching.

"You want to go out?" Clive said.

"But it's pouring," Clover said.

"Oh go on, you big sissy," Kita said. "The soup won't be ready for a while yet, and I'm sick of standing here listening to you two not saying anything."

They walked along the gleaming cobblestones through the steady rain, past a great number of drenched drunks and a few couples huddled romantically beneath their too-small umbrellas. There was a rumble from somewhere off to the east. Up in the sky, a beam of electric light transfixed a cloud bank—Kittyhawk making another assault. Though the plane would have been turned to a similar purpose regardless of his personal contribution, he felt freshly guilty for the part he'd played in its technical development.

"I flew in it once," he said.

Clive hadn't been looking at the plane, but now he did. "Really? What was it like?"

"Terrifying. But also . . ." Clover hesitated.

"Incredible?" Clive offered.

"Yeah. Incredible."

A couple of soldiers materialized out of the mist, but it was dark and they looked to be in a hurry, so Clover wasn't worried about being recognized. One of them did slow as he passed, however, to throw out a cryptic remark: "Keep your eyes on the sky, boys." The other one laughed, and then they were gone.

"What's that supposed to mean?" Clover said.

"No idea." Clive gestured toward a particularly narrow street on their right. "This way."

At the corner, the usual green triangular sign advertised that they were entering the Sixth Quarter. A silhouette behind the shaded window of a cheap apartment block played a sad strain on a violin. A couple could be heard arguing, their baby crying in counterpoint. Occasional gunfire flared up like the first few kernels of corn popping on the skillet. Clive turned down an alley festooned with Protectorate agitprop: THE MINDFUL ARE ENEMIES OF THE STATE. REPORT ANY ACTIVITY TO THE BASTION IMMEDIATELY. The alley dead-ended at a bright red door, music seeping out from beneath it like smoke.

"After you," Clive said.

Clover experienced a moment of vertigo as the door closed behind them. The room was low-ceilinged but vast, lit only with candles: a club of some kind. A man stood just inside the entrance, but he waved them through with a familiar nod at Clive. They took a table just beside the dance floor, where a scrum of bodies moved sinuously to the slow tonk of the band, whose members were all dressed in black-and-white stripes. A waitress arrived with drinks they hadn't ordered—tall fluted glasses full of a bubbling green liquid. She greeted Clive by name and departed with a wink.

"What is this?" Clover said.

"House specialty. Old Church recipe, if you can believe it. Once upon a time, the monks in the outerlands would raise money for their parishes by crafting specialty liqueurs. The practice was outlawed at some point, but the drinks live on. This one's called a Devoçion. Cheers."

They touched glasses. Clive drank deep; Clover sipped. A subtle bouquet of flavors, some of which he knew from his time studying botany—fennel and juniper, something like mint—masked the bite of the alcohol. "Okay," Clover said, as if they'd finally gotten the prologue out of the way. "So just what the hell are we gonna do now?"

"Do? About what?"

Clover gestured around the room as if it were the world. "All this. The war."

"Try to survive it, I guess."

"That's not enough. We have to help. We have to figure out which side we're on."

"They look the same from where I'm sitting."

"But they aren't!" Clover said, surprised by his own intensity. "They're both flawed, but that doesn't mean they're the same." Clive finished his cocktail and signaled the waitress for another; Clover wasn't sure if this conversation would get easier or harder the more his brother had to drink. "Just imagine that you could control everything that's happening, everything that *will* happen. What would you do?"

"I'd stop the war."

"Okay. Good. So how do we do that?"

"We can't. And we shouldn't try. We should leave before things get worse."

"Maybe that's true, but just play along with me for a second."

Clive threw up his hands. "Fine! I guess you'd have to convince Zeno to go back to Sophia and then kill Chang."

"Why not kill both of them?"

"Because Chang needs the war. It's the only reason he's in power, which means he's got no reason to negotiate or back down."

"And Zeno does?"

"I don't know. Maybe."

Clover nodded. "Okay. So all we need to do is kill Chang, figure out if Zeno is willing to call the whole thing off, then kill her too if she isn't."

"Yep. That's all. Easy peasy."

"Easy peasy."

They held each other's gaze for a moment, and Clover felt something thawing between them. It was the silliness of that phrase in contrast with the seriousness of the subject. Clive started giggling first, and then Clover caught the bug. The absurdity only deepened the more he thought about it, the more he and his brother kept repeating the words—*easy peasy*—until he could barely breathe for the laughter.

"Hey, what's going on?" Clive finally said, managing to speak through the tears.

Clover hadn't noticed, but the dance floor was emptying out, the revelers sucked out through the venue's front door like hot air through an open window. Where could they all be going at this time of night? Had they heard about a better party somewhere else?

"Come on," Clive said, downing his second drink in a single swallow.

They joined the exodus, surfing the wave of gasps and mumbles all the way back out to the Silver Road, where they stood with the rest of the crowd and stared up at the sky to the southwest.

"What the hell?" Clive said, taking the words right out of Clover's mouth.

Dashes of orange light were shooting out from the jagged stub that had once been Notre Fille's bell tower and disappearing into the cloud cover. It was a gun, maybe even the same one Chang had used at the Black Wagon Massacre. The Library chemists must have found some way to trigger an incendiary device as the bullets discharged, so whoever was using the gun could track the trajectory of each shot and adjust the aim on the fly. Brilliant.

There was a distant pinging sound; a cloud burst into flame. No, not a cloud: Kittyhawk, streaking out of the mist like a shooting star. The crowd cheered. Those who'd brought their glasses with them raised a toast. The fiery bullets kept coming, making a light show around the central display.

"Did Paz ever tell you about her brother Anton?" Clive said. His voice was strangely quiet, as if he were recounting a dream. "The one who fell off the roof trying to fly a kite?"

"I figured she made him up."

"No, he was real. I think if it weren't for him dying like that, her family would never have left the Descendancy and gone to Sophia. And maybe there wouldn't be any war."

Kittyhawk was a ball of fire trailing a plume of black smoke. Clover thought of the day Burns had destroyed Zeno's phonograph—how it had hurt his heart to see something so beautiful destroyed. If Chang won this war, mankind might never see another airplane.

"We both agree that Chang is worse than Zeno, right?" Clover said.

"Of course."

"So let's start there. First we stop him, then we deal with her."

They watched as Zeno's terrible, glorious creation spiraled down to crash somewhere beyond the Anchor wall. The crowd let out another cheer.

"Okay," Clive said. "But I'm definitely gonna need some soup first."

Clover and Kita hung back as Clive approached the back door of Ratheman Chapel and knocked twice. No one answered.

"*That* was the secret knock?" Kita whispered.

Clive looked back at them. "Why would there be a secret knock?"

"Are you kidding? There's a bunch of Mindful hiding out in there. Of course there's a secret knock!" Kita went up to the door herself. "It's probably something like"—and here she knocked along with the pattern she described—"two knocks, then one, then three, then four—"

The door suddenly swung inward to reveal two extremely unfriendly-looking women holding pistols.

"I guess I got the knock wrong," Kita murmured.

"I'm here to see my father," Clive said.

"Daniel Hamill," Clover added. "He's my da, too."

A rank smell permeated the inside of Ratheman Chapel: too many people living in too little space for too long. Blankets and pillows were set up along the pews, and the sacramental table was laid with the bony remnants of a roast ham, a few clay bowls of overripe fruit, and a glass carafe full of what looked to be either flat beer or apple juice. Clover held Kita's hand as they followed Clive through a sea of suspicious glances and into the vestry. The mirror had been taken off a vanity and leaned against the wall so the bottom half could be used as a table. Daniel Hamill and a bunch of strangers stood around it, looking over an annotated map of the Anchor. They were arguing about something.

"Looks like you've got visitors, Hamill," said the man closest to the door.

Clover's father glanced over at them. His expression shifted quickly from relief to frustration to fear. He signaled one of his associates to roll up the map.

"You don't trust us?" Clover said.

"I don't trust anyone right now."

Clover felt a sudden flash of anger. "We aren't anyone. We're your children!"

"Exactly. You're the children of a man who used to be an Honor, who raised you to believe in the Descendancy."

"Well, we don't believe that anymore," Clive said. "We came here tonight because we all agree that Chang has to be stopped."

"I want to believe that," Daniel said. "I really do. But how can I know for sure?"

Clover looked to his brother, who could only shrug. The assembled Mindful officers were all watching, waiting.

"Do you even know who you're talking to?" Kita said, barreling out into the silence. "Clover Hamill studied in Sophia under Zeno herself. He helped build the airplane that terrorized the Anchor for weeks. He caused a flu outbreak in Edgewise that shut down the whole port. This boy has done more for Sophia than most of you ever will. As for Clive, he broke one of your people out of the Bastion dungeon and got the Protectorate to chase him halfway across the continent." Kita took a deep breath, still not quite spent. "As for me, it was Protectorate soldiers who killed my cousin, Louise Delancey. Some of you probably knew her. She died for the cause, and I would do the same. If that isn't enough for you, then I guess you all can just go to hell." She was practically panting by the end of this speech.

"Give us a minute," Daniel said, taking the other officers aside to confer privately in the corner.

"Not bad," Clive whispered to Kita.

"Not bad?" she replied. "I was amazing."

Daniel returned to the table. "You're all sure this is what you really want?" he said. "What we're doing here isn't easy, or safe. Or sane even."

Clover swallowed his misgivings. "Yes. We're sure."

His father nodded. "Good," he said. With a flourish, he unrolled the map again. It was covered with Xs and Os, like a hundred games of tic-tac-toe that had broken free of their bars. Clover assumed each mark represented a target—for sabotage, for theft, for whatever task Zeno needed done.

Daniel Hamill surveyed the landscape, smiling at all the opportunities it presented. "Now where shall we begin?"

4. Paz

AS IF IN A DREAM, SHE FOLLOWED FLORA THROUGH THE dark streets of a city at once familiar and strange. Though apparently Zeno's airplane had been destroyed a few days ago, the story it had written on the Anchor would take years to efface. A bomb crater or collapsed building awaited around every other corner, bright scraps of clothing and shards of furniture sticking out from piles of brick and stone—each one a kind of burial mound, literally in some cases. Soldiers seemed to be everywhere, hunting for bodies in the rubble, or some clue to the whereabouts of the Mindful, or just somewhere they could momentarily forget their stresses and sorrows. For the first time, Paz understood the logic of the siege. The tension in the Anchor was palpable. Things couldn't go on like this forever; eventually the blister would burst. Anything was better than this perpetual held breath, this emasculating paralysis. People would try to flee the city, even if it meant rushing Sophia's guns. Was that Zeno's plan? Did she hope to thin the herd enough in those initial moments to win the ensuing battle? And what were Chang's intentions? Or Athène's?

They were just people; Paz knew that better than anyone. Yet to think of them now was like thinking of gods—off in some distant empyrean, making their plans with little concern for the people who were hurt along the way.

It took them nearly half an hour to reach Mitchell Poplin's house, and in spite of the chill of the night and the miasma of threat on the air, Paz found herself flooded with a cozy sort of nostalgia at the sight of it. There was the window where "Irene" had spent many a sleepless night scheming her little schemes. Here was the door from which she and Clover had embarked upon their tours around the city, hand in hand like any other young couple in love.

It was quiet and cold inside the house. Paz was struck by the thought that Mitchell Poplin might have died while they'd been away. What with losing both of his granddaughters, to say nothing of Kittyhawk's raids, his old heart might have just up and collapsed somewhere along the line. She overtook Flora and went into the kitchen—a crust of bread and an open jar of honey were on the table, but those could have been there for days.

A soft pulse of light flickered in the stairwell. The steps had always been a little too tall, so that you felt a kind of vertigo walking down them. Paz nearly lost her balance as Flora hurtled past her.

"Who is that?" Mitchell called out.

By the time Paz reached the bottom of the stairs, Flora was already buried deep in her grandfather's chest, heaving with sobs. Mitchell, covered in sawdust and still holding a horsehair brush sticky with lacquer, could only stroke her head with his free hand, tears running down the furrows in his cheeks. Paz gave them a moment before announcing her presence with a cough.

"Gemma?" Mitchell said, squinting in her direction.

"No," Paz said gently.

Mitchell sighed. "Of course not. She's . . . well, I guess you probably know."

"Yeah."

Mitchell looked down at Flora, still bawling in his arms. "You're safe now," he whispered, shushing just for the sound of it. After a moment, he glanced back at Paz. "You'll stay here, won't you? Help me look after her?"

Paz was momentarily nonplussed, moved by this unexpected and undeserved act of generosity. "I wouldn't feel right about it," she said huskily. "You let me live under your roof and I lied to you. You don't even know my real name. The things I've done—"

"You brought my girl home to me. That's all I need to know."

Paz turned away before either of them could see her own eyes welling up. "I'll put a kettle on," she said. To the sound of Flora's sobs, finally beginning to slow, she climbed back up to the kitchen.

Paz sat with her knees hugged to her chest in the clerestory window. Flora was out cold in her bed a few feet away, breathing evenly. Paz had given up trying to sleep hours ago. She gazed down the long avenue opposite the house: utter stillness, like some kind of trompe l'oeil, like a trap.

During dinner, Mitchell had caught her up on the situation inside the Anchor. Apparently Clive's father, Daniel, was alive. He'd publicly disavowed the Descendancy at a Church service, and both he and Clive had been sentenced to death. Paz's heart had been in her throat as Mitchell described the scene at Annunciation Square—the hangman fitting the noose around Clive's neck, Chang's speech, and the last-minute arrival of Kittyhawk. (It seemed to her that Zeno had cut it a little close with that particular piece of theater.) Clover, who'd been staying at the Poplin house since his release from the Bastion, never came back after that day, and there'd been no sign of Clive either.

Had they been killed in the bombing? Were they prisoners of Chang, or of the Mindful, or had they left the city and all its dangers behind? These questions and a thousand more repeated endlessly in Paz's mind, tenacious as the tides, pushing sleep a little further away every moment.

Something moved out in the street. The darkness at the end of the lane shifted as silhouettes rounded the corner. They seemed to glitter, like the flower fairies Paz had imagined populated the forests of her girlhood, but the banal provenance revealed itself a few moments later: uniform buttons and belt buckles, sword hilts and gun butts. At least there was some consolation in solving the mystery of why neither Clive nor Clover had come back to Mitchell's house; they'd both been smart enough to realize that Chang would have eyes on the place—eyes that must have seen Paz the instant she arrived.

Six soldiers: flattering that Chang assumed it would take that many to bring her in.

She considered waking Flora to say good-bye, but she didn't trust that the girl wouldn't try to help her somehow, so she just leaned down and kissed the cheek offered up by sleep. Flora murmured something soft and insubstantial, her subconscious mind refusing to heed the vow of silence, and turned over.

Paz took the stairs two at a time, stopping in the kitchen only long enough to arm herself with a paring knife that still smelled sharply of green onion. The house had a back door that opened up onto a small garden—or what used to be a garden, anyway. Left to his own devices, Mitchell had let the whole thing go to seed. Withered tomato vines still clung to the trellis like crazily articulated spiders' legs, and the raised plant beds were quilted with fallen leaves and insectile seeds. Paz waited until she heard the firm knock at the front door—"Mitchell Poplin, this is the Protectorate. Open up immediately!"—then vaulted the short brick wall into the backyard of the house next door. She clambered over another, taller wall and arrived in a short alleyway connecting two equally forbidding unknowns. Before she could decide which way to go, a flash of red burst out from behind a rubbish bin, and she found herself on her stomach with a soldier crouched on top of her.

"She's over he-*eeeaaagh!*" he shouted, the words morphing into a cry of pain as Paz sank the paring knife up to the hilt in his upper thigh and then slammed the back of her head into his nose. His grip loosened and she slithered out from under him. Standing again, she delivered a quick kick to his temple, stilling him. Just one more callow young soldier unready for the viciousness of a real fight. When Paz had joined the town guard, her father had taught her the cardinal rule of hand-to-hand combat: *If you aren't willing to put your thumbs through a man's eyes, you're gonna lose.*

Paz took off at a sprint, taking the turns as they came, confusing herself in the hopes of confusing her pursuers as well, until at last she arrived, breathless and damp with perspiration, at a bridge arching over the Tiber, not far from where she'd emerged from the aqueducts only a few hours ago. She shivered as a breeze chilled the beads of sweat on her brow, bristled at the feeling of being watched. She looked around and caught the eye of a street urchin encamped in the doorway of a tailor's shop across the street.

"Spare a shekel, miss?" the urchin said as Paz approached.

"Maybe. Depends what you've got for me."

The urchin coughed, shifted beneath the blankets. "What do you need?"

Paz would have to use what she'd learned from Mitchell Poplin to take a stab in the dark. If Clive was still alive, he would probably seek out his father, the disgraced Descendancy minister and infamous defector. "Information. About the Mindful."

A smile, missing some of its key players. Paz realized she couldn't tell if the urchin was a boy or a girl. "I might know something about them."

Paz took off the ring her father had given her on her thirteenth birthday and held it up. "It's gold. Should be easy enough to sell."

"Give it here."

"Talk first."

"I gotta bite it to see if it's real."

"Talk first."

The urchin glanced to the left and right, as if there were anyone around who might overhear. "There's a girl comes out at night to put up posters. Soldiers almost caught her a couple days ago. She had to drop everything. And let me tell you, wheat paste doesn't taste near as good as it smells." The urchin put out a hand. "Ring, please."

"You didn't tell me anything."

"Sure I did. Because that same girl was just here. See?" The urchin leaned out from the alcove and pointed at a poster affixed to the wall of a milliner's shop: THE MINDFUL ARE WATCHING. It was still slick and shiny with paste.

"Thanks," Paz said, handing over the ring. The urchin slid it onto his finger; and it was a *he*—Paz could tell from the hair beneath the knuckles. He held his hand out, admiring the new adornment. "You are going to sell it, aren't you?" Paz said.

The urchin looked genuinely uncertain. "I've never had anything made of gold before," was all he said.

Paz knew how suspicious she looked, walking briskly from street to street in search of Mindful propaganda, stroking each poster to try to discern how recently it had been posted. Twice she was certain she'd lost the trail, only to spot the telltale gleam of moonlight reflecting off wet paper somewhere in her peripheral vision. The last poster had been sopping with paste; she had to be close now. Still, her good fortune seemed to meet its end in a small plaza in the Seventh Quarter. A stone chapel at the center of the square was boarded up, and the sign that would usually advertise the schedule of services read only DAUGHTER PROTECT US. Paz looked everywhere, including a good ways down each of the three roads that fed into the plaza, but came up empty. After a fruitless fifteen minutes, she knew she was beat; the trail would've gone cold by now—or more accurately, dry. She lay down on the steps of the chapel, cold and disheartened, and drifted off to sleep.

It was still dark out when she started at the sound of footsteps on the cobblestones. A girl of fifteen or sixteen, wearing an empty satchel over her shoulder, scuttled around the edge of the plaza and disappeared behind the chapel. Paz stood up, her chilled bones cracking loudly, and followed. Peeking around the corner, she watched the girl speak to someone through the open back of the chapel, then trade out her empty satchel for one packed with rolled-up posters. Paz let the transaction finish; when the door closed again, she stepped into view.

"Excuse me," she said, "is this where—" Lightning quick, the girl reached into the waistband of her jeans and produced a gun. Even in the weak, cloud-diffused starlight, Paz could make out the mark on the barrel. "The man who made that gun is an old friend of mine," she said. "I had one just like it when I served on the Sophian town guard."

"Good for you," the girl replied, cocking the pistol.

"My name's Paz Dedios. I'm looking for Clive Hamill."

"Never heard of him. Or of you."

"I think you have."

The girl considered. "What did you call yourself when you first lived here?"

"Irene."

"How did you stop the Hamill ministry from getting away last year?"

"I filed down the axle so one of the wheels broke off."

"Did you ever love Clover?"

Paz was impressed; the question actually threw her. "In my way. But not how he wanted."

"Daughter on a dill pickle," the girl said, shaking her head as if at a miracle. "You're really her."

"That's right. Now any chance you want to put that gun away?"

"Sure. But I just have to say one thing first. I'm with Clover now, okay? He's mine. So don't go trying anything."

Paz wanted to smile but knew it would look patronizing. "I wouldn't dream of it."

"Good." At last the girl holstered the gun. "Let's go then."

"Go where?"

"Clive and Clover are out on a mission tonight. A big one. Their da told me I couldn't come along, but bein' honest, I was looking for an excuse."

It felt like this night had already gone on forever, but if it meant seeing Clive again, Paz would've gone without sleep for a year. "Lead the way."

5. Clive

CLIVE WAS MANY THINGS AT THE MOMENT. TIRED. A LITTLE scared. Pungent from two weeks without a proper bath. But more than anything else, he was hungry. Since Sophia had set up their siege, nothing had come in or out of the gates, and while Chang had stockpiled plenty of food, one had to produce identification to claim the weekly ration. Many Mindful operatives didn't have the required birth certificate or employment contract; others, such as Clive and Clover, were too notorious to make use of the IDs they had. This meant three square meals a day had become two and a snack, then just two, then one and two snacks. Everyone was a little on edge, a little quicker to anger, a little less happy to carry out his or her share of the endless crimes and morale-destroying displays that were the purview of the Mindful.

Finally, a few days ago, Daniel Hamill had announced that he would be leading a raid on one of the food storage warehouses around the Bastion. The attack would kill two birds with one stone, simultaneously feeding the Mindful and starving the Anchor. Just after midnight, most of the cell decamped from Ratheman Chapel, splitting up so as not to look like the invading army they were. Clive's group was made up only of himself, his brother, his father, and a married couple who'd been won over to the cause just last week. Kita had thrown a Kita-caliber fit about being excluded, but Daniel was adamant that no sixteen-year-old girl would be killed on his watch.

They reconvened outside a shuttered factory in the Fourth Quarter, just southwest of the Bastion proper. The warehouses were well guarded, of course, but Daniel hoped to avoid direct conflict. The cell had spent the weekend spreading a rumor in every café, public house, and brothel in the city that Chang was planning a clandestine disbursal of rations from one particular warehouse at just this time tonight—a gift to some personal friends and relatives. As a result, hundreds of Anchorites had shown up to protest—or perhaps be included in the handout. And this was only one of the Mindful's planned distractions. Those members of the Ratheman cell who weren't here had been tasked with raising as much hell as possible across the city: starting fights, setting fires, posting propaganda—anything to diffuse the Protectorate presence around the Bastion proper.

The warehouse they'd chosen looked much like all the others—built of thin, overlapping steel sheets, crimped like the edges of an apple pie—but it was uniquely large, stretching across an entire city block. The main entrance faced onto the same plaza as the Bastion, so the guards there would have their hands full with protesters. Clive watched as a few Mindful members emptied out their satchels onto the cobblestones—an incomprehensible jumble of machine parts Clover and a few others set to screwing and clicking together with breathless speed.

"What is it again?" Clive said.

"This part's an engine," Clover replied, "like the one that powered

Kittyhawk. It'll provide the electricity to run that." Clover pointed to a disc of serrated steel, the purpose of which was immediately apparent even to a technological simpleton like Clive.

"Is it ready yet?" Daniel said.

"Close," Clover said. "Strike up the band."

Daniel nodded to a trio of men who'd proven to have the loudest singing voices among the Mindful. They linked up arms and began stumbling toward the Bastion, belting out a theatrically drunken rendition of "What a Weight" at full volume.

Halfway through the first verse, Clover pulled a cord on the engine, which sputtered to cacophonous life. The saw spun up, whirring rather pleasantly until its teeth were set to the corrugated steel carapace of the warehouse; the result sounded like a thousand unhappy infants crying at the same time. It took two men to operate the machine, which quickly cut a two-foot-long vertical scar into the wall. The men pulled it out when they reached the ground, lifted it in line with the topmost point of the first cut, and began sawing horizontally. A veritable river of sparks cascaded onto the cobblestones. It seemed impossible that the singers could hope to drown out this terrible noise, but just because the guards heard it didn't necessarily mean they would investigate.

The men turned the saw vertical and cut all the way back down to the cobblestones, at which point Clover switched off the generator. The rectangle they'd cut out was still attached to the rest of the siding by a small tab of steel; it took about a dozen kicks to knock it free. Then Daniel got down on his knees and started crawling through the hole.

"Da," Clive said, "are you sure about this? Someone must've heard all that."

"Too late now," his father said, making the statement true by continuing on into the warehouse.

Clive looked to his brother.

"We picked our side," Clover said—the verbal equivalent of a shrug.

Clive knelt down and followed his father inside. A weak glow filtered through the skylights overhead, illuminating a labyrinth of shelving units piled high with boxes. The air smelled sweetly of cedar and onions. Rats squeaked in the rafters. Clive stood up and dusted himself off.

"Get out of the way," Clover whispered, trying to come through behind him.

"Give me a—"

A Protectorate soldier stepped out from behind a column of crates. "Who's there?"

For a fraction of a second, Clive pitied him. He could remember a time when he too might've stopped to take stock of a situation like this, allowing for the possibility of a misunderstanding. The soldier hadn't yet learned that there could be no room for hesitation or compassion in wartime. And now he never would. *Crack.* The man's eyes went distant and strange; he fell backward as Daniel reholstered his gun.

"Douglas? What was that?" a voice said. Footsteps fluttered on the warped wooden floorboards: at least two or three more soldiers. Daniel had bet everything on there only being guards *outside* the warehouse; now the whole plan was ruined. Clive helped Clo-

TOMMY WALLACH

ver up and the three of them took off to the left, down the corridor made by the towering shelves. They got out of sight around a corner just in time.

"There's a hole in the goddamned wall!"

"They're trying to get in! Draw your weapons!"

Clive plugged his ears against the sound of gunfire. They were on their own now; surely any Mindful still outside would flee. "What do we do now?" he said.

"What we came here to do," Daniel replied, heading deeper into the warehouse.

Clive jogged to keep up with him. "But we can't get any food out now. They've got the doors covered."

"Getting food out was always the icing on the cake."

"So what was the cake?"

They'd reached what looked to be roughly the center of the warehouse. Daniel took a canteen off his belt. "Just enough to get things started," he explained, unscrewing the cap and pouring the contents over the shelves around them. The smell set off an explosion of memory: that moment in Riley's cabin when this all began.

"That's Blood of the Father," Clover whispered.

Daniel shook the last few drops out of the canteen. Of course this had been his plan all along; why would they have left behind what they couldn't carry? The guards were getting closer. Clive drew the gun his father had given him and pointed it vaguely in the direction of the footsteps. He fired twice, neither hoping to nor succeeding in hitting anyone.

The scratch of a match being lit—a face Clive no longer recognized.

"Stop," he found himself saying. "Please." Daniel looked at him, uncomprehending. "It's just women and children who'll starve. Chang's gonna keep his soldiers fed no matter what."

"But those soldiers will have to watch those women and children starve. If it gets bad enough, they'll stop fighting. They'll demand Chang surrender."

Clive shook his head; in this, at least, he knew better than his father. He'd stood face-to-face with Chang. He'd looked into those merciless eyes. "He'll never surrender. Not if he was the only man left standing in this whole city."

"Clive's right," Clover said.

"Then the blood's on his hands, not ours," Daniel replied, and bent to touch the match to the oil-damp wood.

Clive looked to his brother and knew they were thinking the same thing: they couldn't let this happen. Clover started moving first, but it was Clive's foot that found the match and sent it flying out of his father's hand.

A guard shouted, "They're over here!"

Clive dove for the ground just as the soldiers opened fire. Clover was already crawling through an opening between two crates on the bottom of one of the shelving units. Clive followed him, but turned to look over his shoulder at the telltale hiss. His father had lit another match.

"Da, no!" Clive said, but it was no use. Daniel lowered the sphere of cupped light to the puddle at his feet. A phoenix burst to life, flying with exhilarating speed around the whole center section of the warehouse, cutting off the guards. Clive shuffled backward on his knees to get away from the fire. The heat was unbearable, but he

TOMMY WALLACH

stayed long enough to hear the volley of gunshots, to see his father drop to the ground.

Someone grabbed hold of his ankle. He kicked out to try to free himself.

"It's just me!" Clover said. "Come on!"

The flames were only growing higher and hotter; Clive knew there was nothing he could do for his father now. He crawled backward across the shelf and joined his brother on the other side. They beelined for the front of the warehouse and burst through the door together, surprising an unsmiling line of six Protectorate soldiers and ten times that many Anchorite citizens who'd shown up to protest the false rationing report. Everyone went silent; the Protectorate guards were clearly unsure how to react.

"They're handing food out through a hole in the back!" Clover shouted. "It's all true!"

Pandemonium: the protesters surged forward, overwhelming the guards before they could draw their weapons. Clive and his brother moved against the current, making it past the crowd just as word began to spread of the fire inside the warehouse. Retreating to the relative safety of an alley, they watched as the protesters dispersed and the soldiers tried in vain to salvage anything from the inferno.

A clatter behind them—Clive whipped around, reaching for a gun that wasn't there; he must've dropped it back in the warehouse. Two silhouettes emerged warily from the darkness. He recognized Kita first, and then, alongside her . . .

It could only be some sort of supernatural creature, one with the power to look inside the mind of its victim and re-create his dearest desire, his most secret hope.

"I didn't do it," Paz said, her eyes already wet, the words pouring out of her. "I would never have hurt Gemma. Not in a million years. I would've died before I—"

She couldn't say anything more after that, as Clive was holding her so tightly the breath was crushed from her lungs. "I know," he said. "I know."

Of course he believed her. He loved her, after all. And what good was love without faith?

6. Athène

STRANGE TO BE A TOURIST AND AN ENEMY OF THE *state at the same time*, Athène thought to herself as she walked the streets of the Anchor, furred hood pulled tight around her face, gazing on every fresh miracle with a child's wonderment. So many lamps burned in the windows that each apartment became a new constellation. So many buildings towered three or four stories over the street that each boulevard became a sort of canyon. The ingenuity on display awed her, yet it was also frightening to think how the Descendancy had brought nature low, concealing it behind a veil of defanged design. As far as Athène could tell, nearly every tree and flower in sight had been selected and arranged according to some unknowable set of aesthetic criteria, and though she could hear sounds of wildlife—crickets and mosquitoes, even the plangent hoot of an owl—she'd yet to see any animals other than a few stray housecats and a couple large, fearless cockroaches. Did Chang want the whole continent to look like this? Paved over, flat and gray, lifeless beneath the stones? She would hate for her child to grow up in a world like that.

A tin street sign bolted to a wall read VIOLET LN, but at first glance it looked like VIOLENT LN. Athène unfolded the map she'd taken from the Protectorate office in Edgewise and tried to get her bearings. Still surprisingly far to the Bastion—gods, but this city was big. Though it would have been faster to head straight east, she deviated slightly to the north, so as to pass through the celebrated plaza at the center of the city known as Annunciation Square.

It was probably a quarter mile from end to end, surrounded by five-story buildings on all sides. The complex tessellation of gray and red brick underfoot was scarred with bomb craters, only some of which had been filled in with gravel. At the very center of the square crouched the mangled but still imposing Notre Fille, the largest single structure Athène had ever seen, a marvel of granite and glass even in its current state: its eastern facade appeared to have sloughed off, and the resulting wound was covered up with tarp and scaffold. In spite of the lateness of the hour, men could be seen a hundred feet up, working away at the reconstruction. Near the base of the church, a gallows had been erected, and a dozen bodies swung from the high beam in a morbidly balletic near unison. Though Athène was well-acquainted with death, the sight of those corpses left out to rot made her shiver. And was it her imagination, or were those young men smoking in the shadows outside that café paying her an undue amount of attention? She hurried out of the square. It had been a mistake to come here, to allow herself the diversion. Every lane was Violent Lane now, and Athène was just a Wesah woman on her own, surrounded by enemies.

The Bastion was built of huge sandstone blocks the color of dried blood. A guard stood on either side of the front gate, while another pair could be seen pacing the parapet above. Athène pushed her hood back as she approached.

"Who's that?" the soldier on the left said. He was large, almost

TOMMY WALLACH

fat; Athène noticed the bottom button of his jacket wasn't fastened.

"I am Andromède, leader of the Wesah nation," Athène said. "I am here to see the Grand Marshal."

The other guard, skinny and sallow, laughed nervously. "If this is an assassination attempt, you coulda been a bit more subtle."

"I have no weapons," Athène said, having thrown them into the river back by the aqueduct. "I come only to talk."

The soldiers shared a glance. Here was the most perilous moment of the whole endeavor. If the men didn't believe her, or if they simply didn't want to risk wasting Chang's time, they might just kill her on the spot, or throw her in the dungeon and forget about her.

"First things first," the larger soldier said, proceeding to pat her down a little more thoroughly than was necessary. When it was done, he shrugged. "She's not lying about the weapons, anyway."

"So what should we do?" asked the other soldier.

"You should let me in," Athène interjected. "It has been a very long night, and I am tired of standing."

The boldness paid off. After a brief silent dialogue of shrugs and frowns, the soldiers gave in and called up to the guards on the parapet to open the gate. Beyond was a courtyard lined with scalloped pillars and decorated with sculptures of soldiers frozen in strange poses: thrusting a sword up into the sky as if trying to skewer one of the pigeons fluttering overhead; sighting down a bow with no bowstring, one eye squinted shut; gazing heroically off into the distance with one foot up on a perfectly rendered boulder.

"Something funny?" the skinny soldier said.

Athène forced the corners of her mouth back into a reverent, respectful line. "I am liking the—how you say?—the art," she replied, laying her weak grasp of English on as thickly as possible. "Very impressive."

They passed through a set of doors and into the Bastion proper. The walls were constructed of the same red sandstone blocks, here polished down smooth as glass. The halls were empty, likely due to the lateness of the hour. In Athène's opinion, this had always been the most glaring of the Protectorate's weaknesses—the expectation that battles would be fought in the light of day after a long night's rest. How many times had Athène's *naasyoon* struck a detachment of soldiers while they slept, stealing away with a dozen horses before the men managed to get into their trousers and out of their tents?

Another door, this one held open as Athène passed through.

"You'll wait here," the soldier said, before shutting and bolting it behind her.

"*Kaaya!*" she cried out, rattling the handle and giving the door a couple of fruitless thumps. "Come back!"

But no one answered. She turned around and surveyed her prison cell—only to discover it wasn't a cell at all. Here was a bed as large as the one she and Gemma had shared in the Villenaître; there, a cushioned wicker sofa in front of a roaring fire that cast the whole room in a cozy red glow. Paintings in heavy gold frames hung from all four walls—vast, dark landscapes whose detail only became apparent if you got your nose right up against the canvas. A bookcase stood empty but for a few volumes on a middle shelf: a tattered Filia, a thick volume promising an exhaustively dull history of the Anchor, a couple of almanacs dense with statistics. There

TOMMY WALLACH

could be no doubt that this room wasn't for prisoners, but guests.

Athène slipped off her moccasins and squidged her toes in the fluffy mat of the bearskin rug set between the sofa and the hearth. Her eye was drawn to a small marble table, on which someone had set a crystal decanter and four glasses. She took out the stopper and sniffed—sweet and somehow warm in the nostrils, with a bitter undercurrent that made her think of death. Pouring herself a glass, she went to the bookcase and took down the history of the Anchor, propping it on her stomach as she lay back on the sofa. The author used too many large, unfamiliar words, but the general outline was easy enough to follow. If the book was to be believed, the Anchor had been founded nearly a thousand years ago, just after the Flame Deluge. A village like any other for a couple of centuries, it had been set on the path to "greatness" by a man named Gladwell, who founded a church there: the Descendant church. Over time, missionaries from the Descendancy traveled far and wide, up to the cold northern climes and even down to Sudamir. Their fevered exultations persuaded thousands to give up the old religions and move to the Anchor. The author attributed the exponential growth of the city primarily to happenstance—questions of water supply and soil consistency, defensibility and weather, natural resources and a subcategory called "intangibles." Athène didn't recognize the word.

"Gardener's *Anchor History, Volume One,*" someone said.

Athène sat up. Grand Marshal Chang stood in the doorway. She closed the book and touched her finger to the golden *I* embossed on the spine. "So this is not the whole story? There are more books?"

Chang crossed the room to lean against the marble table. "Four more, to be exact. Each one drier than the last. But you can't hope to mold the future if you don't understand the past." He unbuttoned his uniform jacket—a show of relaxed familiarity—and ran a hand across his freshly shaved head. Athène had expected the very sight of him to fill her with rage, but she found herself strangely numb. Here was just a man like any other, pursuing what he believed to be the greatest possible good. The Wesah had merely been in his way. Happenstance.

"I am not thinking I see you tonight," Athène said. "I think you sleep."

Chang coughed out a laugh. "I don't sleep anymore. Too much on my mind. Besides, it isn't often we have Wesah royalty under our roof."

"I am not queen. I am Andromède. No subjects—only sisters."

"Sisters, subjects," he said, as if they were two words for the same thing. "The important thing is that you lead, as do I. I only hope you do a better job of it than the last Andromède." He poured a glass of the amber liqueur for himself and then topped off her glass. "To unlikely visits," he said.

She held his gaze, as her mother had trained her to do, and met his glass with her own. "To unlikely visits."

They drank. Athène could already feel her faculties blurring, like the dark and hazy backgrounds of those oil paintings. A tactical decision of sorts: she would lower his defenses by lowering her own.

Chang sat down beside her. "So are you enjoying the book?"

Athène frowned. "I am learning, but I think also it is wrong about many things. It says the Anchor is here because of the river, because of the rains. All these numbers. But places are more than

TOMMY WALLACH

this. Places have spirits. Where the Wesah hold the *tooroon*, it is not because the sand is this color or the clouds are so big. It is because it is right to hold it there."

"Is that why you're here? Because of the *tooroon*?" Athène was silent. She hadn't intended to bring the subject up at all, but now she was curious to see what Chang had to say. "I won't apologize, if that's what you're hoping for. I requested an alliance and was rejected. At that point, we became enemies."

"And if we had agreed to your offer? You would not have done what you did?"

"Of course not," he said, then smiled slightly. "But we'll never know now, will we?"

She picked up the decanter and refilled Chang's glass, leaving her own as it was. "I am not coming here for an apology, Grand Marshal. I am coming to offer you my help."

"You can imagine how I might find that hard to believe."

"Yes."

Chang leaned back and swirled his drink. "So convince me," he said.

Athène had been preparing for this moment for weeks; she hoped her shaky English would make the speech look less rehearsed. "Sophia is winning the war. Everyone knows this. You are trapped here. Once you run out of food, your citizens will turn on you, and Zeno will strike."

"And you don't want that? I thought your people had always got along with Sophia."

"This is true. But I am thinking Zeno plans this. She is friends with the Wesah for just this moment. Once she wins the war, we must do as she says, or we see a different side of her, just as we see a different side of you at the *tooroon*."

The logs resettled in the hearth, bouncing sparks off the wrought-iron screen. Athène hadn't noticed before, but it was decorated with a picture of an oak tree, complete with tiny squirrels and acorns littering the ground. It looked as if the tree was on fire.

"And you think the Descendancy will treat your people better?" Chang said.

Athène allowed herself a wry smile. "No. I do not."

"So what then? Who are you for? Who do you want to win?"

"Neither of you," Athène said. Here was the greatest risk she would take tonight: telling Chang the truth. "I want the two of you to burn each other to the ground. This is why I offer the Wesah's help. We make sure you and Zeno fight each other fair, army against army. Maybe you win. Maybe she win."

"And maybe *you* win."

"Yes. Maybe both of you end up so weak that you never threaten us again."

"Daughter's love, girl. No wonder they made you Andromède. What a plan!"

"So? Do you accept?"

Chang looked circumspect. "Tell me this: Have you ever heard of 'scorched earth'?" Athène shook her head. "It's a military strategy. The idea is that, as an army moves across a given territory, it should destroy anything its enemies might use—crops, buildings, water supplies, all of it. Grand Marshal Murphy employed the strategy over two centuries ago, during the Ulmann Wars. His forces were overextended, so he called for a retreat. The northern

TOMMY WALLACH

armies pursued. But Murphy destroyed everything as he went, even after he crossed into Descendancy territory, even *fifteen miles* from the Anchor. Which is exactly where he turned on his starving, exhausted enemies and crushed them."

Athène's faculties might have been compromised by the alcohol, but what Chang had just described sounded like madness. "Foolish to destroy your own crops. What good is winning the battle if your people starve after? If one side fights better, they deserve to win. Maybe they make better leader, too."

Chang acknowledged this with a shrug. "Perhaps. But you've faced some of my men in battle. How do they seem to you? Brave? Strong? Experienced?"

"No. They fight like children."

"Exactly. They are soft. But these past few weeks, they've finally begun to harden. The rationing. The Mindful attacks. That fucking plane putting the fear of God in their hearts every night—it's done more to straighten their spines than *years* of training could do. Just a little bit longer, and they'll be ready. Hungry—yes. Desperate—certainly. But ready. This is *my* scorched earth policy, Andromède. I am burning away their hesitation. I am burning away their fear. Only when I'm certain that's done will we fight."

"But how will you fight?" Athène said. "You are trapped here."

"Zeno will come to me. She'll break her own siege."

"Why would she do this?"

Chang raised an eyebrow, as if to say—*that's for me to know.* In that moment, Athène realized she'd made a terrible mistake. Chang was actually *grateful* for his losing position. Whether he was right to be didn't even matter; if he believed the Descendancy was destined to win, he had no reason to accept her offer. She swallowed loudly in the fraught silence. "So you do not want my help?"

"I don't *need* it. But do I *want* it? That all depends."

"On what?"

"On what you're offering. And on what you want in return." He smiled broadly, sipped his drink. "So let's talk details."

7. Clover

MORNING FOUND CLOVER STANDING OVER THE STOVE in the apartment above the Delancey warehouse, preparing to brew the last of the coffee. Clive and Paz sat at the table that he and Kita had made from a couple of sawhorses and some unfinished planks they'd found downstairs. They'd have to drink the coffee black—since the siege began, both sugar and milk had been difficult to procure, but now they would be damn near unattainable. After the Mindful raid on the food storage warehouse, Chang had instituted a curfew from sunset to sunrise. The Protectorate presence on the streets had been vastly increased during daylight hours as well.

"There they are again," Clive said.

Two soldiers with shotguns strapped to their backs walked beneath the warehouse windows.

"How long was that?" Paz said.

Clive glanced at the grandfather clock in the corner. "About fifteen minutes, if that thing runs right."

"Same as last time."

"Yeah."

The water began to boil; Clover poured it over the coffee grounds. "As if it matters," he said.

"Of course it matters," Paz replied testily.

"Why?"

"Because eventually we're going to have to leave this apartment and actually *do* something."

"Why?"

"Because war is coming! A lot of innocent people are going to die."

"And you really think we can stop that from happening?"

"I don't know. Maybe."

"Paz is right," Clive said. "We have to at least try."

"But how?" Clover replied. "We tried to help the Mindful, and look how that turned out."

"That was Da's fault, not ours."

Clover looked to Kita for some support, but she was gazing out the window, seemingly ignoring all of them. He poured the coffee into four of the cracked ceramic bowls that were the apartment's only dishware and carried them two at a time to the table.

"Come on, Clover," Paz said. "Get that big brain of yours working. Chang may not have figured out how to break the siege, but if anybody could, it's you."

"I'm not sure Chang *wants* to break the siege," Clover said, taking a seat at the table. "He could've met the Sophians outside the city walls, but he chose not to. He must have something else up his sleeves."

Paz blew a ghost of steam off the top of her coffee. "Like some kind of new technology?"

"Maybe."

"So let's sneak into Hell and find out," Clive said.

Clover frowned. "It's too well-guarded. But maybe we could—"

"Daughter's love!" Kita said, turning away from the window, her cheeks bright with anger. "Can't the three of you hear yourselves? You're talking like the fate of the whole world depends on us. Well it doesn't! We're children! Children who've nearly killed ourselves over and over again trying to fix things. And all we ever do is make things worse!"

Somewhere in the eaves, a pigeon cooed. Voices could be heard from the street. Clouds flitted across the sky, scattering shadows. The world going about its business, regardless of all their little plans. "So what do you think we should do?" Clover asked.

"We should leave the city. Right now."

At first blush, it seemed absurd. Over the past year, they'd been to hell and back—*literally*, in Clover's case. To simply drop everything and run would be to admit it had all been for nothing. Now that war was finally at hand, Clover felt a sort of responsibility to stay and see how it all played out. But where did that sense of responsibility come from? Except for Flora, who was safe enough with her grandfather, all the people he cared about were right here in this room. If he kept on fighting, what would he even be fighting for?

"It's hard to imagine just up and going," he said. "But maybe it's for the best."

Clive and Paz shared a heavy glance. "When we were in Settle, you told me you wished we could stay there forever," Paz said. Clive didn't answer. Clover felt a twinge of jealousy—or maybe it was just a twinge of memory. "We've done our part, haven't we? Don't we deserve to just be happy? We can go back to Settle. Or better yet, let's go somewhere new. All of us. Together. We can start over." Paz placed her hand at the center of the table. "Who's with me?"

"It was my idea," Kita mumbled, placing her hand over Paz's.

"Anywhere's better than here," Clover said, adding his hand to the pile. They all looked to Clive.

"I think we're making a mistake," he said. "I think we should see this thing through to the end." A pause. "But if this is what you all want, I won't argue." He put his hand on top of Clover's. It was a bitter note on which to leave things, but there was nothing to be done about that.

"So now that we've decided to go," Clover said, "how in the hell are we gonna do it? Zeno's still watching all the gates."

"You think I would've suggested leaving if I didn't know how to do it?" Kita said. She looked to Paz. "Remind me, when does the next patrol come around?"

Clover had never had much cause to visit the Old Town, which was located just east of Portland Park. While plenty of lowlifes could be found around the dance halls and cheap studios of the Second Quarter, it was Old Town where the Anchor's more professional criminal element did its business. Here were the brothels and gambling dens, the gang hideouts and adulterers' hideaways. Clover wouldn't usually have risked coming here even in good times—he couldn't imagine how dangerous the place had become now that everyone had so much less to lose.

"And just how exactly do you know these people?" Paz asked Kita, who was leading them along streets so narrow they felt like wrinkles on the skin of the Anchor. A never-ending cat's cradle of laundry lines blocked out the stars overhead.

"My cousin Louise was this amazing musician, right?" Kita explained. "So she was basically friends with everyone. Folks around here were always hiring her to play their weddings and birthdays and whatnot. I started coming along just for the fun of it, and I guess I made some friends myself."

"Okay," Clive said. "But how are they gonna help us get out of the Anchor?"

"What with all the rules around anathema, people have been smuggling things in and out of the city for centuries. And that's all we're really looking to do, isn't it? Smuggle something out? It just happens to be, you know, us." She stopped in front of a set of black doors. Overhead, a sign advertised THE SILVER BALLS.

"Tell me this isn't a brothel," Clover said.

Kita laughed. "If only. It's a pétanque hall."

"A what?"

"You'll see."

There were no windows inside, and the gaslit air was thick with the smoke from flavored tobacco. The patrons were spread out among the dozen or so rectangular dirt courts built into the floor. The sound of metal balls clanking together was strangely pleasant, almost musical.

"Wait here," Kita said, slipping away past the waitresses scurrying up and down the aisle that ran between the courts.

"Who *is* this girl?" Paz said, her admiration palpable.

"Honestly, I'm starting to think I have no idea," Clover replied.

Kita returned a minute later. "He's busy right now, but I reserved us a court. We just need to wait for the group that's playing to finish."

Clover watched the last few throws without receiving any further insight into the rules of the game. A barmaid brought over a pitcher of ale and four tin cups as soon as they took over the court.

Kita picked up a ball and tossed it to herself. "So you wanna go couple versus couple?"

Over the next half hour, she proceeded to single-handedly trounce Clive and Paz, deftly backspinning the ball in all sorts of crazy ways, overcoming even the utter haplessness of her partner. "We had a court set up behind the workshop," she said after yet another dominant performance, clearly a little embarrassed. They were midway through their fourth game and second pitcher when the summons came. A woman dressed like a burlesque dancer yet somehow maintaining the air of a professional secretary rapped on their table. "Good evening," she said. "My name is Tara. I'm here to take you to Mr. Holmes." The moment they stepped away from the court, another group moved in; Clover heard one of them refer reverently to the girl who'd just "wiped the floor" with her friends.

Tara led them past the bar and through a pair of swinging doors into a chamber where six men sat around a hexagonal felted table, playing some kind of dice game. The walls were covered in black fabric curtains to deaden sound. Tara pulled them apart at some invisible seam and gestured her guests through the opening. On the other side, a short hallway led to a single door painted a garish silver.

"Wait here," Tara said, and promptly disappeared back through the curtain.

Fifteen minutes passed, silent but for a single desperate cry from the room behind them: a bad roll of the dice.

"Do you think they forgot—" Paz started to say, then had to jump backward as the door suddenly swung inward. Strangely, there was no one on the other side who could've opened it.

"Kita Delancey!" said the man sitting at the far end of the expansive office. He was in his sixties, white-haired and clean-shaven, dressed in a natty three-piece suit complete with pocket square and watch chain. His face was long and pointed at the chin, and his heavy-lidded eyes somehow made him look sleepy and menacing at once. He wore a golden die on a chain around his neck, and his fingers were tattooed with a royal flush on each hand—hearts and clubs.

"Hello, Roddy," Kita said.

"And look who you've brought with you. The infamous brothers Hamill and the equally infamous Paz Dedios of Sophia. You three have more lives than a litter of cats, don't you?"

Clover caught his brother's questioning glance and shrugged; it would've been more surprising if the man *hadn't* recognized them, really.

"They're my friends," Kita said.

"And nothing's more important than friendship," Roddy replied. There were no chairs in front of his desk, which was a behemoth of mahogany and leather, its legs unsettlingly carved to look like a goat's. Standing there made Clover think of being called up to the front of class in school. "So what can I do for you all?"

"We're looking to get out of town," Kita said. "I figured if anybody could make that happen, it would be you."

"True enough."

"So . . . can you?"

"Can I indeed." Roddy put a fist on his chin and violently cracked his neck—first right, then left. But instead of answering Kita's question, he turned his attention to Clover. "Mr. Hamill, do you know how I met our friend Kita?"

"She said she used to come around with her cousin, Louise. I guess you met at a concert or something?"

Roddy looked back at Kita, raised an eyebrow. "A concert? Really?"

"What?" she said, suddenly defensive. "The truth would've taken too long to explain."

"What truth?" Clover said.

"The Delanceys and I go way back, back before Louise was even born," Roddy explained. "A smuggler can't smuggle much without wagons. Preferably wagons with a secret compartment or two." Something brushed against Clover's calf—a black cat, tail curling like the top of a question mark, claiming him with its spoor. "By the way," Roddy continued, "I was very sorry to hear about Louise. Seems she fell in with the wrong crowd. Easy mistake to make, these days."

"That's all very interesting," Clive said, clearly uncomfortable talking about Louise, "but are you gonna help us or not? Because if you won't—"

"Clive Hamill, the traitor," Roddy interrupted. "Shame of the nation. Murderer. Why should I help you evade the righteous hand of justice?" He pronounced the last word as if it were a private joke they all shared, but what he said next was anything but funny. "In

TOMMY WALLACH

fact, why shouldn't I turn you all in right now? I'm sure Chang would find a way to show his appreciation."

The black cat leaped up onto the desk and sat back on its haunches, observing them with its nose in the air. Clover had the strange sensation that he was being judged by both animal and master at once. He took a chance, reaching his hand out to let the cat sniff at it. "Are you a gambling man, Mr. Holmes?"

"I've been known to make the odd bet," Roddy conceded.

Clover reached into his pocket and produced a silver shekel. "Heads, you turn us in. Rings, you help us escape."

"Clover, what are you doing?" Kita said.

"He's being clever," Roddy answered. "Your friend here has already worked out that the odds of my deciding to stick my neck out for you are significantly less than fifty percent." He gestured for the shekel, which Clover handed to him. "Such a beautiful object, a coin. I'm told one side is slightly heavier than the other, because of how they're minted, but it's all the same if you don't know which it is." He flipped the coin, flashing end over end, and caught it deftly in his other hand. "Well?"

"Rings," Clover said. Bernstein had told him the same story, as it turned out, along with which side was more likely to come up.

Roddy revealed the coin; Clover had never been so happy to see the annulus.

"I'll admit I was rooting for you," Roddy said, pocketing the coin as if they'd just finished a perfectly ordinary transaction. "Truth is, I've been planning on leaving the city myself. It's gotten a little too hot around here for my taste."

There was a knock at the door; the cat jumped off the desk.

"I'm afraid I have another meeting," Roddy said. "And I prefer that my various business associates don't meet." He pressed something under his desk and a door opened up in the wainscoting behind him, revealing the alley behind the building. "It's been a pleasure meeting you all. Keep a low profile for the next couple of days. I'll reach out when I'm ready."

"How will you find us?" Kita said.

"I'll come to the apartment above the Delancey warehouse," Roddy said, smiling as if this were the most obvious thing in the world. "That is where you're all living now, isn't it?"

8. Paz

ALL MORNING, EYEING HIM ACROSS THE ROOM LIKE some shy schoolgirl, waiting for Clover and Kita to get bored enough to consider leaving the apartment—then having to wait a little longer, until the next Protectorate patrol went past. Listening to the footsteps descending the stairs. Watching the young couple finally emerge onto the street below the window and disappear around the corner.

They would leap at each other then, furious at having to wait, at having to spend chaste night after chaste night in this torturous apartment without any walls or doors, without a single place to be alone besides the definitively unromantic bathroom. She'd thought she'd lost him, would never touch or hold or kiss him again. And even though they'd found their way back to each other, the memory of that loss charged the space between them, made it crackle and spark. She wanted him every moment of every day, wanted to feel his skin on her skin, his stubbled cheek rasp against her smooth one, his desire for her frightening and careless, transcending even love. The only check on their passion was a sop to biology; she couldn't even imagine what it would mean to bring a child into a world so uncertain.

(And where now was Athène, who was well on her way to

bringing forth a child in *spite* of that uncertainty? Had she succeeded in her attempt to woo the Grand Marshal? Just as likely she'd never made it to him, or that he'd gunned her down the moment he saw her—an unintentional double murder.)

They would always dress quickly afterward; it would've been nice to bask in the afterglow, but neither of them wanted Clover to come back while they were still luminescing.

Still, Paz would regret her hurry on days like today, when Clover and Kita hadn't returned to the apartment long after she and Clive had finished making love. She could've used that extra bit of intimacy and consolation; she wasn't sleeping well these days, and not just because of thwarted desire. The city felt like a prison cell whose walls were slowly closing in. There had been a kind of doomsday euphoria for a few weeks there, but with the food stores running low and the curfew making it impossible to blow off steam at night, the tenor of Anchor life had changed irrevocably. Paz couldn't wait to hear from Roddy so they could all get out for good.

But before they left, there was one thing she had to do.

"Where are you going?" Clive whispered.

It was past midnight. Clover and Kita were breathing evenly in the other cot, innocently arranged back to back. Paz wondered if they were secretly indulging their youthful passion as well, on the rare occasion that she and Clive risked a turn around the neighborhood.

"Just getting some water, love. Go back to sleep."

He mumbled something and turned over. Paz put on the green woolen overcoat that she'd taken out of Mitchell's house. It must

TOMMY WALLACH

have been Gemma's once—still smelled of her, in fact. Paz pulled up the hood as she stepped outside, both to obscure her disciplinary tattoos and protect against the autumnal chill. Dangerous to break curfew, but what wasn't dangerous these days? At least she knew her way around the city now and could choose from a dozen different routes from here to there. The first portion of the journey went so smoothly that she let her guard drop a few blocks from her destination—and nearly ran headfirst into a Protectorate patrol. Thankfully, she clocked their laughter just in time to duck behind a rubbish bin and let them pass; she was more careful from then on, slipping from shadow to shadow, stopping often to listen for footsteps.

The doors of Ratheman Chapel were still boarded over, though half the planks had been pried loose, put to use for some makeshift construction project elsewhere in the city. The sign out front had been vandalized, DAUGHTER PROTECT US modified to NO ONE WILL PROTECT US. It was possible the Mindful had moved on since the night of the warehouse raid; when Paz knocked on the back door, she only half expected anyone to answer. But after a moment, the door opened to reveal an unfamiliar and strikingly unwelcoming face. The man was perhaps forty-five years old, with lank gray hair and a gold stud in his left ear. His right arm stopped just below the elbow, and the stump was still bandaged—a recent injury.

"Who the fuck are you?" he said.

"It doesn't matter. I just need to talk to someone who's actually from Sophia, or who's been there recently. I only need a minute."

"Why do you want to talk to someone from Sophia?"

"Because that's where I'm from."

"So what?"

Well, anonymity had been worth a try. She pulled back her hood. "My name is Paz Dedios. I was part of the posse that captured Daniel Hamill. I spent two months being tortured by the Protectorate. So go find me someone from Sophia before I lose my fucking temper."

The man absorbed the abuse impassively, then slammed the door in her face.

"Shit," Paz said. She'd already turned to leave when the door creaked open again.

"Paz?"

She turned back around, blinked as if her eyes were playing tricks on her. Sheriff Evan Okimoto, erstwhile leader of the Sophian town guard, looked much the same as he had the last time Paz had seen him, the night they'd gunned down Ellen Hamill, Eddie Poplin, and poor little Michael. The only noticeable differences were his lack of beard, mustache, and sheriff's badge.

"Hey, Mr. Okimoto."

Paz had lost track of whether the two of them were still on the same side or not. Maybe it didn't matter anymore. All she knew was that seeing him had brought her whole life in Sophia rushing back to her, an overwhelming cascade of guilt and longing and grief. She let him hold her there in the threshold of the chapel.

"Come inside," he said. "We can talk proper."

Paz withdrew, wiping away a tear. "I can't stay. I've got people waiting for me."

TOMMY WALLACH

"The Hamill boys?" Paz nodded. "They stayed here at the chapel for a couple of weeks. Never recognized me."

"Probably for the best."

"Yeah." He laughed, as if there were anything funny about it. "So did you just come by to say hello?"

Paz shook her head. "I haven't had any word about my brothers since I left Sophia. I just wanted to make sure they were all okay. I figured someone here might know."

Something darkened her old friend's face—the shadow of a cloud scudding across the sun. His smile tightened, calcified; he rubbed his cheeks as if to loosen it up again. "Genny Moses moved into your house not long after you left."

"You mean the Widow Moses? From Amestown?"

"That's right. She's looking after the boys and seeing to the farm."

Paz thought back on her few encounters with the old woman, one of those cantankerous crones who hobbled through the world like proud turtles, angrily impenetrable, cold-blooded. Still, she could think of worse guardians; after all, it was the Widow Moses who'd kept Arthur Edwards alive all those years.

"I guess that's good, then," Paz said.

"Yep. It sure is." He coughed unnaturally. "Terrance joined the army."

Paz felt her heart drop. "What? But he's only fifteen."

"He volunteered, and Zeno wasn't exactly checking birth papers."

Paz turned to look over her shoulder, as if she might see through the Anchor wall to Zeno's camp. "That means he's probably out there right now," she said. "He must be so scared."

"Listen, Paz," Evan said, "it's getting pretty late. If you don't mind—"

"Sure. Sorry. Thanks for tellin' me about Terry. I'm glad to know the truth of it."

"Of course." They embraced again. "It's been real good to see you, Paz."

"You too." She held him a moment longer, whispering her last question in his ear. "And Carlos and Frankie? They're okay?"

Evan forcibly pulled away. "Right as rain," he said. Then again, more quietly, with that smile like a skull's, as he shut the door for good: "Right as rain."

She made it back to the apartment in record time, expecting everyone to still be asleep. But when she turned onto Aurora Lane, she made out the gleam of lamplight behind the living room curtains, shadows stretched to monstrous proportions moving frantically to and fro.

"Where have you been?" Clive said as soon as she reached the top of the stairs. Over his shoulder, she saw that both Clover and Kita were also awake—and folding clothes for some reason.

"Ratheman. I wanted to ask after my brothers."

"You shouldn't have gone there alone. It's not safe."

She smiled at his solicitude. "Fair enough. But you shouldn't have woken everybody up on my account."

"I didn't."

"We just got word from Roddy," Kita explained. "We're meeting him in half an hour."

It had been three days since they'd gone to the Silver Balls; Paz had begun to doubt they'd ever hear from Roddy again. "You mean we're leaving tonight?" she said.

Clive shoved an empty satchel into her hands. "That's right. Get packed."

Paz wasn't entirely sure what she should put in the satchel—all her worldly possessions were either on her back or in Sophia— but Kita helpfully donated a few shirts and underthings, as well as what little canned food they had left in the apartment; the bag ended up being surprisingly heavy.

"I think we've got a problem," Clover said. He was peeking out through a crack in the curtains. The rest of them ran over to look for themselves; two Protectorate soldiers stood just below the apartment, staring straight up at the window. "Your friend sold us out."

"He wouldn't," Kita said.

"Of course he would. He's a criminal."

"Wait," Paz said. "Something's happening." Another two figures had just appeared, though it was a moment before she recognized them. "It's Roddy and that girl who works for him."

"Tara," Kita said. "And I *told* you he wouldn't sell us out."

They shouldered their bags and went downstairs. Roddy greeted them with a matched set of firm handshakes. He wore a dapper black suit and carried a cane, while Tara had on an incongruously fancy dress, wispy with taffeta. The two of them looked better prepared for a fancy dinner than a midnight escape.

"You nearly gave us a heart attack," Kita said. "We thought you'd sicced the Protectorate on us."

"Don't be silly," Roddy replied. He gestured to the "soldiers" behind him. "These are just some associates of mine who like playing dress-up. We can't exactly be seen walking around the streets without an escort, now can we?"

Far away, one of Zeno's massive guns began to fire—not an uncommon occurrence, except usually the fusillade lasted for only a few seconds. This one went on and on.

"What's going on out there?" Paz said.

"I can't say that I know," Roddy mused. "What interesting times we live in." He offered his arm to Tara, then tapped his cane on the cobbles. "Off we go!"

Paz threw an amused glance at Clive, who could only shrug. Off they went.

9. Clive

APALL OF MIST HUNG LOW OVER THE CITY, INFLAMED BY a bright crescent of waning moon. Chang's curfew had emptied out the streets but for his own patrols. Thankfully the soldiers seemed to accept Roddy's disguised mercenaries at face value.

As far as Clive could tell, Roddy wasn't taking them toward any of the city's main gates. That made sense, considering Zeno's guns, but it also raised the obvious question of just how they were meant to get past the Anchor wall. Just behind Roddy's men, Clover and Kita walked side by side, whispering to each other. Clive glanced over at Paz, who'd been uncharacteristically quiet ever since she got back from Ratheman Chapel.

"You okay?" Clive said.

She looked through him for a moment, then seemed to come to her senses. "Yeah. Yeah, sorry."

"Something happened, didn't it? Back with the Mindful?"

Paz nodded. "I saw an old friend. He told me my brother Terry volunteered for the Sophian army."

Clive remembered Paz telling him that Terry was only fifteen. "I'm so sorry."

"He's still a child. He should be playing at soldiers and savages in the woods, not actually going to war."

"What about Frankie and Carlos? Did you get a chance to ask after them?"

"Yeah."

"And what did he say?"

"That they were fine. But when he said it—I don't know. Something felt off."

"Off how?"

"I don't know. Just off."

Roddy hissed over his shoulder. "Keep it down, you two. You can chat all you want once we're out."

They turned off the Silver Road just before it would've delivered them to the Bastion, making use of byways so small they didn't even have street signs, and finally arrived at a section of the Ring Road that had been cut off at either end with a makeshift barricade, such that the only way someone could access it would be by way of the exact route they'd just taken. Four men bustled around a strange contraption at the base of the Anchor wall. It looked a bit like a raft—logs lashed together to make a platform—with ropes running to a pulley that ran up along the stonework, disappearing into the mist.

"What is that?" Kita said.

"It's an elevator," Roddy said. "We're gonna ride it all the way to the top of the wall."

"And how are we gonna get down the other side?"

"One problem at a time, pet."

They stepped onto the platform, taking on the four men who'd

TOMMY WALLACH

been there when they arrived. Tara had gone white as a sheet. "You're sure this is safe?"

"Relatively," Roddy said.

The fake Protectorate soldiers began to operate the winch. With each turn, the platform rose a couple of feet and rocked from side to side. Clive held on to one of the ropes overhead for balance, and Paz held on to Clive. In hardly any time at all, they'd made it about a third of the way up the nearly hundred-foot wall, well above the rooflines of the nearest buildings. Bats fluttered between the chimneys and smokestacks. The mist thinned as they went, and soon Clive could see clear to Notre Fille, crouched like a mutilated gargoyle at the center of the city.

"Look there," Paz said. Not far below them was the husk of the warehouse that Clive's father had set ablaze during the raid.

"I think I'm gonna throw up," Tara said.

"Like hell you are," Roddy replied. "My men are working down there."

Another ten feet up and Clive could make out the Southern Gate. Sparks of gunfire regularly lit up the darkness.

"Something's going on down there," he said.

Roddy squinted. "Probably nothing," he said, but Clive could hear the note of disquiet in the man's voice. No one spoke after that, all of them focused on the sounds of battle, on the little squeaks and sighs of the rope passing through the pulley, of their own private fears. They'd risen above the fog now; to look down was to gaze into a misty void, a bowl of ghost milk. The platform jolted; Clive winced as Paz squeezed his arm hard enough to leave a bruise.

After what felt like an hour but was probably only a few minutes, they pulled up plumb with the top of the Anchor wall.

"Thank the Daughter," Tara said, hopping down onto the walkway that ran between the parapets. It was probably fifteen feet wide, curving infinitely away in either direction.

"This part's gonna be a little more difficult," Roddy said, as his men began to draw metal pegs and thin coils of rope out of their satchels. "There's no way we could ride an elevator down the other side. We'd be too visible. So we'll be using individual ropes, like so." He opened his jacket to reveal a leather harness studded with iron loops. "I brought enough for everyone," he said, "but my men can only lower two of us at a time."

As Roddy's men began to fit Tara into her own harness, Clive wandered to the other side of the walkway and looked out over the fields to the southeast of the Anchor. The fog was so thick that he couldn't immediately understand what he was seeing: lights garlanded the city like an annulus, all of them moving so slowly you could almost fool yourself into thinking they were standing still. But no—they were closing in, a noose drawing tight around the Anchor's neck. From this vantage, Clive could see that Zeno's guns at the Southern and Eastern Gates were both laying down cover fire for the thousands of individual Sophian soldiers who made up the ring. He could only assume the same thing was happening at the Northern and Western Gates.

"I think you all need to see this," he said, summoning the rest of the group to the edge of the parapet.

"What's going on?" Kita said.

"Zeno's marching on the city," Clover replied.

"I don't understand," Paz said. "The siege was working. Why break it now?"

None of them had an answer. Clive jumped at a loud *clank*; Roddy's men had begun hammering metal spikes into the parapet.

"You have to tell them to stop," he said to Roddy.

"Why?"

"There are too many soldiers out there. They'll see us on the wall."

"So they see us. They're here to take the Anchor, not kill the people trying to leave." Tara had finished putting on her harness, and now one of Roddy's men threaded a length of rope through the rings in her and Roddy's vests and then tied it off to one of the metal spikes.

"Clive's right," Kita said. "We'll have to find some other way."

"There is no other way," Roddy said. He looked to his men. "We good to go?" He gave his rope a few tugs to test the fit; satisfied, he immediately climbed up onto the parapet and sat down with his legs dangling over the side. "Stay if you want. It's your funeral." With that, he pushed off, falling only a couple of feet before the rope caught him and his men began to slowly lower him down the wall. "Come on, baby," he said to Tara. She stepped up onto the parapet and reeled at the height.

"I'm just supposed to walk off?" she said.

"That's right," Roddy said soothingly. "It's like hanging on a rope swing. Easy peasy."

Clive looked to Clover—but neither of them so much as cracked a smile.

"I hate rope swings," Tara said. "I hate this."

"Don't look where you're going. Face the other way."

"Okay."

She turned around to face the rest of them. Clive wanted to tell her not to go, but he knew it wouldn't make any difference. After thirty seconds of deep breathing bordering on hyperventilation, Tara squeezed her eyes shut and leaned her weight back into the rope. She stepped into clear air and began the descent alongside Roddy. They dropped quickly, and even though the ring of Zeno's soldiers was getting a little bit closer every second, Clive began to wonder if maybe he'd been wrong; maybe this really was their best chance at escape.

One of Roddy's men cursed as the rope slipped off its peg, audibly abrading his palms before he managed to get a grip on it again. Tara screamed as she plummeted ten feet in an instant. Maybe it was the scream that did it, or the sudden movement—or maybe the Sophians had noticed as soon as Roddy first clambered over the parapet. Tara screamed again as the first few desultory shots ricocheted off the Anchor wall.

"Hurry the fuck up!" Roddy shouted, his voice distant, his face already obscured by the fog. His men tried to play out the rope more quickly, but they could only do so much. Roddy wasn't even halfway to the ground when the first bullet found its mark. He looked up at them with the astonishment of a gambler who'd just lost everything on a single bet. Then his eyes rolled back in his head and he went limp. Tara had started gibbering in anticipation of what was coming, so it almost seemed a mercy when the next volley arrived to silence her. For a few moments, they all watched the two bodies swinging there, as if awaiting some miraculous resurrection. But then the Sophians began to target the silhouettes at the top of the wall. Roddy's men let go of the ropes and dove for cover. Clive stayed just long enough to see the two bodies tunnel down through the mist and land in an illegible heap of blood and bent limbs.

No one spoke on the way back down the elevator, and Roddy's men dispersed as soon as they'd all reached the ground. Clover was comforting a tearful Kita, stroking her hair and shushing. Clive was surprised to find Paz crying as well. Could she really have come to care that much about Roddy and Tara in so short a time?

"What is it?" he said.

"I know why Zeno is breaking the siege," she whispered. There was something fanatical in her eyes—epiphany and grief and rage all mixed up. "They're dead, Clive. Frankie and Carlos are dead."

10. Athène

CHANG DIDN'T SHOW UP TO SEE HER OFF—WHICH REALLY shouldn't have come as a surprise; Athène hadn't spoken to him since that first day, when they'd talked and drank late into the night, cementing their arrangement. He'd apologized, but she'd have to remain in the Bastion until he determined that his "scorched earth" approach to morale in the Anchor had reached its apotheosis. Then he would release her on the Sophians "like Zeno unleashed her plague in Edgewise."

That was what she'd become: a weapon, a vector of death.

All told, Athène spent three days as an "honored guest" of the Protectorate. Three days wandering the halls of the Bastion, eating sinfully decadent meals in her room, and going on brief sorties into the city—though never without an escort. She'd seen the towering bricolage monstrosity they called the Library, the manufactured serenity of Portland Park, the twisting alleys of the Second Quarter where the craftspeople and artisans of the Anchor still plied their trade. Her initial wonderment at the sheer scale of the city had been tempered by her gradual discernment of its flaws; it was as if the streets, starved of light by all those tall buildings, had been starved of something else—empathy, maybe, or love. So many beggars offering up their hands in the shape of a bowl; so many desperate women offering up their bodies in exchange for a few coins.

She'd only been Andromède for a matter of weeks, but Athène had already begun to interpret the world primarily through the lens of leadership. Though she could see many of the Descendancy's shortcomings, she wondered if she could've done any better, had she been in charge. Convincing a few thousand like-minded sisters to follow you into battle was one thing; convincing a hundred times that many people—spread out over innumerable villages, towns, and cities—to share a single overarching government and social covenant was quite another.

Just before sunset on that third day, a group of soldiers showed up at her quarters and escorted her back to the secret passage through the aqueduct. There was no going-away party, no last meal, just a scribbled note from Chang: *Deliver my message.*

Twenty minutes later she found herself back on the other side of the Anchor wall. In the failing light, her sisters' tents looked like triangles cut out of the hills to the south. She imagined she could feel the heat radiating off their fires from here. But she would discharge her duty before she returned to them—not for the Grand Marshal, of course, to whom she owed nothing, but for herself.

Since Athène had last seen Zeno, the Sophian leader had set up hundreds of electric lights all around her camp, including a few searing spotlights pointing at the massive central tent. The engines that powered all this artificial illumination could be heard from over a mile away, and the combination of noise and light created an admirable ambiance of threat. The Protectorate soldiers stationed along the Anchor wall had to spend all day gazing out at this intimidating spread of technology and manpower, to say nothing of the guns themselves, which stuttered out an explosive reminder of their existence every hour or so. Until a few days ago, Athène had felt certain Chang couldn't hope to win the war without the help of the Wesah. Now she wasn't so sure. Circumstances were shifting every second. All one could do was stay as flexible and treacherous as possible.

Athène's arrival at the Sophian camp inspired the expected soldierly posturing, but as soon as she made her identity known, the guards escorted her into Zeno's tent.

The director was alone this time. Her giant war table had been covered with a sheet, but Athène could still make out the models and figurines beneath the fabric. Zeno sat cross-legged on a thin mat before a plant in a nondescript ceramic container. It resembled a miniature tree, and Zeno was pruning it with a tiny pair of scissors.

"I am thinking this is how the gods work," Athène said.

"How so?" Zeno replied, clipping off a section of branch no larger than a fingernail.

"To make every tree, it must be like this. A little bit at a time: snip, snip. Very hard work."

"It relaxes me."

"Maybe for the gods, too. Maybe it is relaxing to build worlds. Certainly more so than waging wars."

Zeno ran her hand along the smooth curve of the miniature tree's foliage. She found an imperfection: *snip, snip.* "I hope you won't be offended to hear that I didn't expect to see you alive again."

"No. I would be thinking the same."

"Good. Then the offense can be mine alone." Zeno finally

TOMMY WALLACH

deigned to look up from the tree. Her eyes, ringed with sleepless-ness, were an accusation. "I sent men to die so you could get into the Anchor. So you could kill Chang. And yet here you are." Athène didn't speak; she'd anticipated something like this. "If you'd tried and failed, you would be dead. If you'd succeeded, my spies would know, and you would also be dead. So you didn't try."

"I did."

"Then how did you survive?"

"The Grand Marshal let me go."

"Why would he do that?"

"So I could give you a message."

"What message?"

Athène considered reneging on her promise to Chang, but what good would it do? Surely he'd find some other way to deliver his revelation to Zeno, and the delay would serve no one. The sooner the two armies met on the field of battle, the sooner they would destroy each other. So she delivered Chang's message, along with a threat of her own. As she spoke, the vicious words unspooling like black ribbon from a spindle, she watched Zeno's cool superiority melt from her face like tallow. She left the tent in silence, confident that the final battle for the soul of the continent was finally about to begin.

It was scarcely an hour's walk from Zeno's encampment to the Wesah's, but Athène took her time, hoping the brisk breeze might blow her doubts away. She felt sullied by the events of the past few days. Though she'd only agreed to help Chang because doing so helped the Wesah, it still made her sick to think that she'd shared a drink with the man who'd murdered thousands of her sisters in cold blood, to say nothing of having just done his bidding.

No theoretical nausea after all: Athène doubled over and emptied the contents of her stomach out into the mud. It felt like a judgment, a rejection of all her excuses and equivocations. Though she'd yet to feel her daughter quicken, she could sense the girl's spirit inside her—like a second conscience, appraising her every decision.

"What else would you have me do?" she asked, but her child-to-be didn't respond.

She reached the outskirts of the Wesah camp. During the raid on Edgewise, the tribe had taken on a dozen new missives—all under the age of fourteen, still malleable enough to adapt to their new circumstances without too much bitterness. They crouched around the fires, tending to the meat in silence; missives weren't allowed to speak English to each other, and these boys had yet to learn more than a handful of Wesah words. Watching them now, Athène realized that the time would come when this practice would have to be abolished. Though most missives eventually came to think of themselves as members of the tribe, that didn't change the fact that they began their lives with the Wesah as slaves. How could Athène claim the moral high ground over the Descendancy or Sophia when she was complicit in treating human beings as mere chattel?

"Andromède," said a young warrior called Elodie, whose arms were heavy with battle trophies. "You are back." Her voice betrayed her disappointment.

"Summon the chieftains to my tent."

"Many are out hunting."

"So bring me the ones who aren't. Go."

Athène wasn't surprised at the girl's dismay; she'd only been Andromède for a month, after all. More than a few of her sisters had probably hoped she wouldn't return from her mission to the Anchor, so some more worthy warrior could be promoted in her place.

Seven chieftains had survived the massacre at the *tooroon*, but only three arrived at Athène's tent within the following hour, after which she set a guard outside to bar further entrance. Three was an auspicious number, and the tribe was now small enough that it could be effectively administered with this many. Two of the chieftains—Lyra and Delu—had led *naasyoon* in the southern reaches, and both had the burnished bronze skin and gilded leather armor common to those places. The third was her mother's ex-lover Nephra—the only one Athène really trusted.

"Where have you been?" said Lyra. Of the three women, she was the one most obviously skeptical of the new Andromède. Athène appreciated that; true disloyalty always came disguised as flattery and fawning. "We have been sitting here doing nothing for days."

"I went to the Anchor and offered Chang a temporary alliance."

All three chieftains reacted viscerally; even the usually dispassionate Nephra looked disgusted. "Why would you do this?" she asked.

"The Grand Marshal is no better and no worse than Director Zeno. We cannot trust either one."

"So why ally ourselves with either?"

"Crow is not an ally of Fox or Wolf, but she has been known

to help both when it serves her. We are Crow. We are death itself."

Delu seemed confused by this conflation of the mythological and the real. "So we're going to kill them both?"

"We are arranging it so that they kill each other. If one side wins too easily, then even afterward, they will still be too strong for us to fight. I helped the Grand Marshal because he seemed to be in the weaker position. Even if I was wrong about that, by delivering his message, I have moved us one step closer to our goal."

Two missives appeared carrying a wooden tray laden with seasoned beef, heat-puckered ears of purple corn, and sweet pudding.

"What message?" Nephra said.

"After the *tooroon*, Chang sent a portion of his forces east. They hid in the hills north of Sophia until Zeno's army rode for the Anchor. Then they struck."

Lyra swallowed loudly. "You're saying Sophia is destroyed?"

"If the Grand Marshal is to be believed, the town itself is gone. The academy still stands, but the Protectorate soldiers have been instructed to kill one scholar and burn a hundred books every morning from now until the war is over. But that was only one-half of the message I delivered to Zeno."

"What was the other half?" asked Delu, like a child demanding the end of a bedtime story.

"I told her that her siege was a shameful act of cowardice, and that if she didn't move on the Anchor in the next twenty-four hours, we would attack her armies with everything we have. Zeno has no choice now. To hold the siege is to risk the lives of her precious scholars *and* invite a battle on two fronts. Force will meet force, with Crow hovering overhead all the while, waiting to descend."

"*Mafwe*," Nephra said. Lyra was grinning ear to ear, finally appeased.

"Spread the word through camp," Athène continued. "Tonight we feast. Spare nothing, as if there is no tomorrow. Once Zeno enters the city, the hunt begins."

"But who are we fighting for?" Delu said. "Who are we hunting?"

The smoke wafting off the meat was intoxicating. Athène's mouth dripped with saliva, with expectation. "All of them," she said. "We're hunting all of them."

11. Clover

ALCULUS: A SHRINKING CIRCLE OF SOLDIERS, ITS AREA and circumference determined by the laws of derivatives and integrals, its proneness to chaotic dispersion defined by limits and logarithms. Algebra: unknown variables all converging on one location, their values determinable only through combination and elimination, through the resolution of the equation. Arithmetic: problems multiplying, families divided, element of uncertainty added, lawfulness and sanity subtracted. Wasn't that the secret dream of every scholar, to render the seemingly irrational actions of man entirely through mathematics? To see the world in some more fundamental spectrum? Maybe genius was just the marriage of intuition and calculation: a subconscious that could compute. Revelation always arrived as a lightning bolt, but undoubtedly weather patterns of thought had conspired to create the necessary preconditions for the storm.

As soon as Clover saw Zeno's soldiers on the move, he knew that the academy at Sophia was lost. To attack the Anchor now, just as the effects of the siege were being felt, was completely illogical. And what else but personal vendetta could drive the otherwise unflappable Zeno to act illogically?

"Hello? Clover? What are we gonna do now?"

He came to his senses standing at the bottom of the elevator. In his mind's eye, he could still see Roddy and Tara plummeting with that heaviness peculiar to death, just as Sister Lila had done. (Here physics held sway: terminal velocities and parabolic motion, mass and small-g gravity.) Roddy's men had left, and Clive and Paz were locked in a tight embrace at the other end of the barricaded portion of the Ring Road. Clover could hear Paz's sobs even over the gunfire and the nascent patter of rain; clearly she'd solved the problem of the unlikely assault as well, and knew what it implied for her brothers back in Sophia.

He realized Kita was looking at him expectantly.

"Did you say something?" he hazarded.

"I said what the hell are we gonna do now?"

The future was defined by complex crosscurrents of intention and exigency, like the call-and-response of a Descendant gathering. The only comfort was the thought that a powerful enough mind could read them. "I think we should go to the Library," he said.

"The Library? Isn't that the first place Zeno's going to attack?"

"Probably. That's why it's important we help the attendants defend it."

"So now you wanna fight?" Clive said. He'd left Paz over by the barricade to collect herself. "Five minutes ago you were ready to leave town!"

"But that isn't possible anymore. And if we're stuck here, I'm not just going to sit back and watch it all happen. I have to try and save . . . something." He glanced over at Paz but looked away as soon as he caught her red-rimmed eyes—her brothers were probably beyond saving now.

"Then let's go to Mitchell's," Clive said. "Honestly, I couldn't care less about the Library."

"Why would we go to Mitchell's?"

"To look after him and Flora! Remember them? Our friends?"

"They'll be safe as long as they stay put."

"You can't know that!"

"I know that the Library matters more than any of us!"

"It's just a building, Clover."

"It's not and you know it. You're just not thinking rationally."

"Oh really? Because I'm so stupid and you're so fucking smart?" Clive strode forward, and it took all of Clover's willpower to hold his ground. His brother stopped mere inches from his face. A last moment of impending threat, then a sort of miracle: Clive exhaled, and it was as if all his anger dissipated along with the breath. When he spoke again, his voice was quiet, thick with emotion. "You really won't come with us?"

"I can't," Clover said, though it hurt his heart to do it. "If Sophia's really gone, the Library is all humanity has left. I'm sorry."

"Don't be." A brief hesitation, then: "Do you . . . do you need us to come with you?"

Clover would always be grateful for the offer, whatever happened. "No," he said. "You're right about Flora and Mitchell. Someone should check on them."

They stood there for a moment, just looking at each other. Clover realized how much the two of them had changed in the past year, and how those changes had somehow brought them closer together, or made them more understandable to each other, anyway. It was the one redeeming part of all this upheaval, all this destruction. The asymmetries that had made things so difficult between them had all resolved—Gemma, their parents, their prospective careers. Now there was nothing standing in the way of respect, or affection, or even . . .

"I love you, Clover," Clive said.

The words were so unexpected they sounded almost profane. Was one really allowed to speak something so intimate? "I love you, too," Clover said, tears springing foolishly to his eyes.

Clive turned away. "Don't die," he said gruffly. Then he and Paz clambered over the barricade, as Clover took Kita's hand and made for the alley. Behind them, the pulley of Roddy's elevator clanged against the Anchor wall, like a bell tolling in remembrance of the lost.

They moved quickly along the Purple Road toward the Library. Clover no longer worried about being identified by the Protectorate; Zeno's army would enter the city within the hour, and this knowledge had already percolated through the citizenry by way of information vectors every bit as efficient as the gutters that channeled rainwater along the streets and down into the sewers. Despite the lateness of the hour, it seemed as if half the Anchor was running from one place to another, stocking up on supplies or looking for a safe port in the storm to come, while the soldiers who had been so ubiquitous since the curfew went into effect were conspicuously absent; Chang could no longer spare any men to patrol the streets.

They arrived at the Library and found the gatehouse empty and the gates wide open.

"I don't like it," Clover said. "It looks like a trap."

Kita sighed. "And yet we're still walking into it."

The garden trees were bare, and the rain had already turned the sweeping lawns to puddled swamps. Skeletal leaves dissolved under their feet like wet paper. They reached the large double doors that opened into the Library proper, and still there was no sign of either Library attendant or Protectorate grunt. Clover tried the handle.

"At least *these* are locked," he said. Then, knocking, "Hello! Is anyone in there?"

"Get away," said a muffled voice from inside. "There are a thousand soldiers in here. They'll blow you to pieces."

Kita snorted. "Will they now?" she said. "Then they'll have to get through the eighteen dragons we've got out here."

The peephole grate slid open and a palsied and veinous hand stuck a knife through, swinging it wildly from side to side. "I said get away!"

Clover jumped back on instinct, though the knife wasn't anywhere near him. "We're not with Sophia," he said. "I'm a friend of Attendant Bernstein."

The knife stopped its impotent air-stabbing. "You mean Grand Attendant Bernstein?"

"Yes. I'm . . . we're here to help."

Finally the weapon was withdrawn. A pair of cloudy eyes magnified by pince-nez appeared at the peephole. Kita gave a little wave. "Hello," she said. The grate slid closed and the door opened.

"Sorry about that," said the old man on the other side. The bottom half of his face was a mass of white beard, above which loomed a craggy nose like a mountain peak poking through the clouds. "I'm Attendant Garula."

"Clover Hamill. And this is Kita Delancey."

"Hello again," said Kita.

The grand foyer of the Library, usually bustling with distracted attendants and beleaguered apprentices balancing towers of books in each hand, was empty. Scraps of paper crinkled underfoot, and all but one of the teardrop-shaped gas lamps had been extinguished. Garula led them past the central staircase to what were known as the Innocent Steps—in the Library's early days, the servants known as innocents were compelled to traverse the building by very specific routes.

"Where are the soldiers?" Clover said.

"Who knows?" Garula replied. "Chang cleared almost all of them out yesterday morning."

"Why? He must know how important the Library is to Sophia."

"I guess we aren't a priority. Look there." They were just passing through the third floor along the course of the spiral stairway. A single soldier could be seen pacing the long corridor. "A couple of men on every floor. That's what we've got to defend against an entire army. Honestly, I don't even know why Chang bothered leaving anyone at all." He cupped his hands and called out to the soldier. "You're doing God's work, Grady!"

The soldier turned. "What?" he shouted. But Garula was already climbing the stairs again. Kita followed him, but Clover hesitated for a moment. "What?" the soldier repeated—almost like an admission of something, or an apology.

"Nothing," Clover said. He took the stairs two at a time to catch up with Garula and Kita, who'd arrived at the fifth floor and were already halfway down the hall.

"How much have you got left?" Kita asked the attendant, continuing some conversation that Clover had missed the beginning of.

"Well, that's hard to say. The records are less accurate than we expected. I'd say we've transcribed about a third of what I'd view as critical information."

"What are you talking about?" Clover said.

"See for yourself," Garula replied, opening the door to the Rotunda.

It was the largest single chamber in the Library—three stories tall, with a vaulted ceiling on which were painted various scenes from the Filia relating to books and knowledge, along with a re-creation of the constellations as they would have been arranged on Landfall Day. Clover had been here hundreds of times before, usually chasing down some niggling question of Bernstein's. He could remember tiptoeing across the marble floor so as not to disturb the attendants silently poring over their texts at the long shared tables. Today, however, the room was anything but silent; what had to be most of the attendants and apprentices left in the city were on hand, all of them furiously scribbling away in twine-bound notebooks. At the center of the room, the circular desk where two or three attendants were typically stationed—there to fetch volumes requested by other scholars—was manned by only one person.

"Bernstein!" Clover shouted.

The spark of recognition, a warm smile—immediately giving way to concern. "Clover, what are you doing here?"

"We came to help." An attendant arrived at the desk and picked up a big stack of books, which he carried straight back to his table. "Just what is it you're all doing up here, anyway?"

"Copying," Bernstein explained, as he set out another stack of books for the next attendant. "We've been doing it in secret for weeks, but after Chang cleared out most of his men, we moved into the Rotunda. The soldiers he left behind don't seem to care what we do."

"What's the point of having two copies of everything in the same place?" Kita said.

Bernstein seemed to notice her for the first time. "Who are you?"

"Kita Delancey. Clover's sweetheart."

That got a gruff laugh out of the old man. "Ah. Well, let's hope you're more trustworthy than the last one."

"I am."

"To your question, the books aren't in the same place. We're sealing the copies into barrels and dumping them into the Tiber."

Clover remembered Paz mentioning that she'd seen something floating down the river when she and Athène came through the aqueduct; it must have been one of the barrels. "Why not just send the originals, if you're worried about Zeno taking the Library?" Clover said.

"I couldn't care less who ends up with the manuscripts. I just don't want to see them lost or destroyed. Two copies in two places mitigates the risk."

A woman in attendant's robes snapped for Bernstein's attention. After a brief whispered conversation, she scurried off across the Rotunda. "Is she an attendant?" Clover asked.

"We lifted the ban on women working at the Library after the

Archbishop died. He was the one who insisted on the rule, probably to justify its corollary in the Church hierarchy. We needed the help."

"What did she say?" Kita asked.

"The Sophian army is inside the city. You two have to leave."

"Shouldn't *everybody* in here leave?" Clover said. "Zeno will probably come for the Library first."

Bernstein shook his head. "We all knew what we were signing up for. We'll keep working until the last possible moment."

"Then so will we," Kita said.

Clover turned to her. "Do you even know how to read and write?"

"No," she answered, visibly bristling. "But I'll find a way to make myself useful. I always do."

Clover was assigned a desk and a treatise to copy: *On the Chemical Properties of Different Varieties of Tree Bark*. Kita acted as a go-between for the scholars and the central desk, carrying books and papers back and forth as necessary. Though they could hear nothing of the battle raging outside, the Protectorate guards received occasional updates by way of semaphore sent and received from the roof. Apparently, Zeno had abandoned her guns outside the city, perhaps to encourage Protectorate soldiers to desert, and her forces had entered through all four gates at once. Though it seemed inevitable that at least one of these divisions would come for the Library, no reinforcements from the Protectorate were forthcoming. Again, Clover wondered why the Grand Marshal didn't see fit to better protect the seat of centuries of Descendant erudition and history.

Hours passed. Clover's hand cramped into a claw; he shook it out and kept on writing. At some point, food arrived—massive steaming pots of rice decanted into bowls and sprinkled with salt and pepper—but no one stopped to eat. Some time later, Clover set his head down on his arms to rest a moment and passed out. When he woke again, the sun was rising. He could feel hot breath on his ear, someone whispering for him to *wake up already*.

"What is it?" he said groggily.

Kita clearly hadn't slept; the circles around her eyes were the same green-black hue of an old tattoo. "I followed one of the soldiers upstairs, just to see what he was doing."

"You're lucky he didn't catch you."

"They have Blood of the Father, Clover. Whole barrels of it."

"What? Why would they—"

He'd answered the question before he was finished asking it. Chang had left just enough soldiers behind to carry out a simple directive: if it looked as if Sophia might take the Library, they were to set the whole place ablaze. The Grand Marshal was like a spoiled child with a toy—if he couldn't have it, no one would. And if both the Library and the academy at Sophia were destroyed, the world would be cast back into a dark age that would take centuries to escape, if not millennia.

"We have to stop them," Clover said.

Kita nodded. "I know."

12. Paz

THEY PASSED A LARGE HOUSE IN THE SECOND QUARTER, immaculately kept, with a walled garden out front decorated with hedge sculptures—a bull, a mermaid, an annulus. White sheets hung from each of the eight street-facing windows. They'd gone sopping wet in the rain, sticking to the granite blocks like a shroud, but the message remained clear enough: no one in the house planned to put up resistance to the Sophian incursion. A few blocks on, citizens who lived in the apartments around a market square hefted furniture out of their windows so those waiting on the flagstones below might fashion them into a barricade. There didn't seem to be any Protectorate soldiers on hand, yet somehow there were plenty of guns—mostly long rifles with knives sticking out from under the flared barrels. On the smaller roads closer to the Poplin house, people ran this way and that, half of them carrying pitchforks and axes toward the sound of battle, the other half carrying stuffed satchels and bulging valises away from it. The pubs and dance halls were all dark; the cafés were populated only by upturned stools and the flashing red eyes of the rats.

Paz saw all this, but registered none of it. All she could think about was Frankie and Carlos. Which one had the Protectorate gotten first? Had their deaths at least been quick? Would she ever know?

"Paz," Clive said.

She returned to herself. They were only a few blocks from Mitchell's place, but Clive had stopped walking. Somewhere nearby, the wail of a baby abruptly died out. "What's wrong?" she asked.

"Now that the siege is over, there's nothing keeping us here. We can get Flora and Mitchell and go. Just like we planned."

"What about Clover?"

"Clover can take care of himself. He's proven that by now. But if you want to stay, so you can look for Terry, I'll understand."

Terry, the oldest of her brothers, the most likely to still be alive—just one more faceless soldier in Zeno's army. He was almost certainly inside the city walls now, but how could she ever hope to find him? "I can't protect Terry any more than you can protect Clover. If we can get Flora and Mitchell out of here, we should."

Clive nodded. "Okay, then," he said. "Let's do it."

The windows of the Poplin house were dark, and the front door was open, banging loudly against the frame every few seconds.

"Could they have gone somewhere?" Paz said.

"Where would they go that would be safer than their own house?" Clive replied. He pushed the door open with the tip of his shoe and peeked his head around the jamb. "Hello? Mr. Poplin? Flora?"

They searched the kitchen and living room first, and then Clive went to check the upstairs bedrooms. The house was bone cold. Paz opened the stove and sniffed—no one had cooked anything here for at least a day. The door down to the workshop stuck in the frame. *Houses breathe*, her father used to say. She'd tried to explain the science to him—how wood expanded in the summer due to increased humidity—but he preferred to live in the metaphor. She shouldered open the door to a sour exhalation, as of food left out to rot, which overpowered the more familiar scents of wood scraps and polish. She thought back on the months she'd spent living here as Irene, the late-night talks with Gemma, the weekend she'd donated to Mitchell, helping him to finish painting a set of chairs for a tiny client in the First Quarter. Something tapped her cheek, buzzed past her ear. Why was there something so foreboding about going down a staircase? The vertiginously tall steps, each footfall landing like a heartbeat, like a countdown. Too dark to see anything—Paz fumbled to her left, to the gas lantern Mitchell always left hanging there on a peg. Clover had designed it to spark its own flame when you turned the dial. The room flickered into color.

Paz gasped, nearly gagging as she drew the rotten smell deep into her lungs. Splatters across the dirt floor. Dried patches on the tables, tinting the sawdust red. Spots sprinkled around the walls like raindrops on dark clothing. Mitchell sat in a chair before his treadle lathe, still as a painting, head resting on his chest. His tools were scattered around him, all of them covered in gore; he'd been tortured in too many ways and places to take in at once. Had this happened the night she'd fled the house? She'd assumed the soldiers would leave Mitchell and Flora alone if she ran, but that had been foolish. Yet another corpse left in her wake; yet another stain on her conscience.

One of Mitchell's hands—furred at the joints, thick-veined and calloused—had been nailed to the lathe along with a note.

TOMMY WALLACH

Clive and Clover Hamill: I've taken the girl. Please report to the Old Temple for your orders.

—Your Grand Marshal

Paz heard the creak of steps as Clive descended, the sharp intake of breath, silence as he read the note.

"I should've known Chang would come for them," he said quietly. "This is my fault."

"No. It's mine. The night I arrived in the Anchor, they were watching the house. They came here because of me."

"It's both our faults, then. Or neither. I don't know anymore."

A tear ran slowly down her cheek. She'd liked Mitchell. He'd welcomed her when she first came to the city, had treated her as if she were a member of his family. He'd deserved so much better than this. But that wasn't why she was crying. "We're never going to run away together, are we?"

Clive wiped her tear away with his thumb. "Let's face it," he said. "We've only ever been good at running *into* trouble anyway."

"So the Anchor was actually built over a deep network of tunnels, like the one you and Athène used to go through the aqueducts," Clive explained, as they jogged briskly from overhang to awning, trying to keep out of the downpour. He seemed preternaturally interested in the gutters, which were running heavy and fast as a freshet. "A few hundred years back, there was a big earthquake, and the church at the center of the Anchor ended up collapsing into those tunnels. A bunch of people died, but the city planners decided it was God's will, so they rebuilt underground. But I guess people hated it, because after a while the Church abandoned the place. They laid a fresh foundation over the top and started building Notre Fille. Anyway, people call *that* church, the one they left underground, the Old Temple."

"So what's Chang doing down there?"

"The sewers crisscross the whole city. They'd be a good way to move around without Zeno knowing. That explains why there are so few soldiers out on the streets." Clive abruptly stopped walking. "Here we go." He gestured toward a storm drain. Water poured through, splattering against the stones some unknown distance below.

"Seriously?"

"I'm sure there are more pleasant ways in, but I couldn't tell you where." He sat down on the cobblestones and put his legs through the drain, holding the lantern he'd taken from Mitchell's workshop under his jacket. "Wish me luck," he said, before sliding the rest of his body through.

She didn't hear him land. "Clive? You all right?"

"I'm fine!" he called back. "Just wet. Come on down."

Paz sighed. At least she was wearing Gemma's old jeans and not a dress. She went through on her back, swallowing a mouthful of gutter water as she passed under the cascade. Clive caught her before she plunged into the artificial river that ran down the middle of the brick-walled chute. She tried not to look directly at it; even though the sluiceway ran deep with rain, undoubtedly there were things in there she'd rather not see.

They started walking. Rats scurried out of the lantern's bolus of light, as if it might burn them. Curious cockroaches waved their antennae from the mossy fissures between the bricks. Every few

TOMMY WALLACH

hundred feet, another drain would empty from above, pouring over iridescent patches of mold and fungal blooms that looked uncannily like human ears. The smell alone was enough to knock you on your back; Paz had to keep her sleeve across her nose for the first few minutes, breathing through the fabric until her eyes stopped watering.

"You know where this temple is?" she asked.

"Not exactly. But the sewers all empty into the Tiber eventually, so I figure we should just head upstream."

Screams slipped into the tunnel through the drains. A stutter of gunfire left an image momentarily frozen on the iris. They walked beneath a war zone. After about half an hour, they turned a corner to find a string of electric lights running along the wall. Elegant glass bulbs with thick filaments were connected each to each by long stretches of copper wire.

"Chang must have been planning this for a while," Paz said.

"How do you mean?"

"Well, look at these brackets. They're rusting. That doesn't happen overnight."

Clive shook his head. "We keep underestimating him, don't we?"

"Everybody does. It's why he's winning."

The passage zigzagged for a few hundred feet, then abruptly opened up. They found themselves standing on what felt like a cliffside, gazing out over a massive chamber illuminated by powerful lights mounted on the walls. Paz was surprised to learn that the Old Temple wasn't a single structure, but a complex of many buildings, most of them crumbling stone sheds of one or two stories. The largest of them was the church itself, built in the traditional round shape, with a roof of moldering terra-cotta shingle. Thankfully, no one seemed to be guarding the path by which they'd entered the Temple chamber, nor did anyone notice them descend to the level of the complex. A lone soldier sat outside the church, scratching himself and smoking.

Paz ducked behind a chunk of gray stone that had probably been there since the earthquake that created this place. "Look," she whispered. Clive knelt next to her and peeked around the stone. One of the single-story sheds had shiny new bars over the windows. "You think they're holding Flora in there?"

"It's worth a look."

As quietly as possible, they sprinted from cover to cover until they reached the shed. Clive tried looking through the window, but it was too high up.

"Give me a boost," Paz said.

Clive made a stirrup with his hands and lifted her to the window. "What do you see?"

She squinted. The only light inside the shed was what little penetrated through the cracks in the roof. A glint—there, and then gone. "Something's moving. It must be her."

Click. Paz would have known that sound anywhere. "Shit," she said, dropping back to the ground. The soldier held a cocked gun in one hand and a lit cigarette in the other. He had a ridiculous long mustache—probably a struggling artist or merchant who'd enlisted in the hopes of surviving to claim those twenty gold shekels.

"You came," he said. "The Grand Marshal was starting to lose hope."

"Now you can let Flora go," Clive said.

The soldier looked genuinely confused. "Flora?"

"The girl in there!" Clive pointed to the shed. "She's done nothing wrong."

"When Chang gets back, I'll be sure to tell him you feel that way. Now if you'll be so kind . . ." He gestured with his gun toward the front of the shed.

Clive started to walk, but Paz hesitated. "That's a single-shot pistol," she said.

"Excuse me?" the soldier said.

Paz couldn't help but smile a little as she explained the situation to Clive. "When Chang opened up Hell, he was suddenly looking at a couple centuries of weapons development all at once. Case in point, that gun right there needs to be reloaded after every shot."

"So if he shoots one of us, whoever's left can kill *him*?" Clive said.

"That's right."

Clive frowned sagely, as if cogitating on an interesting riddle. "So who should we let him shoot?"

"I'm fine either way."

"I've been shot before. I can take it."

"How gentlemanly of you."

"Wait, wait, wait!" the soldier said, backing away with his hands up. "Let's not do anything crazy." He looked around, then dropped his voice to a whisper. "I don't even want to be here. I should be at home with a glass of whiskey and a good book."

"I couldn't agree more," Paz said. "So why don't you give us the key to that shed and run along home?"

"You'll really just let me go?"

Paz nodded. "Swear to the Daughter."

He fumbled at his belt and took off the key. "Listen, there are about a hundred soldiers just on the other side of that wall." He pointed toward the church. "So whatever you're gonna do, do it fast." He handed her the key, then took off running toward the nearest entrance back into the sewers.

Paz threw Clive an amused glance. "Who said diplomacy was difficult?" she quipped.

Clive was still chuckling quietly as he unlocked the shed door. It was a mess inside, full of old construction materials and broken furniture. All of it was wet and rotten from the rainwater that filtered first through the streets above the Old Temple and then through the shabby roof.

"Flora?" Clive said. "Flora, are you there?"

The voice that answered was weak and raspy, but unmistakably male. "No Floras, I'm afraid," it said. "Check back next week." This cryptic statement was followed by a peal of wild laughter.

Clive scrambled over the rubble. Paz followed him, and through a gap in the shelves, she could finally make out the figure chained to the back wall. He smelled of infection progressed past the point of no return, of rotting flesh, of the beginning of the end. Or maybe the end of the end.

"Da?" Clive said. "Da, is that you?"

An eerie white line appeared in the darkness—a grimace and a smile at once. "Who's asking?" Daniel growled.

TOMMY WALLACH

Interlude

ROM THE SAFETY OF THE WESAH ENCAMPMENT, Grandmother had watched the Sophians abandon their great black engines of death and converge on the Anchor, where they were swallowed up by its tall arched gateways. The plains and hills went dark, abandoned by all but the Wesah. Even the usually busy roads around the capital were empty, as if the world had magically reverted to some simpler, earlier time.

The woman now known as Andromède had given her orders to the tribe not long after Sophia's advance. She was tempestuous, this one—half Fox and half Wolf. Or perhaps half Fox and half Crow. Her strategy was certainly clever enough; it was also dangerous, fueled by fear and thoughts of vengeance. Though Grandmother mourned her fellow sisters and wished to see Chang punished, there could be no question that the tribe's best chance of survival was to flee north, as the old Andromède had planned. To continue to fight now was to court total annihilation.

But fight they would. Such was their new chieftain's command. Only the gods knew if she was wise beyond her years or foolish in line with them.

Three tribeswomen had been ordered to stay back and protect Grandmother, but she'd quickly shamed them into leaving her alone by accusing them of cowardice. She watched them ride off toward the city, the sun rising like a flat red stone behind the Anchor skyline, and couldn't help but feel the thrill of the hunt in the air. Perhaps that was a flaw of their people, that hunger for danger, for victory; but perhaps it would also be their salvation.

On a whim, she took up her walking stick and abandoned the otherwise empty encampment, crunching over the dead, gray ash where the missives had prepared the tribe's last meal, and made her way over to the Peretemps River—what the Anchorites called the Tiber. Rain pattered gently on the grassy green banks, falling from a sky of mottled granite. Fat salmon slipped between the rocks, disturbing the minnows. A frog splashed into the water and paddled off with its herky-jerky, illogical limbs. The *otsapah* picked a cattail and let it dangle beside her as she went, drawing lines in the mud. She was just about to head back to camp when she spotted something odd floating toward her. At first she thought it had to be a carcass of some kind—the wrong shape for a person, but perhaps a cow or horse. But as she and the mystery converged, it smoothed out into a metal cylinder, dully reflecting the clouds as it turned over. It stopped with a clang a few hundred feet upstream, caught between a pair of river rocks. White water gushed out from beneath it like a geyser. Grandmother found a place where she could descend to the waterline, though it was treacherous going, and she nearly slipped more than once.

She stepped gingerly across the wet stones that lined the riverbank. "Careful," she said to herself. At her age, and on her own, there were falls she might not get up from.

It was an iron barrel, stenciled on either end with the outline of

TOMMY WALLACH

a book. Though it could have arrived there by accident—rolling off a wagon and into the river, for example—the *otsapah* sensed a purpose in it. The barrel was newly made, the paint freshly applied. The symbol was almost certainly a literal description of the barrel's contents, which made sense; both Sophia and the Descendancy had always been obsessed with books. The *dahor* were so terrified of losing their stories, of forgetting and, by extension, being forgotten. The Wesah kept their stories alive by telling them. Paper burned, disintegrated, faded; memory was the hardier medium by far.

So here was a barrel full of books riding the river like a canoe. In the face of possible extinction, the Anchor was sending its stories out into the world, finally sharing that which it had always insisted on keeping to itself. Grandmother planted her feet in the muddy bank and reached out with her walking stick. The first thrust skittered across the top of the nearer river rock. The second plunged past it into the water. On the third, she drew a sonorous *pong* from the barrel and knocked it free. It landed with a splash and sped off downriver, toward its intended destination.

Or maybe there was no destination, no more intention here than in the cry of a dying animal. Maybe the only hope for this desperate exudation was that someone—an old woman left behind by her sisters because she was no use in a fight, for example—would take notice of it. In the aftermath, if this old woman were still around, she might let people know about the barrel of stories she'd seen in the river. Maybe those people would manage to recover it.

It was even harder getting back up the bank than it had been coming down, but the *otsapah* managed it. She could no longer make out the sun for the clouds, but from the disposition of light, knew it had to be past noon. The Western Gate was wide open, unoccupied but for the corpses of Sophians—the sacrificial lambs of the vanguard. By now, the Protectorate would have retreated to some more defensible position elsewhere in the city. The sounds of battle carried across the plains like a Wesah drumbeat, its rhythm gone feral, unpredictable.

Gunfire like feet crunching on gravel.

Swords and daggers clashing like an iron barrel banging along the rocky bottom of a river.

Screams like curses. Curses like screams.

The end was near. Grandmother would not watch it from a distance. These were her people; this was her fight. She said a quick prayer to Crow, then another to Wolf, then another to Fox. The gods would forgive her fickleness; today the Wesah nation needed all the help it could get. She set her gaze on the Western Gate and began the long, slow walk.

TOMMY WALLACH

Part III
VICTORS

If you live long enough, you'll see
that every victory turns into a defeat.
—*Simone de Beauvoir*, All Men Are Mortal

1. Clover

CLOVER WATCHED THE CENTRAL DESK WHERE BERNSTEIN sat, turning first this way and then that to address the questions of one or another attendant. Kita had left the note with him a few minutes ago, but only now did he pick it up and glance at its contents. An impressive impassivity—he put it down and casually answered another couple of requests before excusing himself and coming to stand over the desk where Clover and Kita were sitting.

"You're sure?" he said, with the bland expression of someone asking after the weather.

Kita nodded. "I know what Blood of the Father smells like. My parents helped to smuggle it into the city a few times."

"I should have guessed," Bernstein said. "Why else would Chang have left so few soldiers? It's not as if they could hold this place against Sophia."

"So what do you think they're waiting for?" Clover asked. "Why haven't they started burning the place down already?"

"I suppose they've been told to wait until they're certain the Library is about to fall into enemy hands."

"How many are there?" said Kita.

Bernstein frowned. "How many soldiers? In the whole building? Twenty. Maybe twenty-five."

"Well, you've got nearly ten times that many attendants! Tell them to fight!"

"Chang's men are armed to the teeth. My fellows don't know one end of a sword from the other."

Clover tried to picture all those attendants, many of them hunched and squinty-eyed from a lifetime spent poring over books, going toe-to-toe with two dozen Protectorate soldiers. He could see the fat leather-bound volumes used as shields, quickly cloven in two with one downward swing of a sword. He could hear all their well-reasoned pleas and propositions cut short by the eloquent rebuttal of a pistol. No, Chang's men could never be convinced to spare the Library. They had no respect for knowledge, no understanding of what it would mean for humanity if all these books were lost.

But perhaps the Sophians were different.

"I have an idea," Clover said. "But it means Kita and I will have to leave."

"So go on, then," Bernstein replied. "I never wanted you up here in the first place."

They sat against the trunk of one of the skeletal apple trees in the Library gardens. Clover had hoped it would shield them from the rain, but the branches only collected the water and delivered it in larger, more irritating drops. There were tiny diamonds in Kita's eyelashes, and he noticed, maybe for the first time, that she really was quite pretty.

"I'm sorry I got you into all this," he said.

TOMMY WALLACH

She smiled, let her head drop onto his shoulder. "I could say the same."

They stayed like that for a while, watching the sun climb through the clouds and waiting for the inevitable to arrive. The sounds of battle came over the wall that separated the Library from the rest of the city, growing louder every minute. At last they appeared at the gates to the Library gardens, filing through three or four abreast. No uniforms or pageantry—just a few hundred of the men and women Zeno had drafted from the towns and villages around Sophia, who believed in her message of progress. Clover scanned their faces. He'd hoped the director herself might lead this division, but no such luck; she knew better than to expose herself to such a dangerous mission.

"I still can't believe you're going to try and talk your way out of this," Kita said.

"Well, I'm a whole lot better at talking than I am at fighting, so I figure it's my best shot." Clover stood up and brushed off his pants. "Stay here, okay? I know you don't usually listen when I ask that, but—"

"Good luck," she said, taking his hand and kissing it.

He walked downhill toward the gates, toward the fifty guns trained on him from the moment the Sophians noticed his approach. One woman came forward to meet him, and they shook hands beneath the eerie, outstretched branches of a squat oak tree. She was perhaps forty years old, her brown hair shot through with gray, and she wore two silver pistols at her waist and a bandolier glistening with brass bullets over her shoulder. Bloodstains spattered her thin leather jacket.

"Is this a parley?" she said with playful threat.

"Something like that," Clover replied.

"Somehow I doubt a boy your age has been tasked with speaking on behalf of the Descendancy."

"I'm speaking on behalf of the Library."

"The Library is the Descendancy."

"Not anymore. Not since Chang."

The wind picked up, whipping rain across the gardens. "Say your piece, child."

Clover took a deep breath. "The Grand Marshal's given orders to destroy the Library if you all try to take it."

"He's not defending it?"

"There are a few soldiers inside, but not enough to hold you back. They're probably watching us right now. If you go any farther, they'll burn the whole thing down."

The woman raised an eyebrow. "You gotta admit, this would be a pretty clever way to try and trick us into turning around."

"It would."

The woman spat, turned to look at her ragtag army. "See those folks there? A whole bunch of 'em just found out that their hometown's been destroyed. That they've got nowhere to go back to. And now you're telling me I should help you preserve whatever's inside this . . . this . . . *castle* here?"

"Whoever wins the war is gonna need what's in that castle. Zeno as much as Chang."

The woman considered for a moment. "Fuck me," she said. Then she wiped her wet hands on her wet trousers and plodded back through the mud toward the other Sophians. Clover retreated to the apple tree where Kita waited.

"Did it work?" she asked.

Clover shrugged. He could see the woman gesticulating, hear her voice as a whisper on the wind. Other voices were raised in response. Faces twisted up in anger. One man shoved another, and it took a dozen people and a couple of warning shots to break up the fight. Shoulders slumped; heads grudgingly nodded. The woman turned to Clover and raised a hand: a valediction. Clover waved back as the army began to retreat. A few minutes later, the last of the Sophians passed back through the gates.

He looked to Kita and smiled. "Not bad, huh?"

"Not bad at—" She was interrupted by the sound of glass shattering. Clover looked up just in time to see a body plummet from one of the Library's highest windows and land with an audible crack in some interior courtyard; through the broken glass, he could make out the flicker of fire.

Too late. All for nothing. They sprinted back to the Library and once again took the Innocent Steps up to the fifth floor, tearing down the hallway and through the Rotunda doors.

The tranquil reading room that they'd left scarcely twenty minutes ago was now like an image out of the most harrowing chapters of the Filia's Book of Ivan. The walls of books were all alight, along with most of the desks and tables; flaming pages flapped around the room like phoenixes, setting new fires wherever they landed. Corpses littered the floor, and some of those were on fire as well; the smell of cooked meat was subtle but undeniable. Though the soldiers had abandoned their guns for fear of friendly fire, they still had their swords, and while those attendants still standing fought tooth and nail, they were hopelessly outclassed.

Clover scanned the room for Bernstein, praying the old man wasn't among the fallen.

"Look out!" Kita cried.

He reacted just fast enough to dodge a graceless, plunging sword strike and turned to face the soldier who'd snuck up behind him. A boy about Clive's age, holding his sword with both hands— he feinted a couple of times, laughing at his opponent's seeming helplessness. Meanwhile, just behind him, Kita was lighting a broken chair leg off one of the many local fires. All she had to do was touch it to the soldier's uniform to send him screaming, swinging his sword at the air.

There was no time to celebrate. Clover had just spotted Bernstein and a couple of attendants struggling to pull a large bookshelf away from the wall.

"What happened?" Clover shouted over the clamor. "I talked to the Sophians! They were going to leave us be!"

"As soon as the guards heard those gunshots outside, they made their move," Bernstein shouted back. The bookshelf fell forward, landing in a shower of sparks and ash and revealing the secret door behind it. Bernstein pulled it open and gestured the closest attendants through.

"What's in there?" Clover said.

"A way out," Bernstein said.

"You don't have to tell me twice!" Kita said, and dashed through the doorway. She was quickly followed by another few attendants.

"We have to put the fire out!" Clover said.

"Absolutely," Bernstein replied. "We'll find a way once we're out of here. Go on!"

TOMMY WALLACH

"But that doesn't make any sense. How can we put out the fire if—"

The old man wasn't particularly strong, but he caught Clover by surprise, shoving him backward through the doorway. A large attendant came in just behind, knocking Clover off balance, and by the time he found his feet again, the door had already slammed shut. He ran to it, pounding on the wood.

"Bernstein! What are you doing?"

Kita pulled at his jacket. "Clover, come on. He's giving us time to get away."

Clover shook her off, placing his ear against the door, as if he might discern some word of farewell, of consolation—but there was nothing.

He couldn't remember exactly what happened after that. Flashes of room after room full of fire. The smell of burnt paper, burnt fabric, burnt flesh. In one hallway, the surreal image of a man wreathed in flames sprinting as fast as he could away from them, toward some imaginary succor. The very stones seemed to weep heat; strata of smoke stretched from ceiling to floor. A couple of older attendants went down on their knees coughing and never got up again. At last they found a stairwell, but it became impassable two floors down, masonry toppled where the wooden ribs of the building had given way, so they had to find another route downward through the labyrinth, led by blackened and bloody attendants whose tear tracks were visible through the soot on their cheeks. Time passed—a minute? An hour?—and then they were suddenly free, having escaped through some side door Clover hadn't even known existed, which opened onto the portion of the garden where herbs and vegetables were grown. The rain was still falling, but not nearly heavily enough to slow the fire, which could now be seen blazing in dozens of windows up and down the Library's facade. They stood and watched—Clover, Kita, and those attendants who'd survived the massacre in the Rotunda—as the collected knowledge of the centuries turned to cinders.

Eventually they stumbled on, back through the gardens, through the ash falling like snow all around them, and out through the gates.

Kita screamed, reared like a spooked horse. Before them stood a pile of at least two hundred human bodies. Clover recognized the face of the Sophian woman who'd convinced her fellow soldiers to leave the Library in peace. She was near the bottom of the pile, eyes wide, an arrow through her neck.

Something moved at the end of a nearby alleyway. Then several somethings.

Clover pulled Kita close. "Who's there?" he said.

2. Paz

DANIEL HAMILL'S LAUGHTER DEVOLVED INTO A BREATH-less coughing fit. He spat blood into the dirt. "You shouldn't have come here."

"We had to," Clive said quietly. "Chang has Flora."

"I saw her." Cough. "Wouldn't say a word to me." Cough. "Or to anyone."

Paz couldn't believe Daniel was still alive. It had been days since he'd been shot. Chang must have given him some measure of medical attention—though it looked as if the efficacy of those treatments had reached its limit. But why not just let him die? "What does Chang want with you?" she said.

"Information. He wants to know if Zeno has any other tricks up her sleeves."

"Does she?"

Daniel smiled a mouthful of red-rimmed teeth—fresh blood. "Always."

"You didn't tell him anything?" Clive asked.

"Not a word. I imagine that's why he told you to come here. He thought I might break if I had to watch him torture you."

"Would you have?"

Daniel hesitated, hedged. "It doesn't matter now. You took too long to get here. Chang's not coming back. He's gone to make his stand. Gone to . . . to . . . ." His eyes fluttered, rolled back in his head.

"Da!" Clive said.

But Daniel was out cold; his chest quivered disturbingly with every breath.

"We have to get him out of here," Clive said. "You keep a lookout, and I'll try to find something I can use to—"

"Clive," Paz interrupted, "you see how he is. Even if we . . . he won't . . . ." She trailed off, unable to bring herself to finish the thought.

"I know," Clive whispered. "Of course I know. But not here, okay? Not chained up in the dark."

Paz thought of her own father, cut down outside Riley's pumphouse. Was there anything she wouldn't have done to make his final moments a little easier? To say a proper good-bye? "Fine. But we have to move fast."

Daniel's chains were affixed to metal hooks sunk deep into the stone wall behind him. There was no hope of breaking the thick iron links, but maybe the hooks themselves could be pried out— with the right tool.

"Sometimes it feels as if all I've done for the past year is escape from places," Paz said, running her hand along one of the crudely mortared walls. "I'm beginning to feel like a prisoner who keeps breaking out of her cell only to end up in the cell next door." A pointed jag of granite wobbled under her hand like a loose tooth; she pulled at it once, twice, and on the third tug it came free. "This might work," she said.

She positioned herself above the hook securing the shackle

attached to Daniel's right leg and began hammering away. It came loose after only a few dozen blows. She immediately moved on to the next hook while Clive finished pulling the first one free.

"You're the Sophian girl." Daniel had woken again at the sound of stone on metal. "The one who followed us from Wilmington."

"That's right."

"I wish I'd known back then that you were on the right side of things. I could've saved Emma. I could've saved everyone."

"I wasn't on the right side of things," Paz said. "There is no right side of things." The second hook came away from the wall in an explosion of stone dust.

"Tell that to the Wesah that Chang slaughtered. Tell that to the men Epistem Turin forced to live underground, developing weapons in secret. Tell that to all the . . ."

He kept on talking, but Paz stopped listening, choosing instead to focus on the task at hand. The chains binding Daniel's arms were affixed to the wall about six feet off the ground, which meant she couldn't get nearly the same leverage on them as on the ones that had been attached to his fetters. She struck at the left hook a hundred times to no effect—other than the sensation that her arms were about to fall off. Clive took over after that, but made no more progress than she had.

"It's no use," he said.

"No use," Daniel repeated, though it wasn't clear if he even knew what was happening.

"Maybe we can pull out the whole block," Paz said. She took the jagged rock back from Clive and went at the mortar around the stone that the hook was attached to. It turned out to be even more degraded than she'd expected—probably on account of the year-round damp down here—coming away in fat flakes at every blow. It took the two of them working together nearly an hour to chip off the mortar and shimmy the two stones out of the wall. They immediately set to work on the second block, which came loose slightly faster. When they were done, Daniel was left manacled to a good fifteen-pound weight at the end of either chain—but at least he was free.

They each took one of the stones and then shimmied under Daniel's arms, half-carrying him out of the shed. He radiated the heat of infection but shivered as if he were freezing; Paz nearly retched at the smell. The coast was clear outside, though a few soldiers could be seen through the glassless windows of the church a few hundred feet off.

They made their way back to the passage that led to the city sewers, but were pulled up short by the sound of voices—distant, but definitely coming toward them.

"Who's there?" Daniel said, fading in and out of consciousness. "Is that . . . who is that?"

"Quiet," Paz said. Then, to Clive, "What now?"

They looked out over the Old Temple. There were at least a dozen tunnels out of the chamber, but only a few had been fitted with electric lights, signaling them as the most likely to lead back to the surface. Paz gestured with her head toward the closest one, and Clive nodded his agreement. Luck was once again on their side, and they made it around the chamber without being spotted. Paz sniffed the air outside the passage, hoping for a hint of fresh air, but could smell nothing over the miasma emanating from Daniel. The narrow corridor began to slope almost imperceptibly downhill—a bad sign for its potential as an avenue of escape—meanwhile aggregating the secretions of the city overhead in a rivulet that ran slow as molasses alongside them. The three of them were hardly moving much faster; Daniel continued to fade, which meant she and Clive had to shoulder even more of his weight—along with the stones attached to his wrists.

"I didn't tell them anything," Daniel said. "Let Ariel know I didn't say a word."

Ariel—strange to think of Director Zeno having a first name, or having some kind of relationship with Clive's father. "Is there anything left to tell?" Paz said.

"I know what's coming." He made a sound that was either a laugh or a cough. "It'll be here soon."

"What will?"

"You don't hear it?" This thought seemed genuinely upsetting to him. "It's so loud." He looked up at the slick ceiling of the tunnel, as if he might see the sky. "Loud as thunder."

"What's loud as thunder?" Paz pressed.

"He's feverish," Clive said. "He doesn't know what he's saying."

Daniel's breath was acrid, decaying. "The angels," he said. "The avenging angels."

And now Paz did hear something, only it wasn't thunder: footsteps, echoing along the corridor behind them. Perhaps they'd been seen coming out of the shed after all, or else Daniel's disappearance had been clocked. It felt like some kind of existential joke when the corridor chose that exact moment to fork—two paths curving symmetrically away in either direction. Paz looked to Clive, who shrugged: same difference. They chose the right one and sped up as much as they could manage.

"There's something up ahead," Clive whispered.

A chain-link gate secured with a padlock prevented access to a large opening in the right-hand wall of the tunnel. Paz could hear the sound of rushing water on the other side. "It's the aqueduct," she said. "It would take us right into the Tiber, if we could get to it."

The rivulet at their feet joined up with one coming from the other direction and emptied into the aqueduct.

"The annulus," Daniel said. "We're inside the annulus."

Paz's heart dropped as she realized what he meant. In front of them, the tunnel kept on curving; they were in a loop, just like the annulus. The footsteps of their pursuers came from both directions at once, like something out of a nightmare. Though it hardly made a difference now, somehow continuing on the way they were going felt safer than turning back. They tried to move silently, but the tunnel was like the brass bloom atop Zeno's phonograph, amplifying every little click and scrape of their boots. Light flickered in the distance—a lantern. They turned around and headed back the other way, but ended up facing the same thing a few minutes later; the soldiers had divided themselves up between the two forks, a classic pincer maneuver. Paz and Clive, now practically dragging Daniel between them, retreated to the place where the tunnel fed into the aqueduct. Paz rattled the gate, not caring how much noise she made anymore. The footsteps reverberating through the tunnel quickened—the soldiers smelled blood.

"Clive," Daniel said urgently, placing his hands on his son's

TOMMY WALLACH

cheeks, "I was so wrong. My whole life I was wrong. And you—" He choked up, set himself to coughing again. "I let you down."

"You did your best," Clive said.

From somewhere farther along the tunnel, a soldier called out: "Whoever's there, lay down your weapons and put your hands on your heads!"

"Step back," Daniel whispered.

"It's over, Da," Clive said. "They've got us."

"I said step *back*!"

Suddenly Daniel pushed both of them away, hard enough that they dropped the stones they'd been carrying for him.

A lantern burst into view: the first group of soldiers. "Don't move!" one of them yelled.

Daniel closed his eyes and began to growl; the growl became a roar as he lifted the stones by their chains. With a bloodcurdling scream, he slammed both of them into the padlock on the gate. The second group of soldiers arrived. Guns were cocked. A black bloom had begun to spread across Daniel's shirt—his injuries reopened. He emitted an unearthly, inhuman noise as he raised the stones again. There was a sound like skin splitting, like ribs cracking, and this time when the stones met the padlock, it broke open.

"Go," he rasped.

Paz pulled off the padlock and pushed through the gate, clinging onto the chain links as she swung over the aqueduct.

"Clive!" she said. "Come on!"

She watched the two men regard each other in the flickering torch light. Both of them knew that Daniel wouldn't be coming with them; he could never stay afloat with those stones attached to his wrists.

"Good-bye, Da," Clive said, ducking through the gate as the first shots rang out and Daniel twisted up, somehow not blown off his feet right away, as if in these last moments he'd become invincible. Paz let go of the gate and fell backward into the aqueduct, trusting it to take her somewhere better than here.

3. Athène

THERE WAS A KIND OF LIBERATION TO BE FOUND IN moving through the world as a pure predator. The Wesah had no allies in the Anchor, nothing that should inspire their pity or humanity. If it moved, you put an arrow through it. If it survived—or if you missed, but you did not miss—you stalked it to its hiding place and finished it off with your knives.

There were some who'd refused to enter the city at the last moment, either out of cowardice or conscience. Athène had allowed these "objectors" to retreat to the Villenaître, with the understanding that they were sacrificing their eligibility ever to be either chieftains or mothers. In the end, she was left with what she'd guess was slightly less than thirty-five hundred warriors. A paltry number next to the armies of the Anchor and Sophia, but if all went well, it might just be enough. Once inside the Anchor, she divided her warriors up into ten *naasyoon*—Wesah always hunted best in smaller groups—and directed each one down a different road. The warriors rode off screaming through the rain, hair slicked back, knives out. Athène's heart swelled with pride at the thought of the terror they would inspire.

"Where should we go?" asked Nephra. By rights, the woman

should've been leading her own *naasyoon*, but Athène needed someone to act as her counselor.

"Wherever blood is most likely to be spilled." Athène spun a slow circle, taking in the small plaza just inside the Southern Gate. Bodies were strewn everywhere, the bloodstains already washing away in the rain—Protectorate soldiers mostly, killed trying to hold the gate against the Sophians. In the silvery early-morning light that filtered through the clouds, they looked posed, almost peaceful, like a bunch of children's dolls arranged just so.

The warriors Athène had kept with her gazed about at the fruits of the Descendancy's ingenuity—filigreed metalwork around clear glass windows, the scalloped iron bases of the gas lamps, the cobblestone roads like so many elaborate beaded necklaces. A crow cawed, then flew off at the sound of gunfire. What good were signs you couldn't interpret?

"Have you been to the Anchor before, Nephra?" Athène asked.

"When I was very young. My *naasyoon* brought furs to trade. Relations were different then. We came and went from the city as we pleased."

"What changed?"

"Perhaps we were too aggressive in our recruitment. But we could have come to an understanding if the Descendancy had been willing to negotiate. Instead they began killing us on sight."

So there was plenty of blame to go around, it seemed. There usually was. "This is a war between knowledge and faith, yes?"

"False faith," Nephra corrected.

"Even so. I know of a place in the city where knowledge and faith join together. I learned of it while I was a prisoner of Chang's

TOMMY WALLACH

hospitality. There is bound to be some blood shed over it."

"And what will we do there?"

"Shed more, of course."

The Library was tucked away behind its own wall, like an Anchor inside the Anchor. It bloomed vociferously, chaotically, a mish-mash of incongruous additions made at various times over the centuries—if Athène's memory of Gardener's *Anchor History* served. Turrets rose from turrets, as if the various corners of the building were competing to see which could reach closest to the heavens. Windows were few and far between, mostly high up on the facade to keep any unwelcome eyes from seeing inside.

A lone soldier stood outside the cracked gates that opened onto the gardens beneath the Library. Though soaking wet from the rain, he'd managed to light a drooping cigarillo that hung from his bottom lip. It fell when the arrow pierced his heart, landing in a puddle at his feet with a tiny hiss.

"Hold!" Athène shouted to the *naasyoon*. She approached the gates and peeked through the crack between them. A few hundred people were congregated about a quarter mile away, across an autumnal collage of fallen leaves and naked trees. They had plenty of guns but no uniforms, which meant they were Sophians. They must have come here to take the Library, yet it was clear that the assault had yet to commence—which made it all the more surprising when they turned away from the building and began walking back across the gardens.

"Position the bulk of our warriors out of sight down these alleys and put our best archers on the rooftops," Athène said to Nephra.

"Tell them not to strike until every Sophian has come out of those gates."

Nephra frowned. "But they are unprepared. They do not even know we have named them our enemies."

"So?"

"So what honor can there be in—"

"This is the only way we survive," Athène interrupted. "If there's no honor in this, then there is no honor in anything but dying. Now do as I commanded."

"Yes, Andromède."

When the entire *naasyoon* was hidden, Athène climbed up the side of one of the buildings herself, vaulting from a rubbish bin to a balcony, then clambering across some diabolically slippery terracotta tiles to reach the apex of the peaked roof. From this vantage, she could see out over a large portion of the city. She counted eleven columns of smoke whose source fires were powerful enough to withstand the rain; Zeno was certainly making her presence felt.

The company of Sophian soldiers began to stream through the gate a few minutes later. When they'd all reached the other side, a woman who was clearly their leader climbed up onto an old apple crate and began to speak.

"I understand that a lot of you aren't happy with this decision, but it was mine to make, and I'll take the blame if it comes to that. Now, Zeno said we should converge on Notre Fille once we'd finished here, so that's where . . . what is it?"

The woman had noticed that some of her fellow soldiers were pointing back up at the Library, and soon the entire Sophian contingent had turned to look: one of the turrets had just caught flame.

TOMMY WALLACH

Squinting, Athène could make out an orange flicker behind many of the windows. A black halo of smoke was beginning to form around the topmost spires.

The confused murmuring of the Sophians made it clear they were surprised by the fire; but if they hadn't caused it, who had?

Athène drew her bow and nocked an arrow. Perhaps someone would be alive at the end of this who could answer that question. Or perhaps not. She blinked rainwater from her eyes, then gave a single sharp bark.

From every conceivable angle flew the slim brown bolts. There was no need even to aim; the Sophians were congregated so densely around the gate that a third of them were incapacitated or killed within the first few seconds. They drew their guns and began firing back, a thunderous fusillade that shattered windows and cracked stone but failed to slow the hail of arrows plunging into belly and chest. The Sophians scattered, breaking for cover. Athène picked off two of them before noticing a few of her warriors were pinned down in an alley just beneath her, crouched behind an empty vendor's stall. A group of Sophians had armed themselves with a piece of metal grating they'd pulled off the Library gatehouse and were slowly encroaching on the stall; the holes in the lattice were just large enough to fit the barrel of a pistol, but too small to admit a Wesah arrowhead.

Athène waited until they were almost directly beneath her, then gritted her teeth and rode the smooth soles of her moccasins down the steep roof. The Sophians saw her flying through the air and responded just as she'd hoped—by angling the grating upward, giving her a nearly flat surface to land on and forcing all of them to the ground. She had both her daggers out, and though she could only get an inch or so of the blades through the grating, that was more than enough. The Sophians screamed as she stabbed out again and again, blood gushing up everywhere, like a ship beginning to founder. Though many of them were badly wounded, they eventually found the presence of mind to push the grate away. Athène held on as it tilted back up to vertical, finding her feet at the same moment she found herself looking down the barrel of a gun.

"I have daughter," she said in English. "Please!"

"I've got three kids," said the Sophian woman holding the gun. "So fuck you."

Athène braced herself for the shot, but before it could come, the warriors who'd been crouched behind the vendor's stall leaped up and threw themselves at the grating, sending the whole thing down to the cobblestones again. She went along with it, still holding tight to the lattice, and screamed as her right index finger was crushed between the grate and the shinbone of one of the men trapped beneath it. The warriors made short work of the helpless Sophians, but by the time Athène was able to extricate herself, her finger was mangled beyond recognition, a shaft of red, molten pain; she would never use a bow and arrow again.

The square was silent now but for the falling rain. Athène ordered the *naasyoon* to pile up the Sophian bodies while she cut a strip of cloth from a corpse's shirt to wrap her finger. The cracks between the cobblestones were full of blood. The pile reached halfway up the garden wall.

"Andromède," Nephra said, "we've just seen more people com-

TOMMY WALLACH

ing out of the Library. Not Sophians this time. They'll be here any moment."

"How many sisters did we lose?"

"Forty, forty-five. Maybe more."

"Then we can still fight. Order everyone back into position."

The *naasyoon* once again made itself invisible. Athène remained at street level this time, watching from behind a carriage at the side of the road as the gates slowly swung open.

Frizzy black hair, dark skin coated with a thin layer of ash, brown eyes cracked with red and heavy with sadness. *The smartest person I've ever known*, Gemma used to say. But Clover Hamill didn't look so smart today; he looked devastated, defeated. Athène hadn't seen him since the day she'd first met Gemma, but she felt as if she was about to reunite with an old friend; Gemma had loved him like a brother. Behind him came a young woman and a dozen men in blue robes, all of them singed to a greater or lesser degree. They didn't appear to have a single weapon between them, unless one counted the titanic volumes that a few of them held to their chests like talismans.

"Hold!" Athène shouted, stepping out of cover.

Clover blinked hard, as if he couldn't believe his own eyes. "It's you, isn't it? Athène?" He spoke in a surprisingly fluent and unaccented Wesah.

"In the flesh," she replied, also in Wesah. She felt the strange urge to embrace him, as you would anything so long-lost, yet she demurred. "Tell your friends from the Library to flee the city now, or they'll end up like these Sophians."

Clover relayed the message and the attendants quickly scurried off along the Ring Road. The young woman stayed at Clover's side—a romantic partner of some sort, if the baleful expression she cast at Athène was anything to go by: *you'll have to go through me first.*

Clover gestured toward the pile of bodies. "I guess you killed them?"

"Yes."

She could see his mind working, trying to make sense of things. "You're helping Chang?"

"Not anymore."

"But you did."

"I did what I had to, so that the two sides would be evenly matched."

"Why?"

"Have you ever seen two wolves fight?"

"No."

"When two wolves fight, it doesn't mean either one will win. Sometimes it is only a question of which dies first. Then it is the crow and the vulture who win."

Clover nodded his understanding. "So where are you going now?"

"To the church at the center of the city. I think it is where all of this will end. Would you like to come?"

Clover looked surprised. "You'd have us?"

Athène shrugged. "How do you say it"—and switching to English, tried on the platitude—"the more the merrier?"

Clover started to smile, then abruptly stopped. "Do you hear that?" He looked up at the sky, and Athène realized that many of her warriors were already doing the same. There was a humming sound, obscured by the patter of raindrops on brick and stone but growing a little more distinct every second. A beam of light cut through the clouds. Then another. And another.

"She has more planes!" Clover said. "Find cover!"

The bombs began to drop through the rain-streaked sky. Athène ran.

4. Clive

A SHOCK OF COLD LIKE SOMEONE SLAPPING EVERY inch of your skin at the same time. The afterimage of a man torn apart by bullets, contorting as if enacting some morbid, primitive dance. Clive swallowed what felt like an icicle, daggering down from his throat to his belly. The water ran fast here, channeled by the aqueduct and amplified by the downpour, and it wasn't long before they emerged into the light, dumped into the Tiber at the northern edge of Portland Park. Clive caught sight of Paz's head bobbing a dozen feet in front of him. He could hear gunfire ricocheting across the city like so many cracks of lightning, and beneath it, something new but familiar. A hum, like someone bowing a single note on the double bass: Zeno's airplane had somehow returned from the dead.

Entranced by this martial music, he drifted into the wall of the aqueduct, smashing his knee hard enough to jolt him back to reality. From the angle of the light, he could tell it was a few hours past noon. Usually the park would be busy around this time, but not today. No proud new parents strolled along the river pushing a carriage. No furtive lovers tiptoed down the bowered paths of the Maple Garden. Clive swam with the current and caught up with Paz. Together they made their way over to the grassy bank and hauled themselves out of the water. The cold, which adrenaline had kept at bay until now, set Clive's whole body to shaking. Paz's teeth were chattering so hard he thought they might just shiver to pieces.

"We gotta get warm," he said. "Come on."

They stood up and started walking. A bridge painted white and gold leapfrogged to a small island in the middle of the river, then another carried them over to the eastern side, where they passed a family carrying their belongings in tied-off sheets flung over their shoulders. Clive guessed a lot of people had abandoned the city since Zeno's forces had arrived.

"Where did you live?" Clive called out after them, and was surprised when anyone bothered to answer.

"Thirteen Quernmore Road!" cried a girl no older than Flora.

She was roundly shushed by her pretty older sister, but too late. Quernmore was close. They left the park and reentered the city proper, immediately passing a barricade that told an efficient and tragic story without words: the slow advance of the enemy, the heroic last stand, the corpses with their empty holsters and glazed eyes. The door of 13 Quernmore was locked but gave way with a couple of kicks, revealing a leatherworker's shop on the ground floor and an apartment above it. The hearth fire upstairs had only just been extinguished, and the few small, sordid rooms were blissfully warm. Clive tore some pages from the Filia on the mantle and used them to get the fire going again. Then he and Paz stripped down and laid their sopping clothes just in front of the grate.

Naked, they searched the apartment. The closets and dressers in the bedrooms had been emptied out but for a pair of socks in need of darning and a scrap of black silk. In the kitchen larder, however, they found a huge jar of pickles and a pot of strawberry preserves. They brought this bounty back to the fire and set to it.

"It's funny," Clive said, though it was anything but. "I thought he was dead for so long—I don't even know how to feel now that he's really gone."

"He did the right thing, in the end," Paz said. "I mean, what a father ought to."

"Yeah."

They were silent for a moment, and in that silence Clive heard the rat-a-tat of Chang's guns atop Notre Fille. "Zeno has another plane. Or maybe more than one."

"Chang was ready for it, though," Paz said. "Why else would he have moved all his soldiers underground?" She crunched into a pickle. "So what do we do now? How do we find Flora?"

"I don't know. I guess we just have to hope she's still with Chang."

"And where is he?"

"I don't know that, either. He could be anywhere."

Paz ran her index finger along the bottom of the jam jar, sucking the last globule from her empurpled knuckle. "We're coming up on the end here. Chang's gonna have to be where the action is."

"And just where is that?"

Paz pointed out the window, toward the gnarled finger of Notre Fille. "Where else?"

Their clothes weren't entirely dry when they put them on again, but they'd delayed long enough. Back on the streets, they passed at least a dozen families packed for travel, including one riding in a wagon being pulled by two desperate-looking milk cows. He and

Paz didn't speak much, as it was nearly impossible to hear anything over the whine of the plane engines, the occasional deafening reports of their payloads, the vicious tattoo of Chang's antiaircraft guns, the clash and cry of soldier-to-soldier combat, and the crackle of innumerable fires pulling buildings down all around their ears. Here was the second coming of the Daughter, the Flame Deluge, the apocalypse. Here were the fruits of war.

They made it to Annunciation Square. At least five thousand people were congregated in front of Notre Fille—the bulk, if not the entirety, of the Sophian army. Clive imagined they'd been ordered to gather here so the planes would be free to bomb the rest of the city with impunity—and to try to take the church, of course, which would be an enormous symbolic victory for Zeno. The Sophians, however, were having some difficulty getting in: the doors appeared to have been reinforced somehow from the inside.

"Chang has to be in there," Clive said.

"Great," Paz replied. "So how do we get to him?"

Clive had spent a fair portion of his childhood coming and going from Notre Fille; his secondary school education had been carried out on the building's third floor—a kind of pre-seminary that privileged Filial study above every other sphere of knowledge; he rued all that wasted time now. "A lot of the buildings around the square are offices of the Descendant Church. There are passages connecting them to Notre Fille, so all those old men don't have to trudge through the snow in the winter."

"How civilized."

"The closest entrance is over there." Clive pointed at one of the four-story townhouses on the west side of the square. It was known as the SLO, or Sudamiran Liaison Office—the organization that arranged the Church's official missionary ventures to the dark continent. Clive's father had considered spending a year down there spreading the word of the Daughter, before his wife had unilaterally quashed the notion.

The sun was beginning to set, but the storm was only growing stronger. Behind the scaffold laddering up Notre Fille's eastern facade, the canvas flapped loudly, briefly exposing fragments of the church's innards. Clive felt equally exposed walking around the edge of Annunciation Square, but no one seemed to notice them.

"Look," Paz said, gesturing toward the southern entrance to the square. One of the big guns that Zeno had used to keep the Anchorites trapped in the city was being rolled slowly down the Green Road on a flatbed wagon. Maybe the Sophians were hoping to blow their way through the front doors of Notre Fille, or else they planned to use it on Chang's army—if said army ever showed up. Clive felt strangely disconnected from all of it, as if the battle had already been decided and this was merely a reconstruction. All that really mattered to him now was finding Flora and getting her out of the city.

The door to the SLO was locked, and though the windows on the ground floor were all covered with elaborate bronze grates, Clive was able to use them to climb up to a second-floor balcony, where the windows were unprotected. Just as he'd done at the Delancey warehouse, he took off his jacket and wrapped it around his fist so he could punch through the glass and unlatch the window from the inside. Pulling Paz up onto the balcony after him, he noticed a group of Sophians coming toward them from across the square, guns drawn.

"And I thought we were being so subtle," Paz said.

"Nothing we can do about it now. Come on."

The sounds of war diminished as they took the stairs back down to the ground floor of the SLO, dying out completely as they descended to the basement, which was packed to the ceiling with crates of Sudamiran wine. The entrance to the underground passageway was half-hidden behind a rack of dusty green bottles. As they were pushing it aside, the whole thing collapsed; a good fifty magnums shattered on the concrete floor, causing a minor flood and filling the air with the heady scent of fruit and ferment. The wine poured down the steps and along the passageway, keeping pace beside them like a pet snake. There was less and less light as they went, until it became so dark that Clive had to test each step with a little kick into the void. The smell of the wine faded and was replaced with the usual subterranean dankness—at least it was easier on the nostrils than the sewers had been. After a few minutes, his kick met resistance: a door. He cast about for the handle and breathed a sigh of relief when it turned.

They found themselves on one of the floors of Notre Fille where the Honors kept their offices. There was a bit more light here, directed through narrow shafts artfully built into the ceiling, but it would be gone when the sun finished setting.

"Which way are the stairs?" Paz said.

But Clive was already moving in the opposite direction; his father's office was just down the hall. Unfamiliar at first glance—it took him a moment to realize that some other Honor must have moved in months ago. More surprising, however, was the fact that this interloper had chosen to keep some of the preexisting decoration, including the sword mounted behind the desk. It had been a gift from the mayor of an outerlands town called Tyreal just after its incorporation, which Daniel Hamill had overseen.

Clive slid the sword out of its scabbard. It had never been used, and though the blade was blunt, the point was keen enough—it was better than nothing, anyway. He looped the scabbard through his belt and re-sheathed the weapon.

They took the western stairway, hoping to climb it all the way to the top of Notre Fille, where Chang was most likely to have set up shop. But the stairwell had been purposely blocked off with an impassable barricade just a few steps past the ground floor, and the only available door led directly into the nave of Notre Fille. The chamber lay empty, eerily lit by a dozen braziers making wavering shadows on the stone walls. There was an enormous hole in the ceiling where the bell tower must have fallen through. It had been roughly patched with wooden planks and canvas, but not well enough to stop a steady stalactitic stream of rainwater from drumming on the marble floor. The tower itself had long since been cleared away, the crushed pews replaced with new ones; if not for the great dripping fissure overhead and the shattered tiles underfoot, one might not even know the church had ever been bombed.

Clive glanced at the Dubium, its curtains pulled tight.

"If I had to recite my sins now," Paz whispered, "I'd be in there for a week."

"You and me both."

They passed out of the nave and into the church's massive narthex. The ceilings here were just as high as in the nave itself, a

TOMMY WALLACH

good hundred feet to the frescoed dome, but Clive's attention was immediately drawn to the front doors. A grid of iron bars had been driven deep into the stonework all around the frame; even if their guns ripped the doors themselves to pieces, the Sophians wouldn't be getting in here anytime soon. Paz immediately made for the grand main staircase, which led up to the church's balcony seating and on to the offices and meeting halls on the higher floors, but Clive grabbed her wrist and held her back.

"It's too exposed."

"Is there another staircase?"

"Yeah, on the other side of the building. Unless it was destroyed in the bombing."

They jogged across the narthex, but all the doors leading into the east wing were bolted.

"I guess that's that," Clive said.

"What if we tried—"

But Paz's question was interrupted by a far more pressing one: what to do about the five Sophians who'd followed them through the tunnel and had just now emerged from the nave.

"Don't move!" shouted an older man holding an oversize pistol. "Hands up and walk slowly over to me!"

"Don't do it," Paz said under her breath. "Make them come to us."

"Why?" Clive said.

"Just trust me."

"Hello?" the Sophian man said. "Are you two deaf or something?"

When it was clear neither Clive nor Paz had any intention of obeying his order, the man conferred briefly with his companions.

They began a wary crossing of the cavernous chamber, guns drawn. When they were perfectly centered in front of the doors, Paz called out.

"You should stop there," she said.

"Why would we do that?" one of the Sophians replied.

"Because some of the tiles are traps. You come any closer and you're like to lose a leg."

A few of the Sophians began looking around nervously, but the older man only laughed. "You expect us to believe that? This is marble." He stomped on the floor for emphasis. "Probably a foot thick. There's nothing you could put in here . . ." He trailed off, some part of his consciousness registering a shift in the ambient sound that bled through the front doors from Annunciation Square—a subtle presage of something extremely unsubtle. The first bullets ripped into the wood a moment later, sending splinters flying through the spaces between the bars. Plaster dust exploded from the stairs and walls. A sculpture of Noach lost an arm. Most of the Sophians made the mistake of trying to run instead of ducking; they immediately took a dozen bullets between them. Only the older man, standing a few steps ahead of the others, had the good sense to dive forward. The fusillade lasted for about thirty seconds, and when it was done, the last rays of sunlight shone through a thousand ragged gaps in the doors. The sole surviving Sophian, spattered with the blood of his compatriots, had his gun trained on Paz's forehead.

"I knew you were fucking with me," he said. "And now I'm gonna fuck with—"

A deafening crack opened a hole just above the man's nose, something obscenely intimate leaking down around his lips and pooling on the marble. Clive traced the angle of the shot backward to find the Grand Marshal Ruzo Chang standing on the landing of the stairway. Beside him, holding the smoking gun, was Flora.

"Nice shot," Chang said, casually plucking the gun from her hand and using it to beckon to Clive and Paz. "Get a move on, you two. We haven't got much time left."

5. Clover

THIS DOESN'T EVEN FEEL REAL," KITA SAID QUIETLY, AS IF from the depths of a dream.

And maybe they were dreaming; where else but in a nightmare would you find yourself walking through an unending hellscape of fire and smoke; of bombs exploding and masonry tumbling; of arrows twanging out into the rain-rippled darkness, each one representing a life cut short; of seeing everything you knew falling down around your ears and nothing you could do to stop it?

Where were they even? Wandering a city he used to know, only all the landmarks had been scrambled, all reference points lost. It was like trying to read a book with half the words turned upside down. Clover still wasn't sure why Athène had invited him and Kita to travel with her, but he guessed it had something to do with a lingering sense of responsibility toward Gemma. Otherwise, the woman now wearing the mantle of Andromède showed no mercy toward anyone not of the tribe. She and her blood-drunk army of marauders killed indiscriminately, ecstatically. Sometimes it was a cadre of Protectorate soldiers, other times a wayward clutch of Sophians. And sometimes it was a family clearly trying to escape the Anchor, clutching their bags and their babies, their only crime being in the wrong place at the wrong time. The Wesah seemed to care for little now but destruction for destruction's sake, and Clover couldn't imagine a more efficient vector for mayhem than these zealous and pitiless warriors.

About half an hour ago, one of Zeno's planes had finally succumbed to the perpetual barrage from the guns atop Notre Fille, but that still left two to terrorize the skies over the Anchor. Clearly they were landing somewhere just outside the city to refuel and load fresh explosives. How had Zeno transported them from Sophia without anyone knowing? How had she found the time and resources to build them in the first place?

"This way?" Athène said in Wesah.

Clover tried to orient himself, but the stars were hidden behind the storm clouds and he didn't know the street. "Maybe."

Slowly but surely, they were making their way toward the heart of the city: Notre Fille. Everything had an inexorable quality to it now, a sense of predestination. Clover had to remind himself that this was only in his imagination. In reality, almost nothing was determined. The war was poised on a knife-edge; the smallest gust of wind could change the outcome—and here they were standing in a hurricane.

He stepped close to Kita and spoke under his breath, though there were few in Athène's party who could understand them and even fewer who cared what they had to say. "Who do you think should win?"

"Win what?" She raised her eyebrows. "You mean the war? How should I know?"

"I keep trying to choose a side, but maybe it really doesn't make a difference anymore."

"Just because there isn't a simple answer doesn't mean there isn't an answer. Didn't you ever study math? I thought you were supposed to be smart."

"I don't feel smart anymore." Athène, walking a few dozen feet ahead, glanced back at him. Was that solicitude in her eyes, or suspicion? "But you're right. There must be an ideal outcome."

"So what is it?"

"I don't know. But I'm starting to think it doesn't have anything to do with who wins."

"What else could it have to do with other than who wins?"

"*How* they win," he said, and sensed the rightness of it even if he wasn't completely sure what it meant.

At last they reached an area of the city Clover recognized—only a few blocks from Notre Fille. Athène called the *naasyoon* to a halt in front of an old warehouse. A broken padlock swung from the doors, but there was no one inside. Immediately the Wesah began to pile up furniture to make a fire. Clover was still considering the ramifications of his recent epiphany when Nephra, Athène's second-in-command, tapped him on the shoulder.

"Andromède want us," she said. Then, to Kita: "Not you."

"That's rude," Kita said to Nephra's back.

"Get dry if you can," Clover said. "I don't think we'll be staying here long."

"I'll do my best."

Athène was waiting for him and Nephra just outside the warehouse. She'd found a ladder affixed to the side of the building, and though it was missing two rungs and moved in unsettling ways as they climbed, they were able to use it to reach the roof. From there they leapfrogged between the closely spaced buildings until they reached a place where they could see out over Annunciation Square.

Nobody was fighting yet; in fact, as far as Clover could tell, there wasn't a single Protectorate soldier in sight. Thousands of Sophians were arrayed behind one of the big guns Zeno had used to maintain her siege. It had just finished reducing the doors of Notre Fille to splinters, but some kind of iron grating had been constructed behind the wood, so there was still no way to get through.

"This is only one army," Nephra said in Wesah. "Where is the other? Hiding?"

"The Protectorate army is much larger than Sophia's," Athène replied. "They have no reason to hide."

"Chang must have a plan," Clover said, grateful yet again for the uninterrupted weeks he'd spent studying Athène's language. "If the Sophians make it into Notre Fille, it'll only be because he wants them to."

Athène frowned. "Our scouts say they saw many hundreds of Protectorate soldiers going into the church all day. Chang must have blocked off the doors within the last few hours."

"Why?"

"Only he knows," she said, tapping her temple—the only place a secret could ever be truly safe. Clover hadn't noticed before, but her index finger was badly injured, bent at an ugly angle and wrapped in a bloody cloth. Unfortunately, he didn't have the medical know-how to reset the bone.

"Your finger won't heal like that," he said. "It needs to be splinted."

"The *otsapah* can look at it, when the war is over," Nephra said.

But Athène shook her head. "Some wounds aren't meant to heal. It will be my way of remembering all this."

"I think I'd remember it just fine without a broken finger," Clover said, proud to earn even half a smile from the leader of the Wesah nation.

Athène's strategy was predicated on the Protectorate and Sophian forces annihilating each other, so there was nothing for the Wesah to do now but wait. The three of them stayed up on the roof as the sun went down and the square lit up with torches, by whose light they could track the slow progress of a large log floating through the crowd as if down a river on the way to the mill; ostensibly the Sophians planned to use it to batter down the grate. Clover realized he hadn't heard Zeno's planes in over an hour. Perhaps she'd deemed the skies unsafe; the rain was coming down harder than ever now, a downpour that dominated the senses—muffling sound, blurring vision, washing even the smells of sulfur and cordite from the air.

The log finally reached the church, where it was fitted into an apparatus that appeared to have been repurposed from the gallows that had nearly been the site of Clive's execution. Clover wondered where his brother and Paz were now. He hoped they'd escaped the city safely with Flora, rather than tried to do something heroic—but somehow he doubted it. Clive had never been one for sitting on the sidelines, and Paz was even worse. Not that Clover was anyone to talk; it seemed none of them had ever learned the art of walking away from a losing hand.

He was jolted out of his reverie by the sound of the battering ram colliding with the iron bars behind the bullet-riddled doors of

TOMMY WALLACH

Notre Fille. After about a dozen blows, a cheer went up from the crowd; though Clover couldn't see it through the rain, the grate must have given way. The Sophian army began to stream into the church.

Clover was struggling to understand why Chang was letting the battle play out this way. The Protectorate's numbers advantage could only be brought to bear on a relatively open battlefield; in the close quarters of Notre Fille, manpower would be far less important than firepower, and though Chang had manufactured an impressive arsenal in a short span of time, his soldiers still weren't particularly well-trained in gunplay.

"We're missing something," Clover said to Athène.

"Like what?"

"Like . . . like . . ." He trailed off as a white eye opened on a nearby rooftop, followed by another one across Annunciation Square: two enormous floodlights illuminating the stupefied faces of those soldiers who'd yet to enter the church. A moment later, the facades of several buildings simply fell away like sloughed skin—a marvel of engineering that Clover guessed involved a great number of small explosives—revealing guns even larger than the one the Sophians had brought to bear on Notre Fille. The air filled with the rat-a-tat of their rotating barrels, all pointed inward at the corralled Sophians. Simultaneously, Protectorate soldiers began pulling themselves up from the black holes of sewer grates along the roads that fed into the square, blocking off any avenue of escape other than the church itself. Here was Chang's masterstroke; he'd made sure the Sophians had seen his soldiers entering Notre Fille throughout the day, then used the underground tunnels to bring his men into the sewers and back around again. The Sophians thought they were surrounding, but ended up surrounded. They returned fire on the Protectorate soldiers, but only to give their rearward ranks time to escape into Notre Fille itself.

"It begins," Athène said to Nephra. "Prepare the tribe."

Nephra nodded, quickly disappearing into the sheets of rain. Chang's guns had stopped firing as soon as the last of the Sophians were either dead or safely through the doors of Notre Fille. Athène looked down on the devastation with an inscrutable expression.

"How they win," she said in English.

"What?"

"I heard you speak to your friend. You say it does not matter who wins. Only how. How do you think we should win, little Clover?"

He gestured toward the charnel-house scene beneath them. "Not like this," he said.

"Why not? This is war. War is ugly."

"Maybe. But even if you take the city this way, you won't be able to keep it."

"I don't want the city. I only want my sisters to be able to live without fear."

"Fine. Then you abandon the Anchor, and some new leader rises to power, one who remembers what the Wesah did here, who promises vengeance. Is that what you want?"

Athène wouldn't meet his eye. "No. But what other choice do we have?"

The square was still now, almost silent. Clover imagined that if he could only yell loudly enough, the whole world might hear him; but what good was being heard if you didn't know what you wanted to say?

6. Paz

IN A KIND OF DAZE, THEY FOLLOWED CHANG DOWN HALLS and up narrow corkscrew stairways, through reading rooms lit by a few guttering lanterns throwing the shadows of reliquaries and dusty Filia against the walls, past dozens of spartan offices that reeked of erudition and boredom, and on past the uric tang of the lavatories and the sweat stink of the dormitories where thousands of divinity students had tossed and turned over the years. Flora walked just beside Chang, who had one pistol drawn and another in the holster at his waist. The Grand Marshal seemed different today—calmer, more civil—as if he had finally finished setting all his plans in motion and was now content to sit back and let them play out. Of course Paz still hated him for what he'd done to her, and to the Wesah, and to Mitchell Poplin, but she was curious why he'd bothered to save her and Clive from the Sophian man down in the narthex—curious enough not to immediately choke him to death where he stood, anyway.

"Here we are," Chang finally said, pushing through a set of solid mahogany doors inlaid with elaborate gold filigree. "Can you believe that old bastard Carmassi used to make this climb every day? It's a wonder he lasted as long as he did."

Even if Chang hadn't named him, Paz wouldn't have had any

trouble guessing that these were the chambers of the erstwhile Archbishop. The place perfectly balanced pious religious iconography with ostentatious display: an annulus constructed of innumerable strands of silver and gold, paintings of praying saints with glittering gold-leaf coronas, a silver tea set burnished to a shine, thick pile jacquard rugs that stretched from immaculately wallpapered wall to immaculately wallpapered wall. They passed through the antechamber, where a fountain burbled over a sculpture of the Daughter. Across a formal dining room set for service, Paz could see down a hall and into the Archbishop's bedroom; the bed was a gigantic sleigh missing only a harness and a team of draft horses, wide enough to comfortably sleep an entire family. Beyond the cozy library, with its perfectly alphabetized volumes and a fire burning merrily in the gaping hearth, a pair of doors opened onto a tiered balcony-cum-garden. To the stentorian accompaniment of gunfire, the four of them walked beneath pergolas, immune from the pouring rain, all the way down to the railing overlooking Annunciation Square. A rake leaned against a nearby rose trellis, partially enwrapped in the stems.

"Look," Chang said, "it's all coming together."

Paz tried to make sense of the scene below them, which was now cast in stark relief by two enormous floodlights mounted on distant roofs. Bright sparks stuttered from the ground floors of three buildings; Chang must have hidden the guns somehow, and now they were all firing on the Sophians at once. Rivers of shadows ran along the streets that converged on the church, flickering red and gold beneath the gas lamps and then turning black again. Zeno's army had no choice but to retreat into the church itself—

but wasn't that exactly where they'd been trying to get to in the first place?

"Why'd you kill Mitchell Poplin?" Clive said.

"Who?" Chang looked confused for a moment. "Ah. The old man. I didn't authorize that. Apparently he came at my men with some . . . woodworking tool? I don't remember the details. They'd only come to get the girls."

"Girls? Not just Flora?"

"I told you, I was there that night too," Paz volunteered. "I ran as soon as I saw the soldiers. I didn't think they would hurt anyone."

"Don't beat yourself up," Chang said. "Odds are it would've all happened the same way if you'd stayed."

Only Paz knew that wasn't true. She never would've let them take Flora; she'd have died first.

"But why take them at all?" Clive said. "Haven't you tortured us enough?"

Chang pulled a pocket watch from his uniform jacket and wiped its rain-flecked face. "Don't be a hypocrite, Clive. How many people have died so that you and Paz could still be standing here? I took Flora because your father had information I wanted, and I needed leverage to get it." Paz noticed Chang's watch wasn't showing the correct time, or anything close. Even so, Chang looked to be pleased with what he saw there, replacing it in his pocket with a grunt of satisfaction. "In the end, it didn't even matter that he didn't talk. I'd always known Sophia might have other planes. It's why I sent my army underground. If that's really Zeno's best move, then I've already won."

Lightning flashed, illuminating for an instant a thick cable running from a corner of the balcony out into the space above the square. A power line? Only there didn't seem to be anything running on electricity in the Archbishop's chambers. Maybe the Descendancy had developed its own telegraphy—but whom would Chang be talking to now, and about what?

"Where is everyone?" Paz said. "Why is this place empty?"

"Who else would be here? The Church hierarchy was purged weeks ago. My soldiers are out corraling the Sophians. The Library is going up in smoke as we speak, and I imagine most of the attendants are either dead or on their way out of the city. The work is almost finished."

"The work?"

Chang struck a match off the railing and lit a cigarillo. He took a long drag and flicked the spent match through the exhalation. "I realized something over the past few months, and I think I have you two to thank. You can't keep building new things on top of old things forever. It's like a roof. At a certain point, it just gets too damned heavy and the whole thing collapses. You have to be willing to tear off the old layers first. Or better yet, burn everything to the ground and start over again."

"Scorched earth," Paz whispered.

Chang smiled. "You were always quick, Dedios. I'm glad you're not dead. There might just be a place for you in the new world I'm making."

"I think we'll pass."

"Of course. Because of your principles. You're so much better than me, aren't you?" Chang gazed out over Annunciation Square, over this masterpiece of carnage and chaos he'd brought into being.

The sense of accomplishment on his face was unmistakable. "Men like me make the world go round, children. I'll probably be dead by the time you realize the truth of that. Civilization is the world's most effective medicine. The Descendancy has provided order and meaning for hundreds of thousands of people since its inception. It has saved their lives. So yes, I would do anything to protect it. And I have." After a last long savor of the view, he turned back to them. "Let's try this one more time. I know you hate me, and with good reason. But plenty of working relationships have thrived on hatred. So why not join me? Help me rebuild the Descendancy, without all the superstitious trappings that made us vulnerable in the first place. I can forgive your trespasses if you'll forgive mine."

"Why not just kill us?" Clive said.

"I suppose I could try, but it doesn't ever seem to stick with you two, does it?"

"Maybe we should kill you," Paz said icily.

Chang sighed. "Aren't you bored of this game by now? You may not believe it, but I'm a practical man. I'm tired of wasting my energy on you. I'd rather have that energy working *for* me. There's gonna be a lot to do when this war is over, and if nothing else, you two have proven to be absolutely relentless when you put your minds to something. And I can be good to those who are good to me. I didn't hurt Flora here, did I?"

Paz had almost forgotten the girl was there. Clive knelt down next to her. "Is that true? Did he hurt you?" Flora shook her head.

"Won't speak to you, either, eh?" Chang said. "Makes her pretty good company, actually."

Chang glanced at his pocket watch again; Paz took the opportunity to step out from under the protection of the pergola to examine the cable at the corner of the roof more closely: woven steel, without any kind of dampener around the metal. So it definitely couldn't conduct electricity safely, nor was it any kind of pipe or tube. Yet the material and design meant it would be strong, strong enough to bear quite a bit of weight, if someone needed to . . .

She turned back to Chang, who was still holding the pocket watch. "All right, kids. Time's up. Are we working together or not?"

"Not," Flora suddenly interjected.

Chang snorted. "Girl's got a good sense of timing, anyway. Thankfully, it's not her decision to make."

"I think she captured our feelings on the subject pretty well," Clive said.

"Oh, Clive." Chang pointed his gun at Flora. "I'm disappointed in you. After all this time, you're still not thinking practically. I just gave you a chance to save yourself. But do you take it? No. It's more important to get a little dig in. You're incapable of being reasonable, even when it's a question of life or—"

That tendency to gloat had always been the Grand Marshal's biggest weakness; Paz had pulled the other gun from his holster before he'd even clocked her moving.

Chang groaned. "So I shoot the little girl and then you shoot me? That's how you want this to end?"

Paz didn't respond, just made a slight adjustment to the angle of the gun, firing a single shot out into the darkness.

"What are you doing?" Chang said, but Paz could see from the subtle tightening in his expression that she'd guessed right.

"You already killed thousands of Wesah," she said. "You killed the Epistem and the Archbishop. You killed Burns. I won't let you kill again. Tell me how to stop this."

"First off, I did not kill Marshal Burns. I just needed to shake him up a little. I can take you to—"

She fired again. This time she managed to nick the cable; it shook but didn't snap entirely.

"Stop!" Chang cried out.

"How long do we have?"

"Twenty minutes. Maybe less."

"Oh my God," Clive said, as understanding dawned. "You're gonna pull down the whole church."

"Where will it start?" Paz asked.

"It doesn't matter," Chang said. "I couldn't tell you how to stop the damn thing if I wanted to. I didn't build it myself."

A third shot. The cable shook again. "Where will it start?" Paz demanded.

"Behind the fucking nave! Daughter's love, girl, that's our only way out of here. Are you that eager to die?"

She gestured with the gun toward the cable. "Go on, then."

Chang clearly didn't trust the offer, but what choice did he have? He holstered his gun and climbed up onto the parapet. A blinding flash of lightning cracked the sky behind him as he pulled a leather strap from his jacket and attached it to the cable. He reached into his pocket and pulled out three more, throwing them at Paz's feet.

"I'm not a monster," he said, a declaration that nonetheless felt like a supplication. "When this is all over, you'll see that. I'll make a good leader. People will love me."

None of them replied, and when Chang realized they weren't

going to, he gave a slight nod, then threaded his hand through the strap and allowed his weight to drop onto the cable. He hurtled off across the square, gold buttons gleaming as he passed through the glare of the floodlights and on into the black.

Clive bent down to pick up the straps that Chang had left them. Paz watched him consider them for a moment—before casually tossing them over the balustrade.

"Twenty minutes, eh?" he said.

Paz smiled grimly. "Twenty minutes."

As if on cue, one of the woven threads of steel in the cable suddenly snapped, then another, and another, until only one slim silver fiber remained.

Snap.

Paz squinted into the darkness. Maybe Chang had made it safely to the other side. Maybe not. She couldn't have cared less. Meanwhile, down below, the last of the Sophians had finally entered the church. But even as the Protectorate soldiers were celebrating their victory, a new force could be seen approaching Annunciation Square—bows at the ready and vengeance on their minds.

The war wasn't over yet.

7. Athène

THE SURVIVING SOPHIANS HAD ESCAPED INTO NOTRE Fille, but for some reason, the Protectorate soldiers who'd emerged from the ground like worms after a storm weren't following them inside. In fact, they'd abandoned the plaza proper and were congregated at the ends of the streets that fed into Annunciation Square, standing silent and expectant in the rain, like a miniature re-creation of Sophia's siege on the Anchor. From a strategic standpoint, Athène could make little sense of the situation. Clover said there were secret passages in the church that led to various other places in the city. The Sophians would find them eventually, given that their position was readily defensible in the short term. Meanwhile, Zeno still had her planes, which could recommence devastating the city at any moment. So what was Chang thinking?

Athène once again descended from her perch on the roof and returned to where the many Wesah *naasyoon* had finally joined back together, in a plaza a few blocks from Annunciation Square. Clover and Kita were waiting there too, looking forlorn and damp and out of place. Nephra was idly picking crumbs of pemmican out of a bag.

"Nothing any of you do makes any sense," Athène said in Clover's general direction.

"If it doesn't make sense, we're missing something," Clover replied.

"It makes sense to me," Nephra said. "Chang is trying to starve the Sophians out, just as Zeno tried to do to the Anchor."

But Athène had already discarded that theory. "This is not a siege. The Protectorate is waiting for something."

"Like what?"

"I don't know."

"Maybe he's just gonna take out the whole church," the girl called Kita said in English, which Clover then translated for Nephra's benefit.

"He wouldn't," Athène replied in Wesah.

"He would, though," Clover said. "He'd destroy everything to win this war. That's the difference between him and Zeno. It's why she's losing." The boy was suddenly animated, futures unspooling in his mind's eye, as if he'd just drunk a cup of dreamtea. "But if we— that is, you—only while I . . ." He trailed off, lost in his thoughts. A moment later he looked back up at her, eyes bright with epiphany. "I know what to do."

"You are just a boy," Nephra said. "We are not interested in your plans."

"I wouldn't mind hearing what he has to say." All eyes turned to the tent flap. A bent figure, lank gray hair plastered to her robes, shivered with the cold.

"Grandmother!" Athène cried out. She took off the dry blanket some tribeswoman had given her and wrapped it around the *otsapah*'s shoulders. "You were meant to stay outside the city. It's not safe here."

"The times are not safe."

"But you're shaking. You need to lie down."

"Leave me be!" The old woman could still command a room when she needed to—or an Andromède. "Let the boy speak."

All eyes turned to Clover. "Athène," he said, then, blushing slightly, corrected himself. "Andromède, I want the Wesah to survive this war. The world needs you. But right now, I don't like your odds. You have no guns, no planes. And you've made enemies of both Chang and Zeno. You won't win this fight."

"So what do you suggest?" Athène said. "Should we retreat?"

"No. You could never run far enough."

"But what can we do besides fight or flee?"

"I think I know what the boy is getting at," Grandmother said. "All these years, we have treated the Descendancy and Sophia as if they existed in a world separate from our own. But there is only one world. When we fight them, we fight ourselves. When we run from them, we run from ourselves."

"Don't speak in riddles," Nephra said. "Tell us what to do."

Grandmother spread her arms wide. "Help them."

Athène tried to get her mind around the concept; it was like trying to stop a horse galloping at full tilt. "Help them how?"

The *otsapah* frowned—halfway between confusion and amusement. "I don't know. I'm hoping the boy does."

"I might," Clover said. "All those soldiers out there, they're only fighting because they can't see a way through this war *without* fighting. But if I could just talk to them, I think I could make them see reason."

"Even if that's true, how could you ever hope to talk to thousands and thousands of people all at once?" Athène said.

"There's a way. I just need a little time."

"And what if your friend is right, and Notre Fille falls before you're ready?"

"Then Sophia will be defeated, and Chang will come for you."

Athène looked to the *otsapah*, then to Nephra, but their expressions were inscrutable. This was what it meant to be Andromède. The decision was hers to make—and the consequences would be hers to bear.

"You say you need time. How much?"

"Thirty or forty minutes," Clover said. "But that's not all I'll need from you."

Athène sighed. Somehow she'd always known it would come down to this—terrible risk and terrible sacrifice, blind trust in the gods. "All right, Clover. What would you have me do?"

The square was as quiet as it had been in hours, nearly silent but for the patter of the inexorable rain. Athène had arranged her warriors along the spokes around Notre Fille, just out of sight of the closest Protectorate soldiers. She stood at the front of one of these divisions, steeling herself to give the order. Clover insisted that the war could only be stopped if both the Descendant and Sophian forces became equally uncertain about its outcome. Right now the Protectorate believed themselves to have the upper hand; the Wesah had to take that belief away from them.

Even more sisters would have to die—so that the tribe had a chance to endure.

Athène didn't need to speak. She merely raised a hand and brought it down again, a signal understood by every tribeswoman who'd ever been on a hunt. Her warriors streamed past her and were soon joined by the streams from the other roads. The Protectorate soldiers were slow to react; by the time they realized what was happening, the first Wesah were already crashing into their ranks. Athène doubted the soldiers would risk using their firearms. Clover said the rain had probably rendered most of their rifles and pistols unusable—and besides, in a battle such as this one, the soldiers would be just as likely to shoot each other as their enemies. So this was to be a hand-to-hand and blade-to-blade fight; at least it was an honorable way to be annihilated, should things turn out that way.

Athène would've liked to be on the front lines with her sisters, but Grandmother had insisted she stay back. "They've already lost one Andromède," she'd said. "If you fall and the tribe survives, there will be conflict over who leads us next. That is the last thing we need."

Athène's mother used to complain about the way the Wesah chose its leaders, how the process fueled so much bloodshed and bitterness, and Athène would mock her for her soft heart. She could see now that growing older would be a long and humbling exculpation of all her mother's sins and failings alongside a perpetually deepening understanding of her own.

Lightning illuminated a distant cloud bank, striking somewhere in the fields outside the city. Athène waited for the rumble of thunder but heard only a dull thump as something huge and dark landed on the cobblestones just beside her. It lay still for a moment—a satiated vulture, a gobbet of night—then abruptly came alive again

　　　　　　　　　　　　　　TOMMY WALLACH

with something between a moan and a scream. What had seemed only a shapeless mass at first glance now resolved into form and color: maroon-and-gold jacket; silver stubble atop a brown pate; a jag of bloodstained bone like a fresh shoot bursting from the loam. As Athène approached, the man found the presence of mind to draw a gun, but she batted it away like a mosquito. She lifted his chin to get a better look at his face.

Admittedly, faith had never been Athène's strong suit. Part of that, she now realized, had been sheer childish defiance. Her mother's certainties had grated on her when she was young, especially as they always seemed to require something of her: a prayer or a sacrifice, a dance or a song. And truthfully, aside from the visions granted by the dreamtea—which really weren't all that different from the dreams that came with sleep—she couldn't say she'd ever seen any proof that the gods existed, or that the spirits of her ancestors were watching over her, or that there was more to life than dull, material reality.

It wasn't until the day she met Gemma that Athène began to doubt her doubt. This spiritual rebirth hadn't been a result of seeing Gemma's shaking fits, or of hearing Gemma describe her journey with the dreamtea, or of experiencing any tangible manifestation of the divine. It had been the sheer *fact* of Gemma—her smile, her touch, her light. There was the unequivocal miracle, of the sort only an infinitely powerful and benevolent god could manifest. Her death was the opposite, an existential balancing of the scales too devastating to be arbitrary.

And here was one last miracle, literally falling from the sky; after this, Athène would never lose faith again.

Chang held her gaze.

"Do it," he said.

The fingers of her undamaged hand had already closed around the hilt of her glass blade. She drew it slowly, rasping the leather sheath, savoring her enemy's fear. The blade came free. It caught a bit of ambient gleam from the nearer of the two floodlights, casting a spangle onto Chang's gritted teeth. She would not kill him; there was no need for that, and no justice in it. She would leave him exactly as he had left the Wesah—hobbled, terrified, despairing. Let him live with his shame; let it eat away at him. And should he ever return, she would meet him in the fullness of his strength and annihilate him. She would shame him all over again.

"You have to the count of one hundred to be out of my sight," she said in English. For the count itself, she switched back to Wesah, so he couldn't know exactly how much time he had left.

Chang didn't hesitate, but immediately began to drag himself up the street. Both of his legs appeared to be broken; they trailed behind him as if made of stone. Still he kept putting one hand in front of the other. Place, pull. Place, pull. He was quiet at first, but soon his grunts became groans, each one coming a little more closely to the last, like the contractions of a mother giving birth, until they joined together into one continuous shriek, his voice tearing and cracking as if his very soul were on fire. She'd stopped counting long before he'd shrunk to a slinking worm in the distance, before his screams could no longer be heard over the sounds of battle. She turned her attention back to the people who mattered—her people—sacrificing themselves so that a boy she scarcely knew might broker a peace she wasn't even certain she wanted.

She looked to Notre Fille, a hulking silhouette against the pale moonlight, a dead god. Her wounded hand throbbed to the rhythm of her heartbeat. Her sisters cried out. The rain continued to fall.

8. Clive

EXPLOSIVES?" CLIVE SPUTTERED. "WHY WOULD I KNOW anything about explosives?"

"I don't know," Paz said. "I was just asking."

"Do *you* know anything about explosives?"

"Only the basics." They were making their way back down from the Archbishop's chambers as quickly as possible, taking the steps two and three at a time. "I know which chemicals can give you an incendiary reaction when they're mixed and how gunpowder works. But that's about it."

"Will that be enough?"

"I doubt it."

He nearly crashed into her as she stopped suddenly just before the threshold of the seventh-floor stairway. Flora, who'd been keeping pace behind him, slammed into his back so hard it nearly sent all three of them over the edge. There were voices coming from the landing below them—the Sophian army retreating farther up the building.

"We have to get past them," Paz said. "Is there another stairway?"

"They're all blocked off, remember?"

"Well, we can't risk trying to talk our way through. They're as like to shoot us as not."

"So what? You wanna jump out a window and just hope we land on a big pile of . . ." Clive trailed off. It wouldn't have been possible even a few weeks ago, but now . . .

"What?" Paz said.

"Follow me," he said. He used the windows to orient himself, moving east whenever possible, though the peculiar layout of Notre Fille saw them come face-to-face with a number of dead ends before they finally arrived at a nearly lightless corridor and a door bearing a freshly painted sign reading NO ACCESS. It opened onto a hallway that extended for only about a dozen feet before it was completely obstructed by a flap of canvas. The innocents' dormitory used to be on the other side, before Kittyhawk sheared it off the building entirely. That attack had saved Clive's life once already; hopefully it would do so again today.

"Are you kidding?" Paz said.

"You have a better idea?"

She sighed. "You know I don't."

The canvas was tethered in a half-dozen places. The instant they finished unpicking all the knots, the wind ripped the whole flap up and away from the wall; suddenly they found themselves looking out over Annunciation Square from more than a hundred feet up. Clive forced himself to step to the edge, so he could better see the scaffolding that had been put in place to aid in the reconstruction. It was a rickety layer cake made up of flimsy-looking wooden platforms supported by iron rods at all four corners. These rods ran all the way down to the ground in segments of about fifteen feet, each segment screwed into the next.

They'd been lucky; the topmost platform was only about eight feet below them, and one of the four rods—which would eventually be used to extend the scaffold even higher—was only a foot or so from the edge of the truncated hallway. "All we have to do is grab hold of that pole and slide down to the platform," Clive said, though as soon as the words were out of his mouth, it didn't seem nearly as simple as all that. The whole scaffold seemed to be shivering in the lashing rain and wind, as if it were afraid. He looked to Flora. "I can carry you on my back, if you don't think—" Before he could put out a hand to stop her, she slipped past him, leaping to the iron rod and sliding lithely down to land with a thump on the top level of the scaffold.

"Can I ride on your back?" Paz said.

"Will you be offended if I say no?"

"Extremely. You better jump before I slap you."

Clive sat down on the ledge and wrapped his legs around the bar, thinking he might inchworm his way down the same way you'd climb *up* a rope. Instead, as soon as he'd transferred his weight to the rod, he found himself plummeting toward the platform. His feet caught on the edge for an instant but immediately slipped off again. He slid a few feet past the platform, stopping only when his elbows caught painfully on the wood. Flora reached out for him, but he wasn't secure enough to risk grabbing her hand. He tried to use his legs to climb the pole, but the metal was too slippery.

"Clive!" Paz shouted. "I'll come help."

"Wait!" Clive gasped—but too late. Paz landed heavily on the platform, and the vibrations immediately knocked him loose.

He dropped about ten feet, still clinging tightly to the pole, before he was abruptly stopped by a crossbeam. As he fell forward, into the skeletal interior of the scaffolding, he stretched out his arms toward where two iron bars met in an X and just managed to grab hold. He looked down, and saw Annunciation Square roiling like a storm-tossed sea; the Wesah had arrived and were throwing themselves at the much larger Protectorate force.

The wind picked up, whipping the rain into his eyes. With a groan, Clive managed to heave his right leg over one of the cross-beams. Paz was calling out from somewhere above him, but he couldn't spare the breath to answer. He tried to hoist his other leg up but underestimated his own strength; the momentum carried him over the top of the X and left him dangling from the under-side, by his ankles this time, and staring straight down at the next level of the scaffold. It was at least fifteen feet away—too far to fall. He crunched his abdomen and tried to pull himself upright again, but the beams were too slick. Soon he realized there was no hope of climbing up again; it was down or nothing.

He looked to the nearest of the vertical rods that supported the corners of the scaffold—if he could get to it, at least there'd be some hope of using friction to slow his descent. He began to swing back and forth—newly grateful for the Protectorate's excru-ciating conditioning drills. Then, with a deep breath and a prayer, he unhooked his ankles, launching himself through the air. He got one hand on the rod and pulled himself to it as he began to fall, recrossing his ankles around the metal and squeezing as tightly as he could. It seemed an eternity before he finally crashed onto the wooden platform and was sent sprawling. He was still catching his breath when Flora and Paz descended the rope ladder that was the intended means of traversing the scaffold.

"Not your most graceful moment," Paz said.

"Really? I thought I was pretty damn impressive."

A wisp of a smile pricked the corners of Flora's mouth—maybe she was still in there after all.

The descent went smoothly enough after that, though Clive was never quite able to shake the feeling that the entire scaffold was on the brink of blowing away like some great kite. They stopped at the second floor, where Clive used the sword he'd taken from his father's office to slice open the canvas sheet separating the scaffold from the exposed interior of Notre Fille. Finally he found himself back on familiar territory: the church's administrative offices. Papers were strewn everywhere, many of them blackened and torn from that first bombing. The bodies of those who'd been here that day had long since been removed, but bloodstains were still visible on the walls and ceiling.

The three of them moved quickly through the halls and down the eastern stairwell to the ground floor, where they unlatched the door that had been locked when they'd arrived at Notre Fille scarcely an hour ago. Clive peeked his head around the jamb and was grateful to find the narthex empty; the Sophians must all have retreated upstairs. Still, they didn't waste any time sprinting across the marble floor and into the nave.

An impossible quiet descended as he closed the heavy doors behind Paz and Flora. The velvet curtains of the Dubium shifted slightly with the breath of air.

"We should split up," Paz said. "We can cover more ground that way."

"What are we looking for?" asked Clive.

"Anything that hums or clicks or ticks. Anything suspicious, really."

"How long do you think it's been since Chang gave us twenty minutes?"

"Let's not waste time thinking about that."

She ran toward the ambo. Clive looked beneath the pews one by one, while Flora walked around the edge of the room, glancing into the cabinets at the end of every row where the extra kneelers and Filia were kept. He was lying on his stomach checking the rearmost pew when his eye was drawn to a flicker of movement in the Dubium, in the quarter inch of space between the bottom of the curtain and the floor—someone was in there. He walked quickly to the unoccupied half of the box, pulling the curtain open and closing it behind him.

"Who are you?" he whispered, hoping to avoid distracting Paz and Flora from the search.

"Clive Hamill. Everywhere I turn, there you are."

The voice was a lightning bolt of memory: suddenly Clive found himself back in that strange little lean-to fifty miles out from Sophia, watching as his brother fitted the wax cylinder into the phonograph machine. Back when Gemma was still alive and Paz was still Irene and there was reason to believe war might not ever come.

"Director Zeno," Clive said. "What are you doing in here? Aren't your soldiers upstairs?"

"Yes. They still haven't realized we've walked into a trap."

"You knew?"

"Not until it was too late. I assume Chang has a rather large explosion planned. A part of me is curious to see it."

"We can still stop it. Chang told us the explosives were in here somewhere."

"It hardly matters. If the building doesn't kill us, the soldiers outside will. Besides, isn't there something poetic in us being literally crushed by the church?"

"I'm a lot more interested in the science of it than the poetry, being honest." Clive needed to get Zeno's mind working on the problem at hand; luckily he had some experience soliciting help from a genius—you just had to pique their interest. "Can you really blow up a building this big with one explosion?"

"Why not? Structures have their weak points, just like people."

"Such as?"

"The carotid artery. The Achilles tendon."

"I mean in buildings. Like, how would *you* destroy Notre Fille, if you had to?"

A long pause, longer than they could afford—but Clive knew from experience that there was no rushing people like Zeno. "Well, the nave runs the length of the building, so I'd probably start in here," she finally said.

"I already know that. *Where* in here?"

"I'd need to see the plans to know for sure, but I'd target any structural walls, particularly ones that continue through to higher floors."

It wasn't much, but it was better than nothing. "Okay. That's what I'll look for. Now go and gather as many of your people as you can and lead them outside. You've only got a few minutes before this thing blows."

"But Chang's guns—"

"Have already been abandoned. The Protectorate's busy fending off the Wesah."

"The Wesah? They're fighting the Protectorate?"

"That's right. So get moving." But there was no sound from the other half of the Dubium. "Director Zeno? We're kind of in a hurry here."

Zeno sighed. "In the last twenty-four hours, humanity has managed to erase centuries of progress, if not more. We'll have to start all over again. I'm too old for that, Clive. Too tired."

"Starting over is what humanity does. We build things and then they get ruined and then we build them again. That's life. That's all there is."

Silence. "You're so much like him. Your father, I mean. It's a shame that . . . well . . ." A hitch in her voice, a cough. "Good luck, Clive." He heard the curtain draw back; by the time he left the Dubium, the doors of the nave were already swinging shut. Neither Flora nor Paz appeared to have noticed any of it.

No time to dwell. Zeno had mentioned "weak points"—but what would qualify? He glanced around and tried to work out how the architecture of this chamber related to that of the higher floors. He was pretty sure the rearmost wall, which separated the nave from the sacristy, also ran alongside the hallway upstairs.

"What were you doing in that box for so long?" Paz said. She'd placed a chair up against the back wall so she could reach high enough to run her hand along the back of the big annulus behind the ambo.

"Just looking around." Clive tried to open the door to the sacristy, but it was locked. He grabbed a nearby candelabra and managed to get the base between the jamb and the doorknob; it only took a few seconds to pry the old door loose from its frame and reveal the humble chamber beyond.

Tick, tick, tick.

"Daughter's love," he whispered.

The sacristy was completely empty but for the device sitting on a desk at the back of the room. It was about the size of a milk crate, with a small white clock face on the front, counting down the seconds to Armageddon. About a hundred cables emerged from the back of the device and disappeared into holes drilled into the stone wall just behind it, like exposed veins.

Paz ran to look at the clock. "Three minutes left!"

"What do we do?" Clive said.

"I have no idea!" She ran her hands over the device until she located a crack in the smooth metal. A flap opened to reveal a mass of wires and tubes running from one end to the other. "Some of this is electrical, and some is chemical. When the timer runs out, the machine will trigger a reaction, which will light the fuses."

"So cut them."

"There are too many."

"So cut the tubes with the chemicals."

"That might just initiate the reaction immediately."

Tick, tick, tick.

"Well, we have to try something!" Clive said.

"Fine! The fuses, then!"

Clive drew his sword while Paz produced a switchblade from a pocket of her jeans. They sidled in behind the device and began

　　　　　　TOMMY WALLACH

sawing through the cables. Clive glanced at Flora and tried to give her a comforting smile.

Tick, tick, tick.

They finished cutting through the first two fuses, which left at least a dozen more. The clock now said two minutes.

"This is hopeless," Clive said. "We need to run."

"You're right," Paz replied.

But neither of them moved. After a moment, they both started in on the next fuse. Clive watched as Flora grabbed hold of one as well, trying her level best to tear it out of the wall. He would've told her to leave, but he knew she wouldn't go. They were all in this together now, for better or worse.

Tick, tick, tick.

9. Clover

WHAT DO YOU MEAN YOU DON'T KNOW WHAT YOU'RE doing?" Kita said, once they were out of earshot of Athène and the rest of the Wesah.

"I only mean I don't know *exactly* how to do what I know I need to do," Clover replied.

"And what is it that you know you need to do?"

"Get everyone's attention at exactly the same time."

"And by 'everyone,' you mean the thousands of people who are about to start fighting to the death outside Notre Fille?"

"Yes."

"That's impossible."

"Assume it isn't."

Kita harrumphed—channeling a little bit of Burns in the severity of her frown. It saddened Clover to think she'd never get to meet him. In spite of their many disagreements, Clover had come to think of Burns as family. And Daughter knew he could've used the grizzled old man's counsel right about now. "Okay. Then you'd need to be really loud. Could we make some kind of giant megaphone?"

"It would have to be the size of a house."

"What about fireworks? Everybody looks at fireworks. At least you'd get their attention."

"They wouldn't go off in this storm. And most of the soldiers probably wouldn't even see them. They'd have to be looking in just the right direction."

"Well, I don't know how you expect anyone to see *anything* unless it shows up right in the middle of Annunciation Square, where those two big lights are pointing."

"The lights!" Clover kissed Kita on her sopping cheek. "That's it!"

"What's it?"

But Clover's mind was already rushing forward, following the lines of implication, solving what problems he could predict. They'd have to be big, at least three or four feet wide—though it'd be safer to err on the small side, so the shape was right. Should they be paper? No: too flimsy, and the lights probably ran hot. Wood, then, but where to find it? "Your family's workshop. How far would you say that is from here?"

"Five minutes if we run, but why would we—"

"So let's run."

He made it half a dozen paces down the road before he was brought to attention by Kita's piercing shout. "Clover Hamill, you will stop moving this instant!" His body obeyed before he had time to consciously consider the demand. "I need to know what the hell you're planning."

"No you don't."

"You told Athène. Why not me?"

"I only told her because she refused to do what I asked her to otherwise."

"Which is what? I couldn't understand with all of you talking in Wesah."

"I asked her to stop fighting in the middle of the battle, on my signal."

Kita looked appropriately appalled. "And she agreed to that?"

"Yes. Now can we please stop talking and start running? We have a lot to do."

Kita sighed. "Fine. But if I die before I find out what your stupid plan is, I'm gonna be seriously pissed off."

"Duly noted."

It felt like cowardice to flee Annunciation Square just as the battle was beginning. Clover kept glancing over his shoulder, as if something had to be chasing them, but there was only the steep slant of the rain, guttering candles in windows, the moonlight trying valiantly to penetrate the storm clouds. They reached the Delancey workshop without seeing another living soul. The large front doors were unlatched, slamming against the wall with every gust of wind. Rain had encroached deeply into the room, saturating a pile of finished planks in varying grains stacked up beside a workbench. Clover ran his fingers lightly over the topmost plank, collecting a layer of sawdust. In the wild, he'd have been able to differentiate the trees these came from with ease; but here they were literally shorn of context, just so much anonymous plant matter—and none of it useful. The long tables at which the Delancey wainwrights worked were still busy with wood scraps, iron filings, and chalk, but it was impossible to miss the huge chunk of quartz holding down a scrap of parchment. Kita read it aloud.

"'Left the city with what we could fit in a wagon. Headed for

Corning.'" She let the paper float to the ground. "It's Mama's hand-writing. Pa said he was gonna join up with the Protectorate when Sophia came. My brothers, too. They're probably back there in the square, fighting the Wesah." Clearly she wanted comforting, but there wasn't time; every second they wasted was another life lost—or two, or three. Clover appraised the worktables to see if they might serve his purpose. Most were well-made, built from just a few planks perfectly fitted and sanded into a single unit, but a couple were more rudimentary, constructed of a flimsy agglomera-tion of thin sheets of plywood: perfect.

"Did your family leave their tools behind?" he asked.

"I don't know."

"Where do they usually keep them?" Kita was staring off blankly into space. "Kita! The faster we work, the sooner the fighting stops."

"The tools should be in there," she said, gesturing vaguely toward a closet beneath the stairs at the back of the workshop.

The door was too big for its frame, scraping loudly over the blackened arc already inscribed in the wooden floor. Inside, most of the shelves looked to have been recently cleared out, but a few old tools had failed to make the cut. Clover found two saws, both rust-ing where the blade met the handle, one missing half its teeth. He set them out on one of the plywood worktables and cast about for something he could use for an outline; for this to work, he couldn't afford to draw the circles freehand.

He found a small stool and set it on the table upside down: not quite big enough, but it would do for a baseline.

"What are you doing?" Kita said, curiosity pulling her out of her daze.

"You'll see. Hand me that piece of chalk, would you?"

He climbed onto the table and pushed one side of the saw handle up against the seat of the stool. With his other hand, he held the nub of blue chalk to the opposite side of the handle, creating a makeshift compass that he used to draw a circle about a foot wider in diameter than the stool itself. When that was finished, he repeated the whole process six inches to the left, ending up with two blue circles of the exact same size.

"What's so funny?" Kita said.

Clover realized he'd been smiling. "Nothing, really. Just thinking how strange it is that after everything that's happened, the fate of the Descendancy is gonna come down to a question of faith." He handed her a saw. "Now get to work. It has to be exact. And fast."

She took the saw. "I still don't see how two wooden circles are gonna stop a war."

"Well, we're gonna be here for a minute. How about I explain it to you?"

"Really?" Kita set the teeth of her saw to the edge of the table and bore down. "Finally!"

As he mounted the interior staircase of one of the buildings around Annunciation Square, the broad round of plywood tucked awkwardly under his armpit, Clover considered how, in the end, every battle had to be faced alone. Even if you were surrounded by other people, and even if those people wanted to help you in every way they could, the real war was always an internal one. Your fear versus your courage. Your ignorance versus your willingness to learn. Your selfishness versus your selflessness. So there was something fitting

TOMMY WALLACH

about ending up on his own in these final moments. He and Kita had parted ways about fifteen minutes ago, as his plan required synchronized action across a great distance. And though she was as brave and resourceful as anyone he'd ever known, he was still scared for her.

Up on the roof, a humming generator was plugged into the back of one of the giant floodlights Chang had installed to illuminate the square during his grand turning of the tables. Hopefully Kita was standing before the other one by now, or would be soon. From here, Clover could see nothing of that far-off roof but the light itself, round and white as a full moon.

He allowed himself a moment to inspect the floodlight's construction. At least a hundred individual bulbs, each one the size of two fists put together, had been screwed into sockets in a concave steel frame; together, they created a light so potent that he couldn't look directly at it. Even with the rain and the inevitable diffusion, the bright circle it projected onto the square below was distinct. Bodies moved in that circle, blades flashed, lives were ended. But Notre Fille still stood, and as Clover watched, Sophian soldiers began to stream out the front doors of the church. The result was three armies all fighting at once—an incomprehensible and lunatic chaos. They were all there now; all that remained was to deliver the message.

Clover tugged at the cable powering the floodlight until it came free. The light immediately died. He looked back to the other rooftop. "Come on, Kita," he said under his breath. A flicker, as of something passing in front of the light. A moment later it went out, casting the entire square into darkness.

He began to count, just as they'd planned. "Twenty, nineteen, eighteen . . ."

He placed the wooden circle in front of the floodlight, careful not to break any of the bulbs. To his relief, it looked to be just the right size.

"Fifteen, fourteen, thirteen . . ."

He threaded a length of wire through the hole he'd drilled in the top of the plywood and wrapped it around the metal casing of the spotlight, tying it off so the disc hung right in the center.

"Ten, nine, eight . . ."

He adjusted the light so it pointed at the facade of Notre Fille, rather than the ground. A bullet whizzed just past his ear, though whether the shot had been fired intentionally or accidentally was impossible to know.

"Seven, six, five . . ."

The cable nearly slipped from his fingers as he prepared to plug it back in.

"Four, three, two, one . . ."

He jammed the plug into the floodlight just as the other one turned on across the square. Suddenly two perfect annuli were projected onto the front of Notre Fille. The square was silent as the men of the Descendancy gazed upon those light-forged rings—the most important symbol of their religion, a reminder of the philosophy of peace upon which their entire civilization had been founded. And in the reflected light of those rings, the Wesah warriors began to kneel down, just as Clover had requested, lowering their heads and their blades as if offering themselves up as a sacrifice. No one could fail to connect the gesture to the symbol. Swords clattered to

TOMMY WALLACH

the cobblestones as two thousand men in red and gold went down on their knees, their faith revitalized in the face of this impossible manifestation of divinity and humanity at once.

Only the Sophians were left standing now. Clover knew the annuli would mean nothing to them, but he was confident it wouldn't matter. For all her flaws, Zeno was no Chang—she'd never encouraged needless slaughter. It was only a matter of seconds before the Sophians all lowered themselves down to the ground alongside their Wesah sisters and Descendancy brothers.

Out of sympathy, or gratitude, or some tenacious remnant of faith, Clover did the same. He found tears springing to his eyes and let them fall, let the rain wash them away.

It was done. The war was finally over.

10. Paz

IT HAD BEEN ZENO WHO SAVED THEM, APPEARING IN THE sacristy just as the clock began to count down its final minute. She looked like some kind of divine spirit, her hair an aureole of henna red and silver, the hem of her robe brushing softly against the marble floor. They made space for her in front of the explosive device. She examined it for a few seconds, solving the maze of wires with subtle movements of her head, then extended her hand palm-up. "Knife, please," she said.

Paz obeyed. Zeno used the blade to pry up more of the device's casing, and when she spotted the cable she was looking for, she crimped and cut it. The clock finished its countdown about two seconds later, and some kind of chemical spewed out of the tube and splattered fruitlessly on the table. Immediately Zeno turned and strode back into the nave, but stopped momentarily to gaze around the room, taking in the sculptures and the stained glass, the vast painted ceiling and the golden annulus behind the ambo. "I'm glad this place wasn't completely destroyed," she said. It was probably the closest she could come to calling it beautiful.

The three of them followed Zeno outside, where those Sophians she'd managed to round up in the few minutes she'd been gone were just joining the mad scrum already in progress between the Wesah and the Protectorate. The four of them stood at the top of the church steps, watching as death was doled out liberally and at random. Was Terry out there fighting, or was he already among the fallen? Would it even matter if the battle went on like this, or was the inevitable conclusion the annihilation of all three armies? When Chang's floodlights went out and the annuli suddenly appeared on the facade of Notre Fille, she thought it had to be some kind of practical joke: surely you couldn't stop a war with a couple of rings of light.

But then the Wesah were all kneeling, and the Protectorate followed suit. Only the Sophians were left standing. If any of them had looked to the ruined portal of Notre Fille in that moment, they would have seen Zeno there, her figure as distinct as a lighthouse.

"I'll admit it," she said. "I didn't see this coming."

"Who could?" Paz whispered.

Slowly—as slowly as an old empire collapsing—Director Zeno lowered herself to her knees.

The fighting had ceased about two hours ago, but Paz had spent most of the intervening time looking for Clover and Kita with Clive. Though the war was technically over, it felt as if it might start up again at any moment. Men and women who'd just seen their friends and loved ones killed were compelled to walk alongside the killers. The simple beauty of that initial truce had given way to a more complex reality; the three armies still wandering the battlefield in a daze had no common faith or philosophy, no shared history or vision for the future. In circumstances like these, the smallest altercation could quickly escalate.

Eventually Paz and Clive found Clover and Kita, and together the four of them returned to Flora, Zeno, and Athène in the narthex of Notre Fille. It was there that Zeno had half asked and half ordered them to sit somewhere out of the way while she and Athène arranged for the dismissal of their respective armies. Clive had suggested they return to the late Archbishop's quarters, where they'd now been waiting for over an hour.

"This is crazy," he said. "After everything we've been through, how'd we end up stuck in here doing nothing?"

"We have to leave this part to Zeno and Athène," Paz replied. "I'm sure they're as eager to sort everything out as we are."

"But who's going to speak for us?" Clover said.

Paz frowned. "Who's us?"

"The Descendancy. Sophia has Zeno. The Wesah have Athène. We have no one."

It was true. Chang had disappeared; most likely his body was among those piled up in the square, yet to be identified. And with so many Protectorate leaders dead, to say nothing of the culling of the Church hierarchy and the literal destruction of the Library, it would be difficult to determine who had the authority to represent the Anchor in the negotiations that were likely already underway.

"Does it even matter?" Kita said.

"Of course it matters!" Clover said. "Don't forget there are more Descendancy citizens than Sophians and Wesah put together. The people need to have a say in their own future, otherwise we're just planting the seeds of the next war."

"Could one of us represent the Descendancy?" Clive suggested. "We've been in the middle of all this from the beginning."

TOMMY WALLACH

Kita laughed. "No offense, but you and your brother are two of the most famous traitors in Descendancy history."

"I wasn't actually a traitor," Clover corrected. "I was working for the Library the whole time."

"Good luck convincing anyone of that now that the Epistem and Archbishop are dead. Besides, people never really trusted the Library anyway. They thought the Epistem was keeping secrets."

"Which he was."

"Exactly. That's the whole problem with scholars—and with priests too. All those secrets. It's why we ended up with Chang as our leader. Soldiers are easier to relate to."

Paz looked to Clive. She could see in his eyes that they were thinking the same thing.

"We don't know if Chang was telling the truth," he said.

"We could find out."

The five of them descended from the heights of the church and returned once again to Annunciation Square. The three factions had each retreated into its own corner—the Protectorate to the northeast, the Wesah to the south, and the Sophians to the west. There were some promising signs of collaboration—Wesah missives and Descendancy women were tending to the wounded without regard for nationality, and Paz spotted a Sophian and a Protectorate soldier awkwardly hammocking a body away from the battlefield—but the overwhelming feeling was still one of tension and enmity. She didn't let herself look at the faces of the dead; she wasn't ready to know if Terry was among them.

They left the square by way of the Silver Road. Though the

storm had finally broken, rainwater still ran torrential through the city's gutters and thundered down through the sewer grates. Paz wasn't sure what time it was, but it felt as if the sun might rise at any moment. How long could one night go on?

At last they reached the Bastion. Paz was surprised the building had survived the conflict untouched, but on further consideration, it made sense; Chang had abandoned his erstwhile headquarters relatively early on to pursue his strategy of moving through the city underground, and the Bastion didn't have the symbolic value of the Library or Notre Fille. Still, it was strange to see the place looking so pristine after the devastation of Annunciation Square, like something out of a fairy tale—the castle left untouched for a thousand years. The portcullis was up, the gates wide open.

"You know where to look?" Paz said. Clive nodded. "Then lead the way."

Paz remembered all too well the first time she'd come to the Bastion, bound and gagged, praying for some kind of deliverance—be it rescue or death. She'd been tortured here, nearly driven mad, and though most of the words inscribed in her skin were hidden beneath her hair now, she could still feel the burn of the needle as it marked her, the pitiless look in the tattooist's eyes, the soreness that lasted for days afterward. Clive must've noticed the way she stiffened as they passed through the gates.

"All that's done," he said, taking hold of her hand. "Nobody can hurt you anymore."

Paz smiled. "People can always hurt you."

Their steps echoed down the long, empty halls. Some of the

windows looked out on the training fields where she and Clive used to walk, where they'd fallen in love. And were all their troubles really over? Just like that? Were they at last free to stop running and try to build a life together? It seemed too good to be true—and at the same time, frightening.

The Bastion infirmary was a long, high-ceilinged room with red tile floors. A couple dozen beds, their sheets tightly fitted, their pillows perfectly centered, were lined up against either wall like soldiers at reveille. Clive said it wasn't really a proper hospital, merely a place for recuperation for those soldiers who took ill or were injured in the course of training; that explained why none of the casualties from the battle in Annunciation Square had been brought here, and why only one of the beds was currently in use. Its occupant had sat up as soon as the door opened, scrabbling in the drawer of his bedside table and pulling out what appeared to be a letter opener.

"Stay the fuck away from me!" he shouted.

Clive smiled. "Hey, Burns. Long time."

"Clive?"

The marshal dropped the letter opener and slipped out from under the sheets, throwing one leg and one stump over the edge of the mattress; Paz made sure not to stare. His crutches were leaning up against the bedside table, and he took a moment to fit them into his armpits before galumphing across the infirmary. Kita held back as the rest of them all collided in an extremely inelegant group embrace with Burns at the center.

"Daughter's love, I can't believe it's you," he said from inside the clutch. He smelled of disinfectant and tobacco.

"I don't understand," Clover said, after they'd finally separated. "How are you alive? Chang chopped off your leg."

"He did indeed," Burns said, glancing down at the small, neat knot in his left trouser leg. "But I'm not sure he ever planned to kill me. Turns out good advice was in short supply. I told him that's what happens when you purge everyone you see as a threat."

"So you've been helping him?" Clive said.

"More like trying to check his worst impulses. Did it work?"

Paz wondered if Burns was to thank for Chang's decision to spare her and Clive when they ran into each other in Notre Fille. "I think it did," she said.

"So where is he, then?"

"Gone," Clive said. "Probably dead. The war is over."

Burns shook his head and snickered. "And I missed the whole damn thing. So who won?"

"That's a little hard to say. Clover here kinda convinced everybody to lay down their weapons and parley."

"Did he now?" Burns looked to Clover, and then to the girl holding his hand. "And who's this one? She a spoil of war?"

"My name's Kita Delancey. And I'd slap you if I knew you better."

Burns laughed. "Ooh. I like her, Clover. Helluva lot better than the last one." He glanced suggestively at Paz. "No offense."

"None taken," Paz replied, frowning in mock upset.

"So what are you all doing here, anyway? You miss me that much?"

"We're here because Zeno and Athène are going to be talking terms soon," Clive said. "And right now, there's no one around to represent the Anchor."

　　　　　　　　　　TOMMY WALLACH

"And you think *I* know somebody?" There was a pregnant pause. Burns frowned. Then he grunted. Then he frowned again. "You've got to be fucking kidding."

They returned to Annunciation Square with Burns in tow and were surprised to find that the place had almost completely emptied out. A Descendancy woman helping to clear the rubble explained that the Sophian and Wesah armies had left the city—apparently Zeno and Athène didn't want the citizens of the Anchor to feel like they were being occupied. To Paz, it meant only one thing: if Terry was still alive, he might very well be on his way back to Sophia—or whatever was left of Sophia anyway. Paz pulled Clive aside just as the group was entering Notre Fille.

"I need to talk to you. Alone."

"Okay." Clive called out to the others. "You all go on. We'll catch up."

She and Clive walked across the narthex and into the nave. The place was no longer empty—dozens of Descendancy men and women, including no small number of soldiers, were spread out around the pews—praying, sleeping, or just gazing dully at the walls, trying to process everything they'd been through. Paz found a spot far from everyone else, in the middle of a pew near the back of the room. Her heart fluttered with dread as she took hold of Clive's hands.

"I have to go back," she said, already feeling the pressure of tears building behind her eyes. "Before I get caught up in anything else here, before you and I can figure out what comes next, I have to go home and look for my brothers. They were my responsibility, and I abandoned them."

Clive took this in with his usual stoicism. "How long?"

"Long enough to get there, make whatever arrangements I need to make, and come back."

"If you come back."

"Of course I'm comin' back." She squeezed his hands tightly, as if by doing so she might convey the intensity of her intention, the depth of her love. "You can come with me if you want."

"I can't leave Clover and Flora alone. Not right now. Not after everything that's happened."

The first tear came loose from its moorings. "I know."

They held each other, and Paz felt her gaze drawn to the giant annulus above the ambo. It had been a long time since she'd known the comfort of religion, but there was no denying the fact that faith had saved all their lives tonight. That ring—nothing but a geometric shape, nothing but the outline of a tree trunk or the full moon, had inspired thousands of men and women to choose peace, to choose mercy. That had to be worth something, didn't it?

She closed her eyes and imagined the future as she wanted it to be. Riding back down the Teeth with all three of her brothers at her side. Carlos gasping at the sight of the Anchor, still majestic even with many of its tallest buildings reduced to rubble. Terry making some snide comment about Paz's traitorous heart. Frankie worrying about where they'd sleep and what they'd eat and whether he'd make any friends. They'd pass through the Eastern Gate and there Clive would be, holding a bundle of carnations and wearing that anxious smile of his—never quite contented, always waiting for the other shoe to drop.

She pulled back from the embrace and looked Clive in the eye.

"What?" he said.

She leaned forward and kissed him, long and slow, promissory. Foreheads together, breath commingling, she whispered, "I'm comin' back."

11. Athène

WAGING WAR IS THE EASY PART.

Her mother's words, ringing in her ears as she and Zeno sat across from each other at a too-large table, attempting to direct the future of the world. The parley was not going smoothly; Zeno seemed to think the Wesah had done their part and should now be happy to return to the life they'd known before. She would have Athène pretend that the war had never happened, that the massacre at the *tooroon* had never happened, that the cease-fire itself hadn't come about primarily because of the Wesah. The old order lay in pieces; did Zeno really think Athène had come all this way and risked so many of her sisters' lives just to be sidelined when the time came to build a new one?

"I don't mean to offend you," Zeno said, "but you are still a child. You simply don't have the experience needed to run a city."

"This is about more than a city," Athène countered. "It is about a nation. I am wanting for us to make it together."

"The majority of your tribe doesn't even speak English. They can't read. Nations are built on documents. On contracts and treaties. Not songs and rituals."

"I can read. My sisters will learn."

"Maybe. But would you hang the fate of this new nation on whether they succeed?"

"I trust my sisters with my life every day. Can you say the same?"

They'd been going back and forth like this for hours, always returning to the same nut of a problem: she didn't trust Zeno, and Zeno didn't respect her. Come to think of it, Zeno probably didn't trust her much either, given the events of the past twenty-four hours. Athène leaned back in her creaky wicker chair and looked out the window, toward the rising sun. Her warriors were waiting for her outside the city. After what she'd asked them to do, she couldn't return to them with anything less than an unalloyed victory. But what did that even look like in these circumstances?

"How do you make your hair like this?" Athène said, surprising even herself with the banality of the question. "The color is so beautiful."

Zeno touched her temple, where the vibrant red was ceding to gray. "It's a plant. *Lawsonia inermis*. It doesn't grow naturally on this continent."

"So where do you find it?"

"I believe we bought the seeds from a traveling merchant, long before I became director. We grow many rare plants in the academy greenhouse." Her face darkened. "Or we used to."

Athène had momentarily forgotten what Chang had done. She felt an upwelling of sympathy for Zeno, a wisp of kinship. "I am sorry for what you lost," she said.

"And I you." The softness only lasted a moment. "But I'm afraid a shared sympathy doesn't solve our problem."

There was a sharp knock on the door—a warning, not a request.

A moment later it swung open to reveal a mangled husk of a man standing on the other side. Or half standing, really, as one of his legs had been amputated at the knee, necessitating crutches. His face was gaunt and thickly bearded, but Athène recognized him right away: Burns, the marshal who'd been there the day she met Gemma. She caught a glimpse of Clover, Flora, and Kita through the doorway before Burns shut the door.

"Director Zeno," he said. "Andromède." He traversed the room in a few miniature vaults and took a seat at the table—now slightly less too-large than before. "I guess I'm here as a representative of the Descendancy, seeing as everybody else is dead or . . ." He trailed off, reflected for a moment, then shrugged. "Just dead, I guess."

"Does the Descendancy even exist anymore?" Zeno said.

"As much as Sophia does, from what I hear," Burns sniped back.

"We are the same," Athène interjected. "We all are choosing to surrender."

"I didn't surrender," Zeno said.

"You stop fighting. You drop your weapons. This is surrender."

"Perhaps semantically. But practically, a surrender is meant to help differentiate the victorious from the vanquished."

Athène didn't know many of the words Zeno had just used, but the sentiment was clear enough—and it suggested a potential solution. "The Wesah, we have one leader—Andromède—but she speaks for the whole tribe only when it is necessary. Otherwise, all the chieftains are equal."

"Sounds like a shitshow," Burns said.

Zeno snorted. "There are plenty of advantages to decentralized systems of governance."

"I'm sure there are. That's why you shared your authority with . . . who was it again? Oh, right—no one."

"At least we didn't murder the Wesah on sight."

Athène raised her voice to make herself heard over their bickering. "Director Zeno, you are the only leader in Sophia?"

"We were never big enough to require a larger government," Zeno replied testily.

"And Marshal Burns, I am told the Descendancy has three leaders. One for soldiers, one for the Library, and one for the Church."

"That's how it was, yeah," Burns said.

"And there are three of us. This is perfect, no?"

She watched as Zeno and Burns stared each other down, each waiting for the other to veto the plan. But there was only silence.

"Who would go where?" Zeno finally asked.

"This church we're sitting in is still pretty important to a lot of people," Burns said. "I'd say we should govern out of here. You Sophians can take the Library."

"The Library was destroyed," Zeno said. "Chang ordered it burned."

"The walls are still standing. We can clean it up." He looked to Athène. "That means you Wesah would be stuck in the Bastion, if we're planning on using all the same buildings as before."

"That is fine," Athène said.

"You sure? It's pretty small."

"I do not think many of my sisters will want to live in the Anchor."

"This is all well and good," Zeno said, "but there still needs to be a primary leader. When the three of us don't agree, someone must have ultimate authority. I am the oldest here, and the most experienced leader."

"I don't even want to lead," Burns said. "After everything I've been through, I'd much rather spend the next few months either asleep or drunk. But I'm telling you this, the people here aren't gonna accept a Sophian as their, you know, president or whatever we end up callin' it. Not anytime soon, anyway."

"The same is true of my people and you," Zeno countered. "Sophians always respected the Library and the Church, but they despise the Protectorate."

"The Protectorate never terrorized a whole city for weeks with a fucking airplane."

"Only because they didn't have the intelligence to build one!"

Athène realized she hadn't even tried the tea someone had set in front of her when she first arrived. It tasted of bitter herbs and had long since gone cold. She took the cup and went to the window as Zeno and Burns continued arguing. The sun had risen, and it shone now like one of those copper shekels, full and round and red, burnishing the rain-slick brick and stone of Annunciation Square. Athène wished she could go back to the Villenaître now, leave all of this behind, but something told her she wouldn't see that place again for a very long time.

She touched a finger to the crown she wore on her brow, as if to remind herself why it was there.

"There is a third option," she said.

Ridiculous, Athène thought, turning first this way and then the other in the glass. The gown was heavier than wet muslin, made up more of precious gems than cloth, and designed in such a way as to push her breasts up toward her chin, like some kind of perverse offering. She'd refused the absurd vaulted shoes at least, and her weathered moccasins were hidden away beneath the dense folds of the dress like a secret. An hour ago some woman she'd never met had tried to "style" her, daubing her face with white powder and then adding a bit of red back to her cheeks and lips. Now Athène looked decidedly un-Wesah—a shame-faced snowman, a blushing ghost. She hadn't let the style woman touch her hair, but had agreed to brush out some of the kinks herself—a finicky operation she was only too happy to be distracted from by a knock at the door.

"What?" she shouted in English (which was, she had to admit, a better language for shouting).

The door opened to reveal Flora standing on the threshold. Athène hadn't seen her since the war ended two days ago. The girl wore her own monstrous outfit—an elaborate sculpture of pink taffeta and silver lace, bulging at the shoulders and the rear—and her long hair had been sculpted into a pointlessly artful labyrinth of braids and whorls.

"You look almost as stupid as me," Athène said to Flora's figure in the mirror. "I am feeling better already."

Flora closed the door behind her and crossed the room. She was holding a large black box, which she set down on the vanity.

"What is that?" Athène said, returning to the knotty problem of her own hair. Flora shrugged. She still wasn't speaking, which was part of the reason Athène had summoned her—but only part. "Flora, I am asking you here today because I want to make a deal. Is that possible? If yes, just nod your head." The slightest tilt, almost imperceptible. "Good. What is coming for me—not just today, but in all the months and years ahead—it frightens me. You know what it is to be frightened, yes?" Another tilt. "Some of my people will stay with me, but not many, and none that I know well. You are young, but I trust you. I would like you to—*ow!*"

The hairbrush had gotten stuck in a particularly tenacious tangle. Athène pulled at it a few times with little result but pain. Without any prompting, Flora reached out and deftly worked the brush free in a matter of seconds.

"Thank you," Athène said.

The girl nodded, then continued to brush Athène's hair.

"What I was saying is that I would like you to stay with me. Not as a counselor, or a servant, but as a friend. Do you think you could do this?" A moment's hesitation, then another nod. "I'm sorry, but that is not enough. This vow of silence, I have not asked you to break it, not since the day your sister died. But now, if you are to be my friend, I need your voice."

Flora stopped brushing, stopped moving entirely; she seemed paralyzed with indecision.

Athène remembered the box on her vanity. It was heavier than she'd expected, made entirely of leather. The brass hinges opened silently. In a crevice of black velvet perched a filigreed confection of precious metals spun by some empyrean spider. Tendrils curved upward from the base, latticing the hypnotic purple depth of a sapphire the size of a chicken egg. Athène lifted it free and was delighted to discover that the jeweler had done as he'd promised: her old brass crown made up the base of this ostentatious knick-knack. Gingerly she lifted it to her brow—and her delight curdled. It was so heavy! Her old crown dug into her forehead now, and that lattice would surely catch on everything.

In the mirror, she saw the hungry look in Flora's eyes: two birds with one stone. In a single violent motion, she slammed the crown down on the edge of the box, breaking off the delicate new adorn-ments. She put the brass circlet back on her head and then stood up, gesturing Flora toward the chair.

"Sit," she said.

It took some doing, but eventually she succeeded in fitting all the broken ends of gold and silver into the beribboned layer cake that was Flora's hair, bending the ductile metal down to lie flush with the girl's scalp. The sapphire ended up resting right on top of her head, like some dark thought Flora couldn't quite shake.

"There we are." Athène put her hands on Flora's shoulders. Their eyes met.

"It's pretty," Flora said.

Athène smiled. "Yes. It is very pretty."

They moved as a group down the central hallway of the Bastion. The walls were garlanded with long strings of white, red, and yellow roses—three colors to signify the joining of three nations; Athène couldn't remember which was meant to be which. Flora remained at her side, and behind them were various representatives of the Anchor and Sophia, including Zeno and Burns, both of whom had also been trussed and gussied up. The formality fit Zeno well enough, but Burns looked as out of his element as Athène had ever seen him. Still he managed a smile when she glanced at him over her shoulder. Her "coronation," as Zeno had taken to calling it, represented the fruits of compromise, the best option they had. She would be more than a figurehead, but hopefully not *too* much more; power for power's sake had never much appealed to her. Anyway, Zeno and Burns would be there to guide her in the years to come, and she would be there to guide them, too.

The front doors of the Bastion were shut, a guard stationed to either side. Her heart beat hard at the sound of the crowd waiting for her to emerge.

"Are you ready?" Zeno asked.

"They aren't all gonna be happy about this," Burns added. "You're gonna get some jeers. But it'll all settle down before too long. I got a good feeling."

"A good feeling?" Athène said skeptically.

"Sure. Why not?"

She wished her mother could have been there to see her, and even more than that, she wished Gemma were still alive, standing beside her, telling her everything was going to be all right. So many things she wished. Yet this was far from the worst possible outcome. The *otsapah* had seen blood and fire in the future, and there had been plenty of both. But the Wesah were still here, and the fighting was done. There was no reason not to believe a bright and

TOMMY WALLACH

shining future was on its way—other than experience, of course. And precedent.

Athène nodded to the guards. The doors swung open, drenching the dark hallway with sunlight. Her ears filled with the cries of the people, who were her people now. Head held high, she stepped into the brave new world she'd brought into being.

12. Clive

To walk the streets of the anchor now was to subject yourself to a history lesson, to a laundry list of losses. Shops and taverns that had stood for a hundred years had been reduced to a splintered sign atop a pile of rubble. Landmarks you'd used to orient yourself no longer existed, such that the whole city felt as if it had been turned on an axis, or else replaced with some aged, ruined doppelgänger. And was it Clive's imagination, or were there just not as many people around as there ought to have been? Turning onto the Purple Road, he couldn't shake the feeling that he was either late or early for something, that everyone else in the city was attending some event from which he'd been excluded.

It had been two weeks since Athène was named Minister of the Anchor—a new title invented by the Wesah-Sophia-Descendancy triumvirate. There would never again be an Epistem, or an Archbishop, or a Grand Marshal, or a director for that matter. The Wesah still thought of their leader as Andromède, but even that title was unlikely to last. Everything was changing.

Case in point: this ramshackle two-story house in the Sixth Quarter, fortuitously untouched by the bombings but still wearing a mantle of soot—the dust of the fragmented city, washed away with every rain but still swirling around the atmosphere, circling and alighting over and over again, like a flock of scavenger birds. All through his childhood, this had been Gemma's house first and her grandfather's house second. Now both of them were gone, and Clive was learning to think of it as *his* house, or even stranger than that—his *family* house. Clive had the master bedroom, while Clover was in Flora's old room. Flora had moved to Gemma's room; it wouldn't be long before she'd grow into her older sister's clothes, as she was already growing into Gemma's beauty.

"Hello?" Clive called out.

"Upstairs!" Clover called back.

"You almost ready?"

"Just give me a second."

Clive went into the kitchen. At Flora's insistence, the room had been decorated a month early for Landfall Day. Kita had come over earlier in the week, and the four of them had spent the day cutting out paper dolls and hanging them from the ceiling, painting little snow-limned trees on the windowpanes, drinking hot cider, and baking cookies that had somehow only grown more delicious as they went stale. The decorations made the room more cheerful, though the cheer inevitably made Clive wistful for past holidays. It also made him miss Paz, which was strange, as they'd never celebrated a Landfall Day together. Everything made him miss her, really.

His bag was already packed and waiting by the door. They'd be traveling by foot, rather than by wagon or horse, so he'd made sure to keep it light. He was good at that by now.

"They're way too big for me," Clover complained, clomping

down the stairs in their father's scuffed work boots. Both brothers had lost most of their clothes over the past year, so they'd become dependent on their father's wardrobe, salvaged from the old house before it had been sold. "I'm wearing three pairs of socks to keep my feet from sliding around."

"Better than goin' barefoot."

"Is it, though?"

"Yeah. It is." Clive shouldered his bag and led the way back outside.

"How are things at Notre Fille?" Clover asked.

"Madness. As always." Clive had spent that morning as he did most mornings, helping Burns administrate what was now known as the Civic Protectorate; the erstwhile military organization was tasked with overseeing the reconstruction effort—not to mention quite a bit of original construction as well. "Zeno wants the whole city wired for electricity by the end of the year, and apparently we're expected to do most of the work."

"She's right, though," Clover said. "It'll be a lot easier to create the infrastructure now than after everything gets rebuilt."

"I know, and Burns is fine with it, but Athène is making things difficult. She says that she visited Sophia once, and all those electric lights made it so you couldn't see the stars."

"So what?"

"I guess she likes the stars."

Clover frowned. "I kinda like the stars too."

Another shock of dislocation to see the men guarding the Western Gate wearing something other than red and gold; the old uniforms had been retired before a new design could be chosen, so the guards were dressed in their civvies. At Athène's insistence, they were armed only with swords, as if time had turned back to before Chang excavated Hell. They nodded at Clive and Clover—perhaps recognizing them, perhaps not. Inevitably the Hamill brothers had become rather well-known, for reasons both good and bad.

"What do you think Da would've made of all this?" Clive said.

"What part?"

"A Wesah chieftain running the Anchor. A Sophian overseeing the Library. All of it."

"I don't know. The Da we grew up with, I think it would've horrified him. But the one who came back from Sophia—who knows? Maybe this is exactly what he hoped would happen."

"Yeah." Clive hesitated. "I hope I feel it, at some point. Losing him, I mean. It still hasn't hit me. And that doesn't seem right somehow. Like I didn't really love him."

"There's no point thinking about it that way. You feel how you feel."

"I guess."

They didn't speak for a while, and then they did, but not about anything that mattered. Clive shed his wool jacket. The day was cold but they were moving fast, following the course of the Tiber, which itself was only following the inescapable dictates of water and gravity. That was gravity with a small *g* now, gravity that Clover insisted could be scientifically explained—except insofar as any question of cause and effect eventually reached a point of inexplicability, except insofar as everything could be called a mystery, or an aspect of the divine.

When they passed someone on the road, they stopped to shake

hands and discuss the news of the day. When they were hungry, they ate something from their packs. When darkness fell, they stopped and put up the canvas tent, cooked beans over the fire, slept. When the sun rose, they rose with it, continued on. They had a mission, of course, but it was a moving target, maybe even a fool's errand. Clive didn't mind. In fact, he felt this was the perfect amount of intention—traveling as much for the journey as the destination. Three days out and the Tiber deepened, slowed; frost collected in still pockets, cracked underfoot. The road bent up and away from the river, forcing them to hike along the steep, rocky bank so they could remain close enough to see what they needed to see.

Clover was out in front a ways, kicking at stones for the hell of it, when Clive thought of something their mother had once told him.

"You know they wanted to change your name?"

Clover stopped, and for a moment Clive was afraid he'd hurt his brother's feelings somehow. He could still remember the days when the smallest slight could set Clover to brooding for days. But so much had happened since then. So much had changed. Somewhere along the line, his little brother had become a man.

"Really?" he said, turning around. "When?"

"You were about three, so I would've been five, and I guess you wouldn't answer to 'Clover.' Plus people were always getting our names confused."

"Eddie Poplin used to do that all the time."

"Yeah. Michael thought it was the funniest thing in the world."

"And Gemma would always try to cover for it by changing the

subject, 'cause she knew how much I hated being called Clive."

They let a moment of silence pass for Eddie, Michael, and Gemma without needing to acknowledge it.

"Anyway," Clive continued, "they tried to think up new names for you. Da wanted to go with something from the Filia, but they settled on some old family name of Mama's. For a whole week they called you Emmett."

"Emmett?" Clover cried, offended at the very sound of it. "Emmett?"

"You don't remember?"

"No! So what happened after that?"

"Well, at first you didn't seem to notice. But after a couple of days, you started bawling every time either one of them said it. Like you were allergic . . ." Clive trailed off. Clover was squinting at something down in the river. "What is it? Do you see something?"

"Look there, between the rocks."

A glint of silver, caught in a backwater: one of the barrels Bernstein had sent downstream before the Library was set ablaze. A fragment of the knowledge collected over the centuries, one step in an unending staircase that connected the benighted past to the enlightened future—bobbing there as innocently as a duckling. Their job wasn't to bring them back, of course; the Civic Protectorate would come with a wagon for that. Clive and Clover had only been tasked with dragging the barrels out of the river where possible and marking their locations on a map.

"I always loved my name," Clover said. Clive had almost forgotten they'd been in the middle of a conversation.

"Yeah?"

"Of course. It's a plant, first of all. And a good one, by the way. Smells nice. Tastes nice. Horses love it. Bees love it. Plus, it's lucky."

"Some of the time."

"Yeah. Some of the time. Also . . ." Clover paused, and Clive could sense something like embarrassment in the silence. He gave his brother time to work through it, watching the barrel slowly spinning in the scintillant water, like a lazy compass point. "Also, I like that it sounds like your name. I didn't always, but I do now. I don't even know why. I just do." Clover smiled experimentally, seeking the same thing he'd always been seeking, ever since he was a red-faced and squalling selkie gripping Clive's index finger like it was the most important thing in the world. "What about you?" he said.

Clive felt the foolish grin growing on his own face. It was a wonderful thing, when you could make someone happy just by telling them the truth. And suddenly the future didn't feel quite so uncertain, or so frightening. They'd nearly killed each other. They'd ended up on opposite sides of a war. And yet here they were. Still standing. Still brothers. Still friends.

"You know what?" Clive said, throwing an arm over Clover's shoulder. "I feel exactly the same way."

Epilogue

SUNLIGHT—A BRIGHT WHITE LINE BETWEEN THE CUR-tains, slicing open the dark room like a cantaloupe, advertising the quintessential summer day about to begin.

Nora hated sunlight.

She rubbed the sleep from her eyes angrily, as if she might dull the glare that way. If she'd had her way, it would always be raining, or at the very least, there'd be a nice thick layer of clouds between her and the sun, turning the golden light to pewter, casting the whole world in a lovely, morbid pall. Her parents had taken her on a visit to Edgewise a few months ago, and she remembered the difference the weather made to the color of the ocean, which her da explained was functioning as a giant mirror. On a sunny day, it was just one dull, flat expanse of stolen blue. On a rainy day, it became molten silver, cresting and collapsing in a never-ending dance, spackled with droplets, beating insistent as a hungry baby against the shoreline.

She put on an old blouse and ratty jeans—how much more enjoyable it was getting dressed in winter, layering colors and textures, and nothing hardly ever needing washing because you weren't sweaty and smelly at the end of the day—and went to the kitchen. Her father was already out for the morning, and she could hear her mother tending to little Blanca, cooing and tutting as if she were a child herself.

"I'm going for a walk!" Nora shouted, and didn't bother listening to the response. It was always some injunction or another—don't go there, don't talk to him, don't touch the whatever. As if she needed to be told over and over again. She was eleven years old, not four. She knew what was what.

"Morning, Nora!"

That would be Mr. Selman, the old widower who lived in the apartment upstairs. He seemed to spend his whole day looking out the window, checking on everyone. Nora didn't like being watched, so she stuck out her tongue at him, but he just laughed as if she were only *pretending* not to like him. She wanted to tell him that she *actually* didn't like him, but somehow whenever you got into a conversation with Mr. Selman, he'd start talking about some dumb thing and you ended up having to stand there listening for an hour. So she just marched right past him and on down to the Green Road, joining the weekend strollers as they perused the wheeled farmer's stalls that would spend the day rotating slowly around the city, such that each quarter got slightly worse produce, until the Seventh would be left with nothing but rotten apples and wilted cabbage.

She had two bronze shekels of chore money clinking in her pocket and used one to buy a bunch of bananas. As she walked south, she tore one away from its brethren and began to peel it. She did so slowly, and for emphasis, threw in a drawn-out and agonizing scream, as if flaying someone alive. A middle-aged couple gave her a dirty look; she smiled back, chomping lustily into the top of

TOMMY WALLACH

the banana and chewing with her mouth open until they turned away in disgust. Somewhere close by, music was playing—cheery guitar and accordion. Nora hated cheery music. She only liked slow ballads sung by miserable people about how miserable they were. It was best if the balladeer was ugly too, and if her guitar was a little out of tune, or she had a dirty old dog, or no shoes. Then you could believe what she sang about and relate to it without thinking she was just lying to you so you'd throw some shekels in her case.

Nora reached the gate and kept on going around the Ring Road, toward Portland Park and the Tiber. Her plan was to keep walking until she found a place without any people, but this turned out to be harder than she'd expected. It was the first nice day since the warm turn, and a Sunday to boot; the banks of the river were dense with canoodling couples and screaming babies and old people looking all wrinkly and content. She'd probably walked at least a mile already, and had decided she would tell her father it had been five, even though she knew he wouldn't believe her. Sometimes you had to describe things the way they *felt*, not the way they *were*.

The sun beat down a little harder every minute, like some annoying toddler trying to get your attention. She threw a banana at it, but came up a little short, and the fruit ended up landing a few feet shy of the riverbank.

"Hey!"

The boy was maybe a year younger than her, dressed in a leather skirt and a bandanna: a member of some local *naasyoon* come into the city for the day. She hadn't seen him sitting in the bower of a weeping willow whose branches looked like so many fishing lines dangling in the water.

"Did you throw this at me?" he asked in perfect English, holding up the banana.

"No. I just threw it," Nora replied. "Hey, what are you doing?"

The boy had begun to peel the banana. "Finders keepers." He took a bite, chewed thoughtfully, swallowed. "You wanna see my toy?"

"No," Nora said, which wasn't true. "I don't play with toys," she added, which also wasn't true. "But you can show me if you really want."

"Okay. It's here."

She stepped under the shade of the willow. Somehow it was hot even here.

"I hate sunny days," she said.

"Why?"

"Because they make you all sunburned. And because you feel like you're wasting the day if you just stay in the house reading a book, so you go outside, but then there are people everywhere, so you couldn't enjoy yourself even if you wanted to."

"You can't enjoy a thing if other people are enjoying it too?"

"No," she said curtly, rather than think about his question. "So what is this supposed to be?"

The "toy" was made up of a few wooden dowels, a diamond-shaped swatch of silk, and a long spool of twine, all laid out in the dirt at the boy's feet. Nora was annoyed that she didn't know what it was—and even more annoyed that she wanted to.

"I've been waiting for the glue to dry," the boy explained. "But I think it should be ready by now." He picked it up by the frame. The silk had been affixed to the dowels like a sail to a mast. It fluttered in the breeze, light dancing on the surface of the fabric. "We'll need more wind than this. Come on."

Nora desperately wanted to tell the boy she was bored and had better things to do, but she couldn't leave before she knew what his dumb toy did. They left the river behind and scrambled up some big rocks to the south. Beyond was a hilly field where groups of children were playing kickball and tag while the adults lounged about on blankets. The women wore big fancy hats to keep the monstrous sun at bay. The men smoked cigarillos and looked extremely serious.

"Just tell me what it does," Nora said, but the boy ignored her, and she immediately regretted admitting curiosity. He kept walking until he'd reached the top of one of the hills. Then he handed the spindle of twine to her. "Here."

She refused it on principle; nobody willingly gave up anything worth having. "Why? What is it? What does it do?"

The boy laughed. "Are you scared?"

"Of course not."

She grabbed the spindle; one end of the twine was tied to a corner of the toy's frame, like a dog's leash. The boy backed away, twine unspooling as he went. When he was about ten feet away, he stopped. "Ready?" he said.

"For what?"

He turned around and launched the silk diamond into the air. It arced up, and then by some inexplicable magic, didn't fall back to the earth. Instead the wind caught the fabric and held the whole thing aloft. Nora understood the spindle now; without prompting, she gave the line more slack, freeing the diamond to rise even higher into the blue. Some of the other kids in the field had noticed, and now they ran over to try to figure out how the toy worked. Nora also saw an elderly couple glance at the diamond and grimace, as if there were something immoral about it. She liked that.

"How'd you figure out how to make this?" she said to the boy.

He shrugged. "I was watching the leaves swirl around a couple weeks ago, and I thought about how you could probably make your own leaf, if you wanted. That's how I tried it first, with just one sorta spine thing running down the middle, like a leaf has, but it didn't work. I figured it needed to be more—"

"Like a sail," Nora interrupted.

"Yeah."

Something surfaced in her memory, a conversation she'd only half attended to, because it was about her mother's childhood and so boring by definition. "It's called a kite," she said.

"A kite?"

"Yeah."

The wind fought her; the kite gyrated in the invisible eddies of the sky, a metaphor for something she couldn't quite determine. She fed it more line and then reeled it in, back and forth—a delicate, instinctual dance—until finally something shifted irrevocably and the diamond plummeted to the ground like a meteor. The boy ran to fetch it.

"Is it okay?" Nora called out.

The boy held it up for her to see; one of the dowels had snapped clean in half, and the silk was torn. He carried it back to her, stoic on the surface but clearly dejected over the loss.

"I can fix it," Nora said.

"Really?"

Too late to take it back, so nowhere to go but forward, deeper into the unfamiliar waters of voluntary human interaction. "My ma and my uncle both like to tinker with things, so we've got a whole workshop downstairs. At my house, I mean. If you want. You don't have to. It's stupid."

"No, that'd be really nice," the boy said, sniffling a little. "I just have to be back home before dark."

Her invitation accepted, Nora felt no need to be civil anymore. "Obviously. I didn't invite you for a sleepover. You're a *boy*. We'll just fix your dumb toy and then you can go."

"Okay. Thanks."

He walked beside her, cradling the broken kite, not saying anything. Nora had to admit there was something nice about moving silently through the world with someone; maybe her baby sister wouldn't be too much of an imposition after all. Nora would just have to teach her how not to be an annoying idiot, like almost everybody else in the world.

"We might have to be quiet once we get to the house. There's a baby. She's always sleeping, except when you want her to."

"Okay."

"She won't like you. She doesn't like anyone except me and my momma."

"Okay."

The sun disappeared behind a bank of fluffy white clouds just as a breeze picked up. Nora shivered. She and the Wesah boy would fix the kite together. It was fun, fixing things. She'd always liked the idea that with a little effort, you could transform a piece of junk into something useful again. Fixing even the tiniest little thing—a snapped dowel, a torn scrap of silk—was enough to make a person think that maybe *everything* could be fixed, maybe everything wrong could be set right again.

It was enough to make a person hope.